MURDER ONE

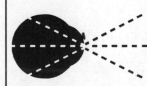

This Large Print Book carries the
Seal of Approval of N.A.V.H.

MURDER ONE

ROBERT DUGONI

THORNDIKE PRESS
A part of Gale, Cengage Learning

GALE
CENGAGE Learning™

Detroit • New York • San Francisco • New Haven, Conn • Waterville, Maine • London

GALE
CENGAGE Learning™

LIBRARY OF CONGRESS CATALOGING-IN-PUBLICATION DATA

Dugoni, Robert.
  Murder one / by Robert Dugoni.
    p. cm. — (Thorndike Press large print thriller)
  ISBN-13: 978-1-4104-3992-5 (hardcover)
  ISBN-10: 1-4104-3992-5 (hardcover)
    1. Attorney and client—Fiction. 2. Murder—Investigation—Fiction.
3. Drug traffic—Fiction. 4. Washington (State)—Fiction. 5. Large type
books. I. Title.
PS3604.U385M87 2011b
813'.6—dc22   2011018945

Published in 2011 by arrangement with Simon & Schuster, Inc.

Printed in the United States of America
1 2 3 4 5 6 7 15 14 13 12 11

To James Fick,
an excellent attorney,
a better brother-in-law,
and a great friend.

I am grateful for all that you
have done to support me.
Peace and blessings.

The credit belongs to the man who is actually in the arena . . . if he fails, at least he fails while daring greatly, so that his place shall never be with those cold and timid souls who know neither victory nor defeat.

— THEODORE ROOSEVELT

ONE

Friday, September 2, 2011
United States Federal District Court
Seattle, Washington

She stood resolute, head held high, refusing to so much as flinch. After a decade as an assistant United States attorney, Rebecca Han had developed thick skin, but she would have needed the hide of an elephant to absorb the flogging Judge Myron Kozlowski continued to administer from the bench.

"Assuming there had been probable cause to establish that Mr. Vasiliev trafficked in drugs — and I am not convinced there was — that does not justify a search of Mr. Vasiliev's car dealership."

"Your Honor —"

Kozlowski's hand shot from the sleeve of his black robe, one bony finger pointing like the Grim Reaper. "Do not interrupt me, counsel. I'll let you know when I'm fin-

9

ished." Each word sounded as if it were scratching the back of his throat raw. "By the government's theory, a legitimate business may be searched any time the owner of that business is suspected of engaging in drug trafficking *anywhere.* This is a dangerous assumption that goes well beyond any tolerable limits."

Han gripped the edge of the podium, holding on and holding back.

Kozlowski looked past her to the media-filled gallery of the modern courtroom. "I am fully aware of the publicity this matter has generated and its significance to certain members of the public. And I am fully aware of what a case such as this could potentially mean to an ambitious young lawyer."

Han pinched her lips, jaw clenched.

"But a United States attorney must be above the sway of the media and of self-aggrandizing, especially in situations such as this."

This time, Han did not attempt to respond. What was there to say? Kozlowski wasn't interested in argument; he was interested in another piece of her flesh.

"Overbroad warrants that authorize the search of every square inch of a defendant's place of business are the type of general

10

searches specifically prohibited by the Fourth Amendment and abhorred by the colonists. That this warrant was in part based upon speculation by Drug Enforcement agents that Mr. Vasiliev associated with members of organized crime — specifically Russian mafia — is equally reprehensible and a generalization no less offensive to the Russian community than it has been to the Italian and Asian communities."

Kozlowski massaged his brow with his thumb and middle finger, leaving his eyebrows like tufts of untended lawn. His face resembled a malnourished midwestern scarecrow, skin stretched over sharp features, wrinkled at the neck and tucked beneath the white collar protruding above his robe. Sunken eye sockets encapsulated stark white orbs. He would have frightened even the most hardened of trick-o'-treaters.

"You've really given me no choice in this matter. As far as I am concerned, the U.S. attorney's office has no one to blame but itself. With a little more diligence, these problems could have been avoided." He shuffled the papers and scratched a pen across a page as he spoke. "I am granting the defendant's motion to suppress."

At Kozlowski's pronouncement, Filyp Vasiliev sat up in his chair at the counsel table, grinning as he ran a hand over his neatly shaved head. The ruling would prohibit the government from introducing at trial much of the evidence the DEA had gathered during a raid of Vasiliev's used-car dealership in Renton, Washington. Without the heroin and the incriminating statements, the government had no case. And everyone in the courtroom knew it.

Kozlowski rapped his gavel and retreated to his chambers before his bailiff had finished commanding the room to rise.

Han seethed, watching Vasiliev pick an imaginary piece of lint from the lapel of a shimmering pin-striped suit, rubbing his fingertips as if brushing aside the criminal charges. Standing, he shook hands with his attorney.

"I told you," he said, accent thick. "No worries."

He patted the man's shoulder and then pushed through the waist-high wooden gate. Han watched as he gained an entourage of media, strolling down the aisle proclaiming his vindication. Just before the alcove leading to the large wooden doors, Vasiliev paused, though not to address a question or offer further comment. He scanned the spectators, finding his target. His nod and grin were nearly imperceptible, but his message delivered loud and clear.

Two

Saturday, September 3, 2011
The Rainier Club
Seattle, Washington

David Sloane just wanted to leave.

Attired in a tuxedo, his pocketbook a thousand dollars lighter and his obligation complete, Sloane wove his way across the ballroom floor shaking hands and offering friendly greetings, advising all that he'd be "right back."

He wouldn't be.

Sloane's goal remained the ornately carved wooden doorway through which he intended to slip out and disappear before the band started to play and every well-meaning person in the room sought to find him a dance partner for the evening.

His speech to promote legal aid services had been his first public event since Tina's death thirteen months earlier. He had initially declined the request, as he had

14

every other professional and personal invitation, but the organization's president had made an impassioned plea, so Sloane relented. His speech seemed well received by the crowd, but people treated a man whose wife had been murdered differently, like something so fragile it might crack if handled too much; better left undisturbed. They pacified him, humored him, pitied him, but they were rarely honest.

Someone called his name. He turned and gave a perfunctory wave as he lengthened his stride and stepped from the room, making his escape. Turning back, he glimpsed the black blur out of the corner of his eye, too late to veer his course or otherwise avoid. They impacted full stride. Sloane, the larger of the two, delivered the more severe blow, sending the other person sprawling. At the last moment he managed to grab a flailing arm and keep her upright while he fought to regain his own balance.

"I'm so sorry," he said. "Are you all right?"

The woman had her back to him, readjusting atop four-inch heels. Turning, she said, "I'm . . ." Her eyes widened. "David?"

Sloane recognized the face but could not immediately recall the name.

"It's Barclay," she said, rescuing him. "Barclay Reid."

Sloane had not seen Reid in nearly a year, since litigating a case against her client, Kendall Toys. Even if he had, he wasn't sure he would have recognized her. In court, Reid had worn bookish glasses, no visible makeup or jewelry, and understated conservative suits. Tonight, contacts revealed jade-green eyes, pearl earrings matched a necklace, and a simple black evening gown accentuated a petite, shapely figure. Her hair had grown to nearly shoulder-length, with a reddish tint Sloane did not recall.

"Barclay, of course. I'm sorry." During his mental gymnastics, Sloane had momentarily forgotten that he nearly tackled the poor woman, which only added to his abject embarrassment. "Are you okay? I didn't hurt you, did I?"

"I'm fine." Reid tugged at a spaghetti strap. "You're in a hurry."

Perhaps still off balance, Sloane uttered the truth. "I was trying to sneak out before the dancing."

"No wonder. Are you always this light on your feet?"

"I was trying to be discreet."

She smiled. "Remind me not to walk near you when you're trying to be obvious."

"Barclay?" Washington governor Hugh Chang approached with an entourage.

Sloane had sat beside the man at the head table, but now the governor's gaze fixed on Reid. She offered her hand, but he stepped through it to embrace her. "It's good to see you," he said. "When are we going to have lunch?"

Reid turned to Sloane. "You've met our distinguished speaker?"

Chang had a politician's grip. "That was a terrific speech you gave tonight. I'd hire you as my writer, but I doubt I could afford you." Sloane smiled. The governor returned his attention to Reid. "When you come to Olympia, we'll discuss that matter you wrote me about," he said before departing.

The band started up, a melody from the eighties — the decade of choice at events attended by people too young to have been a part of the sixties and too old to be hip to modern music.

"That's my cue," Sloane said.

"And mine."

"No dancing for you?" Sloane asked.

"Too many well-meaning friends."

"I know the feeling," he said. "Can I walk you out?"

They retrieved Reid's black shawl and handbag and Sloane slipped the shawl over Reid's shoulders. The act made him wonder why, on a Saturday night, at a black-tie function, Reid was alone. Given what he knew of her — the name partner of a large Seattle firm and the former president of the Washington Bar Association — it surprised him.

A warm summer breeze from an unusually humid September greeted them as they stepped outside. Reid rested a hand on Sloane's forearm as she navigated the steps, and they walked beneath the blue-gray awning of the gabled 120-year-old brick-and-mortar building that resembled an English country estate dropped in the middle of the city, now dwarfed by modern glass-and-steel skyscrapers.

"You look dashing in your tuxedo by the way. Very James Bond."

"You look nice also." He grimaced at the sound of it. This time Reid did not rescue him.

She stopped, hand on hip. "For the amount this dress cost me, I was hoping for something more than 'nice' . . . but I won't fish for compliments."

"I'm sorry; I think I'm still a bit off balance." He cleared his throat. "You look —"

"I'm teasing," she said.

At the sidewalk, a young man in a red vest reached for Reid's valet ticket, but she deferred to Sloane. "You go ahead."

18

"I think I've escaped. Besides, you have to let me show a little chivalry."

She handed the valet her ticket as a second young man approached and took Sloane's. The two jogged across the street to a parking garage.

"Crescent moon," Reid said. At just after nine, the sky had faded but not darkened, revealing a hint of stars and the slice of moon. "New moon Wednesday night."

Sloane had never heard the term. "You mean full moon?"

"Actually, it's the opposite. It's when the moon is in the same position as the sun and its illuminated half faces away from the earth. The part we see is dark. It's called a new moon."

"You're an astronomer," he said.

"Hardly."

A blue BMW pulled forward, and the valet exited, leaving the headlights on and the engine running.

"That's me." Reid stepped from the curb.

"Well . . . I am sorry about . . ."

She smiled over her shoulder. "Forget it."

The second attendant exited the parking garage and made a U-turn, tires squealing as he pulled Sloane's 1964 Cadillac Coupe de Ville directly behind Reid's car. The white behemoth, fins protruding from the rear, dwarfed the import. The Caddy had been a gift from Charles Jenkins that Sloane's stepson, Jake, aptly named Moby, as in the great white whale Captain Ahab had hunted.

"I love it." Reid left the valet holding her car door and walked down the street, running her hand over the hood. "Sixty-four or sixty-five?"

"Sixty-four. You know cars?"

"I know Cadillacs." She spoke across the hood. "My father drove a Cadillac his whole life. He would have loved this." Sloane joined her as she bent and touched the cherry-red interior restored to mint condition. "May I?"

"Be my guest."

She sat behind the steering wheel, running her gaze and hands over the seats and dash. "Power locks and windows." She closed her eyes and inhaled. "I used to stand on the seat with my arm around his shoulders. I can still remember the smell of his Aqua Velva. When we'd get close to home, I'd sit in his lap and he'd let me steer. I'm sure he kept his knee on the wheel, but he still made me feel like I was doing it by myself."

In court Reid had been businesslike-efficient, but now she looked like a teenage girl whose date had just picked her up for the prom. Before he could stop himself Sloane said, "Do you want to drive it?"

She looked up, eyes eager. "Really?"

He handed the attendant a five-dollar bill. "Can you keep her car a while longer?"

Reid took the keys and waited until Sloane slid in the passenger side to adjust the bench seat forward. Settled, she gave him a girlish smile. "Where should we go?"

Sloane shrugged. "You're the driver."

"No requests?"

"Surprise me," Sloane said, though she already had.

Sunyat Chelyakov sat parked down the street from the blue-gray awning. He picked up the disposable cell phone and punched the speed dial, the only number on the phone. For ten dollars, he received eight hours of phone calls and 150 hours of standby service, after which he threw out the phone and chose another from the dozens at his disposal.

The woman stood admiring the white Cadillac.

"She just left the party, but she is not alone," he reported.

The woman slid behind the wheel as the man accompanying her walked around the car and slipped in the passenger door. Perhaps he'd had too much to drink?

"She is getting into a car with a man. She's driving."

"You have the license number?" his contact asked.

He provided the letters and numbers, shut off the phone, and pulled the sedan from the curb.

"Americans and their cars," he mused. It would not be difficult to follow such a large vehicle.

THREE

Pioneer Square
Seattle, Washington

He stood on the sidewalk, staring up at thirteen tusked faces.

"As a girl, I called it the Walrus Building," she said. "Apparently, everyone did."

The walruses' heads, carved in white marble on the exterior of the third floor of the Arctic Club Hotel, peered down at all who climbed the white marble steps and walked beneath the arched pediment. Supported on four columns, the entrance on Cherry Street resembled the entrance to an ancient Greek temple. Inside, Reid explained that the building had been constructed in 1917 by a group of men flush with gold from the Alaska Klondike. Black-and-white photographs of those original members — a men's club when that sort of thing remained acceptable — hung in the refurbished lobby.

"You know a lot about this place," Sloane said.

"It helps when one of your clients purchases and renovates the building." She explained that after decades as government offices, the hotel had undergone an expensive and painstaking renovation to restore the Alaskan marble stairways and foyer, the leaded glass, and the dark wood paneling and ornate cornices. "We had a few disputes, as you can appreciate. I learned more than I or my client really wanted."

"And here I thought you did it all from memory."

"Sorry to disappoint."

Reid led him past the registration desk into the Polar Bar, a room with leather chairs, round tables, and lamps strategically positioned about pillars. A fire burned in the fireplace along one wall, but the main attraction was the blue glow light emanating from beneath the bar at the front of the room — a slab of wood atop thick cracked glass made to resemble large blocks of arctic ice.

"Well?" Reid asked.

"I like it," he said. "Very good choice."

They took a table beneath a navy blue velvet drape hanging from a ceiling curtain rod. A waitress greeted them.

24

"Scotch rocks, if I recall," Reid said.

"You do have a good memory." Sloane had ordered the drink when the two met in the Fireside Room of the Sorrento Hotel to discuss a possible settlement of the Kendall Toy matter. "Okay, my turn." He stared into Reid's eyes as if trying to read her mind and was again struck by the clarity of the green. "Martini. Two olives. No onion."

She arched her eyebrows then looked up at the waitress. "Martini. One olive. No onion."

"I guess my memory isn't quite as good."

"Your memory is fine. I'm cutting back on my olive intake."

"Nice choice," he said. "I've never been here."

"You're not from here, are you? Was it San Francisco?"

"Very good again." Sloane had been raised in foster homes in Los Angeles but had practiced law in San Francisco for the better part of thirteen years, until moving to Seattle with Tina and her son, Jake.

She shrugged. "You made quite a splash in the bar journal after the Kendall Toy victory."

Sloane detected no bitterness. He recalled seeing Harvard on her résumé. "And you? Was it Boston?"

"Just for law school. I was raised in Magnolia and went to U-Dub."

"You're a Husky."

She gave a halfhearted fist pump. "Go Dawgs."

The crack of what sounded like pool balls colliding drew Sloane's attention to a man and woman standing at a vintage table in the corner of the room.

"It was very good, by the way," she said.

"What's that?"

"Your speech tonight; it was very good."

He nodded.

"That was a compliment. Usually, the response is 'thank you.' "

He picked up a drink coaster imprinted with a cartoonish polar bear holding a martini glass and flipped the coaster between his fingers like he'd seen magicians do with a playing card, trying to think of the right word. "Since my wife's death, it isn't always easy to tell if people are being sincere."

She winced, a look he had become all too familiar with. She touched his arm. "I'm sorry. I forgot about your wife. I'm very sorry, David."

Sloane had become adept at redirecting conversations when others brought up the

26

topic of Tina's death, but no words came to mind.

"Well, it was, sincerely, very good." She crossed her heart. "Scout's honor."

"You were a Girl Scout?"

"Is that so difficult to believe?"

"I see you more as a troop leader."

She stood without warning. "Pool table is free."

Two men seated closer looked to be making a play for next, but they were no match for Reid. She reached the table, snatched the cues, and gave the two men a coquettish wink that only an attractive woman in a black evening gown could get away with. As the two men retreated, Reid handed Sloane the longer of the two cues.

"I don't know when I last played," Sloane said.

"It will be fun." She racked the balls at the far end of the table, deftly removing the wooden triangle. "Do you want to break?"

"I wouldn't dream of it," Sloane said. "What are we playing?"

"Eight ball?"

"Call the pocket?"

She eyed him. "You have played."

"A bit."

"Care to make it interesting?"

"It already is."

27

"I meant, care to make a bet?"

"Am I in the presence of a pool shark, Ms. Reid?" She smiled. "What did you have in mind?"

"Loser buys the drinks," she said.

"You're on."

She squeezed her fingers inside the triangular frame to tighten the rack and centered the top ball on the blue dot on the table before slowly removing the frame. Sauntering to the opposite end, she hip-checked Sloane. "I like a little room when I break."

Sloane had an idea he'd be buying the drinks.

She drew the cue back three times before it sprang forward and shot the white ball into the racked pack, hitting with a loud smack and sending balls scattering, three finding homes in pockets, two solids and one striped. The two men who failed to get the table gave a vocal approval. "I hope you didn't bet the house," one said.

Reid chose stripes and sank the 10 and 13 before missing, giving her a four-balls-to-one lead. Sloane lined up the 2, called the corner pocket, and sank the shot. Reid nodded her approval. Surveying the table, he called the opposite corner and, using more force, sank the orange 5, narrowing her lead to four to three. He missed a shot he should

28

have made, and they alternated until each had one ball remaining in addition to the 8 ball. Reid missed, but she didn't leave Sloane much to work with. To sink the 6, he'd have to bounce the cue ball off the side bumper and ricochet it, something he had never been good at. After a moment of contemplation, he shrugged. "What the heck. Six ball, corner pocket."

"Not a chance," Reid said.

Sloane bent, lined up the shot, then stood to chalk his cue.

"You're not nervous, are you, Mr. Sloane?"

"You wish."

He set the chalk down. Then, with a deft touch, he tapped the cue ball against the side bumper. It kicked off and hit the 6. The ball rolled the length of the table, looking as if it would run out of steam at the pocket edge, then trickled in.

The two men cheered. Sloane smiled at Reid. Only the 8 remained — an easy shot into the side pocket. He strolled to where Reid stood. "Excuse me," he said. "I like a little room when I win."

Reid sneered playfully and stepped to the side.

Sloane lined up the shot — a tap would be all it would take. He bent and pulled back the cue. "Eight ball . . ."

"Lunch."

He stood. "Are you trying to distract me?"

She held the cue with both hands, head tilted, her hair brushing softly against her shoulder. Sloane felt his Adam's apple bob.

"Lunch. Loser also buys the winner lunch at the restaurant of her choosing."

The two men gave an "Oooh."

"Don't you mean of 'his choosing'?"

"Does that mean you accept?"

"Why would I pass up a free lunch?"

Sloane rechalked the cue, bent to line up the shot, but could not resist considering her again, something that her grin told him she had expected. He forced himself to concentrate, easing back the stick and letting it slide through his fingers. He tapped the cue ball into the 8 and the 8 into the pocket.

The two men gave another cheer.

Sloane lay the cue on the felt. "I guess I'll have to think of a place for lunch."

Reid smiled. "I wouldn't worry about it if I were you."

"You're not reneging, are you?"

"I would never renege. I won."

Sloane laughed. "How do you figure?"

"You didn't call the shot."

The two men, momentarily stunned,

30

turned to each other and yelped, "Whoa."

"Yes, I —" Sloane started.

Reid shook her head. "No. You didn't. I think you were . . . distracted?"

"You tricked me."

"To the contrary, I played by the rules — your rule. 'Call the pocket.' " She set the cue down. "Looks like our drinks have arrived."

At their table she picked up her drink and quaffed the glass, waiting for him to reciprocate. "I think I'm going to really like the taste of mine," she said. "I hope yours isn't too bitter."

FOUR

Monday, September 5, 2011
Pike Place Market
Seattle, Washington

To the victor went the spoils, and Sloane presumed from the direction they walked that also meant a bite out of his wallet. But Reid continued to surprise. She turned down the Post Street alley and stopped outside Kells Irish Pub, another of Seattle's better-known landmarks and, in summer, a tourist haven.

Kells and the other establishments in the alley had set up outdoor tables, some draped with white tablecloths, and nearly every chair was filled. It painted a quaint scene Sloane recalled from his visit to Europe, a scene he had too infrequently enjoyed in Seattle — a hazard of a profession in which time was money.

"You know, I make a decent living,"

Sloane said as they settled at an outdoor table.

Reid folded her hands and leaned forward. "I consider this my continuing obligation as a Seattle native to further educate the uninformed."

The temperature hovered in the mid-eighties and continued to be unseasonably humid. The air had the thick, tangy smell of the Puget Sound, blocks away. The weathermen had predicted late-evening and early-morning thundershowers, but Sloane did not see a cloud in the sky, only a thin layer of lingering marine haze.

"I love the summers here," she said.

"If only they lasted longer," Sloane said.

"We might not appreciate them as much."

"Glass-is-half-full-type thing?"

"Something like that." Reid wore blue jeans, tennis shoes, and a cream-colored blouse, but she looked as attractive — maybe even more so than — as she had Saturday night. Sloane had avoided the office and spent much of the holiday weekend in the garden — a chore Tina had enjoyed and long overdue — and thinking of Barclay Reid. The image of her beside the pool table in her black dress had lingered.

The waiter brought menus, but Reid declined. "I'll have the Dublin coddle and a pint of Guinness."

"You come here often?" Sloane asked.

She smiled from behind her sunglasses.

"I hate to be ignorant, but what's a coddle?"

"Stew," the waiter replied.

"You'll like it," Reid said.

Sloane handed back the menu. "Make it two . . . and a Guinness."

After the waiter departed, Reid said, "This was a hangout in college. I tried to buy a stake in it a few years back."

"What, running a law firm and hustling guys at pool isn't enough to fill your time?"

"I'm a bit of a compulsive overachiever."

Sloane unbuttoned his cuffs and rolled the sleeves up his forearms. "Is there anything you don't do well?"

"Parenting, apparently." Reid turned her head and looked off, then back. "Sorry."

"Is everything okay?"

She removed the sunglasses. "You don't know, do you?" She seemed amazed by an unexpressed thought. "This has been so public, I guess I just assume everyone knows." Sloane waited. "I lost my daughter to a drug overdose about seven months ago."

The words brought the familiar hurt, a hollow, empty feeling that reminded him he was far from over the death of his wife. "I'm sorry. I took some time off; I've been out of the country."

She looked on the verge of tears. "She was a good kid. It wasn't her fault."

He wondered if the overdose had been accidental or if Reid was simply protecting her daughter, a parental instinct.

She cleared her throat and sipped water. "Carly was a rock climber . . . hiker . . . She loved anything outdoors, really. She and a friend were climbing, and one of her clips failed. She fell thirty feet before her safety rope caught. It jarred her back, like a whiplash. She had chronic pain and became addicted to Oxycontin."

Sloane sensed the direction of the story.

"I didn't know," Reid said, her voice softening. "One of the hazards of running a large law firm. You think you can just throw money at problems and everything will be all right. I sent Carly to a facility in Yakima and thought that would be the end of it. What I came to learn, too late, is that certain people are predisposed to addiction. It's part of their genetic makeup; they can't help it. Carly would text me from college asking for money and say it was for a class or books. I didn't think much of it. I always trusted her. But that's just an excuse I use to get through the day. The truth is, I always had so much going on I didn't have time . . ." She sighed again. "I accepted all the superficial evidence that she was back on track: honor roll, straight A's, active in after-school activities."

The waiter set two pints of Guinness on the table. Reid raised her glass and took a deep breath, regrouping. "Here's to old adversaries and new friends."

He touched her glass. She sipped the beer and used the napkin to wipe foam from her upper lip. Then, like a swimmer who had waded into cold water, she must have decided that having entered this far, she might as well get it over with and submerge herself.

"She was using the money to buy. When Oxycontin wasn't available, she did something called 'cheese.' " Reid explained that "cheese" was formed by combining heroin with crushed tablets of over-the-counter cold medications containing acetaminophen and is snorted. "The heroin content is usually between two and eight percent. Carly got a batch that was more than twenty." A tear rolled down her cheek. She used the napkin to wipe it away. "She stopped breathing . . . the paramedics couldn't revive her."

As tragic as it had been to watch Tina die,

Sloane couldn't imagine the agony of a mother losing a child. It was against the natural order of things for a child to die before a parent, and he had read somewhere that a parent never gets over the loss. He wondered how Reid found the strength to go on, and if she had been alone Saturday night because, like Sloane, she found it easier to be by herself than to pretend she enjoyed the company of others.

"The street dealer was a low-life, a punk. He's sitting in the King County jail. The person I really wanted was a man named Filyp Vasiliev."

Sloane recalled the name from an article on the front page of the metro section of the *Seattle Times*. "The guy who walked out of federal court last week. The car dealer in Renton?"

Reid's voice hardened. "He's not a car dealer. He's a drug dealer. He uses his car dealerships to import the drugs and launder the proceeds."

"What happened? How did he beat the charge?"

"You don't want to talk about this now."

Sloane sensed Reid did. "Only if you do."

She drew a line in the condensation on the outside of her glass. "A King County sheriff — a canine unit — made a routine traffic stop, and the dog alerted for the presence of drugs. Turns out the driver had an outstanding warrant for assault. The sheriff arrested him and impounded the car, which had been purchased that day at auction and registered to Vasiliev's used-car dealership. They found ten kilos of heroin in the spare tire. The DEA had been after Vasiliev for a while. They used the drugs to set up an operation that culminated in a raid of Vasiliev's dealership. Judge Kozlowski ruled that the search violated Vasiliev's Fourth Amendment rights. He threw out much of the evidence, too much to go forward."

"Any chance of an appeal?"

She shrugged. "The U.S. attorney says she's considering it, but you know how difficult the standards are to get a decision overturned."

Sloane had no doubt Reid had discussed the issue directly with Margaret Rothstein, the U.S. attorney for the Western District of Washington, and wondered if it was the matter Governor Hugh Chang had been referring to.

"For weeks after Carly died I couldn't function. Then I decided I wasn't going to let her die in vain, you know? I found out that other states have what are called drug dealer liability acts. It allows for the use of civil laws and civil penalties against drug dealers. Similar laws have been used to bankrupt hate organizations — neo-Nazi groups and skinheads. The rationale is, if you can't put them in jail, you take all their property and get them out of the community. I've been lobbying the Washington legislature to enact a similar statute."

"That would be a wonderful tribute to your daughter."

"It doesn't come close. She was so full of life; she could have done anything." The muscles of her jaw undulated. "And a piece of shit like Vasiliev is living in a mansion in Laurelhurst, free to do it to someone else's child."

The glass shattered.

Beer splashed across the table.

Sloane slid back, knocking over his chair. He used his napkin to dam the flow of beer and took another napkin from a nearby patron to wipe at his shirt and the crotch of his pants. When he looked up, Reid, too, was wiping at her blouse.

That was when he saw the blood.

Swedish Hospital
Emergency Room
Looking more embarrassed than hurt, Reid avoided eye contact and touched the rust-

colored bloodstains on her blouse, though it was well past saving. The hospital had the lemony odor of antiseptic, like a freshly cleaned floor.

"Am I a fun lunch date or what?"

The manager at Kells had wanted to call an ambulance, but Reid resisted. After Sloane applied pressure to stop the bleeding, he used butterfly bandages the manager provided to close the three-inch cut on the heel of her left hand, below the thumb. He wrapped it in gauze and accompanied Reid on the ten-minute taxi ride to Swedish Hospital, though she told him it wasn't necessary.

"I've never left a lunch date behind," he said.

In a strange way, the piece of glass, it seemed, had sliced through not only her skin but also the facade of control and composure she had undoubtedly developed from years of having to project herself as the competent, successful businesswoman and lawyer. Sitting on the bed, her shirt and pants splattered with blood, she looked vulnerable, more the person Sloane thought she must be when she did not have to impress or entertain, when she let down her guard.

"You're going to have to stop apologizing," he said. "You're the one who's hurt, after all."

"With no one to blame but myself."

"I don't know about that. We are lawyers, after all. I'm sure we could find someone to blame if we put our minds to it. Defective glass, perhaps."

"Can I sue myself for stupidity?"

A hand specialist had stitched the wound after determining the cut had not severed any tendons or nerves. They awaited the paperwork to discharge.

"How does it feel?" Sloane asked.

She held up the wrap. "Given the size of the bandage, I wish I had a better story to tell at the office." She smiled as if catching herself slipping back into Barclay Reid, attorney-at-law. "It's fine," she said. "Stings a little bit." A tear escaped the corner of her eye and she wiped it away. "It hurts sometimes . . . you know?"

"I know." And he did.

She cleared her throat. "You're the first person who has said that to me that I didn't feel like punching in the mouth."

"Well, that's a start."

"How do you deal with it?" she asked.

He thought of the advice from the white-haired woman in the cemetery. "The best I can. Moment to moment. Someone once told me that time doesn't heal all wounds, Barclay, it just deadens the pain."

"I'm sorry about lunch."

"We'll reschedule. Never let it be said that David Sloane welched on a bet."

She shook her head. "No."

"No?"

"Let me make it up to you. I know a great restaurant. Let me take you to dinner."

He shook his head. "Barclay, your hand—"

"It's fine. My hand is fine. Please."

"You're sure? You feel up to it?"

"I'm sure. Good food, good wine . . . and no blood."

Queen Anne Hill
Seattle, Washington

They took a cab downtown and Sloane retrieved his car, offering to drive Barclay home to change.

He angled the wheel and let the car roll until the tires nudged the curb, parking alongside a seven-foot wooden fence with Oriental trim and lanterns atop the posts. Bamboo stalks extended three feet above the fence line, and above the stalks he could see the upper floors of a modern glass and concrete structure.

Just north of downtown, Queen Anne was

42

the tallest of the city's seven "fabled hills." At one time Seattle's rich and famous resided there, building ornate Victorian homes, many of which remained untouched by developers. They reminded Sloane of the Victorians he had grown fond of while living in San Francisco.

At the wooden gate, Reid punched in a series of numbers on a keypad, and the lock buzzed. Sloane reached above her to assist in pushing open the gate, surprised by its significant weight. He let it swing shut, hearing it latch, but focused on the drastic transformation. Stone and moss footpaths lined by bonsai trees and Japanese maples meandered through the garden. Water babbled over rocks and trickled through a bamboo shoot into a koi pond surrounding a large boulder and, atop it, a pagoda. The tail of an orange and white fish flicked and darted, leaving ripples on the water's surface.

"It's beautiful," he said.

"I had to fight the city over the height of the fence. They gave in when I reminded them there was no limit on the height of the bamboo trees."

"Why Japanese?"

"After college, I spent a year in the small village of my great-grandmother's ancestors

43

— Takeshi-muri, Chiisagatagun."

"Easy for you to say. So you're Japanese?"

"One eighth and proud of it, so don't make any driving jokes, buster."

Sloane raised his hands in mock surrender.

"I took a lot of pictures. I always wanted to build my own home, but I had to settle for doing a remodel."

Sloane noticed rectangular boxes the size of Jake's iPod mounted below each of the light fixtures and several more along the footpaths. Initially, he thought them to be solar panels, but that would be an ill-suited design for a city where gray skies dominated much of the year. He deduced them to be motion detectors.

A large Buddha greeted them in the foyer. The interior was also Asian decor: black marble, Oriental screens and fans, bamboo floors, plush furniture, and a white marble fireplace. Lanterns hung from the ceiling by nearly translucent wires, and recessed lights illuminated impressionist paintings on the wall.

"Be it ever so humble." Reid shut the door, reapplied the deadbolt, and entered a series of numbers on a panel on the wall. "The alarm," she explained. "I make it a habit."

44

"You have motion detectors in the yard."

"And on the doors and the windows. I'm a single woman on a crusade against drug dealers. I've made my share of enemies."

She stepped out of her running shoes and left them in an impressive pile near the Buddha, exchanging them for slippers.

"Did you rob a shoe store?"

"When you're running long distances, it makes a huge difference. They wear out quickly."

She handed him a pair of slippers.

"House rule. The chef gets mad if you don't." She walked away, finishing the sentence with her back to him.

Sloane slipped off his shoes, considering her comment. He had thought she stopped to change clothes, but they weren't going to a restaurant. He tried to cover his anxiety. "What, are you running a hundred miles a day?"

"Depends on my schedule."

He joined her in the kitchen, where she used one hand to pull vegetables out of the refrigerator and put them on the black marble counter. "I was kidding. Tell me you're not serious."

"I do triathlons. The workout varies with the day of the week." She handed him two bottles of Perrier.

He opened one and handed it back to her. "How do you find the time?"

"After Carly died, time seemed to be all that I had."

Sloane knew the feeling.

She walked past him to a black wrought-iron staircase, climbing the concrete steps. "Make yourself comfortable. I'm going to change."

Sloane sipped his water at a sliding-glass door leading to a small concrete patio that afforded a view of the Seattle skyline, the Space Needle nearly dead center.

"Much better." Reid descended the staircase in a pair of black leggings and an extra-large gray sweatshirt with HARVARD in crimson across the front.

"The view is incredible," he said.

She struck a pose. "Thank you, but what do you think of the skyline?"

He laughed. "The skyline isn't bad, either."

"Sounds like another of your 'You look nice' compliments. Hungry?" In the kitchen, Reid pulled two glasses from a cabinet and poured red wine. "The view is what sold me. I thought I'd prefer something with more land, but this just felt like it could be home."

Sloane had purchased the house at Three Tree Point for the same reason: it had felt like a place he and Tina and Jake could call home. Though he had gone back after Tina's murder, he remained uncertain he would stay. Jake's visits from the Bay Area had become more infrequent what with school and sports commitments; friends and girls were also beginning to take precedence. Though Jake had spent the entire month of August with him, Sloane knew the boy had been bored at times and would have preferred to be in the Bay Area with his friends. They spoke regularly on the phone, and Sloane had learned the art of texting. He had been contemplating a condominium downtown, closer to work, but had resisted for fear work would again consume his life.

She handed him his glass, then retrieved hers from the counter. "Okay, let's try this again." She held the glass by the stem. "To old adversaries."

"And new friends," he added.

She clinked his glass, took a sip, and pivoted back to the stove, pulling out pots and pans.

"What's on the menu?" he asked.

"Putanesca."

"Let me guess, you're a gourmet chef, too."

47

"Actually, I can't boil water. But I can follow directions as well as anyone. I found a recipe in a magazine and wanted to give it a try. Now I have the chance."

"Why do I suddenly feel like one of those lab rats?"

She swatted him with a towel.

"What can I do to help?"

"You know your way around a kitchen?"

"I'm a quick study, and since the chef needs a hand . . ."

She pretended to beat on the pans like drums. "Ba-dum-dum."

For the next half hour, they worked in close quarters, sipping red wine, reading the recipe, and debating — as only two lawyers could — what the directions actually meant. Reid instructed Sloane on the proper way to chop tomatoes, olives and garlic cloves, then the parsley and basil. She added oil to anchovies and capers in a cast-iron skillet and allowed it to simmer before adding the vegetables. The room filled with a sweet fragrance and the smell reminded Sloane that he hadn't eaten since breakfast.

The meal did not disappoint. "My compliments to the chef," he said.

Reid stood. "Okay, grab the wine and follow me."

He hadn't drunk much in the past thirteen

months, not wanting to start down the path of drinking alone at home. He could feel the wine. He grabbed the bottle and his glass and followed her into the living room but she started up the stairs. Sloane had not been with a woman since Tina and had mentally prepared himself only for lunch.

At the top of the second flight of stairs, they came to a locked metal door. Reid keyed a code on a pad mounted on the wall, pushed down on the handle, and put a shoulder to the door, pushing it open and stepping out onto a roof. Sloane caught the door, which, like the gate, was spring-loaded to close automatically and of significant weight.

A wood plank walkway led to a deck with patio furniture and planter boxes filled with bamboo, tall grass, and miniature maples. The planters provided some privacy from the windows of the homes across the street, the lighting subtle. Music filtered from hidden speakers. He was surprised that it was country.

Sloane set the bottle on a table and joined Reid at a black metal-tube railing atop the parapet walls. She gestured to an even more impressive and unobstructed view of downtown, the lights shining in the fading summer sky. "Now, this is a view."

"It's certainly better than nice," he said. "And so are you. Thank you for dinner."

She gave a slight curtsy. "You're welcome."

Reid rested her forearms on the railing, her drink in hand. "Sometimes I come up here to escape from all the turmoil, you know?"

"I used to love to go home and listen to the sound of the waves," he said.

"You live on the water?"

"Three Tree Point. It's a tiny beach community near Burien — our own little oasis. Since my wife's death . . ." He caught himself.

She put a hand on his forearm. "It's okay, David. I know you loved her. Since her death what?"

"I don't much like being home anymore. I find myself making excuses to work late, take on added responsibility."

She looked back toward the skyline. "Oh, how I can relate. Life sure has a way of changing in an instant, doesn't it? I used to wonder what I would do when I saw him face-to-face." He knew she meant Vasiliev. "I contemplated what I would say to him as they led him out of the courtroom in handcuffs to spend the rest of his life in prison." She shook her head, her eyes regaining focus. "If I had known he was going to walk,

I would have just put a bullet in him and been done with it."

The comment surprised him. "No. You wouldn't have."

She glanced at him out of the corner of her eye. "I'm not so certain."

"I am."

Sloane had never told anyone about the night he held a searing fire poker to Anthony Stenopolis's face and threatened to blind the man who had murdered his wife. He hadn't done it, though, realizing that revenge was a poor substitute for justice.

"It's what separates us from people like Vasiliev — and the man who killed my wife." She turned from the view. "I had the chance. And believe me, I thought there was nothing more in the world I wanted to do."

"The paper said they never caught him."

"They didn't."

"Did you —"

"Kill him? No. I didn't kill him."

"What stopped you?"

He debated how much more he wanted to reveal, having also learned there was a fine line between being sympathetic and being pathetic. He wasn't about to start spilling his guts about growing up in foster homes because his mother had been raped and murdered as he cowered beneath his bed.

"I just knew if I pulled that trigger, I'd be stepping through a very dark doorway that I'd already escaped once. And I didn't want to go back."

She squeezed his arm. "I've never brought anyone up here before. There was never anyone I wanted to share it with." She pushed onto her toes and gently kissed his lips. Sloane felt a dozen different emotions. Together, they paralyzed him. She pulled back. "I'm sorry . . . I shouldn't have . . ."

"No." He touched her shoulder. "It's just that I haven't . . . not since my wife died."

"I understand."

"I don't think you do." He put his glass down. "There hasn't been anyone, Barclay. So I might be a bit rusty when it comes to compliments and things, but you have to understand, you didn't just take me by surprise the other night; you took me someplace I haven't been in a long time. And it all feels a bit foreign."

"There's no rush, David."

He pulled her close, wanting to feel the warmth of another human being.

This time, when she inched onto her toes, he bent and met her halfway.

FIVE

Tuesday, September 6, 2011
Queen Anne Hill
Seattle, Washington

He stared at the blank ceiling over Barclay Reid's bed, but in his mind he saw the face of Albert Einstein — the black-and-white print hung on his office wall, the genius with a twinkle in his coal-black eyes, a mischievous, elflike grin, and his trademark silver hair as wild as the bristles of an exploded broom.

A person starts to live when he can live outside himself.

John Kannin, Sloane's law partner, had hung the print where Sloane would always see it. No one would ever accuse Kannin of being subtle.

After Tina's death, Sloane became absorbed by so much sorrow and guilt it had left him physically ill. He had little appetite, frequently forgot his train of thought, and

53

lacked energy to the point that getting out of bed became a struggle. His world lost color, everything a dull, ugly gray. Though work had once been his refuge from the loneliness of his life, even there he could not function. Finally, Kannin gathered Charles Jenkins and his wife, Alex, and Sloane's secretary, Carolyn, and together they orchestrated an intervention in Sloane's office. It was nothing dramatic, just a heart-to-heart suggestion that Sloane take some time off. He had resisted, not because he thought their assessment wrong, but with Jake living with his biological father in California, work was all Sloane had.

"Someplace warm," Kannin had suggested. "Heat is good for the soul."

Sloane spent a week considering his options. He dismissed Hawaii, which he associated with honeymoons. Europe, with so much history, would only make him feel even less significant. Africa, vast and open, would exacerbate his loneliness. Undecided, he sat one evening surfing channels, not really watching, but stopped when he came upon a movie starring Morgan Freeman and Tim Robbins. Robbins, it seemed, was a man falsely convicted of murdering his wife and sent to prison. The topic wasn't exactly what Sloane needed. About to change the channel, the movie went to commercial and he learned he was watching *The Shawshank Redemption.* A lifelong Stephen King fan, Sloane decided to watch.

In the climax, Robbins tunneled his way through his cell wall, a decades-long endeavor, moving one pocketful of rock at a time. When he had finally punched through, he pulled himself to freedom through a sewer pipe, sliding out into a rain-swollen drainage ditch to exact justice on those who had wronged him. Then he fled to a quiet fishing village in Mexico called Zihuatanejo.

And Sloane found his answer.

Zihuatanejo was not the quiet 1940s fishing village Robbins described in the movie, but Sloane still found it therapeutic. He rented a house on a quiet street at the foot of the Sierra Madres and spent three months without any schedule, doing whatever he wanted: reading, lying in the sun, swimming in the Pacific Ocean, and exploring other villages on a bike. The days of the week blended. He often didn't know if it was Monday or Friday and didn't care. After several months he awoke to a recollection of another scene from the movie. Just before his escape, Robbins had turned to Morgan Freeman in the prison courtyard and proclaimed it time to either "get busy living or get busy dying."

Sloane returned to Seattle apprehensive but ready to at least try to get busy living.

Over the next several months, his progress felt at times like digging one pocketful of dirt from an endless tunnel. Now he thought he had maybe broken through the wall. He was living outside himself again — thinking not of his grief and misery but of Barclay Reid.

Sloane opened the note Reid left on her pillow.

I'm on the roof. Join me for breakfast. P.S. Put some clothes on. It's cold!

His shirt and pants hung in the closet and he found his slippers on the closet floor beside a silver box with a combination lock on top.

At the top of the staircase, he encountered the heavy door. About to knock, he noticed a second sticky note on the alarm touch pad.

Password: LEENIE

Sloane keyed the corresponding number for each letter, heard a small click, and pushed down on the handle. Reid reclined in a silk bathrobe on one of the lounge chairs, her legs bent beneath her, bandaged hand holding the handle of a ceramic mug, *The Wall Street Journal* in her lap.

"Look what the cat dragged in," she said. "Or out. I knew you plaintiff's attorneys kept bankers' hours."

Steam emanated from the spout of a ceramic teapot, and beside it, a bowl of mixed fruit, two smaller bowls, and spoons. "You're ambitious this morning," he said.

Reid poured Sloane a cup. "I worked up an appetite." She grinned. "Tea?"

Sloane took the cup and sat on the end of her recliner, the note still stuck to his fingers. "Leenie?"

"Carly's nickname," she said. "Another one of my secrets. Now you have to eat the note."

"And the gun?" he asked. "Sorry. I saw the box on the closet floor."

She shrugged. "Like I said, I'm a single woman on a crusade."

"How bad has it been?"

"The night we went for a drink?"

"Saturday?"

"We were followed. We were also followed yesterday. If you look over the railing, you might see a silver Mercedes with blackened windows."

Sloane went to the railing but did not see

57

a car fitting the description. "How long has this been going on?"

She shrugged.

"You've told the police."

"I have, and they sent a patrol car to my house, and an officer stayed with me for a few days and it stopped. But the police don't have the resources to follow around a private citizen twenty-four/seven. They suggested I hire my own security, but that posed the same problems, not to mention the expense. So I put in the alarm."

"What about when you're not at home? When you're out running or swimming, or riding your bike?"

"If Vasiliev was going to do something, he would have already done it. He's a scumbag, but he's not stupid. I've been pushing the investigation by the U.S. attorney hard. Anything happens to me, they'll come down on him like a sledgehammer. It would be bad for business. He knows that."

"Why didn't you tell me about the car Saturday night?"

She laughed. "Sure. 'You want to go for a drink? You don't mind that I have the Russian mafia following me, do you?'"

"You think Vasiliev is mafia?"

"I know it. Look, they want to scare me so I'll back off. I'm not about to do that. So

I live with it."

"You can't live this way forever."

"It won't be forever."

"How's it going to end?"

"One way or another."

He sat, thinking about the situation.

"You're having second thoughts," she said. "Most guys would."

He slid closer. "No."

"I've never done this with anyone, David."

"Have tea on the roof? You should. It's a great view." He put a hand on her thigh and leaned forward. The kiss lingered. Her cell phone rang.

She checked caller ID. "This would be my assistant, wondering why I'm not at my desk preparing for my meeting at nine."

He considered his watch. "And if I'm any later, Carolyn will declare a firm holiday, go shopping, and hand me the bill."

Reid unfolded her legs and stood back in attorney mode. "Towels in the bathroom."

"You just get ready for your meeting. I'll drop you off and grab a shower at the Washington Athletic Club."

She laughed, a bark. "Hah! Like I can work the magic that quickly, especially with this thing." She lifted her bandaged left hand. "You go. I'll get a cab."

He thought of the silver Mercedes. "You

going to be all right?"

"Are you going to watch me twenty-four/seven? I'm a big girl. I can handle myself." They started across the rooftop on the wooden walkway. "Do you have lunch plans?"

"Not anymore."

"There's something I want to talk to you about, an idea that came to me this morning."

"What about?"

"I want to do some research before we discuss it."

"Another one of your secrets."

"A woman has to have secrets," she said. "That's what makes her interesting."

Law Offices of David Sloane
One Union Square
Seattle, Washington

There was little chance he could sneak into his office and quietly grab his gym bag and the fresh shirt he kept on the hook behind his door without Carolyn asking him a dozen questions. So Sloane decided on plan B — misdirection.

When he entered, Carolyn moved with the dramatic flair of a Broadway actress. She considered her watch and arched her eyebrows. "And where have we been? Strike

60

that. I know where *I've* been. Where have you been?"

"I got home late and decided to sleep in." He picked up the stack of mail from the bin outside her cubicle.

"From lunch?"

Momentarily stumped, Sloane didn't say anything.

"You remember lunch, don't you? 'Carolyn, I'm going out for lunch, be back in a couple hours.' That was yesterday around noon? That would be the last time we saw or spoke to each other, though I did try."

If he told her he'd turned off his phone, it would raise a whole host of questions, but if he told her he had chosen not to answer or return her calls, that would raise a whole different series of questions.

"I left my phone in the car."

"You drove to lunch?"

"Yes."

"You sound uncertain."

"No. I drove."

"Lasted a little longer than anticipated, did it?"

"It did."

"Must have been great company."

"Charlie," he said. "Hadn't seen him in a while."

She nodded. "Well, no wonder; whenever

you and the Jolly Green Giant get together, it's trouble."

"He's a bad influence."

"Was there drinking involved?"

"A few beers."

"I suspect more than a few, since you didn't return my calls."

"I decided to go home, get a good night's sleep."

"You certainly look well rested," she said.

"I bought a new mattress." At least that was not a lie. He had thrown out his mattress as another way to move forward along with buying all new bed linens.

"You also appear to have gotten some sun. You have a bit of a glow."

He started for his office. "The restaurant had an outdoor patio." He stopped, trying to make it look spontaneous. "Oh . . . anything on my schedule for lunch?"

"I'll have to check. Are you two going to stage a repeat performance?"

"Unfortunately not. This is work-related. If there is anything, could you reschedule?"

"What if it's something important? What if it's a hearing or a meeting . . . or the president has asked to see you?"

"Mr. Obama will just have to reschedule. Book me the conference room and order in sandwiches."

"How many sandwiches will I be order-ing?"

"Two. Unless you're hungry, then make it three."

"You're awfully generous this morning. Anyone I know joining us?"

"Barclay Reid."

"Barclay . . ." She made a face as if she'd caught a whiff of a bad odor. "From the Kendall matter? What does that bimbo want?"

"She wants to discuss a matter with me."

Carolyn remained standing watching him with arms crossed, a pleasant smile.

"Anything else?" he asked.

"Nope."

"You're sure?"

"Yep."

"You're going to check my calendar?"

"Can't wait."

Sloane pushed open his office door. Charles Jenkins stood by the floor-to-ceiling windows, cell phone pressed to his ear.

"What, you're not answering your phone?" Jenkins looked and sounded genuinely concerned. His biceps strained the sleeves of a black short-sleeve shirt, trademark sunglasses clipped to the collar. In boots, he stood nearly six feet seven.

63

"Do you have any colors in your wardrobe besides black? You look like Johnny Cash on steroids."

"I tried you at the house yesterday and your cell this morning. Carolyn said she couldn't reach you, either."

"Thanks for that."

"What's the deal?"

"I had my phone off."

"Why?"

"I had lunch with a friend yesterday."

Jenkins cocked his head. "Would this friend be female?"

Sloane nodded.

"Shit, she was right."

"Who?"

"Alex. She said maybe you were out with a woman. I don't know how the hell she knows these things. It's scary." His tone brightened. "So . . . how did it go?"

"It went fine."

"Just fine?"

Sloane considered his answer. Jenkins was his best friend. "It went well."

"How well?"

"Charlie . . ."

Jenkins grinned. "Anyone I know?"

"Barclay Reid."

Jenkins looked puzzled. "How do I know that name?"

"She was the attorney for Kendall Toys."

"That's right. Mousy . . . thing." Jenkins lowered himself into one of the chairs across the desk. He made it look small. "Yeah? So, give me some details."

"I ran into her Saturday night at that event I spoke at and we decided to get a drink and ended up playing pool. She won. Loser had to buy lunch. Yesterday we went to Kels, and one thing led to another. She cooked me dinner."

"And you spent the night? How was it?"

Reid had been both a patient and passionate lover, and when they had finished, Sloane felt a warmth and comfort he had not felt since Tina's death.

"It was great."

"You like this woman?" Jenkins asked.

"I do."

"You don't think you're going too fast?"

It hadn't occurred to him. "Why?"

"These things take time. You suffered a huge loss. Emotionally, I mean, you're in a vulnerable position."

"Wait a minute . . . that's Alex talking."

"Okay, yes, it's Alex."

"How could Alex know?"

"I told you, when I couldn't get ahold of you yesterday or last night, she speculated, you know, that maybe . . . And Alex just

65

said you might be with a woman, though she hoped not."

"She hoped not? Why?"

"She said you needed to take time. Hell, you know how women are. She just said she hoped you didn't jump in bed with the first woman you met, that you need to try on a few pairs of shoes to make sure it's the right fit."

"Try on a few pairs of shoes?"

Jenkins sat forward. "Humor a condemned man, will you? She's going to kill me."

"Why is she going to kill you?"

"I have to tell her."

"No, you don't."

"Come on. You know I can't keep a secret from her."

"Just tell her I appreciate her concern and won't go too fast."

"She'll want to meet her."

"Soon."

"Don't say that; she'll be bugging me to call and invite the two of you to dinner. I'll tell her you're not ready."

"Fine."

Jenkins leaned the chair onto its back legs. "Okay, I did my duty. I can report back to Alex with a clear conscience. So, how was it?"

The door pushed open, Carolyn hustled

in. "Hold on. Hold on. If there are going to be details, I want to hear, too."

"There are not going to be details," Sloane said. "We had a nice evening. Let's leave it at that."

"Oh, that sucks." Carolyn picked up the stack of papers from the out-box on Sloane's desk and trudged out.

Sloane asked Jenkins, "Did you drive all this way just to check up on me?"

Jenkins considered his watch. "Pendergrass has a prevailing-wage case, a union screw job against a nonunion contractor in Eastern Washington. The DLI is blackmailing his client to pay more employee wages or they'll blackball him from bidding public jobs."

"Sound like the DLI. They're in the unions' pockets."

"He wants me to find some workers for him, prove they were correctly paid. You want to have dinner on my way back through?"

"Sure. Call me. We can meet at the Tin Room."

Jenkins grabbed the door handle. "All right, but this time, if I can't get ahold of you, you're on your own. I'm not going to come looking for you again."

The scariest part of the man wasn't the bald pate or his sheer immensity but his complete lack of emotion. The unexpected visit had caught Vasiliev unaware, and he fumbled to end a telephone call. He hung up, apologizing profusely. Sunyat Chelyakov shrugged, unconcerned. Vasiliev had seen the same expression just before Chelyakov shot a man in the head to determine whether his gun worked.

"Would you like some coffee?" Vasiliev swiveled his chair, bumping the wall behind him, leaving another black scuff mark.

Chelyakov raised a hand the size of a catcher's mitt. "Too much caffeine is not good for a man. It makes him jumpy. There are better vices," he said, his voice ragged from years smoking unfiltered cigarettes and drinking vodka.

Vasiliev returned to his seat. He knew Chelyakov had been raised on a farm in the Ukraine. It was said when the family ox died during one particularly harsh winter, Sunyat had pulled the plow himself. He was, as the Americans liked to say, "country-strong." And everything about him was big. His bald head resembled a small watermelon and his ears two lettuce leafs. The

68

cigarette in his left hand all but disappeared between fingers as round as sausages, and his body obscured the chair in which he sat. At the moment his right hand rested on his thigh, which looked about to split the seams of his slacks; there was no way he could cross his legs.

"I'm sorry about this fucking heat," Vasiliev said.

The portable office, located at the back of his Renton used-car dealership, was little more than a construction trailer with cheap wood paneling and fluorescent lights, and it was barely tolerable. With the heat and humidity the past three days, it had become unbearable. The air-conditioner broke, and the trailer had become a sweatbox even with the windows open.

Chelyakov again raised his hand. Smoke filtered from between his fingers, weaving upward. "A man cannot control the weather."

"No —"

"But he can control his business."

They had reached the purpose for the visit. Those to whom Chelyakov answered were not happy with the U.S. attorney's investigation. They considered it the direct result of poor business practices, using a man with outstanding warrants to pick up the car at the auction. Chelyakov's visit was to determine whether to continue doing business with Vasiliev.

"Everything is under control, Sunyat."

"Is it?"

"We have altered the shipments and the transport. And we are no longer using a landline. Everything now is discussed outside of this box and only on TracFones. I can assure you there will be no further problems."

"Except payment, of course, for the shipment you lost."

The drugs were supplied on credit and payment made upon subsequent sale, with the profit reinvested in the business — in this case, the half a dozen used-car dealerships through which Vasiliev helped to launder the organization's money.

Chelyakov blew smoke from his nostrils. He looked like a bull. "And what of the attorney?"

"She is not going to be a problem, Sunyat."

"No? It seems Ms. Reid has a boyfriend, a wrongful-death attorney of some repute," Chelyakov said.

"Wrongful death? What is this?" The string of red, white, and blue flags strung from the corner of the building and crisscrossing the lot flapped in a light breeze but just as quickly fell silent.

Chelyakov sucked on the cigarette, his whole face pulling in the nicotine. "He sues others when someone is killed."

"For money? How is this possible?"

"It is America. Anything is possible." An infrequent smile revealed teeth too small for his mouth.

Vasiliev slapped the desk. "Whitlock did not mention this," he said, referring to his criminal defense lawyer. "He said the charges would be dropped, that I had nothing to worry about."

"He did not consider it."

"For the amount I fucking paid him, he should have considered it."

Chelyakov took another drag. The tip glowed red. Smoke escaped his nose and mouth as he spoke. "The amount you paid?"

It pained Vasiliev to take orders from a man like Chelyakov. Who was he to be giving him orders? Who was he? A fucking farm boy who spent his youth buggering the family ox. Vasiliev was a multimillionaire. He brought the organization tens of millions of dollars, a hundred million some years. So who was Chelyakov to be giving orders?

"Do not forget who you work for," Chelyakov said.

And therein lay the problem. Vasiliev knew very well who he worked for, and even more so, who Chelyakov worked for: Petyr Sakorov, the Russian billionaire. But that was not his problem at the moment. His problem was the lawyer.

"You think she plans to sue me for money?"

"She and this lawyer have become familiar."

"Then Mr. Whitlock will have to defeat him, too."

Chelyakov shook his head. "Whitlock is not a civil lawyer."

"Someone else, then."

"You're not listening, Filyp." He crushed the butt of the cigarette beneath a foot as wide as a salad plate. The chair creaked as he gripped the arms and stood. His head nearly brushed the ceiling tiles. "I think Mr. Sloane should know it would not be wise to do business with Ms. Reid."

Law Offices of David Sloane
One Union Square
Seattle, Washington
Barclay spoke as soon as Carolyn closed the door to the conference room behind her. "I

want to sue Filyp Vasiliev for wrongful death."

"What?" Sloane asked.

"That's the idea that came to me this morning. Am I crazy?"

"The drug dealer?"

Reid paced near the floor-to-ceiling windows. "This morning I read a case in the *Law Journal:* a mother in California, unhappy with the sentence a judge handed down to a drug dealer who supplied her son drugs, sued him in a civil suit."

"What was the cause of action?"

"Intentional tort and intentional infliction of emotional distress. She alleged he was responsible for her son's addiction and should be held responsible for all of his medical bills and the cost of rehab."

Sloane tried not to sound skeptical. "How did it turn out?"

"It hasn't gone to trial and likely won't ever get that far. They'll settle, I'm sure, but that's not a possibility for me. Carly's dead. No amount of money will bring her back. I won't settle."

Sloane knew of celebrated cases in which criminal defendants had been sued in civil court for wrongful death. The most infamous, of course, was the $33 million verdict against O. J. Simpson following his acquittal of the murder of his wife, Nicole, and her boyfriend, Ron Goldman. The standard of proof in civil cases obligated a plaintiff to prove a defendant guilty by a "preponderance of the evidence," or 51 percent. The burden was far less onerous than the criminal standard of "proof beyond a reasonable doubt."

"Has it ever been done?"

"I don't know. But who better to blaze that trail than you?" She paced again. "I had an associate do some preliminary research this morning. Remember I mentioned how some states have enacted drug dealer liability acts?"

"You said Washington doesn't have one."

"It doesn't. But this is the same concept; if you can sue a drug dealer in a civil action for an intentional tort, why not for wrongful death?"

Reid was not a typical potential client. Still, Sloane felt compelled to determine if she had thought the matter through. He tried to slow the pace of the conversation. "Assuming for a moment that we have a viable cause of action, you know there's an argument that Carly assumed the risk of injury by ingesting a dangerous drug."

Reid stopped pacing. "My daughter didn't choose to be addicted. Before she hurt her back, she didn't even take aspirin. She was a fitness freak. Her addiction wasn't her fault."

"You're preaching to the choir."

She took a deep breath. "Sorry."

"All I'm saying is that Vasiliev's lawyers will argue that the potential of dying from the use of heroin is a known risk." Reid started to interrupt, but he raised a hand to allow him to finish. "They'll bring up Carly's drug history and drag her past through the mud. It could be painful."

Reid had the same determined look Sloane recalled from the courtroom, a woman not to be denied. "It won't be any more painful than having to identify my daughter's body in a morgue. I'm numb to the pain, David. I've been numb since I received that first phone call. This morning is the first time in a long time that I've had hope that maybe Carly didn't have to die in vain."

"And they'll argue that the man who supplied Carly with drugs is in jail."

"He's just a pawn."

"He's the dealer."

"*He* doesn't exist if guys like Vasiliev aren't importing it."

"Neither does Vasiliev if there aren't guys supplying him. How high up does this go?

Where do we stop?"

"I want Vasiliev. I'll worry about those above him after I get him."

"He hasn't been convicted of anything."

"He walked on a technicality. There is a lot of evidence he was dealing drugs through his car dealerships and laundering the proceeds. With the reduced burden of proof, you can convince a jury."

"If it ever gets that far; they'll file motions to dismiss, summary judgments."

Reid approached. "I'm not going to lie to you: I want to win this case, but barring an outright win, the publicity alone could be what I need to get the Washington legislature to seriously consider passing a drug dealer liability act."

Part of Sloane wanted to take the case because he knew how much it meant to her — and also because he was concerned how it might impact their relationship if he declined. He had been cautious in his comments with Charles Jenkins earlier that morning, but he couldn't deny that he had quickly developed feelings for Barclay Reid.

"The U.S. attorney's office will help," she said. "I spoke to Rebecca Han this morning." Reid was off again, pacing, thinking aloud. "If we can get an O.J.-type verdict, thirty to thirty-five million, we can take everything Vasiliev owns — his cars, his house. I can put the money into a foundation to educate kids in high school and college about drug use. We can do something good with bad money." She considered him. "Look, I know I'm asking a lot, David, maybe too much. But please consider it."

"You already have them following you, watching your home."

"I'm not afraid of them. The more we let people like Vasiliev get away with it, the more chances he has to do it to someone else's child. I'm not going to live my life in fear. I will do what I have to do to avenge my daughter's death."

Six

Law Offices of David Sloane
One Union Square
Seattle, Washington

Sloane threw his gym bag into the backseat and slipped behind the wheel, not bothering to check the clock on the dash. He was late. He'd worked out longer and harder than intended. He needed it to clear his head, to think through what Barclay had asked of him. He had a bad feeling it could be one of those cases in which, no matter how it turned out, there would be no winners. But what option did he have? He had seen the intensity in her eyes and heard it in her voice. She was committed.

The V8 engine echoed in the underground garage before settling into a melodic rumble that sounded like a boat engine. To park in one of the stalls beneath the building, Sloane had to inch the front bumper until it touched the stucco wall. Even then the back fins stuck out farther than any other car in the garage. A compact it was not. At least the car on his left had departed, which would make it easier to maneuver the behemoth from the space.

He shifted the handle on the steering column into reverse, causing the emergency brake to automatically pop, and started backward, cutting the wheels to avoid a pillar on his left, never seeing the black Mercedes until he felt the jolt and heard the crunch of metal and glass.

The car had come around the corner fast, too fast, but his insurance company wouldn't care. He'd pay a deductible, and his premiums would go up — all because some guy was in a hurry to get home.

Sloane pushed out of the car, angry. The Mercedes driver shouted and gesticulated about the damage to the front of his car.

"Look! Look what you have done." He had a heavy accent, gel-spiked hair, a diamond stud in one ear, and wore fashionable clothes — jeans that, to Sloane, always looked to be in need of a wash.

"Hang on a second. I didn't even see you."

"Because you don't look."

"Because you came around that corner too fast."

The man pressed closer, about Sloane's

size, over six feet, and stocky, with a square jaw. Sloane guessed late twenties. "You're the one who came backward." He made a screeching noise and used his hand to demonstrate the Caddy shooting from its spot.

"The screeching was *your* tires coming around the corner," Sloane said, his adrenaline pulsing.

"Then how come you don't stop?"

Sloane stepped around him to the back of the Cadillac, took one look at the damage, and fought the urge to laugh. The fin barely had a scratch on it, but it had embedded in the hood of the Mercedes and destroyed its front-left headlight.

"You are going to pay for this damage," the man continued.

Sloane turned. "Look, just get your —"

The man held open his leather car coat, displaying the butt of a handgun. A second man, also wearing a car coat despite the heat and humidity, got out of a nearby parked car.

And everything registered.

Vasiliev.

Auto World
Renton, Washington
The hand at his back encouraged Sloane

toward a rectangular wood-sided modular structure. Part of the skirt hiding the foundation had pulled away to reveal that the building sat on cinder blocks. Overhead, multicolored flags strung from the corners of the building hung limp. A sign indicated Auto World was having an end-of-summer sale.

The building shook as Sloane followed one of his escorts up two stairs and stepped inside. Cluttered desks perpendicular to the walls left an aisle down the middle. Sloane smelled burnt coffee.

"You might want to turn that off." He pointed to a stained coffeepot on a Formica counter. "Hate to see a fire burn down such a fine establishment."

One of his escorts flipped the switch. The second man encouraged Sloane to an office at the back with a large metal desk. Behind it, a man in an open-collar silk shirt leaned back in his chair, leg crossed, scratching the bottom of his socked foot. The room smelled of perspiration poorly masked by too much cologne.

"Looks like I missed the memo on leisure-suit attire. Or did you guys miss the seventies?" Sloane said.

Vasiliev slipped the loafer over the sock, smiling. "Come in, come in." He gestured to the cheap cloth chairs, a lime-green color. "Mr. Sloane. Yes, come in. Thank you for agreeing to see me."

"I assume you're Vasiliev."

"You see, we are already knowing one another." Vasiliev nodded to the escorts, who stepped back and took up posts at the door. "Please, be seated."

Sloane considered the stained chairs. "Do I have a choice?"

"Only if you wish to be more comfortable. Do you wish for coffee?" Vasiliev had a tattoo on his neck, a crest of some sort, partially hidden by the collar of his shirt and the links of several gold chains.

"No, thanks. The jolt I got in the car was enough. Maybe I have whiplash. I'm thinking about suing you."

Vasiliev laughed. "An unfortunate accident, but this is why we have insurance, yes? I have repair shop. Bring in your car, and I will see that it is fixed. No charge."

"That's very sporting of you, but I think the Mercedes absorbed most of the damage."

"They don't make cars like they used to." Vasiliev shrugged. "You are a Cadillac man. You know what they say about a man who must drive such a big car?" Vasiliev held his fingers two inches apart, bringing chuckles from his two bodyguards.

"No. But I know what they say about a man who has to carry a big gun."

The Mercedes driver quit laughing.

Vasiliev winked. "Which is why I don't need a gun. I'm a businessman, Mr. Sloane."

"Then why don't we cut the pleasantries and get down to business. Why am I here?"

Vasiliev tried to recline but his chair hit the wall. When he attempted to cross his leg, his knee hit the desk. He had a nervous habit of jiggling his foot. He also intermittently bit his fingernails, which had been worn to the nubs. "I wish to make you a business proposal. Man to man."

"I'm all ears."

"I wish for you to . . . to persuade Ms. Reid to let bygones be bygones, as they say in your country."

"I'm not familiar with that saying. Why don't you explain it to me?"

Vasiliev's mouth widened into a broad smile. He chuckled and wagged a finger. "I think I like you, Mr. Sloane. Yes, I think I do. I think you must be very good lawyer. Perhaps someday you would be my lawyer."

"I don't think so, Filyp."

"Yes, call me Filyp. May I call you David?"

"No."

"Don't be so quick to judge, Mr. Sloane. This is America. We are entitled to an attorney, no? Innocent until proven guilty. I have many businesses; you could make a lot of money. I pay very well my attorneys."

"I don't need your business."

"A man with no price? Very rare. Tell me, what is nature of your relationship with Ms. Reid?"

"I don't think so."

"You don't think so what?"

"I don't think I want to tell you the nature of my relationship. So if you don't mind, I have someplace to be and someone waiting for me." He started from the chair, but Vasiliev looked at his men, and one put a firm hand on Sloane's shoulder. Sloane sat. "You do realize kidnapping is a crime in this country."

Vasiliev bit at his thumbnail, his left foot continuing to jiggle. "Is it business, this relationship, or do you just like fucking her?"

Sloane didn't answer.

Vasiliev pointed. "I think you do like fucking her. I know I would. Perhaps someday I will have chance. But me, I would do her in the ass, like a dog. Maybe she would bark, yes? Does she bark for you, Mr. Sloane?"

Vasiliev wanted Sloane to come across the desk so the two goons could beat him down, put him in his place. He was a punk. A dangerous punk, but still just a punk.

"I don't think that's going to work, Filyp. She doesn't sleep with guys who don't have a gun."

One of the two men behind Sloane snorted, and Vasiliev's eyes quickly found him. "You are funny man, Mr. Sloane. But I am not so much in mood for humor."

"And here I thought we were all getting along swimmingly."

"You will tell Ms. Reid not to pursue this."

"Not to pursue what?"

"Ms. Reid thinks I have something to do with her daughter's death. The papers say she is on crusade."

"Did you have anything to do with her daughter's death?"

Vasiliev held up his hands, the universal sign for "who knows." "So she comes to hire you, and you will seek to know that answer. Am I wrong? No, I don't think I am wrong."

"You said you had a business proposal?"

"Yes, you will convince her not to pursue this foolishness further." Vasiliev sat back. "You will talk to Ms. Reid and we go our separate way. Bygones."

"Let me ask you something, Filyp. What

85

makes you think she would listen? What makes you think she wouldn't just find another lawyer?"

Vasiliev waved the finger as if Sloane were a misbehaving student. "I don't think so. You can be very persuasive, no? You will convince her." The smile disappeared. "You will convince her because you are familiar with the consequences."

"What does that mean?"

Vasiliev spoke Russian to the men behind him. The man on Sloane's left stepped forward, tapped him on the shoulder, and handed him a cell phone.

Vasiliev said, "I believe this call is for you, Mr. Sloane."

Sloane took the phone and pressed it to his ear, hearing it ring, then a familiar voice. "Hello?"

Sloane felt his heart sink. "Jake."

"Dad? I can barely hear you. Why did your phone come up as a private number?"

The Tin Room
Burien, Washington
They sat beneath an umbrella at a wooden table. The first drops of rain intermittently splattered the deck, leaving large black spots — perhaps the beginning of the thunderstorms the weathermen had been predict-

86

ing. Dan House, the owner, put pints in front of Sloane and Jenkins, and asked Sloane how he was doing before moving on to serve another table. When Tina had been alive, the bar and restaurant had been their favorite hangout. Since her death, Sloane had frequented it less, but that hadn't stopped House from treating him like a member of the family.

"Do you need to go?" Jenkins asked.

Sloane ran a hand over his face, still feeling the rush of adrenaline from his meeting with Vasiliev. He had assured Jake everything was fine and told him he'd call when he got home.

Jenkins rapped on the table with his knuckles. "Do you need to go?"

Sloane shook his head. He had called Reid on the drive but she had left for a workout. When she called back she refused to check into a hotel.

"She won't leave her house. Maybe that's best. It's like a fortress. She's safer there than at a hotel."

"Not if they can't find her. What about you? You still have that gun?"

Sloane kept a .38 Glock in the top desk drawer of his home office. Not that it had done him any good the night Anthony Stenopolis murdered his wife. He now took it upstairs when he went to bed, leaving it on the nightstand.

"What are you going to do?" Jenkins asked.

"What do you think I should do?"

"I think I gave up telling you what to do a long time ago."

Sloane asked, "Should I let it go?"

"Like I said . . ."

"But now I'm asking."

Jenkins sipped his beer. "What about Jake?"

"He and Frank leave at the end of the week." Jake's biological father and grandparents were taking him to Italy. With the commercial real estate business still in the toilet, Frank's father had found his son a consulting position on a hotel project. It was the opportunity of a lifetime for a high school kid.

"Tell him to pack a bottle of ranch dressing," Jenkins said. He and Alex had honeymooned in Italy and Jenkins complained he could get only oil and vinegar on his salad.

Sloane's legs ached, the adrenaline giving way to lactic acid. "I'm tired, Charlie. I'm tired of people threatening me, threatening my family."

"I'd say you have a right to be tired."

"Do I court it? Do I go looking for this shit?"

The black spots on the concrete and wood decking multiplied. When the waitress appeared, Sloane handed her his menu without ordering. Jenkins did the same.

"You're not thinking of doing anything stupid, are you?"

Water began to drip off the edges of the umbrella. Sloane looked into the restaurant. Dan House stood with his hand on someone's shoulder, talking and laughing.

"Like I said . . . I'm just tired."

"If this guy Vasiliev is connected, he is not to be taken lightly, do you hear me? They're cowboys, the Russians. They're smart, but they're crazy." Sloane did not respond. Jenkins said, "And to answer your question . . . no. I don't think you court it. Sometimes bad things happen when you do the right thing."

"Yeah, that's me," Sloane said, picking up his beer. "The guy who always does the right thing."

SEVEN

Kinsington Rowe stepped from the blue Impala and grimaced, sucking air through his teeth and blowing out the pain until the initial wave passed. He bent back inside the car and retrieved his black go bag, which resembled a tool bag with multiple pockets and interior compartments. Rowe clenched the blue laser light on his key chain between his teeth as he rummaged through boxes of sterile gloves, booties, and evidence containers until he found the small plastic bottle and slipped it into the pocket of his windbreaker. Overhead, the blades of a helicopter thumped, a white light spotting the residence along the shores of Lake Washington. If the storm hadn't kept the neighbors up, the helicopter certainly would.

It had been raining hard when Rowe left

the Justice Center in downtown Seattle at midnight, the end of his shift, and he'd heard a steady patter on the roof shingles and skylights when he got home. He climbed into bed in time for the thunder to frighten awake his three-year-old son and had barely calmed him when his cell buzzed on the nightstand, never a good thing when you were the homicide detective on call.

Though the rain had passed, the storm had not cleared the humidity, and Rowe was glad he opted for the windbreaker and not his patrol jacket. A long morning was likely to become a long couple of days, making comfort important. He'd slipped the windbreaker over a white polo shirt, blue jeans, and patrol boots.

Rowe flipped open his notebook and wrote the time of his arrival beneath the time he received the call from his detective sergeant: 3:22 A.M.

"Rise and shine, sunshine, we have a homicide."

Beneath the time, Rowe had written "ANONYMOUS" in capital letters, underlining it twice.

He wedged the notebook at the small of his back beneath the windbreaker, and ducked beneath the strand of yellow police tape strung across the road. A uniformed

91

officer handed him the crime-scene log and a pen, and Rowe dutifully signed his name and noted his badge number and time of entry. Anyone who stepped beneath the yellow tape would have to do the same.

Handing back the pen, he made his way toward the cluster of dark shadows standing in the street. His partner, Tracy Crosswhite-Jones, held a notebook and talked with the sergeant supervisor, Billy Williams, who had likely reported the homicide to their detective sergeant.

"Long time no see," Crosswhite said. She and Rowe had left the Justice Center together.

"I knew I'd see you in the middle of the night sooner or later, Professor."

Everyone in the unit referred to her as either Crosswhite or Professor, the latter a reference to the fact that she had taught chemistry at a local high school for fifteen years. After a divorce she decided she needed to change more than just the man in her life. Having competed in pistol-shooting contests into her late teens, she enrolled in the police academy.

Rowe noted the Prius parked outside a second strand of tape strung chest-high across the street, halfway down the block. "I see you got the first pick from the motor pool."

She groaned. "I feel like I'm driving a sewing machine."

The detective team on call took a car home from the motor pool. Everyone else was supposed to drive a personal vehicle, but some kept the cars longer than necessary, and the pickings got slim. The Prius was last choice. Crosswhite had little room to complain as the low woman on the homicide-detective totem pole, having been recently elevated to one of the highly coveted positions. An opening in the fifteen-person unit was rare, the promotion of a woman rarer still — Crosswhite being the first and only. In seven months, Rowe was already her third partner. The first, a veteran of thirty-two years, flat-out declined to work with a woman. The second relationship lasted until her partner's wife met Crosswhite at a party and couldn't deal with her husband being professionally wed to a tall, athletically built blonde who looked more like a fashion model than a police officer. Rowe's wife had expressed similar reticence but solved the matter diplomatically: she told Rowe she'd kill him if he screwed around.

"If there's not a dead body, this is a cruel

practical joke," Rowe said.

Crosswhite pointed in the direction of the residence.

"The body is in a room off the patio at the back of the house. Shooter apparently shot through the sliding-glass door."

"Through it?"

"So I'm told," she said, indicating Williams.

"Who was first in?" Rowe asked, meaning the first officer to respond.

She checked her notes. "Adderley. He's waiting on the porch down the drive."

The sloping aggregate driveway forked as they descended. The straight shot continued along the east side of the property, where Rowe could make out the strand of yellow tape strung between trees. The other path turned right and led to the residence. As Rowe pulled out his notebook to write down the address, his right foot slipped on a patch of moss, and pain shot from his hip, causing him to stop and grimace.

"You okay?" Crosswhite asked.

He removed the bottle from his windbreaker, shook out two anti-inflammatory tablets, and chewed them.

Crosswhite winced. "Jesus, Sparrow. I hate it when you do that. Why can't you swallow them like the rest of the world?"

Most thought his nickname a derivation of his last name, but he had actually received it while working undercover narcotics. He'd grown his hair long, along with a scraggly goatee, and one of the members of the unit likened him to the pirate Jack Sparrow played by Johnny Depp in the *Pirates of the Caribbean* movies. Nobody called him Kinsington, his mother's maiden name, or even Kins, which had been his nickname growing up.

"Never could," he said, "even as a kid."

"But you can *chew* them?"

"Everyone can chew."

Crosswhite shuddered. "It gives me the willies." They continued down the path. "Why don't you have the surgery?"

The hip had been a problem since Rowe's senior year playing football for the U. The team doctor had called the injury a hip pointer, and Rowe had played through the pain. More extensive X rays later in life revealed a fracture that had developed avascular necrosis from a decreased blood supply to the head of the femur. Rowe fell back on his degree in criminology and applied to the FBI but couldn't pass the medical exam, so he joined the police force. He would eventually need an artificial hip.

"Because I only want to go through this once."

"Don't they use titanium now? I thought that stuff lasts forever."

"Twenty to thirty years, according to my doctor."

"I hope someone lets Boeing know."

"Boeing?" he asked.

"I read they make airplanes out of that stuff now."

At thirty-nine, Rowe felt too young to be walking around with an artificial hip. But every time he stepped on the front lawn to play football with his sons, reality replaced fantasy; the pain inched him closer to pulling the trigger. Until he did, he chewed the ibuprofen.

A Mercedes Roadster sat parked near the front entrance.

"So this is how the other half lives," Crosswhite said, looking over the car and the three-story residence. Rowe estimated the house to be nine thousand square feet, several million dollars, at least. Expensive home, expensive car — the owner had money or a lot of debt.

Two uniformed officers approached.

"Who's Adderley?" Rowe asked.

The taller of the two, African-American, adjusted the utility belt around his waist.

"That would be me." The bulletproof vest beneath his navy blue shirt puffed him up like a marshmallow.

Rowe introduced himself, and Adderley explained that he had received a call from dispatch, an anonymous report of a prowler.

"A prowler? Not shots fired?" Rowe asked.

"Prowler."

Under the word "ANONYMOUS" in his notebook, Rowe wrote: *Prowler?* And beneath that: *Thunder and lightning.*

"What next?"

Adderley explained that after backup arrived, he radioed dispatch to try to reach someone inside the home to tell them not to shoot him in the ass. "I asked that they keep the air open while we walked the perimeter. We found the victim in a room off the patio. Shooter shot through the sliding-glass door. I called it in 'person down' and held for more resources."

"Did you attempt to enter?"

Adderley shook his head. "No."

Adderley and the second officer both wore black gloves. "You wearing your gloves, then?" Rowe asked.

"Haven't taken them off."

"Show us."

Adderley led Rowe and Crosswhite to a concrete patio at the back of the house. The sliding-glass door was shut, the glass pierced by a single hole that had caused a spider-web of cracks, though the glass had not crystallized. Blood splattered the interior, and Rowe could see the bloodied back of a head resting on the arm of a leather sofa. A pool of blood had accumulated on the hardwood floor where the Persian rug did not reach. The flat-screen television mounted on the wall remained on, a movie Rowe did not recognize.

"When SWAT arrived, we cleared the house, taped it off, secured the perimeter, and waited," Adderley explained.

"Did you do anything else? Talk with anyone? Go anywhere else on the property?"

Adderley shook his head.

"Search the yard?"

"Just a visual from the patio. Something else, though."

"What's that?"

"I asked dispatch to run a background check."

"Why'd you do that?"

"Thought I recognized the name of the owner."

"And . . ."

"This is the guy who was in the papers. The feds were after him for dealing heroin. He owns a bunch of used-car dealerships."

Sloane exited the Cadillac and wiped beads of perspiration dripping down his face with the front of his sweatshirt. He heard a car engine and lowered the shirt in time to see a Volvo station wagon roll through the intersection, unconcerned about other cars at four in the morning. The neighbor down the block worked for one of the local television stations. No one else in his right mind would be awake and up this early.

Sloane pushed through the gate in the hedge and trudged up the back steps, his legs leaden. Just inside the door, he hung the keys on the life-size cardboard cutout of Larry Bird, Celtic legend, and filled the kettle with water, putting it on a lit burner. He retrieved a ceramic mug — world's best dad, a birthday gift from Jake — and set it on the counter, then pulled down the box of tea and set a bag inside the mug. He pulled a cup from the shelf and filled it with tap water. He had drunk half the glass when he felt his throat constrict. He gagged and dropped the cup into the sink. The muscles of his stomach contracted, and he threw up the water, then endured half a dozen dry heaves.

He gripped the counter, trying again to

catch his breath. The vomiting began not long after he returned to Three Tree Point following Tina's death, a physical manifestation, he assumed, of his guilt and anxiety. Research on the Internet said such things were often associated with PTSD — post-traumatic stress disorder. The first time had been a Friday afternoon, Sloane's first trip back to the Tin Room. He had taken a seat toward the back, sipping a beer, trying to relax but unable to slow his mind or get rid of the image of Tina standing on the steps, calling out to him just before her chest exploded in a red bloom. The image flickered and clicked in his head like a movie reel in constant rewind. He had gagged, began to retch, and barely made it into the alley before throwing up.

On the drive home, he had passed the St. Francis of Assisi church. Raised with no faith, Sloane had never been religious, but shortly after they moved to Three Tree Point he began attending mass with Tina and Jake. He hadn't experienced any epiphanies; it had been a way to spend more time as a family. He parked and went into the church alone and sat in the pew staring up at the cross. Every so often a person would step from one of three doors at the side of the church, and another would enter, mostly older women. After about half an hour, when there was no one left in line, the middle of the three doors opened and Father Allen, the young Catholic priest whom Sloane knew through Tina and Jake, stepped out. If Allen was surprised to find Sloane in the pew, he didn't show it. He asked how Sloane was coping, what he was doing to keep busy, and sought details about Jake's life in California.

Sloane returned the following Friday, but neither the priest nor anyone else entered or exited the three doors. A woman at the rectory informed him that the three doors were the confessional and available only the third Friday of the month. Father Allen, she said, was in the schoolyard.

Sloane found the curly-haired priest wearing shorts that extended to his knees and high-top tennis shoes, shooting a basketball. When Allen tossed Sloane the ball, Sloane buried a jump shot from the top of the key. When Sloane buried a second shot, the priest challenged him to a game of horse, which Sloane lost. Horse led to what started as a friendly game of one-on-one that became a battle that left Allen, fifteen years Sloane's junior, the victor and both men spent. The pickup games became part basketball, part counseling. During one of the games, Father Allen got down to the crux of their discussions. "You wanted to kill him," he said, meaning Stenopolis.

"I thought I did."

"And you're wondering if that makes you a bad person to have those kinds of thoughts."

"Does it?" Sloane had never given the concepts of heaven and hell much thought, but now, with Tina gone, he wondered.

"Thoughts of revenge are natural, David. You suffered a great loss, a great injustice. You wanted someone to pay for it. But always remember, it's our actions that define us, not our thoughts, and even then God will forgive those who seek His forgiveness."

"What about an eye for an eye? I thought I read that somewhere."

"That's the Old Testament. That was not Christ's message. *Love* was his message. Even your enemies."

"I'm afraid that's not something I can bring myself to do."

"Most of us find it a hard concept."

"And if I can't?"

"Then you'll be like ninety-nine-point-nine percent of us. Imperfect." That caused Sloane to smile. "You're not alone. You only think you are."

"I don't have your faith, Allen. The only time I've ever really prayed was when Tina was dying, and that didn't turn out too well."

"And what about when you punished this man? Did that make you feel any better?"

"No."

"And do you think it would have if you had pulled the trigger?"

"You're asking . . . if I had the chance, the chance to do it again . . . would I pull the trigger?"

The kettle on the stove whistled.

EIGHT

A crowd loitering in the street of an upscale neighborhood before dawn would normally generate police interest, but in this case, police interest had generated the crowd. Rowe had put everything on hold to prepare a search warrant, a necessity since he could not be certain the victim lived alone, and therefore he could not rule out if anyone else had a privacy interest in the residence. With the sleeves of his windbreaker pulled up his forearms, Rowe continued to hunt-and-peck on the laptop keyboard balanced on his knees, the screen a blue-white glow. At least he wasn't lonely. Three CSI detectives, women dressed like triplets in black BDU cargo pants and black T-shirts and vests with gold letters proclaiming CRIME SCENE INVESTIGATOR on the back, sipped coffee and waited. The detective team next

104

up in the rotation had also arrived, though Rowe had directed them to canvass the neighborhood, photograph license plates, and talk with the neighbors to determine if one of them had made the anonymous call or had seen or heard anything.

Rowe didn't think so.

Normal cell phones registered the number with dispatch, making it a simple matter to run a reverse directory to get a name and address. But dispatch had indicated that the number of the anonymous caller was not registered, which meant the caller had likely used a disposable TracFone, which could be bought for ten dollars at almost any store.

Why?

Rowe had written that word in his notebook along with a reminder to determine if they could trace the phone to a particular retail store. If so, they could check sales receipts to determine whether the buyer used a credit card. Fat chance. The store might also have a video camera that recorded the transaction, including a beautifully clear picture of the purchaser. Even fatter chance. Rowe had also made a note to determine if they could use cell phone towers to triangulate the call to at least determine the GPS coordinates when the call was made.

Crosswhite approached. "He's the only registered owner. Three in the morning. If someone else lived here, you'd expect to find them home."

Rowe drafted the subpoena with that assumption. He wanted it as broad as possible, because his initial impression — shot fired through the sliding-glass door — was that the forensic evidence would be minimal. However, if Vasiliev had been moving large quantities of heroin and using his used-car businesses to launder the proceeds, he had to have kept records to account for the shipments and the money. Rowe had learned from his time on the narcotics unit that the drug trade was a cash business, and distributors like Vasiliev had suppliers and distributors to pay. If he had been executed, and it certainly appeared that way, Rowe wanted to spread a wide net to identify the man's known business associates. Maybe someone would talk.

"Is that the search warrant?" Rowe looked up at the sound of a familiar voice and watched Rick Cerrabone make his way down the driveway wearing a blue and red Boston Red Sox cap.

Rowe made a dramatic gesture to check his watch. "Nice team spirit, Morty," he said, borrowing a line from his favorite Bill

Murray movie, *Meatballs.*

"Some of us need more beauty sleep," Cerrabone said. "I'd recommend a week for you, Sparrow."

"Everyone's a comedian this morning."

Cerrabone, a King County senior prosecuting attorney, was a member of the Prosecutor's MDOP unit. The Most Dangerous Offenders Program had been started to involve the county's most experienced prosecutors in the earliest stages of violent crime investigations. Some detectives weren't thrilled to have an attorney peeking over their shoulders. Rowe had been one of them until a four-month stint sitting beside Cerrabone at a homicide trial gave him an appreciation of what Cerrabone and his colleagues were up against. It didn't take much for an enterprising defense attorney to exploit even the most insignificant mistake and blow it up to look like grievous police misconduct. Involving the prosecutor early in the game was intended to minimize those mistakes.

Rowe smiled. "Yankees ever going to win another pennant, Rick?"

Cerrabone shifted the hat back, revealing a bald spot. "Fucking Red Sox."

Cerrabone's language became more colorful and his Brooklyn accent more distinct when he discussed anything Boston. A diehard Yankees fan who resembled the former skipper, Joe Torre, with his thinning hair, high forehead, hangdog eyes, and perpetual five o'clock shadow, Cerrabone had somehow managed to marry an equally diehard Red Sox fan — a clerk for the Superior Court.

"Dustin Pedroia? Are you kidding me? The guy had a career year. He'll never sniff those numbers again."

The annual bet was widely known around the courthouse. The spouse whose team finished lower in the pennant race had to wear the other team's hat for one solid week, night and day, Cerrabone's court appearances being the only exception.

Crosswhite provided Cerrabone with a five-minute snapshot of the crime scene and Vasiliev's likely ties to the local heroin trade. Cerrabone reached for the laptop. "Let me take a look."

Rowe stepped aside and stretched his back, walking out the kink in his hip, which burned despite the ibuprofen. He could feel his shirt sticking to his chest.

"Tell me something," Crosswhite said to Rowe. "How many people in this neighborhood would know that when you call in a gunshot, especially on a night with thunder, you might get a patrol out here within the hour?"

They were starting to think alike. A common misconception among the public was that a report of gunshots would bring a cavalry of police. In reality, such calls were common and usually false alarms. The police had become somewhat desensitized. Call in a prowler, however, and the response could be instantaneous. That and an anonymous caller on an untraceable cell phone made the situation unusual.

Cerrabone handed him the laptop. "Looks good . . . broad. I'm not sure you'll get the computer records."

"Who are you thinking about calling?" Rowe asked.

The judge who issued the warrant was automatically disqualified from being the trial judge on the case, if it ever got that far. So the PA ordinarily didn't want to burn one of his first trial-judge choices. But in this instance, they were also seeking a search warrant broader in scope than normal, and Cerrabone would want a judge predisposed to granting expansive searches.

After discussing a few names, Cerrabone said, "Let's call O'Neil."

Rowe attached the recording device to his cell phone, plugged in the earpiece, and called Judge Thomas O'Neil's cell phone. When the judge answered, he apologized for the hour and explained the circumstances. O'Neil swore him in as the affiant of the facts to justify issuing the warrant, and Rowe read what he had typed, including the time of the 911 call to dispatch, the fact that the residence was registered only to Vasiliev, and everything Adderley had related. Then he got to the request.

"I am requesting a warrant to search the residence for firearms, weapons, and bills and receipts." And now the reach. "I am also seeking all computers and business records located inside the residence."

"Computer records?" O'Neil's voice sounded like a smoker's, deep and brusque from the early hour. "What for?"

"The victim was recently the subject of a federal investigation for trafficking in narcotics. Heroin."

"What was the outcome, Detective?"

"The matter is unresolved."

"And the reason you want the computer records?"

"Given the manner in which the victim was killed, Your Honor, I would like to pursue known associates. I think this could have been an execution related to the victim's involvement in narcotics. Forensic evidence is likely to be minimal."

"Alleged involvement."

"Alleged involvement. But I believe it to be a logical theory to pursue based on the physical evidence."

Rowe looked to Cerrabone, who shrugged.

After nearly a minute, O'Neil said, "All right, Detective. I'm orally granting the search warrant. Have a written copy sent to my chambers today, and I'll sign it."

Rowe disconnected the call, shut off the recorder, and removed the earpiece. "We're in," he said.

United States Attorney's Office
Federal Building
Seattle, Washington

The last time Sloane had been in the green-copper-trim Federal Building, it had led to the forced resignation of the secretary of defense. He held no such lofty expectations from his visit this morning. Reid had set up a meeting with Assistant U.S. Attorney Rebecca Han to discuss the Vasiliev investigation. Sloane thought it best to meet Han alone so she could be as forthright as possible.

After greeting Sloane in the lobby, Han led him to her office on the fifth floor — small, utilitarian, and cluttered. A stack of

111

files teetered on the edge of her desk, the shelving units equally well stacked.

Han gestured to seven Bekins boxes lining a wall. "Filyp Vasiliev. I've spent more time with him the past six months than my husband."

"I can't say I'm looking forward to it."

"You've met him?" Han asked.

"Unfortunately," Sloane said.

"I felt like showering every time I got within five feet of the man." Han adjusted a headband. She had a small mole just above her right eyebrow. "So . . . wrongful death, huh?" She sounded skeptical.

"Maybe. Just looking into it at this point."

"I wish you didn't have to. Kozlowski's ruling was flat-out wrong."

"Will you appeal?"

"They're still kicking it around upstairs, but I don't think they'll pull the trigger."

"Why not, if the ruling was wrong?"

"We've spent a lot of money already and without a guarantee that we'll get it reversed . . ." She sighed. "I wanted to challenge him, but we don't like to do that, either. It sets a bad precedent."

A challenge allowed an attorney to ask a judge to recuse himself from a case for any number of reasons, but often because the attorney didn't think the judge could be impartial. It was not an accusation to be made lightly, especially by a member of the Justice Department against a federal district court judge. For Han to suggest she had considered it piqued Sloane's interest.

"On what grounds?"

"It's pretty widely accepted in the office that Kozlowski's had a thing against women attorneys since his divorce. Frankly, I thought it was BS, but he's been a burr in my ass for the past year."

"But not exactly a good reason for a challenge," Sloane said with a smile.

"Not exactly. Whatever the reason, he isn't doing wonders for my career. But this one I know I did by the book."

"So what happened?"

Han explained the months-long investigation. "The DEA had been after Vasiliev for a while. Then they came to us to get wiretaps."

"Let me guess," Sloane said, though his recollection of criminal law was fuzzy. "Kozlowski ruled there was no probable cause for the initial decision to search the trunk of the car."

"Vasiliev's lawyer argued that because the driver had a thick eastern European accent, the police officer had racially profiled him."

"You're kidding."

"The joke in law enforcement is if you say the words 'Russian mafia,' it's redundant. Kozlowski ruled the heroin inadmissible, and since the wiretaps were obtained as a result of the heroin . . ."

"Tainted fruit," Sloane said, recalling that any evidence uncovered as a result of the original misconduct was considered tainted and subject to being excluded.

"I don't have a problem with him finding no probable cause for the initial search but I do have a problem with him linking that to evidence subsequently uncovered through an operation done by the book. Are you hiring? I might need a job."

Sloane knew Han to be joking, though at the moment there wasn't much humor in her voice. "Barclay said you could help with the chain of distribution."

"Maybe. Our case against Vasiliev was for drug distribution. Barclay and the U.S. attorney are acquainted. She wanted us to go after Vasiliev for supplying *the drugs* that killed her daughter. Given who she is in the legal community, I was told to try. But without first getting a conviction for distribution, that couldn't happen."

"So you don't have much on the organization."

"Vasiliev didn't keep the drug records with

114

his business records, and likely for just that reason — in case he ever got raided. He probably kept them at his home or someplace else. If we could find where the money goes, what offshore accounts, we might be able to trace it to determine who is ultimately profiting."

Han looked at the clock on the wall and walked around the desk to shake his hand. "I have to cover a hearing. Listen, I'll help any way I can. If I get the word we're not going to appeal, I'll send you what I have." She slipped into a blue jacket that matched her skirt and adjusted her hair over the collar. "I'd like to see *someone* wipe the smile off Vasiliev's face."

A female voice called out over the speakerphone on Han's desk advising that she had a call from Jeff Behrman.

"Put him through." Han spoke to Sloane. "He was the lead DEA agent on Vasiliev. If you think I'm pissed, you ought to talk to him."

Han picked up the receiver. "Were your ears burning?" She didn't say much after that. When she did, it was brief. "You're kidding. When? Okay. Call me back when you know more." She hung up.

"More bad news?" Sloane asked.

"Depends on your perspective; I don't

have to worry about confidentiality any-more. I can give you the whole file."

"No appeal?"

"No need. I don't have a case. But neither do you. I've heard you're good, but I don't think even you can sue a dead man."

Laurelhurst
Seattle, Washington

Search warrant in hand, Rowe and Cross-white donned blue nitrile gloves and boo-ties to walk the house with Kathy Stafford, the lead CSI detective. Because of the breadth of the subpoena, CSI made a call to the latent's unit at the Washington State Patrol crime lab and asked that it send out civilian fingerprint analysts to assist with the process.

Passing through a room with a vaulted twenty-foot ceiling, thick white rug, and leather furniture, Rowe considered a large painting of St. Basil's Cathedral in Red Square hanging above a river-rock fireplace. "Who said crime doesn't pay?"

"The guy in the other room with a bullet in his head," Crosswhite said.

Upon entering the back room, Stafford noted the single hole in the sliding-glass door, calling it a defect. They were trained not to say "bullet hole," as it could be considered a conclusion that a good defense attorney might later try to exploit.

A fireman on scene took two seconds to confirm Vasiliev dead, which was also standard procedure, even though the "defect" had blown away half his skull. Rowe deduced a large-caliber weapon, a .38 or a .45. Given the damage to the front of Vasiliev's skull, and because the bullet had to pass through the double-paned glass, he doubted the shooter had used a hollow point, which was designed to peel open upon impact to maximize damage and usually stayed inside the body. Rowe expected to find something like ball ammunition.

"I'm guessing it's around here somewhere," Rowe said, meaning the bullet. "What do you think about getting Barry out here?" he asked Crosswhite. With the forensic evidence looking more and more likely to be thin, he figured they could use all the help they could get, and Barry Dilliard was as good as it got. The supervising forensic scientist for the Washington State Patrol Crime Lab, Dilliard was generally considered the guru on everything to do with firearms.

"Can't hurt," Crosswhite said.

"What about the tracker?" he asked.

After finding footprints in the lawn, Crosswhite had suggested they call for Kaylee Wright, a man-tracker with the King County sheriff's office special operations unit. Crosswight had used Wright on another investigation and said she could evaluate shoe prints and broken vegetation to determine the number of people at a crime scene, where they stepped, and whether they were running or walking.

"On her way."

"Can she put her ear to the ground and hear the buffalo, too?"

Crosswhite rolled her eyes. "Nice, Sparrow. You'll like her. She's your type. She breathes."

"Funny." He considered his watch. "My type is at home asleep or cooking breakfast for three boys."

They agreed CSI should roll up and take the Persian rug, along with the sofa. Though the killer had shot from outside, it was possible he and Vasiliev were acquainted. If so, the shooter might have been inside Vasiliev's home at some earlier time and left behind a print or a DNA sample they could match to a weapon, were they ever to find one.

It would take CS I nearly an hour to photograph the house and the backyard, after which the fingerprint experts would go to work on the interior. Two detectives worked on the crime-scene sketch.

In the backyard Crosswhite introduced Rowe to Kaylee Wright, an athletically built woman who stared out across the lawn toward the lake. Except for the auburn hair and dark complexion, she and Crosswhite looked like they could be related.

"What do you need to get started?" Rowe asked.

"Nothing," Wright said. "I'll do a cut around the house for footprints."

"We had two patrol officers . . . dispatch reported a prowler. They walked the house trying to gain access."

"I'll need to talk to them and eliminate their boots. They look like Danner," she said, referring to the boot preferred by patrol officers.

"We also had a lot of rain last night," Rowe said.

Wright shrugged. "It's the Northwest. This is typical for me."

They left Wright alone when Stafford advised they had found the bullet wedged in a piece of hardwood molding at the base of a wall. Though the bullet was distorted, Rowe's hunch had been right — a .38 ball round.

When Rowe returned to the backyard half

an hour later, the lawn looked as though a greenkeeper at a miniature-golf course had gone berserk with tiny red and yellow flags.

Wright provided her initial impression. "There are three distinct sets of prints. They lead from the water to the patio and back to the water."

"So three people came?"

"Can't say." She led him to a narrow strip of beach and pointed out a lone print in the sand on the far right of the property. "See how the ball of the print is deeper than the heel? The person pressed down and vaulted onto the bulkhead." She pointed to a straight line of yellow flags leading to the concrete patio.

"The person who made this print also made those prints," she said. She walked him up the yard to the patio, then pointed out sand and dirt granules. "The person stood here." Wright turned and pointed toward the water. "See the red flags?" The red flags delineated a path from the patio to the water, though it veered to the left into a thicket of trees. "The same person started for the water, diverted to the trees, then continued on to the water. What time did you say dispatch got a call of a prowler?"

"Right around three," Rowe said.

Wright nodded. "These prints were made

within that time period."

"How close can you get?"

"Within four hours."

"And those flags over there?" Rowe pointed to yellow and red flags on the left side of the lawn.

Wright ran him through the same analysis, starting with multiple shoe prints on the beach. "They also came out of the water and moved up the lawn quickly." The prints were bigger, size 101/2 and 12.

"Could one of them have been the shooter?"

"That's not my area of expertise. That's for Barry. They left, running. As they approached the bulkhead, they slowed to climb down the wall. The footprints in the sand are twisted in different directions." She used her hand to demonstrate.

Rowe considered it. "If someone had a boat, they'd jump down, turn around — maybe while untying a rope — and jump into the boat." He pointed across the property to the flag for the lone print. "So what the hell was that person doing way over there?"

"Don't know, but that person got to the patio first."

"I thought you could only limit the time to within four hours."

Wright led him to a spot containing both a red and a yellow flag. "See how some of the blades of grass in the smaller impression are lying flat in the direction of the concrete patio? That's the person walking to the back of the house. Now, see how some of the blades of the larger print are lying over the top of those diagonally? That tells me they were made after the smaller print . . . but by how much, I can't tell you."

Columbia Center
Seattle, Washington

Sloane stepped from the elevator onto the fifty-fourth floor, wiping sweat from his temples. He asked the receptionist for Barclay Reid's assistant, Nina Terry. His calls to Reid's cell phone had gone immediately to voice mail. When he called the office, Terry said Reid was in a morning meeting. She reiterated that information when she met Sloane in the reception area but said they were finishing up.

"I'll wait," he said.

Terry led him to an interior conference room without windows and brought him coffee. Ten minutes passed before the door pushed open and Reid entered with an uncertain smile. "David?"

122

"I'm sorry to take you from your meeting."

"Is everything okay? Nina said you called."

"I just came from Rebecca Han's office."

Reid's shoulders sagged. "She won't help?"

"No, that's not it. While I was there, she got a call from her chief investigator on the Vasiliev matter." He paused. "Vasiliev is dead, Barclay. Someone shot him last night." Reid did not immediately react. Then she pulled out a chair and sat, eyes focused on the tabletop. "Are you all right?"

"I don't know. I don't know what I feel." She looked up at him. "I'm not going to lie . . . part of me is glad he's dead. But part of me feels like he just cheated me all over again."

"Do you want to get a cup of coffee, take some time?"

She shook her head. "I have meetings this morning and this afternoon . . ."

"You could reschedule —"

She cut him off. "No. I'm not going to let him affect my life any more than he already has. Thanks for letting me know. I appreciate it."

"Anything I can do?"

She seemed to give it some thought, shook her head, and left without another word.

123

Rowe and Crosswhite locked down the crime scene and posted two uniformed officers, one at the front and one at the rear of the house. Throughout the day, the neighbors had gathered behind the police tape, along with the media and the curious, who always seemed to find their way to a crime scene. That number would only increase as word spread. A murder in upscale Laurelhurst would be a top news story, especially if the victim had been a suspected heroin-dealing businessman living among them.

Crosswhite accompanied the packaged evidence to Park 95, the CSI processing building on Airport Way south of downtown. Rowe headed to the Justice Center on Fifth Avenue to get the initial paperwork started.

Stepping from the elevator onto the seventh floor, Rowe passed two robbery detectives escorting an inmate in red scrubs and handcuffs through the beige and gray hallways in the direction of the interrogation rooms. An underground tunnel connected the building to the jail, making it easier to interview suspects in custody. In addition to the homicide unit, the Justice Center housed the sexual assault, gang, and domestic-violence units, along with the brass — the

124

chief of police, lieutenants, and captains.

The homicide unit consisted of fifteen cluttered cubicles positioned so that partners sat across aisles from one another, the desks facing away from the windows. Entering, Rowe heard the Mariners' play-by-play announcer from the television mounted from the ceiling. He contemplated checking the score, but the smell of food, perhaps even pizza, had greater appeal. He hadn't thought about eating until the drive back to the office.

Rowe draped his windbreaker on the "skull of death" hooked over the top of his cubicle. The skull signified the detective team next up to work a homicide — gallows humor, but so far, unlike the T-shirts embossed with OUR DAY BEGINS WHEN YOUR DAYS END, there had been no memos from above. The skull would hang on someone else's cubicle by morning.

He followed the smell to the small kitchenette. His optimism soared at the sight of a pizza box on the Formica counter then plummeted when he found the box empty. "Bastards."

He stuffed two bucks into the lockbox, poured a fifty-cent cup of tea, and grabbed a bag of chips and a bag of miniature cookies. What more could a starving man want?

At his cubicle he munched the chips as he logged on to the computer, opened a new file, and began typing in his notes.

"When did you get in?" Ron Mayweather held a napkin with two slices of pizza in one hand, and a two-inch-thick stack of papers in the other.

"Tell me the pizza is for me and I might marry you."

"Sorry, Sparrow, you're not my type." He handed him the pizza anyway. "But I thought I better save you a couple slices; the people around here are vultures."

"Bless you, my son." Rowe made an exaggerated sign of the cross and took a large bite.

Mayweather set the documents on the desk. "This guy's a real piece of shit."

Rowe had called and asked Mayweather, their unit's fifth wheel, to run a triple-I check on Vasiliev's criminal history, then call the Seattle DEA's office to get a copy of whatever file they had generated during the investigation that led to his arrest. Rowe wanted to know if Vasiliev had rolled over on someone or agreed to testify against anyone.

"Any deals?"

"Hell, no. The guy at the DEA said he was an arrogant prick, acted like they'd never get him. Burned his ass when Vasiliev turned out to be right."

Rowe took another bite as he flipped through the documents, which included newspaper articles on a federal judge's decision to grant a motion to suppress evidence seized at Vasiliev's car dealership in Renton.

"They're sending their file over without the sympathy card," Mayweather continued. "The guy said whoever did kill him should be charged with a misdemeanor homicide."

"Yeah, well . . ." It was a law enforcement joke, but not to Rowe.

The phone on his desk rang. He wedged it under his chin so he could use both hands to continue flipping through the documents. The receptionist said a caller claimed to have information that might relate to the Laurelhurst murder. He and Crosswhite would receive and follow up on dozens of such tips, including the usual nut jobs and loose bolts who claimed to be channeling spirits and demons.

"All right, put him through," he said.

"You need anything else?" Mayweather asked.

Rowe covered the receiver. "No, I'm good."

Rowe introduced himself and listened, taking another bite of pizza. As the caller spoke, Rowe set down the documents and went to write the caller's last name in his spiral notebook. "Can you spell that for me?"

He continued to scan one of the news clippings as the caller continued, then he came to an abrupt stop. "Excuse me . . ." His eyes shifted to the name he'd written on his notepad. "Dr. Oberman? Can you give me that name again?"

Rowe scanned the article again. "Where are you now?" He wrote the address. "My partner and I will see you in half an hour."

As if on cue, Crosswhite rounded the corner and tossed her purse in her cubicle closet, the front lined with photographs.

Rowe hung up. "Holy shit."

"You talking about the pope again, Sparrow? Otherwise, there is no such thing. There's just shit, and we're stepping in it at the moment." Crosswhite nodded to the remaining slice of pizza. "I hope you saved that for your partner."

Rowe swiveled his chair to face her. "You remember how I said this had all the markings of an execution?"

NINE

Queen Anne Hill
Seattle, Washington

The aroma of spices — ginger and basil and onions — seeped from the white cartons in the two plastic bags on the seat beside him. Sloane shut off the engine and tried Barclay's cell phone again. When she did not answer, he checked the time on the phone. She had told him she was going to get in a workout, but she should have been home by now.

After delivering the news of Vasiliev's death, Sloane had gone back to his office and called Ian Yamaguchi, a reporter at the *Times* who covered the courts. Yamaguchi said the police were not releasing any details of the crime and likely wouldn't for a while; what he knew was Vasiliev had been shot in the head and would be returning to the Ukraine in a box. The man who had intimidated through violence had died a violent death, and wasn't that the way it always seemed to be?

Sloane spent the better part of the after-noon resisting the urge to call Barclay, but like a man weaning himself off cigarettes, the urge became stronger with each passing hour. Late that afternoon she had called. She said she didn't feel like going out but wanted to see him. He offered to pick up dinner.

Sloane watched a runner turn the corner at the bottom of the steep incline, arms and legs pumping like pistons, churning up the hill in the fading daylight. As the runner neared, he saw the bandaged hand and pushed out of the car. Barclay arrived with a final burst, breathing hard and dripping sweat.

"Sorry." She walked in circles, hands folded on top of her head. "I didn't realize the time. I sprinted the last mile so I wouldn't miss you."

Sloane considered the hill. "I might be dead if I tried that."

She blew out a breath, hands on hips. "I needed to burn off some energy."

"I hope you also worked up an appetite." He lifted the bags from the seat and fol-lowed her inside the front gate.

"Exercise became my therapy after Leenie's death. The psychologist said I was clinically depressed. He wanted to put me on antidepressants, but after what I had just been through, I wasn't about to go that route. The alternative was exercise. It progressed from there. Sometimes exercise was the only way I could get to sleep."

Sloane knew the feeling. "You changed the wrap." He pointed to the smaller dressing on her left hand.

"The other one was too bulky." Inside, she walked into the kitchen and pulled out a large plastic bag. "I'm supposed to keep it dry." She kissed him, her hand on his chest. "I don't imagine I smell anywhere near as good as the Thai food. I'm going to slip on a plastic bag and jump in the shower. How's that for an invitation?"

Reid sipped her glass of Syrah, the plate in front of her full. Though she had been uncharacteristically quiet, Sloane hadn't pushed her on the topic of Vasiliev's murder. She sat back, holding the glass of wine. "Sorry I haven't been better company. I really haven't had much of a chance before now to digest what's happened." She put down the glass. "I just had such high hopes for the civil suit, for what it could do. I'm not really sure where to go from here."

"You can still lobby the legislature."

Sloane heard a series of chimes, and Rowe considered the clock on the mantel over the fireplace. "Doorbell," she said. "Late for visitors. Probably a solicitor." The chimes rang again. She put her napkin on the table. "Let me get rid of them."

At the front door, Reid hit the button to the intercom. "Are you a solicitor?"

"Barclay Reid?"

"Who's this?"

"Seattle Police Department. May we come in?"

Reid gave Sloane a shrug. He pushed back his chair and walked to the door. "Maybe he has news about Vasiliev."

"Ms. Reid?"

"Yes, I'm sorry." She pressed the button freeing the lock on the gate.

Through a sidelight, Sloane watched a man and woman, casually dressed, enter and momentarily consider the garden before proceeding up the walk. Barclay punched in the code to deactivate the alarm, unlocked the deadbolt, and pulled open the door.

"I'm Detective Rowe. This is my partner, Detective Crosswhite. May we come in?" They held identification and badges.

"Certainly."

When Rowe stepped over the threshold,

he stopped to consider the pile of shoes.

"I do a lot of running," Barclay said, closing the door. "But you can leave your shoes on."

"You sure?" Rowe asked. "I just put in hardwood floors myself."

Rowe looked to Sloane, who extended his hand and introduced himself. When Crosswhite heard the name, she said, "I saw you on TV. You represented the family of that National Guardsman killed in Iraq."

"That's me," Sloane said.

"We were just finishing dinner," Barclay said, gesturing to the table. "Can I get you anything to drink — water, cup of coffee?"

The detectives declined and Reid invited them into the living room. They all remained standing.

"Is this about Filyp Vasiliev?" Barclay asked.

"Why do you ask?" Rowe replied.

"Well, I understand he was shot this morning."

"Where did you learn that?"

She motioned to Sloane. "David told me."

Rowe turned to Sloane. "How did you find out?"

"I heard it while I was at the U.S. attorney's office this morning. Under the circumstances, I knew Barclay would want to know."

"The circumstances?" Rowe asked.

"Vasiliev was under investigation by the DEA and the DA's office for drug trafficking," Barclay said.

Rowe directed his question to Sloane. "What interest was that of yours?"

"I had the interest, Detective," Barclay continued. "I believed Mr. Vasiliev's operation distributed the drugs that killed my daughter; she died of an overdose about eight months ago. It's been in the news."

"I'm sorry," Rowe said. "My condolences."

"Last Friday a federal judge granted a motion to exclude evidence. I went to see David to discuss the possibility of bringing a wrongful-death suit against Mr. Vasiliev if the U.S. attorney decided not to appeal the judge's decision."

"Wrongful death? You mean like O. J. Simpson?" Crosswhite asked.

"Exactly," Reid said.

"You can do that?" Rowe asked.

"We were hoping to find out," Sloane said. "Obviously, it never got that far."

"So you had a personal interest in the criminal investigation," Rowe said to Reid.

"Very personal."

"Were you upset by the outcome of that

investigation?"

"I wasn't happy about it." Her remark sounded flippant. Then she became more serious. "I thought Judge Kozlowski made a bad decision that let a drug dealer back out into the community." She started again toward the kitchen. "Are you sure I can't get you something to drink? A glass of water?"

Rowe said, "You own a handgun, Ms. Reid."

It wasn't a question, and it stopped Barclay's progress. "I do. A Smith and Wesson thirty-eight Special." She smiled. "But don't ask me anything more, because that pretty much exhausts my knowledge."

"Where do you keep it?" Rowe asked.

"In a gun box in my bedroom closet."

"Can we have a look?"

She looked to Sloane, then back to Rowe. "May I ask why?"

"Let's see the gun first," Rowe said. "Then we can talk."

Barclay led them up the stairs to her bedroom on the second floor. Her bathrobe lay on the goose-down comforter where she had left it after they exited the shower. Barclay slid open the closet door and started to kneel.

"We'll open it," Rowe said.

She stepped back. Crosswhite bent on her knee and opened the box.

Golden Dragon Restaurant
International District
Seattle, Washington

Jerry Willins felt sick to his stomach, and judging from Julio Cruz's constipated expression, Cruz didn't feel much better. The aroma of Chinese food, pungent and greasy, wafted up from the restaurant below, exacerbating Willins's nausea. He stifled a burp, which brought an acidic burn to the back of his throat.

The third man in the room, Micheal Hurley, silently dissected them over the top of his folded hands, elbows propped on the pale yellow, wood-laminate desk that looked to have been scavenged from a 1950s science classroom and wedged in the room like an SUV in a compact parking space. An open book lay flat on the desk. Reading the spine upside down, Willins determined it to be poetry by Robert Frost.

"Where were you?" Hurley directed the question to Cruz, his voice flat and even.

Cruz hesitated. "In the head."

In between the clang and clatter of pans and the shrill shouts of the cooks speaking Chinese, Willins detected the faint smell of

136

tobacco — restaurant employees on a cigarette break in the alley.

Hurley's eyes, coal black in contrast to snow-white eyebrows, shifted to Willins. "I thought I made it clear that I wanted audio *and* visual."

"You did. It was raining and —"

"Then you should have seen who put a bullet in his head. Did you see who put a bullet in his head?"

Willins knew the question to be rhetorical. Cruz apparently did not.

"We didn't see nothing. It was black out. No moon or stars. And the storm."

Willins said, "It was seconds, at most. By the time I even figured out it was a gunshot and not thunder, it was too late."

Hurley sat back. His barrel chest rose and fell while he rubbed at a goatee as white as his eyebrows. "How am I going to explain this?"

This time Cruz exercised better judgment and did not answer. They'd had high hopes for Vasiliev, and the cost associated with the operation had not been insignificant. Hurley turned to the opposite wall, considering a chart with rectangular boxes stacked like a family tree, some blank, some penciled in with eastern European surnames.

"Maybe they knew," Cruz offered. "Maybe

137

someone found out."

Hurley said, "He was alone."

Willins understood. "If he had suspected anything . . ."

"Maybe he didn't," Cruz said. "That's my point. Maybe he didn't know."

"Chelyakov spoke to him?" Hurley asked.

"At the dealership," Cruz said. "Day before."

Willins nodded. "He told him they had a problem with that attorney, that she was talking to a civil lawyer . . ." He looked at his notes. "David Sloane. Chelyakov said he didn't want the woman pushing any more lawsuits. He wanted Vasiliev to handle it. Couple hours later, Vasiliev has his two guys bring in Sloane and he threatens him — tells him to convince the woman to let it go."

"What was this guy Sloane's response?"

"Sloane . . . he didn't sound intimidated, man." Cruz's accent became more pronounced. "Not at all. Said he'd kill him if he touched his family."

"Said he'd kill him?" Hurley asked.

" 'Touch my son and I'll kill you,' " Willins said.

"Didn't sound scared, neither," Cruz added.

The room, a windowless, colorless box, radiated white. Overhead fluorescent lights illuminated the nicked and scratched metal table and three chairs. Light blue soundproofing foam covered the upper half of the walls to deter a suspect from shouting to an accomplice in one of the adjoining rooms.

The unit referred to the room as a "hard" interrogation room, though the "soft" interrogation rooms, located on the same narrow hallway, weren't significantly bigger and didn't come with any additional amenities. With the doors shut, the rooms brought the claustrophobic feel of a prison cell, which was the point — to let a suspect know they were deep in the soup and the only way to keep from spending a very long time, perhaps the rest of their lives, in a room just as small and just as sparse was to cooperate, maybe even confess.

Rowe didn't expect that to happen tonight.

"What do you think?" Rowe asked.

Rick Cerrabone and Crosswhite watched Barclay Reid from behind one-way glass. Around them knobs and lights on the video and recording equipment flashed yellow and green. Before transporting Reid to the

Justice Center, Rowe had called Cerrabone to give him a heads-up. He'd googled Reid on the Internet and knew of her status in the community — a former president of the Washington Bar Association. They would need to do everything by the book. The brass would be breathing hard down their necks, and since they were located in the same building, they wouldn't have far to go.

"How did she react when you opened the box?" Cerrabone asked.

Rowe had kept his focus on Reid when Crosswhite opened the gun box, revealing the Styrofoam cutout where the gun should have been. Reid's eyes had widened, and she brought up a hand to cover her mouth.

"Not much. She looked more confused than concerned. She didn't panic," Rowe said.

"Does she look like the panicking type?" Crosswhite asked.

Rowe and Cerrabone considered Reid again. She sat with her legs crossed, cleaning the ink from her fingertips with an alcohol wipe. She looked as if she'd just painted her nails and was waiting for the polish to dry. Rowe had interrogated a lot of witnesses, and few looked as calm as Reid did at that moment — even the few who turned out to be completely innocent.

After opening the box, Rowe had handed Reid a search warrant he'd procured from Judge O'Neil to search her house and to impound her car. Rowe was interested in determining if they might find sand or water in the carpet.

"She didn't ask for an attorney?" Cerrabone scratched the back of his neck behind the ear. With bloodshot eyes, dark bags, and sagging cheeks, he resembled a basset hound scratching at a flea. "Didn't want to call anyone?"

"She *had* an attorney with her," Crosswhite said. "A good one. David Sloane."

When Crosswhite mentioned the name, Cerrabone stopped scratching. "Why do I know that name?"

"He's the attorney whose wife was murdered last year," Crosswhite said.

"His wife was murdered?" Rowe asked.

She shook her head. "Do you listen to anything I say? I already told you that."

Rowe made a note in the spiral notebook. "I'll check with Bernie," he said, referring to Bernie Hamilton, the detective assigned to the cold-cases unit.

"I already have," Crosswhite said.

Cerrabone said, "Sloane also handled that matter involving Argus a few years back — the one on the National Guardsman. And

141

didn't he have that magnet case against Kendall Toys last year?" Cerrabone didn't wait for an answer. He nodded, answering his own question. "He did. In fact, if my memory serves me . . ." He stopped and looked at Reid. "She was the attorney for Kendall."

"Strange bedfellows," Rowe said.

Cerrabone looked at him. "Figure of speech?"

Rowe shrugged. "Their hair was wet and the bed looked like someone just gave it a good workout."

"Why would he let her come down here without him?" Cerrabone asked, though they all knew that technically, there wasn't much Sloane could have done. Rowe had another search warrant in his pocket for Reid to provide her fingerprints and the DNA swab had she refused to voluntarily provide them, and Sloane had no right to be in the interrogation room unless she requested he act as her attorney.

"He advised against it," Rowe said. "He told her not to say anything."

"What did she say?" Cerrabone asked, nervousness sneaking into his voice. "Did you write it down?"

Crosswhite flipped the pages of her notebook. "She said she wanted to quote,

142

'cooperate,' end quote, and quote, 'get to the bottom of the matter,' end quote. She told him she would call him later. Then she asked if she could change her clothes."

"Ask her again," Cerrabone said. "Get it on tape."

"Look where she sat," Crosswhite said. Reid had taken a seat on the side of the table with two chairs rather than the side with just the one chair. "Why would she sit there?"

Rowe shook his head. He'd never had anyone do that either. Seemed everyone understood the etiquette of an interrogation was to take the hot seat.

Rowe looked to Crosswhite. "How do you want to play it?"

Normally, they interviewed witnesses together, though one or the other might leave to run up information on something the suspect said. Sometimes they agreed upon a ruse — the "good cop, bad cop" routine or the "we know more than you do" ruse. But Rowe was not inclined to try to outsmart the name partner of a Seattle law firm.

Crosswhite said, "Why don't you handle it."

"I was going to suggest *you* handle it. You know, woman-to-woman–type thing."

Crosswhite spoke to the glass. "I don't think so. Women like her sometimes feel the need to prove themselves to another professional woman, show them how competent they are, how smart. I think you'd do better without me. If I think of something, I'll come in."

Cerrabone agreed with the strategy and told Rowe to play it straight up. "She has a lot of contacts," he said, "including the governor."

Three Tree Point
Burien, Washington

Sloane turned off the engine and sat back, staring at the overgrown laurel hedge. He wondered if, subconsciously, he'd deliberately let the hedge grow, like the bamboo inside Barclay's fence, his own way of further isolating himself from the world.

Every instinct told him Barclay should have declined to talk voluntarily to the police without a lawyer present, but she had refused his advice.

He stepped from the car but did not push through the gate, instead walking down the easement to the bulkhead. With the tide in, only a sliver of rocks remained between the water's edge and the cement wall on which he stood. He considered an evening sky painted hues of colors man seemed incapable of duplicating. A breeze from the southwest caused rippled waves and rocked the boats tied to the buoys. The heat and humidity that had brought the thunderstorms seemed to have finally passed.

If I had known he was going to walk, I would have just put a bullet in him and been done with it.

Sloane had dismissed her words as rhetoric, the type of thing someone says when angry but would never actually do.

If I had known he was going to walk, I would have just put a bullet in him and been done with it.

Most people never had the chance to do it, to kill someone.

Sloane had, and he knew how close he had come to squeezing the trigger. Ultimately, he had refrained from shooting Anthony Stenopolos, but he could not deny that he had felt the primal urge for revenge, and it had been as strong as any he'd ever had, though not as strong as his instinct to protect Jake. And that was what had ultimately stopped him. It had not been his conscience or some burst of morality, good triumphing over evil. No, the reason he had not pulled the trigger had been something much more practical than divine. About to

145

shoot, he had thought of Jake and the promise he had made to Tina that he would always care for their son.

Barclay had no such concern.

She had no such obligation.

Vasiliev had taken that from her.

What did it do to a mother to lose a child?

If I had known he was going to walk, I would have just put a bullet in him and been done with it.

Tina had been his wife, perhaps his soul mate, the person with whom he had chosen to spend the rest of his life. But she was not of him. She did not have his blood, his genes, his chromosomes. He had not carried her inside his body for nine months, given her life, nurtured her, watched her grow, guided her. That was a bond no man could ever truly understand. That was a bond only mothers knew. Sloane had come to realize something of it with Jake, whom he truly believed he loved as much as any father could, and still he knew it was a fraction of the love Tina had for her child.

What does it do to have that bond severed, to have your child killed?

If I had known he was going to walk, I would have just put a bullet in him and been done with it.

What does it do to a person?

Sloane turned from the view and walked back up the easement, pushing through the wooden gate to the back porch. He pulled open the screen door, about to unlock the Dutch door, when he noticed light on the staircase leading to the second floor. He left two lights on timers — one in his study and one in the kitchen. The light in the study could be seen from the front and the south sides of the house. The light in the kitchen, the room where he normally entered, could be seen from the west and north sides. There was no timer for an upstairs light, and he wouldn't have left a light on.

He unlocked the door, pressed a hand on the glass to keep it from rattling, and nudged the wood from the frame, stepping in. At first he heard nothing but the creaks and moans of an empty house with which he had become all too familiar. Then the floorboards overhead creaked, the seventy-year-old wood unforgiving, someone walking upstairs. His bedroom.

He stepped from the kitchen into the living room, maneuvering around the sofa and coffee table to his study, hearing the person or persons moving through the rooms overhead. In his study, he slid open the desk drawer and removed the .38.

As he started from the office, he heard the

person at the top of the stairs. He put his left foot forward, legs shoulder width, body turned at a 30-degree angle, bent his knees and leaned slightly forward, left elbow bent.

The person descended, revealing more with each step: black boots, jeans, the bottom of a black leather coat — the kind Vasiliev's two escorts had worn. Sloane slid his finger from the barrel to the trigger. When he saw the head, he shouted.

"Freeze!"

The Justice Center
Seattle, Washington
Before entering the room, Rowe paused in the hall to gather his thoughts. His ego hated to admit it, but his sphincter had tightened when he picked up the news article on his desk that mentioned Barclay Reid, and confirmed it to be the same name the caller, Dr. Felix Oberman, had provided. Oberman identified himself as Reid's ex-husband. He said that two weeks earlier, Reid had told him she'd tired of the legal process and wished she had just put a bullet in the back of Vasiliev's head. When Rowe met Oberman, the doctor confirmed his ex-wife owned a gun and he believed it to be a .38 revolver.

Rowe ran Reid's name through the system

148

and determined she did indeed own a .38 Smith & Wesson J-Frame. Designed to be lightweight — just eleven and a half ounces — the black and gray gun had a shortened barrel that made it a popular choice of civilians who carried concealed weapons or kept guns in bedside stands. The bullet that had killed Vasiliev, a ball round — so named because the tip was rounded and resembled the lead balls fired from muskets during the Civil War — also matched a box of ammunition they found in Reid's closet. Like the .38, the ball round was popular. Cheap, it was often used as practice rounds. Only a ballistics analysis would confirm the bullet had been fired by a particular gun, and without the gun, that could not happen.

Rowe blew out a breath, shook his arms, and stepped around the corner, entering as Reid placed the alcohol wipe, blackened with ink, on the table.

"Sorry," he said. "We aren't built for comfort around here."

"Not a problem, Detective." She gestured to the lone chair. "Did you want to switch sides? I didn't know if Detective Crosswhite would be joining us."

"She might, but we're fine for now." Rowe took the single chair and grimaced when the pain burned in his hip.

"Are you all right?" Reid asked.

"I'm fine."

"My knee acts up every once in a while," she said.

"We appreciate you coming down to get this straightened out."

"I'm happy to oblige. I'd like to know myself what's going on." She sounded genuine.

"Do you want an attorney present?"

She shook her head. Then she looked toward the one-way glass as if to let all know she was aware that Crosswhite, and likely others, watched. "If you need me to sign something, I'm happy to do so, but as I told you at my house, I don't need or want an attorney."

Rowe flipped through his notes, trying to decide where to start. Though he had kept the door to the room open, the room seemed smaller, warmer. "You said the last time you saw the gun was . . . when?"

"Actually, you asked me the last time I fired the gun, and I said I hadn't fired it since I finished a shooting lesson. I'm not sure when I last saw it."

"How long ago did you have that lesson?"

She thought for a moment. "About two months, I think. I'm sure we could get the exact date."

"And where was that?"

"Wade's gun shop in Bellevue. That's also where I bought it."

"How long ago did you buy it?"

"I don't know. It was after my husband and I separated. Ten years."

Rowe considered her. "Any particular reason you decided to purchase a weapon?"

"My ex-husband had become physically and verbally abusive."

"Physically?"

"The divorce file has several police reports leading to a restraining order."

Rowe made a mental note to get the file. If Reid's statement were true — and he doubted she would lie about something so easy to confirm — it cast Oberman's unsolicited tip in a different light.

"So why did you take the lessons two months ago?"

"Because I started to receive threats."

"Threats from who, your ex?"

"No. I don't know who, exactly. I'm a single woman on a 'crusade' against drug dealers. They didn't leave a name. But if I had to guess, I'd guess people who worked for Vasiliev."

"Did you report the threats?"

"Every one."

Rowe made a mental note to also confirm

151

the threats, and knew Crosswhite was writing it down. "Did anyone come out to the house to take a statement?"

"No."

Rowe found his rhythm. "Did you ask them to? Did you ask them to put a wiretap on your phone?"

"The calls came up on my home phone as private. I doubt very much the person was calling from his home."

"It was a man?"

"It sounded like a man."

"Was it the same voice each time? Could you tell?"

"No. But the person had an eastern European accent."

"How many of these calls do you think you received?"

"You can look it up. I reported perhaps half a dozen. I was also followed."

"Followed how?"

"A car, a silver Mercedes, would appear periodically outside my home and while I was driving, shopping."

"Did you ever see the driver?"

"No. The car had tinted windows."

"When's the last time you saw it?"

"Monday night."

"This past Monday?"

"Yes."

"And you believe these threats were because you are on a 'crusade,' as you put it."

"I don't call it a crusade, Detective. The newspaper called it that. After my daughter died, I found out that there is very little the average citizen can do against someone like Vasiliev. I've been an advocate for a drug dealer liability act here in Washington."

"Which is what?"

"It allows for civil penalties against drug dealers."

"What did the caller say? What were the threats?"

She turned her head, her gaze on the wall. " 'Keep your nose out of other people's business or your daughter will have company. Keep pushing and you'll be next.' That was the gist of it."

"Anything else you can remember?"

"He equated me to a female dog and made explicit reference to one of my body parts."

Rowe could guess which one. "So you took the shooting class after you received these threats?"

She nodded. "I'd also taken classes when I purchased the gun. They offered it, and I decided it was prudent. I hope I never shoot it again."

"Why is that?"

She leaned forward, forearms on the table, hands folded. A cross on a simple gold chain around her neck dangled near the second open buttonhole of her shirt. Before leaving her home, she had changed into blue jeans, a light-blue silk blouse, and flat shoes. Judging by the fragrance Rowe detected when she got into the car, she had also taken the time to put on perfume. Now he realized from the soft contours and the movement of the silk that Reid was not wearing a bra.

"I didn't appreciate the power . . . it scared me. Is that a bird?" she asked.

Rowe lifted his eyes. He couldn't be certain, but Reid seemed to have the bemused look of a woman who had caught a man's eyes wandering. "Excuse me?"

"The tattoo." Her fingers brushed the ink on the inside of his forearm.

"It's a sparrow."

She sat back, still making eye contact. "Why a sparrow?"

Rowe could not recall ever hearing the buzzing noise in the room, like a swarm of invisible insects. "Can I get you a glass of water, cup of coffee?"

"I'm fine. But if you need a break . . . Is that your nickname? Sparrow?"

He was certain someone had turned up the thermostat. "And you haven't touched the gun again?"

"Again?"

"Since you brought it home after your final lesson."

"Not that I recall. It's been in the box."

"Even after the threats? You never felt the need to take it out, make sure?"

She shrugged. "It's in my bedroom closet. I guess I figured I could always get to it if I needed it."

"You live alone?"

"Yes."

"Anyone else have access to your home? Maid? Cleaning service?"

"It's just me, Detective. I can be a slob, but there's really not much to clean."

"What about your ex-husband?"

"We don't see each other, for obvious reasons."

"So he hasn't been in your house?"

"Not that I'm aware of."

"When was the last time you had contact with him?"

Reid's brow wrinkled. Her middle finger tapped her bottom lip. "Carly's funeral?" she said. "No, wait . . . I ran into him at a function about two or three weeks ago. I can't recall the date."

"What kind of function?"

"The symphony, a fund-raiser."

"Did you and your ex-husband speak?"

"Briefly."

"What about?"

"What do two people with nothing to say to each other talk about? It was small talk. It wasn't comfortable."

Rowe waited.

"As I said, it got ugly. He was showing up at my office and at home, making all kinds of wild accusations."

The domestic-violence unit was located in the same building. Getting reports to confirm the allegations would not be difficult.

"Anyone else you can think of who could have had access to your home?"

"I didn't say my ex had access to my home, Detective."

"I meant can you think of anyone else besides your ex?"

She shrugged.

"What about Mr. Sloane?"

"What about him?"

"He was in your home tonight; has he been in your home before?"

She looked bemused again and fingered the gold chain around her neck, her eyes finding his. "Yes."

Rowe forced himself to maintain eye contact. "Did he know you had a gun?"

Reid didn't answer immediately. She sat

back. It was the first time she seemed reluctant. "He commented on it."

"What did he say?"

"He said he saw the gun box in the closet that morning."

"What morning?"

"Tuesday morning." She looked about to say something more, then stopped.

"Something you want to add?"

She shook her head. "Nothing."

"You looked like you wanted to say something."

She smiled. "I'm a lawyer; I always look like I want to say something."

"Who would know the code for the gun box?"

"Just me, but it wouldn't really matter; I don't lock it."

"You don't lock the box?"

She shook her head. "Like I said, I'm the only one there to worry about, and I didn't want to be fumbling with numbers in the dark if I needed to get to it in a hurry."

"What's your relationship with Mr. Sloane?"

"We're friends."

"And you asked him to file a civil action against Mr. Vasiliev?"

"Yes."

"How did you meet?"

"I had a case against him last year. He won. I don't lose, Detective. For someone to beat me, he has to be good. He's also quite prominent. I hoped his notoriety would help my 'crusade.' " She used her fingers to demonstrate quotations.

"How long ago did you retain him?"

"I talked to him about it that same day."

"What day?"

"Tuesday. We met for lunch in his office, and I asked him if he would consider it."

"And did he agree?"

"Not right away. He wanted to talk to the U.S. attorney who had handled the criminal case."

"Where were you last night?"

"I knew we would get around to that question sooner or later. You mean my alibi? I don't have one, unless you consider reading in bed alone an alibi."

"When did you arrive home?"

"I left the office around four to get in a bike ride."

"Where'd you go on your ride?" Reid provided Rowe with what she called "her normal route," and he commented, "That's a long way."

"About twenty-five miles, round-trip."

"You always ride that far?"

"Farther on the weekend."

"And judging from the shoes piled by your front door, can I assume you also run?"

"And swim. I'm in training for triathlons. I'm hoping to do my first Ironman next year."

"That's what, running, biking, and swimming?" Rowe asked.

"Reverse order. It's swimming, biking, and running. I did a run tonight," Reid said.

"How far did you go?"

"Seven and a half miles."

"You usually run farther?"

"Sometimes."

"And when you swim, how far do you usually go?"

"As much as I can stomach; I like it the least."

"Why is that?"

"I bore easily, Detective."

"When did you get back to the house after your bike ride Tuesday night?"

She shrugged and showed him the ACE bandage wrapped around her wrist. "I didn't have a watch. Dusk. So I would guess about eight or eight-thirty. Give or take a half hour."

"What happened to your wrist?"

"My hand, actually. I cut it on a piece of glass."

"And you still went for a ride?"

She shrugged. "The back tire brake is applied with the right hand."

"Did you ride with anyone?"

"No, by myself."

"Stop anywhere along the way?"

"If I stop, Detective, I'm liable not to start again."

"And what did you do after you got home?"

"Nothing." She drew the word out, smiling as she said it. "I try to make my evenings my time. It's really the only time I have to myself. If I kept to routine, I made a protein shake, watched a little television, climbed in bed, and read until I fell asleep, which usually doesn't take long."

Rowe looked at his notes. "Did you make any phone calls that night, talk to anyone?"

Reid thought for a moment, shaking her head. "I don't remember if I did or not, but I'm sure you could subpoena my phone records if that becomes necessary."

"What about Mr. Sloane? Did you and he talk?" Rowe had been taking notes. When the answer did not come as quickly as the others, he looked up. It was the second time she had hesitated. Both questions involved David Sloane. "Did you hear the question?"

"I talked to David."

"What time was that?"

"I don't remember."

Rowe sensed sudden reticence. "Do you remember what you talked about?"

"He was upset."

"Did he say why?"

"Two of Vasiliev's men had staged a car accident and forcibly escorted him to Vasiliev's car dealership in Renton."

"Did he say what happened?"

She paused. "He said Vasiliev threatened him, threatened to hurt his son."

Rowe sat back, watching her. "Has Mr. Sloane ever been in your bedroom when you weren't present?"

She bit the lip again. "Yes."

"When?"

"That same morning."

"Tuesday morning?"

"Yes."

The day before Vasiliev was killed.

Three Tree Point
Burien, Washington

If the trigger pull on the Glock had been any less, Sloane would have shot him in the head.

He slid his finger back along the barrel and lowered the gun, breathing heavily. Light-headed, he reached for the door frame. Realizing this would not keep him

161

upright, he took two steps backward and slumped to a sitting position on the edge of his desk, his eyes closed. He felt a chill.

"You okay?" Charles Jenkins descended the remaining stairs and stood before him. At the sound of Sloane yelling "Freeze!" Jenkins had fallen backward against the railing, hands raised, eyes wide.

"No, I'm not okay. What the hell are you doing here? I told you I wouldn't be home tonight." A thought came to him. "Where's your car?" Jenkins's eyes shifted to the gun in Sloane's hand. "What?" Sloane asked.

"Did you do it?"

Sloane tilted his head, uncertain. "Do what?"

"Did you kill him?"

"What are you talking about?"

"It was on the news."

"I know."

"I made a call; the bullet was a thirty-eight."

"You have to ask me that question?" When Jenkins didn't respond, Sloane said, "You were there. I could have blown Stenopolis's head off."

When Jenkins still didn't respond, Sloane held out the gun. Jenkins took it and sniffed the barrel for gunpowder residue. Sloane walked past him into the living room and

162

pulled a bottle of Scotch from the antique cupboard that served as a hard-liquor cabinet. "You want one?" Jenkins shook his head. Sloane fought to steady his hand as he poured the amber liquid and took a drink. He went out on the covered porch, facing the plate-glass windows.

Jenkins followed him. "So why are you home?"

"The police came. She owns a thirty-eight revolver. It's missing."

"Missing?"

"She keeps it in a gun box in her closet. It isn't there. They asked her to go with them for questioning."

"You didn't go with her?"

"She wouldn't let me." The sun had set, just a faint glow above the Olympic Mountain peaks. He heard Jenkins's boots on the wooden porch behind him. Sloane didn't turn from the view. "She didn't do it."

"How do you know?"

Sloane shrugged, turned from the view. Jenkins leaned against the door frame. "I just do," Sloane said.

"Who, then?" Jenkins asked.

"I don't know." He felt the Scotch burn the back of his throat.

"You said you were tired of people threatening you; tired of people threatening the people you love," Jenkins said, as if to explain.

"I am tired. Damn tired."

Before Jenkins could respond, someone knocked on the front door.

The Justice Center
Seattle, Washington

His adrenaline normally continued to pump long after an interrogation, but after an hour with Barclay Reid, Rowe left the room feeling fatigued. It'd been a long day, and it would be an even longer next couple of days. He wondered if he was coming down with something, a flu or a cold. One of his kids had been sick earlier in the week, throwing up, a twenty-four-hour stomach thing.

Crosswhite and Cerrabone turned from the window as he walked in. Rowe shrugged, the universal gesture: *What do you think?*

Crosswhite said, "We were just asking each other the same thing. I don't know. Something's not right. She's too calm."

Rowe slumped onto a plastic chair. "Maybe it's like she said. Maybe she has nothing to hide."

Crosswhite gave an emphatic shake of the head. "All the more reason to be concerned, Sparrow; most people would be shitting bricks sitting in that room, especially if they *didn't* do it."

"I don't think she's most people," he said.

"Exactly. She knows the legal system."

"You think that's why she offered to take a polygraph?"

Reid had made the offer out of the blue. She said she wanted to get the matter resolved.

"She's a lawyer," Crosswhite said. "She probably knows it's not admissible. It's a hollow gesture."

"Not if she fails."

Crosswhite paced. "Something doesn't add up, her reactions . . . She was flirting with you."

Rowe scoffed. "She didn't flirt with me."

Crosswhite rolled her eyes. "Please. Every man in the world thinks every woman in the world is flirting with him. Now you have one who is, and you don't recognize it?"

Rowe looked to Cerrabone. "What did you think?"

Cerrabone raised a hand. "I've been married so long I wouldn't know flirting if a woman took off her top in front of me."

"Yeah? That ever happen?" Rowe asked.

"Not when I was single, and definitely not since I've been married."

Crosswhite's voice rose. "Come on. She

touched your forearm." She softened her voice. " 'Is that a bird?' What type of a question is that? She's being questioned about a murder, and she's acting like she's having coffee at the local Starbucks."

Rowe looked to the window. Reid had pushed her chair away from the table to cross her legs, the index finger and thumb of her right hand kneading the gold cross. As his gaze found the soft outline of her breasts, her head turned, as if she had sensed him, and despite the glass, she seemed to make eye contact.

"Sparrow?"

"Huh?"

"What do you think?" From her tone, he knew he'd missed the question.

"About what?"

"Let's call her on it," Cerrabone said. "Let's have her take the polygraph. What, does she think she can beat it?"

"Can we get somebody now?" Rowe asked.

"Have her come back tomorrow," Cerrabone said.

Rowe stood, pulled the keys from his pocket. "I'll thank her for coming in, drive her home."

Cerrabone said, "Have a patrol car take her home." Rowe looked over at him. "In

166

case she's right," he said, giving a nod to Crosswhite.

Crosswhite stood and stepped past him. "Forget it. I'll let her know."

Three Tree Point
Burien, Washington

The front door of Sloane's home faced SW 170th Place, but it was not visible from the street behind the laurel hedge, a freestanding single-car garage, and twenty feet of lawn. People who knew him used one of the two gates off the easement, which led to the porches outside the kitchen and the backyard. Only solicitors knocked on Sloane's front door, but it was late, even for the most brazen and persistent. Sloane had a hunch whom he'd find even before he looked through the peephole.

Detectives Rowe and Crosswhite weren't selling anything.

"Sorry to call on you so late," Rowe said, though he didn't sound like it. "May we come in?"

Sloane followed them into the living room, where Charles Jenkins stood as big and imposing as the darkened view out the plate-glass windows. Sloane introduced them.

"What can I help you with?" Sloane asked.

167

"We'd like to ask you a few things, get some time lines straight."

"You've spoken to Barclay?"

"We're just trying to corroborate a few things. Would you mind?"

Sloane knew they hadn't made the drive to corroborate anything. "No, I don't mind."

They sat in the living room, Sloane on the leather sofa, Rowe and Crosswhite across the glass coffee table in two matching chairs. Jenkins remained standing.

Rowe started. "Could you tell us the nature of your relationship with Ms. Reid?"

"She's a colleague and friend."

"That friendship has been recent?"

"Yes, though we had a case against each other about a year ago."

"But that did not develop into a relationship?"

"I was married at the time, Detective. My wife died about fourteen months ago. She was murdered. I haven't been in any shape for a relationship."

"I'm sorry," Rowe said. "Was her murder ever resolved?"

Sloane had a sense Rowe knew it had not been, at least not as far as a police investigation would ever reveal. "How is this related to Barclay?"

"How well do you know Ms. Reid?"

"What do you mean?"

"You've spent the night at her home?"

"Is this relevant?"

"Were you with her last night? The night Mr. Vasiliev was killed?"

"No."

"She indicated you spent Monday night together at her home."

"That's correct."

Rowe flipped a page in his notebook. Sloane got the impression it was for show. "And it was the next day, Tuesday I believe, that she came to you with this idea of suing Mr. Vasiliev in a civil case?"

"That's right. She wanted to sue him for the wrongful death of her daughter. I told her I wanted to speak to the U.S. attorney first and find out what information she had that could link Vasiliev to the drugs that killed Carly. Barclay set up the meeting."

"And what chance of success did you give Ms. Reid's case?"

"It hadn't really gotten that far, Detective. I wanted to talk to the U.S. attorney first."

Crosswhite asked, "Has a wrongful-death case against a suspected drug dealer ever been successful, to your knowledge?"

Sloane shrugged. "Again, everything was preliminary. Barclay was excited about the prospect; she thought it could help with her efforts to lobby the legislature to pass a drug dealer liability act."

"Had Ms. Reid ever displayed any anger over her daughter's death? Did she ever blame Vasiliev?"

In his head, Sloane saw the glass shatter, beer spraying, then the blood.

If I had known he was going to walk, I would have just put a bullet in him and been done with it.

"Those are two separate questions."

"Feel free to choose either one," Rowe said.

"All right . . . As to whether she ever blamed Vasiliev, I'd have to assume she did, since she was in my office and wanted him held responsible. As to whether she ever expressed any anger, no, I don't recall that she did."

Rowe flipped backward through the pages of his notebook. As he did, Crosswhite jumped in. "So you saw Ms. Reid Tuesday morning . . . what time did you leave her home?"

"Around eight, I think."

"And then you saw her again in your office at . . ."

"Noon."

"Why didn't she just talk to you about suing Vasiliev that morning?"

170

Sloane shrugged. "Ask her. We were both late getting to work. She said she wanted to do some research first . . . I would guess to see if it had ever been done."

"Did she say what was the result of her research?"

"She'd found a case in California that appeared promising."

"Did you have any further contact with her that day?" Rowe asked.

Sloane realized where Rowe was headed. He had called Reid that afternoon to tell her Vasiliev had threatened him. He also realized something else. He'd had access to Reid's gun that morning. They had discussed it on the roof deck.

"I spoke to her on the phone late that afternoon, early evening," Sloane said.

"Why did you call?" Rowe asked.

"I was concerned about her."

"Why?"

"As I was leaving work that afternoon, Mr. Vasiliev sent two men to my garage to invite me to talk with him."

"You mean they forced you."

"They staged a car accident as I was backing out of my space."

"Did they have weapons?"

"Both men were carrying guns."

"And they brought you to meet Vasiliev?

171

What did he want?"

"Mr. Vasiliev was concerned Barclay might file a civil suit against him."

"He knew about it? How?"

"I don't know how. But he knew."

"So what did he say? What did he want?"

"He wanted me to convince Barclay it would be better if she let bygones be bygones."

"And if she didn't?"

"He didn't say."

"Did you report it to the police?"

"No."

"Did he threaten you?"

"Yes."

"But you didn't report it."

"My wife is dead, Detective. My stepson lives in California with his biological father and leaves for Italy tomorrow for three months."

"What about you?"

"What about me?"

"Didn't you feel threatened?"

"I told you, I took it as a threat."

"But not enough to involve the police?"

"Vasiliev's threat was *if* I filed the case. I hadn't filed the case yet."

"Do you own a gun, Mr. Sloane?"

This was where things could get tricky. The .38 that Jenkins had given Sloane was not registered. His possessing it could get them both in trouble.

"No, I don't own one."

"You were aware that Ms. Reid owned a gun."

It wasn't a question. "I saw the gun box in her closet with you and Detective Crosswhite."

"Is that the first time you saw it?"

"No. I saw it Tuesday morning."

"The day before Vasiliev was murdered."

"Yes."

"You talked to Ms. Reid about it."

"I expressed surprise that she had it."

"And what did she say?"

"She said she was a single woman on a crusade against drug dealers."

"You said you saw the box. Did you see the gun in the box?"

"I didn't open it."

"Because there was a combination lock?"

"Because I didn't think it would be appropriate to go through her things."

"So you never actually saw the gun?"

"No."

"You don't know if it was in the box at that time or not."

"I don't."

Rowe looked to Crosswhite, then back to

Sloane. "Where were you this morning, by the way?"

TEN

Thursday, September 8, 2011
Interstate Five
Burien, Washington

The following morning, as he sat in bumper-to-bumper traffic on I-5, inching his way toward downtown, Sloane reconsidered the second search warrant Rowe had handed him after he declined to voluntarily provide his fingerprints and a DNA sample.

Sloane's cell phone rang. The number seemed familiar, but he couldn't place it. He recognized the voice: Ian Yamaguchi, the court reporter for the *Times.*

"Ian, this is not a good time. Can I call you back?"

"I was hoping to get a comment."

"On what?"

"On the article we ran in this morning's paper."

175

The amount of brass in the conference room could have made musical instruments for a marching band. Rowe and Crosswhite sat on one side of the table with their detective sergeant, Andrew Laub. Several copies of the *Seattle Times* lay scattered across the wood surface, the article of interest in the power position, top left-hand column. To say the article had come as a surprise would have been akin to saying the iceberg surprised the *Titanic.* Citing an anonymous source, Ian Yamaguchi had reported that two prominent Seattle attorneys, Barclay Reid and David Sloane, had been questioned by police in the murder of Laurelhurst resident and suspected heroin dealer Filyp Vasiliev. The fallout had been like one of those phone trees on Little League teams where the first person who gets significant information calls the next person on the tree who in turn calls the person beneath and so on down the line. This tree started with the chief of police, Douglas "Sandy" Clarridge, ended with Rowe and Crosswhite, and included a whole lot of people in between.

"They directed us to their lawyers," Laub said to the assembled in the conference room. "They're calling it a confidential source."

"Neither of you, I hope to God." Clarridge directed the comment to Rowe and Crosswhite.

"Never spoken to the man," Rowe said.

"We directed all questions on Vasiliev's murder through media relations," Crosswhite added.

Media relations was Etta Kimble, who sat at the table and had also sworn that she had released no information on any suspects, persons of interest, or anything else.

"Well, somebody let them know," Clarridge said. "And now I have the governor calling, a state senator, and two city council members asking what the hell is going on." Clarridge's cheeks had lit up like red Christmas bulbs, a dramatic contrast to his otherwise Slavic complexion.

"Nobody in this unit," Laub said. "Not a chance."

Clarridge sat back. "So what *do* we have?"

Crosswhite gave the assembled a detailed accounting of the investigation, something she, Rowe, and Laub had agreed upon prior to the meeting. Rowe tended to get confrontational when questioned about his decisions. Crosswhite, the ex–high school teacher, was used to it.

Rowe's testiness also stemmed from a lack

of sleep. His joints ached, and his hip burned from the lack of rest, and he had a plethora of better things to do than sit in a room pacifying nervous bureaucrats. Before going home, he and Crosswhite had made an extensive to-do list while wolfing down Dick's hamburgers, fries, and shakes, and the list wasn't getting any shorter sitting here. They needed to draft and get out subpoenas for Sloane's and Reid's businesses and cell phone records. They needed to review the reports summarizing the interviews of Vasiliev's neighbors and follow up, though they were being told by the interviewing detectives that the neighbors had little information of interest. No one had admitted to being the anonymous telephone caller, or to having made the second and third sets of shoe prints. No one had heard the gunshot. Initial attempts to track the phone used to report a prowler had been unsuccessful as well.

Also on the list were interviews with Sloane's and Reid's assistants, colleagues, and neighbors, and Rowe wanted to talk again to the tracker, Kaylee Wright. He'd reviewed the report from the K9 unit that had arrived late in the afternoon of the murder. Freddy, a Belgian Malinois, had alerted to three distinct scents that followed the same trail laid out by Wright, except Freddy did not stop tracking at the single shoe print on the beach. He'd continued twenty yards south. A phone call to the dog's handler revealed that Freddy had continued to track the person's scent even after they had entered the water and likely swum parallel to the shore. Harbor Patrol had searched the area at Rowe's request and reported a wooded public access half a mile from Vasiliev's home. Rowe wanted Wright to determine whether she could match any shoe prints at that easement with the prints found in Vasiliev's backyard. They'd already lost a day, and if the access was open to the public, it meant a greater chance that what evidence might have been there had already been destroyed.

"Ms. Reid is a triathlete; she runs, bikes, and swims long distances," Crosswhite continued. "We've confiscated five pairs of running shoes. All size seven. We're waiting on a further comparison of the soles to determine if any are a match with the print in the sand."

Wright had said there were two websites containing photographs of the soles of hundreds of different models of shoes. Unlike the automated fingerprint system, there was no automated system to compare and match shoe prints. It had to be done by hand and could be laborious.

"What about the other shoe prints?" Clarridge asked. "Can we eliminate them?"

Crosswhite nodded. "They were not made by the shooter. Dilliard is working on it, but initial reports are that the angles are off. The shooter was the size seven print."

"Tell me about the ex-husband," Clarridge said.

When Rowe and Crosswhite interviewed Dr. Felix Oberman in person he had quite the story to tell about his ex-wife. Then again, Reid had pretty much predicted what he would say — blaming her for everything, bitter and angry. Rowe had asked Mayweather to pull the Superior Court file from their divorce and to speak to the attorneys for both parties.

"He's certain about the statement she made, but the divorce appears to have been acrimonious . . ." Crosswhite considered her choice of words. "Let's just say that the husband might have his own reasons for being vindictive."

"What's her alibi?"

"She has none," Crosswhite said. "At home in bed, asleep."

"And this guy Sloane?"

"Initial indications are the other sets of

shoe prints are size ten and a half and size twelve. Sloane wears a twelve. We dropped off his shoes early this morning for comparison."

"And you say Vasiliev threatened him? Threatened to harm his son?"

"Day before," Crosswhite confirmed.

"Sloane's a marine," Rowe added. "I think we can assume he knows how to handle a gun."

"Does he own one?"

"He says he doesn't," Rowe said, "and I found no record that he does."

Clarridge looked to Cerrabone. "What do you think?"

Cerrabone took up the torch. "I agree that these are inquiries that absolutely have to be pursued," he said, confirming what Rowe liked so much about the man. Some prosecutors could be namby-pants when it came to charging crimes, but Cerrabone had a pair of cajones, and they had just grown a size larger, in Rowe's opinion. More than ever, Rowe would need to keep Cerrabone involved in every step of the investigation.

Clarridge reconsidered Rowe and Crosswhite. "You said she's coming in for a polygraph?"

Rowe looked at his watch. "Within half an hour."

"I want the results as soon as you have them." Clarridge pushed back his chair, signaling an end to the meeting.

Sloane stared at his one-inch-square mug shot just below a similar size picture of Barclay Reid — canned shots newspapers kept on file for people in the news. The paper had used the same picture of Sloane in the article reporting Tina's death. Most people would have glossed over the photographs without interest but for the headline immediately above.

Prominent Seattle Attorneys Questioned in Drug Dealer's Killing

Sloane had declined Yamaguchi's request for a comment, pulled off the freeway, and bought a newspaper. The article was cryptic though accurate. Citing an anonymous source, Yamaguchi reported that both Sloane and Reid had been separately questioned but could not be reached for comment. Seattle homicide had further declined to confirm or deny the accuracy of the report. Sloane knew Yamaguchi to be a good reporter and doubted he would have published the story unless the source had been reliable. The question was whom?

182

Yamaguchi led with the most sensational facts, though he tempered those by also reporting that Reid's daughter had died of a drug overdose and the federal government had recently conducted an investigation of Vasiliev for dealing narcotics. The implication was that the police could have been questioning Reid because of those circumstances. There was no such excuse provided for Sloane.

Halfway through the article, Sloane's cell phone rang. Carolyn.

"I'm reading it now," he said when she told him about the article. She said the phone at the office had been ringing off the hook and that the morning news had aired a short segment.

"Tell anyone who calls I'm not in and won't be commenting on the article or on Mr. Vasiliev's death. And let the security officer in the lobby know no one is to be allowed access to our offices."

"When will you be in?"

"Later this afternoon." When he disconnected, he pulled Detective Rowe's business card from his pants pocket.

Rowe hung up the telephone and downed his second Red Bull of the morning. Crosswhite remained entrenched in a telephone call. When she hung up, he said, "That was Sloane. He saw the article."

"What did he have to say?"

"Knew nothing about it until the reporter called him this morning to get a comment. He declined. He said he's not the source and wants to know if we have any idea who is."

"When is he coming in?"

Rowe tossed the can across the aisle, aiming for Crosswhite's trash and missing off the rim with a clunk. "On his way. Asked if there was a private entrance in case the anonymous source was someone in the department and a horde of reporters is gathering at the front gates."

Rowe had told Sloane that was unlikely, but as a concession, he'd advised him to drive around the back of the building and enter the parking garage from Sixth Avenue. He'd agreed to meet Sloane and escort him into the building. That was as private as it would get.

"Good, because that was Mayweather," Crosswhite said. "One of Sloane's neighbors says she saw him early yesterday morning in a sweatsuit and that he looked to be out of breath and sweating."

Rowe retrieved the errant shot. "How early?"

"Around four A.M."

Rowe crushed the can. "What's the neighbor doing up that early?"

"She's a technician on the morning news for KIRO. She gets up at three-fifteen and leaves her house at four."

"She got a clear look? She's positive it was Sloane?"

"She told Mayweather it was still dark when she drove down the street, but she thought it was Sloane."

"Thought?"

"She said the person was standing by Sloane's white Cadillac, bent over, like he was catching his breath, and using his shirt to wipe his face."

"Or maybe trying to conceal it," Rowe said.

"She kept watch in her rearview mirror and said the person pulled open the wooden gate and went into Sloane's yard."

Rowe dropped the can in the wastebasket. "She ever seen Sloane up that early before?"

"Let's hope Mayweather thought to ask."

The phone on Crosswhite's desk rang. After a few sentences, she hung up. "She's here," she said, meaning Reid. "I'll bring her up."

Crosswhite met Barclay Reid in the lobby

off the Fifth Avenue and Cherry Street entrance. No horde of reporters waited to hurl questions at them. Reid signed in at the security desk, and Crosswhite led her to the bank of elevators.

"I assume you saw the article in the newspaper?" Reid asked, sounding testy.

Crosswhite nodded.

"Any idea of the anonymous source?"

Crosswhite shook her head. "You?"

"It's not exactly something I would advertise, Detective."

"Nor would we."

Crosswhite led Reid from the elevator through the halls. The polygraph examiner, anticipating a test that morning, had already set out signs advising others that a test was in progress and requesting quiet. Unlike the hard — or even the soft — interrogation rooms, the anteroom outside the two rooms where the polygraph tests were administered was all about comfort — an open space with leather chairs, a potted plant, soft lighting. The goal was to put the examinee at ease. It was a fallacy that a polygraph detected a person lying. What it tracked was a person's physiological responses, their breathing and heart rate while answering questions. The calming atmosphere was intended to minimize any argument that the environment had caused anxiety. For the same reason, the examinee was provided the questions in advance — to eliminate argument that a question had been a surprise and falsely registered as an elevated physiological response. The examiner started with simple control questions, such as asking name and date and place of birth. This established a baseline physiological response. After having established a baseline, the examiner could measure the elevation in the person's physiological response to a particular question, as well as the decrease in tension after the person answered it.

If Reid were the least bit intimidated or nervous, she hid it well. Attired in a navy blue pin-striped suit with a cream-colored blouse and a strand of pearls, she walked into the anteroom with her arm outstretched and greeted the examiner like a fellow attorney before a deposition. "Let's get started," she said.

The file dropped from above, landing with a thud. Rowe jerked back from the computer screen, nearly knocking his coffee mug off the edge.

"What the fuck, Bernie?"

Bernie Hamilton's grin stretched his thick black mustache from cheek to cheek. With dark curly hair and black-framed glasses, he looked like a guy at a costume party wearing a Groucho Marx disguise. "Christina Anne Sloane," he said.

Rowe opened the file. "The wife? What does it say?"

"Says she's still dead. Hey, did I tell you this one? Knock knock."

"I got the husband coming in any minute, Bernie. What does the file say?"

Hamilton thrust his hands into his pockets. "Home invasion. Sloane gave a statement. Said he was in his office late when a man suddenly appeared in the doorway with a gun. Sloane and the guy got into it, and Sloane took a bullet in the thigh and one in the shoulder. The wife came down the stairs, and the guy shot her once in the chest. The son called nine-one-one."

"How old was the kid?"

"I believe it says fourteen."

"Did he confirm the shooter?"

Hamilton nodded. "Said the shooter pointed the gun at him but fled when he heard the sirens."

Rowe studied the file. "They never caught the guy?"

"Nope."

"No known motivation for the break-in?"

Hamilton shook his head. "Sloane has had

a series of high-profile cases. He's no stranger to controversy. He represented the family of that National Guardsman a few years back. You remember? He took down that chemical company . . . what was its name?"

"Argus," Rowe said, continuing to review the file.

"Right. Argus International. And North-cutt had to resign. That I was glad about, he was a prick —"

"He had a gun."

"That's usually where bullets come from, Sparrow," Hamilton said, but Rowe had stopped listening.

Sloane wiped the ink from each of his fingertips with an alcohol swab.

"You mind if I ask you a few more questions?" Rowe had sat through the finger-printing process. Sloane didn't think he was being friendly.

"The newspaper seems to think I'm a suspect, Detective."

"They didn't get that from me or anyone in this unit."

"Am I a suspect?"

Rowe folded his arms across his chest. "You're a lawyer, Mr. Sloane. I'm not going to bullshit you; you can figure it out. You were in Barclay Reid's home and had access to her gun the morning before Vasiliev was shot. The gun is missing. Vasiliev threatened you and your family."

Sloane continued to wipe off the ink. "Sounds like I'm a suspect."

"So help me clear it up."

"I thought I did last night."

"A neighbor says she saw you out early that morning, between three-thirty and four A.M." The paper had not reported the time Vasiliev had been shot. "You said you were home in bed that night," Rowe said.

"I was."

"So that wasn't you?"

"I went to bed that night close to midnight and woke up early and went for a run."

"So she did see you."

"I don't know if she saw me or not. But yeah, I went running that morning."

"You always run that early?"

Sloane tossed the alcohol wipe in the wastebasket. "Since my wife's murder, I get insomnia. I either can't fall asleep, or I wake up early and can't get back to sleep. So I went for a run."

"Do you always drive to go for a run? She said she saw you getting out of your car."

"You've been to my house. I'm not in any shape at present to run up those hills. I drive

190

up the hill to the middle school and run around the track or the flat area." Sloane was eager to leave. "Anything else?"

"You told me last night you don't own a gun."

Sloane's mind raced. "I don't own a gun."

"Have you ever owned a gun?"

"Why are you asking?"

Rowe reached behind his back and handed Sloane a document folded lengthwise that he'd had in his back pocket. Sloane considered it as Rowe continued. "You gave a statement in the hospital after you were shot."

Sloane's eyes scanned the statement and came to the sentence as Rowe spoke.

"You said you couldn't get to the gun in your desk drawer that night. So I'm wondering . . . if you've never owned a gun . . . what gun were you referring to?" Rowe leveled his gaze. "And where is it now?"

Camano Island
Washington

Charles Jenkins called out as he walked in the back door. "Alex?" The kitchen smelled like sausage.

"I'm in the study," Alex replied.

She sat with her hands on the keyboard. She had the stereo on low, listening to the

191

Shania Twain CD he'd bought for her. As he walked in, Sam rose from her slumber long enough to bark. Max, his pit bull, didn't even bother to raise his head from his paws, looking at Jenkins with an arched brow.

"Nice watchdogs," Jenkins said.

He had intended the room at the back of the house to be his "man cave" when they rebuilt following the fire, a place where he could retreat and watch television, maybe smoke a cigar. That explained the wood paneling, the dark-colored furniture, and the forty-two-inch flat-screen on the wall. But the mess on the desk belonged to Alex, who used the room as her office.

"So what happened?"

Jenkins had rushed from the house upon learning that Vasiliev's killer had used a .38 and spoke to her only briefly on the phone to tell her he'd spend the night at Sloane's, promising to fill her in when he got home.

"He went in to get fingerprinted. I told him I'd call later today." Jenkins picked up the mug from the desk, the tea lukewarm.

She manipulated her black curls into a ponytail. "They can't really be considering him as a suspect."

"They can and they are."

She had the sliding-glass door to the deck

open to allow fresh air. Jenkins walked out onto the deck, the dogs following. The view looked like something painted on a canvas. A blue, cloudless sky hung over two Appaloosas grazing on a field of yellow-brown grass that stretched across their acreage to the adjacent dairy farm's rolling green hills.

She joined him. He handed her back the empty mug. "Where's CJ?"

"Preschool. And don't change the subject. What's wrong?" Her eyes narrowed in question. "You're worried."

"Of course I'm worried. He's my best friend."

But she knew him better than that. "Don't dismiss me. You're not worried about the police . . . about the investigation. You think he could have done it. Is that why you told me to try to get in touch with John?"

Jenkins had asked her to call Sloane's law partner, John Kannin, who had criminal law experience but remained on vacation somewhere in the Amazon. "Did you?" he asked.

"Not yet."

The Appaloosas raised their heads in unison, turning to the barking of the neighbor's dog. Sam waggled out onto the porch to consider it. Max had closed his eyes.

"I think he's been through a lot," Jenkins said. "An awful lot."

"He wouldn't do it," Alex said.

Jenkins knew otherwise. In Vietnam, he'd seen good men break from the stress and anxiety — shoot women and children — men who would not have deliberately stepped on a bug when they first arrived in-country. And he'd been there the night Sloane had nearly blinded Anthony Stenopolis with a fire poker. He'd seen the rage.

I'm tired, Charlie. I'm tired of people threatening me, threatening my family.

"Every man has his breaking point," he said. "Every man has that potential."

"What are the police saying?"

"Nothing directly, but between the lines, they're saying someone shot Vasiliev in the back of the head with a thirty-eight." Jenkins removed the Glock from his pocket and clicked free the clip, putting both on the deck railing. He knew what she was thinking, that if they ran a ballistics test, it could rule out the gun.

"I couldn't take the chance," he said. "I don't think it's been recently fired, but . . . Barclay owns a thirty-eight Smith and Wesson. It's missing. David had access to it that morning."

She gave this some thought. "Okay, but you said Vasiliev didn't threaten him until later that day, after he left her house."

"Maybe the threat wasn't the motivation." Jenkins had the hour-and-a-half drive to consider it.

"What do you mean?"

"Maybe it's like he said, Alex. Maybe he's just tired of people threatening those he loves."

"He told you he loves her?"

"He didn't have to."

Alex paused again, seeming to digest the information. "Then why would he take her gun? Why would he put her in that position?"

Jenkins had also considered that question. "Why would he take on an unwinnable case against the U.S. government? Why would he go after Kendall Toys when he knew it could create problems?" He sat on the bench seat built into the deck. Alex sat beside him. "He asked me if he courted it."

"Courted what?"

"Danger . . . cases that put those he loves in jeopardy."

"That's ridiculous."

He glanced at her. "Is it?"

A cool breeze blew the hair from her face. "What are you saying — that he took her gun so she would need him?"

"It does add to the confusion, doesn't it?"

She shook her head as if not believing it

possible, but she had not been there when Jenkins had asked Sloane point-blank if Sloane had killed Vasiliev.

Did you do it?

Do what?

Did you kill him?

What are you talking about?

It was on the news.

I know.

I made a call; the bullet was a thirty-eight.

You have to ask me that question? You were there. I could have blown Stenopolis's head off.

Sloane hadn't answered the question.

The Justice Center
Seattle, Washington

Rowe munched a PowerBar as he made his way back to his cubicle. The unit was in full swing, and he could hear the voices of his colleagues on the phone or in conversation. Two were discussing the Mariners game from the night before, when the bullpen fell apart and the Angels came back to win.

"It was a belt-high fastball . . . I could have hit it out."

Rowe wished he had the time. He found Crosswhite at her desk reading, but the tiny shake of her head gave away her mood even before she opened her mouth. It was the

196

shake she gave when she didn't believe what she was hearing or, in this case, reading. She tossed the document to him. "She passed."

"What?"

The head shake again. "The polygraph. She passed it."

His eyes immediately saw the initials ND on the document — "no discernible deception."

He rolled his chair closer to her cubicle, sat on the edge of his seat, and handed her the second PowerBar as he continued to go through the report.

"I talked to Stephanie," Crosswhite said, meaning the examiner. "She said she's never had anyone with that low a baseline before. Reid displayed little if any signs of being anxious or nervous."

Rowe flipped the pages, looking at the attached charts. He wasn't great at deciphering them. Most people didn't take polygraphs anymore. With the Internet and other sources of information, most people had learned they didn't have to or that the reason polygraphs weren't admissible was, in part, because the science behind them wasn't completely accepted. But he understood enough to know the charts should have been filled with peaks and valleys where the pen had scratched across the paper. Reid's chart looked damn near like an EKG readout of a patient who had flat-lined, as straight a line as he had ever seen on the few reports he had read.

"How does Stephanie explain it?" Rowe asked.

Crosswhite shrugged. "She can't."

He slumped back against the seat. "What about the fact that Reid's an attorney?"

"What about it?"

"Well, we don't get too many people as educated or with as much experience asking and answering questions. She's probably been in similar situations — depositions and trials — a hundred times before. She's used to the stress."

"Yeah, except in those situations, she's the one asking the questions, not hooked to a machine answering them as a suspect in a murder case."

"Agreed, but my point is, she's been in stressful situations before, a lot more than most people. Maybe she's learned how to control her emotions better; she doesn't get as worked up."

Crosswhite pointed to the report. "That good? I don't think anyone's *that* good, Sparrow. Besides, the test is designed to find the person's baseline, and that's what everything is measured against. Even if she were the most cool, calm, and collected person in the world, the test should still register fluctuations."

He scratched the side of his face. When he didn't shave, his skin itched. "So where does this leave us?"

The tiny shake of the head again. "Either she didn't do it, or she beat the test."

"Stephanie ever have that happen before?" Rowe also knew from the Internet that people had access to a lot of information on how to beat a polygraph by doing things such as altering their breathing patterns, or biting their tongue to induce pain, even putting a tack in their shoe and pressing down on it during certain questions to create a false physiological response. But the examiners had become savvy to these tricks, and the test accounted for them.

"Not to her."

"But she's heard of it?"

"She said it's in the literature. The test depends on the normal human psychology of anticipation and release of tension."

"You said 'normal.' Who wouldn't anticipate it, someone abnormal?"

Crosswhite shrugged. "Sociopaths, apparently."

ELEVEN

Burien
Washington

Unable to concentrate at work, Sloane told Carolyn to clear his calendar and went home early. As he drove down SW52nd Street, he saw the sign for the Saint Francis of Assisi School. He thought of the young priest, Father Allen, who he had not seen for a while.

He turned at Twenty-first Avenue and drove past the brick-and-glass one-story building, parking in front of the rounded steeple.

With Jake no longer living with him, Sloane had stopped measuring the months by the school year and was surprised when he got out of the car and heard the din of unseen children in the playground behind the buildings. It was the start of a new school year.

Inside the building, the woman behind the

counter advised that Father Allen was out on the playground but Sloane could not join him. She didn't have to explain further that school rules frowned upon unknown adults wandering the grounds. She told Sloane she could text the priest if it was urgent. The comment made him smile — a priest who texted. What was next, confession via cell phone? Sloane didn't know what "urgent" was to a priest — maybe someone dying? He told her not to bother. "Just tell him David stopped by to talk?"

Sloane was slipping on his sunglasses as he walked back to his car when he heard someone shout his name and the sound of leather sandals slapping the sidewalk. Father Allen jogged toward him in his brown Franciscan robe, the knots of the rope tied around his waist bouncing in rhythm with his mop of curly blond hair. In his left hand, he held an iPhone. "Hey, I just got a text that you were here."

"I told her not to bother you," Sloane said, wondering if there was something about the way he looked or sounded that had caused the woman in the office to determine on her own that his visit was urgent.

"No bother." Father Allen removed a handkerchief from the pocket of his robe, like a kangaroo's pouch, and wiped at a trickle of perspiration. "You saved me. Wall ball is not my sport, especially not in sandals." He stuffed the handkerchief back in the pouch. "How have you been? It's been awhile."

Sloane wasn't sure how he had been. "You haven't seen the paper this morning?"

The priest shook his head, and the mop of hair shimmied. "I saw that the Mariners lost and dropped another game behind the Angels and that my chances of going to a play-off game this year suck at the moment."

"This was on the front page. *I* was on the front page."

The school bell rang, loud and long. When the echo faded, Father Allen said, "You want to grab an iced tea or something up the street?"

It being early afternoon, the crowd in the Tin Room amounted to a couple of men on stools, beer glasses on the bar. A soccer game played on the overhead television. Another man sat at a table finishing a hamburger and fries beneath a vintage photograph of a tinsmith's tools. Sloane and the priest took a table at the back of the room, but the music was loud — Tom Petty

— so they opted for the wooden deck, sitting under the shade of a table umbrella. Allen asked, "So I assume you being on the front page was not good news."

It was a long story without any logical beginning. "I've been seeing someone."

"Yeah?"

"We were both on the front page."

"Oh. Well . . . you've piqued my curiosity."

As Sloane explained his relationship with Barclay, Kelley, who had worked at the Tin Room since it opened, brought their iced-tea orders and a plate of nachos. Allen poured two packs of sweetener into his tea. "How do you feel about this woman?"

"She's a lot like Tina — independent, intelligent, athletic, competitive . . . funny."

The priest sat back. "And you're physically attracted to her?"

Sloane said he was.

"Do you think you could be in love with her?"

Sloane contemplated an appropriate answer for a priest. Was it too soon to be in love again? Would Allen frown upon their physical relationship, even between two consenting adults? He didn't know. He knew only that he'd come to view Allen as more of a confidant and friend than a priest.

"I think so."

"You're uncertain."

"Not about her, about . . . With Tina, I thought I'd found a life, you know, something I had wanted, a family. But then it seemed I was always doing something I knew could jeopardize that — the case against Argus International, then Kendall Toys. I guess I've had moments when I doubted whether I really loved Tina, or only loved the thought of her and Jake, of being part of a family."

"Why would you say that?"

"Because if I loved her as much as I believed I did . . ."

"You would not have taken cases that placed them in jeopardy."

"I'm wondering if I have a destructive streak. You know, something that makes me do things that could potentially destroy what I think I want . . . that puts me and those I love in harm's way."

Allen contemplated this for a bit. Then he said, "I don't doubt for a moment that you loved Tina, David, as well as the situation — a family, a husband . . . a father. There's no reason to separate one from the other. It was part of what you found appealing about her as a person. But tell me something, did your feelings for Barclay begin before or after she found herself in trouble with the law?"

"Why do you ask?"

Allen just smiled. "You know why; you're an intelligent person."

"You think I'm attracted to women in trouble?"

"I think you're attracted to . . . causes, David. I think you're attracted to *people* who *need* you. I think that it's a manifestation of what you told me happened to your mother, how you felt powerless to help her. You have a weak spot for people in need, for people who turn to you because they have no one or no place to go."

"It's my job, Allen. I'm an attorney. People don't come to me unless they need me."

Allen smiled, sipped his tea. "You're preaching to the choir. But there's a difference between it being your job and it defining who you are as a person."

"I guess I don't completely follow. Tina was incredibly independent and self-sufficient. She'd raised Jake for years on her own. She went back to school, had a job. She didn't need me."

"No? Didn't you tell me that when you first met her she had a bad marriage and a husband who didn't pay her any alimony or child care, didn't spend any time with his own son?"

"But I knew I liked Tina the minute we met, before I even knew her circumstances. There was a spark."

Allen laughed. "Of course there was. She was an incredibly attractive woman that just about any man would have been physically attracted to. And physical attraction leads to interaction, and interaction is what allows us to become better acquainted and decide if we want to be intimate. When you did, you found a good woman who'd been dealt a bad hand and could use some help."

"Is there anything wrong with that?"

"To help others? Of course not. But I think you also loved being the husband she never had and the father Jake wanted . . . and the person who could take care of them. That's part of the reason for the depth of your pain now. You blame yourself for her death because you saw yourself as not just her husband, not just Jake's father, but their guardian, the person who would protect them, the person who was supposed to prevent bad things from ever happening to either of them again. And you believe you failed."

"I did fail."

"Bad things happen to good people, David. Tell me, if Tina had been stricken with cancer, would you have blamed yourself?"

"No."

"Then how can you blame yourself for an act of violence equally as random? And now you have found another woman, divorced, alone, a person hurting inside, as are you, from a terrible loss, something that most people, thankfully, can never truly understand — but that you can."

"And you think that's what I'm attracted to?"

"Not entirely, no. But I think it is a part of who you are."

"So what do I do?"

"Just understand your vulnerabilities."

"Such as?"

"There's a huge difference between love and need. Someone who needs you will put themselves first. Someone who loves you will put you first."

The Justice Center
Seattle, Washington

As promised, Rowe delivered the report on Reid's polygraph to his detective sergeant, Andrew Laub. Laub said he would advise Sandy Clarridge, though he neither looked nor sounded happy about having to do so. He asked Rowe where the investigation was headed in light of the test. Rowe didn't have a ready answer and didn't want to bullshit him. He told Laub they were awaiting certain CSI reports, including the analysis of the shoes by the special operations unit. He also told Laub about the neighbor who saw Sloane early on the morning of the murder, and said they were following up on that lead as well.

The neighbor was certain she saw Sloane minutes before four in the morning, because she left every morning at that time to be at work by 4:30. The anonymous phone call reporting Vasiliev's death had been logged at 3:12 A.M. The drive from Vasiliev's home in Laurelhurst to Sloane's home in Three Tree Point was just over twenty-eight miles and, according to MapQuest, took about thirty-four minutes — likely less at that hour, without traffic. Therefore, it was conceivable Sloane could have shot Vasiliev and still had time to drive home to be seen by the neighbor. That was well and good, but it did not comport with Kaylee Wright's analysis that *three* people had run through Vasiliev's backyard at about the same time and that one of them, with a foot size much smaller than Sloane's, had been the shooter. It also didn't comport with Rowe's working theory that whoever had killed Vasiliev had left via the water, either swimming or by boat. DMV records revealed Sloane owned a boat but he never could have piloted between his home and Vasiliev's in the requisite time, because to do so would have required that he navigate the boat from Lake Washington through the locks to the Puget Sound.

As Rowe stood to leave Laub's office, Laub didn't exactly send him off with the rousing motivational speech he had hoped for.

"I'll cover your asses as much as I can, but you better have all your i's dotted and t's crossed on this one, Sparrow."

Rowe made his way back to his cubicle asking himself the same question his father used to ask whenever his son failed at a task: "What the Sam Hill happened?"

Crosswhite approached carrying her purse and his windbreaker, which meant they were going somewhere.

"How did he take it?" she asked.

"You might want to get that schoolteacher résumé updated, and let me know if you find any openings for a janitor."

"You think we're having fun now? We're just getting started."

He followed her down the interior stairwell. "Now what?"

"Latents are back."

"Already?"

She pushed through the door to the parking garage. Her voice echoed. "I called for an initial assessment. I was hoping we'd find Reid's print at the site, blow her alibi, and move directly to accepting our commendations for a job well done."

"You really don't like her, do you?" He walked past the Prius to the Impala parked two stalls farther down. "I'll drive."

Crosswhite picked up her pace. "Like has nothing to do with it. I think she's lying."

"Polygraph says otherwise."

"Women's intuition says the polygraph is wrong."

They slipped into the car and clipped the seat belts.

"Maybe we should have hooked her up to you and asked the questions. Let me guess — I shouldn't dust off my dress blues for that commendation ceremony anytime soon."

"I wouldn't. But you may be right about Vasiliev providing more information dead than alive . . ."

Rowe had his hand on the key in the ignition, waiting. "So how long are you going to hold me in suspense?"

"Latents has positive AFIS IDs on five other prints found inside the home —

including three guys with a history of dealing and one woman with a history of solicitation. I got uniforms rounding them up now. Mayweather and Simonson are lined up to find out what they have to say."

"Okay, but you said five. Math was never my best subject in school, Professor, but three plus one was four in my grade school."

Crosswhite smiled. "I'm saving the best for last."

"Yeah, and what would that be?"

"Take a left out of the garage."

Drug Enforcement Administration
Second Avenue West
Seattle, Washington

Half an hour later, Lucas Finley, the special agent in charge of the DEA's five northwestern states — Washington, Oregon, Idaho, Montana, and Alaska — sat looking like a man who took a wrong turn while deep in thought and came out of it wondering where the heck he was and how he had gotten there.

"Honestly, I have no idea who this guy is or where he could have come from. I don't recognize the name, and I've been SAC here six years and an agent eight before that."

Finley sounded convincing, but Rowe wasn't completely buying it. Maybe his

211

reluctance to accept the man at his word was because Finley, tall and lean with gunmetal-gray hair, a set of perfect white teeth, starched white shirt, and conservative blue tie, looked and sounded like the team doctor who had told Rowe there was nothing seriously wrong with his hip and that continuing to play wouldn't harm it further. Rowe also knew the DEA had spent seven months chasing Vasiliev, and he wasn't convinced they would have just walked away because a Federal District Court judge threw out the evidence on a technicality. But if they'd kept Vasiliev under surveillance after the court hearing without proper authority, maybe without the Justice Department's blessing or knowledge, there could be a lot of questions to answer for a guy with not long to go before vesting for that cushy federal pension.

"I need to know whether you guys had him under surveillance," Rowe said. One of the latents had come back as a match for a federal DEA agent named Julio Cruz. "Because if you guys fucked up my homicide investigation, I'm really going to get pissed."

Finley sat forward. Two bull moose locking horns. "I told Detective Crosswhite on the phone I'd look into it, and I'm telling

212

you now, face-to-face — one, we didn't have Vasiliev under surveillance . . . why would we? We had enough evidence to put the son of a bitch away for a very long time if Kozlowski hadn't come down with that bullshit decision. And two, I have no idea who the hell Julio Cruz is. He doesn't work in this division. I can tell you that."

Rowe took a deep breath, blowing out the frustration. "What about another division?"

"I got a call in to human resources in Virginia," Finley said, meaning the home office and *I'm way ahead of you, pal.* "When I know, you'll know. And then we'll both know."

Three Tree Point
Burien, Washington
Sloane looked up. He had reached the end. He had kayaked around the point to the south of his home many times, just a short distance from where he put in, but he had never reached the point to the north. He hadn't planned on it this trip, either, but he'd found a rhythm to his stroke, like a runner lost in his footfalls, and when he looked up, he had done it.

After leaving the Tin Room and dropping Father Allen back at the school, he took advantage of the weather, as initially intended. With the sun still bright and the tide out, he pulled out the kayak to get some exercise. He now sat bobbing in the waves, letting his arms and shoulders rest, sweat trickling from beneath his 49ers cap and darkening his tank top beneath the life vest. He looked across the Puget Sound, considering a ferry boat crossing between Vashon Island and West Seattle, much larger than in the view from his home. From the wave action, he judged the tide to have shifted. The breeze had also picked up, and it felt good on his skin. He heard the bark of an unseen seal, which was becoming more and more rare.

He pointed his kayak toward home and let the paddles cut through the water, allowing his mind to drift again. He wondered how someone as young as Father Allen had become so perceptive. It was tough to argue with logic, and that was exactly what the priest had put squarely in Sloane's face, forcing him to consider that maybe he did see himself as a knight in shining armor, the person to whom others went when justice could not be obtained elsewhere. The priest had said there was nothing wrong with that, so long as Sloane didn't let it define him or his relationships.

The journey home seemed shorter, the

tide with him and the wind at his back, but he was also pushing the pace and felt the strain in his shoulders. His breathing grew labored. He lifted his head to gauge his path and noticed someone walking along the beach, a blue dot in the distance. As he approached, the dot grew and the features became recognizable — the color of her hair, the tiny frame, the casual way she moved. Nearing, he saw that she wore a pin-striped suit, holding her shoes by the straps, walking in stocking feet. Barclay.

He shouted her name and waved, drawing her attention. Then he gave a few final, powerful strokes to beach the kayak in the sand and pebbles. He stepped out into ankle-deep water, grabbed the tie line at the front of the skiff, and pulled it farther up the beach.

"How did you find me?"

"Carolyn said you had gone home early. She gave me directions."

"Decided to get some exercise," he said, pulling his bib overhead, which stretched over the opening of the kayak to keep water out. He threw it and the paddles inside the hull.

Reid looked out across the sound. "It's beautiful. Now I know what you meant about living on the water." She tilted her chin and smiled up at him. "I've been afraid to call."

He nodded. "I was concerned about the police, about how it might look."

"That's not what I meant." She looked again at the view. A tear trickled from beneath her sunglasses. "I'm sorry I got you involved in this, David. It never should have been your problem. I never should have asked you to take the civil case. It was wrong of me."

"I appreciate that," he said. "But I'm a big boy."

"I took a lie-detector test this morning."

The news alarmed him. "Do you think that's wise?"

"I wanted to. I don't want there to be any doubt."

"Do you think it will convince them?"

She removed the sunglasses. "I'm not worried about convincing them."

"I don't have any doubt, Barclay."

She took a deep breath, cleared her throat. "Thank you. But right now this isn't fair to you, not after what happened to your wife . . ." Another tear pooled and trickled, like a slow leak. "That's why I came out here . . . to find you . . . to tell you that I'm not going to see you anymore — not until this is over. Not until it gets resolved, and then only if you still want to."

He stepped forward, took her hand that was not holding the shoe straps. Her nylons had run railroad tracks up her shins and calves. "It is resolved," he said. "For me, it's resolved."

He bent to kiss her, a movement she only momentarily resisted.

Second Avenue West
Seattle, Washington

Crosswhite slid into the passenger seat. When the driver's-side door didn't open, she turned and looked out the back window. Rowe stood a couple of strides down the sidewalk, near the rear bumper, hands on his hips, facing north. She got out of the car and walked around the back, considering the direction of his gaze, seeing nothing but parked cars, buildings, and trees on the sidewalk.

"What is it?"

He tilted his head a bit, not really looking at her. "What the Sam Hill is going on?"

"Sam Hill?"

"We got a suspect who passed a lie-detector test, another who logic dictates wasn't there, footprints that lead to no-where, and the fingerprint of a DEA agent who, agency records indicate, retired twenty years ago."

Lucas Finley had indeed received a call from the home office, but the information had done little to clear up the mystery of Julio Cruz. If anything, it deepened it. According to personnel, Cruz had been a DEA agent in the Florida field office, working mostly in Miami before retiring in the late 1990s. His last known address, the one where his retirement pension was mailed each month, was a P.O. box in Miami. His last known phone number had been disconnected. They had no idea where he was, which meant they couldn't rule out Seattle.

Birds chirped in the trees. "Maybe we got a rogue agent who got a taste of the money and decided he liked it," Crosswhite said.

"So he comes all the way across the United States to work with Vasiliev? What, he can't find any drugs coming into the country in Miami?"

"Just thinking out loud." She squinted against the bright sun. Her sunglasses remained on the dashboard. "Finley said he would look into it."

Rowe pointed down the street, and though he wore wraparound sunglasses, she realized he wasn't pointing at anything there. He was seeing the green lawn behind Vasiliev's house, leading to the concrete patio and the sliding-glass door.

"We got two sets of footprints running up the left side of the lawn to Vasiliev's back door, then running back to the water, likely to a boat. If it was this guy Cruz, and we have to assume latents didn't fabricate his print out of thin air, he wasn't there by chance."

"Or alone."

He glanced at her. "Or alone."

"Vasiliev was under surveillance," she said.

"Seems the logical conclusion, doesn't it? What other explanation is there?"

This time she sensed he wanted her to play devil's advocate. "Okay. Maybe this guy Cruz and the second guy were working with the shooter. They drop the person into the water, and the person swims to shore, pops Vasiliev. Once he's done, they drive the boat in, check the handiwork, and . . ." She stopped her train of thought.

"Except we know the shooter detoured to the bushes and, thanks to Freddy, left swimming in the opposite direction," Rowe said, verbalizing the problem with her theory. "It doesn't fit, which brings us full circle to Sam Hill."

"Never heard of him." That got a tiny smile. "Finley says they didn't have Vasiliev under surveillance. Why would he lie?"

"Maybe he isn't."

"It was a Seattle operation. How could he not have known?"

"Maybe it wasn't a Seattle operation. His office had the evidence they needed and put it in the U.S. attorney's hands." He turned his head to her. "Remember the weather the morning Vasiliev was killed?"

"Thunderstorms."

"So let's say someone has Vasiliev under surveillance, for whatever reason. Where would be a good place to keep an eye on the house?"

"Given all the windows, the side facing the water," she said.

"I agree. So they're watching from a boat, only they can't really see or hear too clearly because of the storm. They hear a noise, sounds like thunder. When they look, they see him slumped over on the sofa. Now they're moving quickly to the shore, up to the patio. He's dead. Nothing they can do about it."

"Why call it in?"

"That's where I'm going. How many times have we asked neighbors if they heard gunshots and gotten a positive response?"

"Only in the city," she said, where the houses were close, sometimes side by side.

"Right. And who would know that most

gunshots go unreported until the victim is found?"

"Someone in law enforcement."

"And who else but law enforcement and criminals would think to have an untraceable phone?"

"So where are you going with this?"

"I don't know."

"So let's focus on the print. How does it get on the door?" she asked.

"It's instinct. Remember, Adderley said he could hardly remember exactly what he did because his heart was pumping so fast. Maybe Cruz can't stop himself in time and touches the door."

"Okay, so how does the shooter play in to all of this?"

"I'm not sure he or she does. We saw all three as working together, but maybe not. Maybe the shooter got there thinking she would kill Vasiliev and swim off. She picked the night because of the storm, and everything is going according to plan until she hears a boat engine approaching, so she hides in the bushes and waits until they leave."

"Except Reid passed the test," Crosswhite said. "She passed the polygraph."

He smiled. "But not the Crosswhite test. And you had what, fifteen years to evaluate every possible lie a high school kid could conjure up."

"Doesn't matter if we can't break her alibi, put her at the scene."

"I know." Rowe removed his sunglasses, squinting as he rubbed the bridge of his nose.

"It's good, Sparrow," she assured him. "It makes sense. It's progress. Let's get something to eat and some caffeine. We'll go back and digest everything we have and go over it again. Maybe latents will have processed Sloane's fingerprints and Wright will have good news on the shoe prints. Then we go to work on finding the other suspect."

He nodded and turned for the car, stopped. "What other suspect?"

"Sam Hill," she said.

Three Tree Point
Burien, Washington
They made love with the windows open, feeling the light breeze and hearing the sound of waves lapping on the shore. Afterward, they lay atop the rumpled sheets, sweat glistening. Tendrils of light streamed through the two skylights, which had been the extent of Sloane's architectural contribution when he and Tina bought the home and set to remodeling it. He wanted to be

222

able to lie in bed at night and look up at the stars, like he had as a kid when one of the foster families gave him a room in the attic with a window.

Barclay lay beside him trying to catch her breath. She gave an audible moan with each exhale. "I hope your neighbors aren't home," she said, making him laugh. She sat up and put her feet on the floor, arching her back, pulling air into her lungs. "I need a glass of water."

"I'll get it," he said.

She reached back and put a hand on his chest, stopping him. "You've done enough. Just point me in the direction."

Sloane stretched out a lazy arm toward the stairs. "Kitchen, left cupboard as you face the sink."

She kissed him passionately. "I'll get two," she said.

"I'm fine."

"Maybe for now, but after what I have in store for you, you might very well be dehydrated."

She rolled off the bed, standing, seemingly not the least bit bashful about her nakedness. She had the body of a dancer, with sinewy muscles and no detectable fat. "I'll need to borrow a bathrobe," she said, "unless you want the neighbors to see me as well as hear me."

"Back of the bathroom door," he said.

She emerged, rolling up the sleeves of his navy blue terry-cloth robe that fell to her ankles. Sloane had given Tina's clothes to Goodwill.

"I liked the show better before you drew the curtain," he said.

She turned at the doorway with an impish grin. "Really? Well, the next screening will be . . . downstairs." She dropped the robe and took off running.

TWELVE

Laurelhurst
Seattle, Washington

They would not get the caffeine they needed or the food they craved, but Rowe didn't care, and he knew Crosswhite didn't, either. Though neither would say it aloud, like baseball players sitting silent in a dugout for fear of jinxing a pitcher in the midst of throwing a no-hitter, each was optimistic this could be the break they needed, the break every investigation needed.

Andrew Laub had called as Rowe maneuvered through afternoon traffic on their return to the Justice Center. A woman in Laurelhurst had called and asked to speak to the detectives in charge of the murder investigation — "the one in Laurelhurst," was how she put it. She said she might have some information; she didn't know, so she was calling. They had received dozens of tips, but this lady, Laub said, had been modest and quiet, like maybe she really did know something.

Rowe and Crosswhite would find out soon enough.

Mary Beth Blume answered a cathedral wood-and-lead-glass door. She appeared too small and demure to be living in such a grand expanse of overindulgence, but her demeanor fit Laub's description of her voice on the phone — "tentative." Dressed in a pair of designer jeans, a V-neck cashmere sweater over a white T-shirt, and gold-colored slippers, the kind with a rubber tread, Blume briefly considered their badges, seeming much more interested in the unmarked blue Impala parked in the street.

"Is it okay there?" Crosswhite asked. "Would you like us to move it?"

"No . . . it's fine," she said, letting them in and closing the door.

Rowe deduced it would not have been fine had it been an actual police cruiser, visible to all the neighbors and likely to be the subject of interest and subsequent questions.

Blume had straw-colored hair that curved just below her chin and looked to have been recently brushed. "My husband is on his way home," she said, seeming uncertain what to do next. "He thought he should be here."

"That's fine," Rowe said, trying to maintain an air of calm. "We're in no hurry." He looked about, hoping it might spur Blume to invite them to sit down. His hip burned.

"You have a beautiful home," Crosswhite said.

That could have been the understatement of the year. The entryway was bigger than Rowe's master bedroom and bathroom combined, with black and white marble floor tiles, gold-leaf mirrors on wallpapered walls, and an elaborate chandelier hanging from a domed ceiling above a newel-post staircase that curved down from the upper floor.

Blume stopped fidgeting with her hands long enough to point to an adjacent room. "We can wait in the living room." She stepped down into a sunken room mostly champagne-colored but for a black baby-grand piano near a bay window that provided a view of the manicured front yard.

"Do you play?" Crosswhite asked, moving toward the keys.

Rowe knew his partner hoped to relax Blume by talking about a comfortable subject. The poor woman looked as though she might throw up at any moment, which, in a perverse way, made Rowe optimistic she might have some information of value.

"Not too much anymore," Blume said. Then, as if to explain, "My mother thought it was important for me to learn an instrument. But I haven't had much time lately. We've been in the middle of a remodel."

Of course they were, Rowe thought. A three-to-four-million-dollar home clearly needed a face-lift to make it presentable.

"Sounds like we had similar mothers," Crosswhite said.

"You play?" Rowe asked.

She gave him the eye roll. "Twelve years."

"My son plays," Blume added. "Though now he mostly plays his guitar. He's in a band."

Rowe heard regret in the woman's voice. The purr of a car engine drew his attention to the bay window as a canary-yellow convertible Porsche pulled up the driveway and parked in front of one of the four garage bays. The personalized license plate read BLUME. The only thing missing now was the golden retriever or yellow Lab.

"That's Richard," Mary Beth said as a short, balding man wearing designer sunglasses popped from the car fixing his windblown hair, and jogged in the direction of the front door. Mary Beth met her husband in the entry with a look that clearly conveyed, "They're here."

Richard walked past her without so much as an acknowledgment, dropped his keys on a table abutting the staircase, and fixed his silver sunglasses atop his head. He stepped down into the living room, hand extended, all business, dressed like his wife in designer jeans, a gray cashmere sweater pulled up his forearms, and loafers. After introductions, they remained standing, again seemingly uncertain of the next step. Rowe couldn't take it anymore and blazed a trail to the sofa. Crosswhite joined him, and Richard and Mary Beth sat to Rowe's right in the two matching chairs. When neither initiated conversation, Rowe said, "My detective sergeant indicated you might have some information that relates to the shooting."

The Blume home was half a mile south of Vasiliev's home — Rowe and Crosswhite had clocked it — and across from the public easement.

Richard sat forward, forearms on his knees. Despite strands of gray in what hair remained atop his head, his goatee was solid black. He looked too young to be living in a house so grand, driving a car so expensive. Rowe deduced him to be either a trust-fund baby or one of the lucky ones who hit the

229

Internet start-up craze at the right time and got out before the crash.

"I need to know whether we have any liability here . . . before we talk, whether I should call my attorney."

What was it with rich people and attorneys? Rowe wondered. They talked of attorneys as if they kept them on leashes like other people kept dogs.

"I don't understand," Rowe said. "I was told you may have some information. Do you think there could be some liability?"

Blume looked at his wife. The woman sat chewing her thumbnail, grimacing. "No. It's not that." Richard paused, lips pursed. "We just don't want his name in the paper — the publicity."

"Whose name?" Rowe asked.

Blume again looked to his wife, but this time his expression was more of a question. "I'm sorry. I thought my wife told you all of this."

"We were waiting for you," Rowe explained.

"It's our son, Joshua. He was out the other night; he shouldn't have been, but he was. He snuck out." The picture began to sharpen for Rowe, and with clarity, the butterflies of anticipation again began to flutter. "That's why we didn't come forward earlier. We didn't know. Joshua was afraid of the consequences because we'd told him we'd ground him if we caught him sneaking out again."

"Your son was out the morning Mr. Vasiliev was shot," Rowe said, trying to move the story along.

Mary Beth pointed in the direction of the bay window. "He was coming up the street. His bedroom is off the porch in the back. He was . . ." She stopped speaking when her husband raised a hand. Rowe could only imagine what Crosswhite was thinking. She would have pistol-whipped Rowe if he ever similarly disrespected her.

"He was out with friends," Richard said. "They dropped him off down the road so we wouldn't hear the car engine. He has a room in the back with a slider. Anyway, he saw something. It scared him, actually."

"What did he see?" Crosswhite asked.

"There's no liability here, is there, for not coming forward earlier? I mean, if this even amounts to anything . . . there's no repercussions?"

"There's no repercussions I can think of," Rowe said. "Except maybe between you and your son." He smiled. Richard Blume did not. "Why don't you just tell us what your son thinks he saw?"

231

"I think maybe it would be better if Joshua told you," Richard said, standing.

Three Tree Point
Burien, Washington

Sloane chased her down the stairs, hand sliding on the railing. When he hit the landing, the entire house shook. When he rounded the corner for the kitchen, Barclay dodged him, but he got a hand on her waist and pulled her to him, wrestling with her from behind until she suddenly stopped, looking past him. He turned to see Charles Jenkins at the kitchen door, about to knock. Instead Jenkins pulled back his hand and quickly retreated down the steps.

"Shit," Sloane said.

She covered a grin. "A neighbor?"

"My investigator . . . and friend."

She laughed. "Sorry. I'll go upstairs."

Sloane pulled open the door, standing behind it. "Hey. Hey!"

Jenkins turned at the gate. "I'll call you later."

"Hold on. Let me get some clothes on. Just . . . wait." He went back upstairs and slipped on a pair of sweatpants and a cutoff sweatshirt.

Barclay stood in the bathroom wearing his robe, still smiling. "Did he see the show?"

232

"Enough of it."

"I'll take a shower. I'm not sure I can look him in the eye at the moment."

Sloane found Jenkins in the easement, standing beside the Buick.

"In my defense, I was about to knock."

Sloane shook his head, the situation now amusing. Seagulls cawed overhead. "Sorry about that."

"You and me both. The last thing I needed was a glimpse of your hairy ass."

"So what's up?"

"Nothing. I tracked down some more employees for Pendergrass and stopped to give him a report." Pendergrass lived nearby, in the city of Des Moines. "Thought I'd check in and find out how it went at the Justice Center."

"I'm sorry, I should have called. I left work early and took the kayak out. Barclay surprised me."

Jenkins waved it off, but Sloane knew it bothered him.

"I should have called. I'm sorry."

"So how *did* it go?"

"Well, I'm not in handcuffs . . . but Rowe had the file on Tina's murder. I forgot I gave a statement about the gun, not being able to get to it. He called me on it."

"What did you tell him?"

"That it had been Tina's gun before we got married and that I got rid of it after her death."

"Rid of it how?"

"Dumped it off the boat into the Sound. Said it was a nine-millimeter."

"Do you think he bought it?"

"No."

Jenkins looked back up at the house to the second-story window.

"Something else?" Sloane asked.

"Just kind of strange . . . seeing her here."

Sloane understood. "I know."

"You love this woman?"

Two dogs, a golden retriever and a mutt, ran up the easement from the beach, nails clicking on the pavement, tongues out, panting. Not far behind, two women made their way up the slope in a power walk. Sloane greeted them as they passed, then turned back to Jenkins. "I think I might," he said.

"She makes you happy?"

"Well, it's been pretty trying lately . . . She took a lie-detector test. She took it for me."

"For you?"

"She didn't want there to be any doubt. She wanted me to be certain."

"So she passed?"

"Apparently."

"And is there?"

"Is there what?"

"Any doubt?"

Laurelhurst
Seattle, Washington

Joshua Blume had his father's dark hair and olive complexion, but judging from his meek demeanor as he shuffled into the room, gaze fixed on the floor, shoulders slumped, hands thrust into the pockets of faded and torn blue jeans that hung below his waist, he was more his mother than his father. A mop of black hair extended over his forehead and all but covered his eyes. Rowe's initial thought was the kid had his head down to see where he was walking. Then another, more troubling thought came to him — how the hell could he have seen anyone or anything through all that hair, in the dark of night?

When introduced, Joshua responded with a limp handshake and the briefest of eye contact. Rowe didn't take it personally. He'd met enough of his son's teenage friends to know that some kids had either been taught how to look an adult in the eye or had the self-confidence to do so on their own. Others did not and never would.

His father directed Joshua to the chair

235

where he had been sitting and motioned for his wife to move, banishing Mary Beth to one of two brown leather stationary chairs in a corner of the room near a bookcase and reading lamp. Rowe doubted anyone ever sat in the chair and read, but it was part of the facade, along with the baby grand nobody played and the convertible car that anyone who lived in the Northwest knew to be completely impractical.

"Sit up," Richard Blume said to his son.

Joshua dutifully sat up, though it was a matter of degrees and had little impact on his overall posture. He wore a black T-shirt with the words GOD'S NAILS and the silhouette of a guitar. Teenage acne pocked his chin and cheeks and likely his forehead, though the hair prevented Rowe from knowing.

Rowe decided to get to it. "Joshua, we understand you may have some information about something you saw the other night."

The kid nodded. "Yeah."

"Yes," Richard corrected.

Rowe thought he saw the kid roll his eyes beneath the bangs.

"Yes."

"Why don't you tell us what you saw?" Rowe asked.

The boy pointed in the direction of the

bay window. "I saw someone down near the road."

"Okay, Joshua, I'm going to need you to be more specific. Should we go outside so you can show us exactly where you saw this person?"

"Do we need to do that?" Mary Beth blurted.

"What time was it when you saw this person?" Crosswhite asked in a gentle voice only a former schoolteacher could muster to calm everyone and let Rowe know he was going about it the wrong way.

Joshua frowned in thought. "About three-thirty, maybe three-forty-five. Around there."

"Are you sure about the time?" Crosswhite asked.

He glanced in the direction of his father before nodding. They'd obviously had a conversation, and Richard likely had demanded to know, to the exact minute, the time his son had returned home.

"Yes," Richard said.

"Yes," the son said, sounding annoyed.

"How can you be certain?" Crosswhite prodded.

"Because we left the club around three, and I told my friends I had to get home or my dad was going to kill me."

"Oh, Joshua." Mary Beth tried to put a dismissive lilt in her voice, but she sounded more nervous than amused. "You know your father would never hurt you." She leaned forward to enter the inner circle. "We don't believe in physical punishment. Joshua has never even been spanked."

"Mary Beth. Please," Richard said.

Rowe thought it was Richard who could have used a few good spankings as a child.

"Your friends drove you home?" Crosswhite asked. "And where did they drop you off?"

The boy gave another vague gesture in the direction of the window. "Down the street. It's a couple of houses."

"There's an easement, a path at the back of our house. He uses it to sneak out and in," Richard said, making it sound like the boy had tunneled out of prison. "It leads past our backyard. It's not really an easement, but the kids have made it one. It cuts between the two houses and comes up through our side yard. He hops the fence."

"Is that right, Joshua?" Crosswhite asked, never looking at Richard.

He nodded. "Yeah . . . Yes."

"And your friends dropped you off there so your parents wouldn't hear the car engine?"

Joshua nodded.

"And they left?"

"They left."

"Then what happened?"

"I heard a noise, like something moving in the bushes."

"We have raccoons," Richard said.

Crosswhite ignored him. "What did you do when you heard the sound?"

"I ducked behind some bushes. And that's when I saw this person getting a bike out from a hedge. Then they got on it and rode down the street."

"Can you describe this person?" Crosswhite asked, careful not to suggest a gender. A good defense attorney would imply the police had suggested a suspect to a witness.

"Black . . . I don't know what you call them, like tights or something. One-piece."

"A wet suit?"

He shook his head. "It seemed thinner than a wet suit, but . . . I don't know."

"What color hair did the person have?"

"I couldn't really tell because of the bike helmet. But I think it was dark, like . . ." He searched the people in the room, his mother, then Crosswhite, and finally, Rowe. "More like his, maybe, without the gel."

"And you got a look at this person's face."

He nodded.

"A good look?"

"Like, a couple seconds."

"Do you think you could pick out the face if we came back with a group of pictures for you to look at?"

"I don't know. I think so." Joshua paused and, for the first time, brushed aside the tips of his bangs, revealing blue eyes.

Rowe asked, "How old are you, Joshua?"

"Sixteen."

"What club were you at?" He knew that underground clubs didn't get too hung up on things like the legal drinking age and fake IDs. Rowe and Crosswhite would have to confirm the boy's story and find out what he'd been doing. But that could be done later.

Joshua's voice became tentative again. "We were just listening to music. Another band we know."

"That's fine, but I need to know the name of the club," Rowe said. "I'm going to have to confirm some things."

"Are you going to talk to my friends?"

"Right now I don't think that will be necessary," Crosswhite said. "We can get their names later if we need them."

Rowe backed off.

Crosswhite sat forward. "Joshua, I need you to be honest with me. Did you drink any alcohol or use any drugs that night?"

Richard Blume moved farther to the edge of his seat but resisted the urge to stand. "I don't think I want Joshua to answer that question. I think I'd rather have my attorney here."

Rowe tried to stay even-keel. He wanted to say, "Listen, idiot, if you think that was a tough question to answer, wait until an experienced criminal defense attorney gets your son on the stand."

Crosswhite maintained the demeanor and tone of the schoolteacher trying to get to the bottom of a situation. "Mr. Blume, as we explained earlier, any time you desire, you can have your attorney present, that's not a problem. If you would like to make a call, please do. We're just trying to make sure Joshua is certain of what he saw. As I said, any *family* rules Joshua may have broken are between you, your wife, and your son. But why don't we leave that question for another conversation."

"I had a couple of beers," Joshua volunteered, not waiting for his father's permission, his voice defiant.

Ordinarily, Rowe would have asked the witness to accompany them to the Justice Center to consider a montage of photographs, but he had deduced that asking the

Blumes to do so for Joshua's trip down memory lane would be far enough outside Richard Blume's controlled environment to get him to follow through on his desire to call his attorney. Legally, there was not much a lawyer could do, but that never stopped some from becoming as big a pain in the ass as possible.

"We'll bring back some pictures tonight for you to consider, if that's all right," Crosswhite said, letting Rowe know they were on the same page. They would keep things within the comfort of the Blume castle walls as long as they could.

"That would be fine," Richard said.

Rowe looked at Crosswhite, only one more question to ask, and they both knew it. Crosswhite nodded. Rowe sat forward.

"Joshua, this person you saw . . . Can you tell us if it was a man or a woman?"

Camano Island
Washington

Charles Jenkins entered from the garage, about to drop his keys on the counter, when he saw the ghostly silhouette at the sliding-glass door and didn't want to disturb the image. Bare-chested and barefoot, his pull-up diaper sagging almost to the floor, CJ stood in the fading light with one hand on the glass, the other holding a bottle. Head tilted back, bottle angled, he sucked on the nipple as he watched his mother hose off the patio furniture. Water dripped down the glass, and Jenkins deduced why even before Alex turned and shot a blast from the hose, causing CJ to slap the glass, stiff legs dancing with delight, and emit a sound of pure pleasure.

Who was Jenkins to judge?

When Alex had told him she loved him, his first thought had been it would never work. Midfifties, he was twenty-five years her senior. He liked the Rolling Stones and the Beatles; she listened to Sting and Tom Petty. He had been drafted and spent thirteen months in a hellhole in Southeast Asia. She had graduated from college and backpacked through the same country on vacation. No one would have given them two minutes, let alone two years. And yet it had worked somehow. When she told him she wanted a child, he had the same doubts: thinking how stupid he'd look at the school events, everyone believing he was the child's grandparent, not possibly his father. But next to Alex, CJ had been the single greatest joy of his life. That, too, had worked, despite the odds.

So who was he to judge?

Jenkins made a loud raspberry with his tongue and lips. CJ startled, and turned, wide-eyed. When he saw his father, he beamed, the nipple stuck between his teeth. "Wa-ter," he said, slapping at the window. "Wa-ter."

Jenkins picked him up and felt the significant weight of his pull-up, another indication that CJ had been banished to the house after he got his clothes soaking wet. With the sun going down, the temperature had dropped. They watched Alex together. Her black hair was pulled back in a ponytail, and wisps of curls hung free about her face. She wore Dolfin running shorts and her pink skintight running top with the zipper, the one Jenkins loved to slowly unzip and watch her breasts emerge. With the suds running down her forearms and thighs, it reminded him of the scene in the movie *Cool Hand Luke* when the woman washed her car wearing only a sundress while dozens of inmates cleared weeds along the road.

He tapped on the glass with his wedding ring. Seeing him, Alex shot another blast. CJ squealed and threw his bottle, then, alarmed to have lost it, he reached down, squirming. Jenkins lowered him to the ground and watched his son hurry off in a stiff-legged gallop to retrieve his bottle.

As Jenkins slid open the door and stepped onto the patio, Alex turned and pointed the nozzle, causing him to flinch. "Don't!" She laughed and gave Jenkins a short mist.

"Are you hosing me down *before* I even try anything?"

She held the nozzle at her side like a gunslinger. "On the count a three, I'm a-gonna draw, partner. And I don't mean draw with a pencil." She chortled, the way she did when she found herself funny.

"You're getting a big kick out of yourself, aren't you?" he said.

"Somebody has to."

He walked closer. "You know I think you're funny."

She whipped the nozzle at him. "Back off. You're not touching this zipper until I finish the patio furniture."

"Why so motivated?"

"I gave the dogs a bath." The dogs lay sprawled in the grass where a patch of sun still remained amid the shadows. "So I decided since I had everything out that I'd tackle the deck, too. Help me with the table."

He helped her turn over the table, then stepped back as she soaped and hosed down the underside.

"Did you talk to David?" She wrung out

the sponge and looked over at him.

Jenkins had not just stopped by Sloane's house to find out what had happened at the Justice Center. He had information. Alex had checked with the organization that held the event at the Rainier Club, the one at which Sloane had been the speaker. Barclay Reid had not preregistered for the dinner; she had provided the organization with a credit-card number that day. By itself, it meant little, but it bothered Jenkins, who didn't believe in coincidences.

"He loves her, Alex."

She put the sponge on one of the chairs. "Are you sure?"

"He said he did. And they sure looked like it."

"She was there?"

"In her birthday suit. Him, too. In the kitchen."

She covered her smile with her hand. "Tell me you did *not* walk in on them."

"It's not funny," he said, though he laughed.

Alex removed her hand, no longer smiling. "You didn't tell him . . ."

Jenkins shook his head. "He's happy, Alex. For the first time since Tina's death, he seems happy."

Summer in Seattle, Sloane had concluded, was the reason people in the Northwest tolerated the nine miserable months of gray and rain. God must have chosen Seattle to spend His summers; there was no other way to describe the beauty that befell the place almost immediately after July Fourth. The snowcapped Olympic Mountains to the west looked close enough to touch, and the water brightened from a bland gray to a sparkling blue, with everything beneath a great dome Michelangelo could not have painted better.

Barclay minced cloves of fresh garlic on a chopping block, wearing one of Sloane's red Stanford-basketball T-shirts. Jake had attended a camp at the school in the summer and had given Sloane the shirt. It extended to Barclay's midthigh.

They had spent a lazy afternoon reading books in the two Adirondack lawn chairs. Then Sloane had driven to the grocery store with a list of ingredients for dinner, a necessity if they expected to eat. Since Tina's death, the contents of his refrigerator had ranged between bare and almost bare.

He felt the comforting glow from the red wine as he bent to manipulate the radio, pausing on the Mariners baseball game, hoping to catch the score. He caught the tail end of an inning, the third out, and as they went to station break the announcer informed that the Mariners led the Angels, 5–3. He switched to FM and channel-surfed until he recognized a song by Green Day, a band Jake favored.

"Don't you want to listen to the game?"

He refilled her glass of wine. "I'll catch the score later on the news."

The sound of the knife hitting the wood block stopped. "Warm summer night, screen door open, steaks on the barbecue. Perfect night to listen to baseball."

"You're a fan?" he asked.

She mocked him, wide-eyed. "Oh my God! A girl who likes baseball!" She continued mincing. "My father used to take me to the Kingdome. And the firm has a suite at Safeco."

"A suite? I knew I liked you for a reason." He wrapped his arms around her waist and nuzzled her neck.

She reached behind, massaging the back of his head. "Be nice to me, and I just might take you to a game." He let his hands wander but she squirmed free. "Uh-uh. We have work to do."

He kissed her neck. "We could eat later."

"You'll be busy later." She slapped him lightly across the cheek with a bundle of parsley, then handed it to him. "Chop."

As Sloane set to the task, she scooped the garlic with the knife and lifted the lid on the pot to add it to the sauce. The room filled with the aroma of tomatoes simmering. "What did your friend want?" she asked.

Sloane looked up from the parsley. "Charlie? Nothing important. He's working on another case in the office, a prevailing-wage claim. He just stopped by on his way home."

"What does he think about us?" Sloane didn't have a ready answer. "He's worried, isn't he?"

"He's my friend. He wants what's best for me."

She continued chopping. "Everyone needs a friend like that. You'll let me know, won't you?"

He looked over at her. "Let you know what?"

"If it's moving too fast. If you're not ready."

"I'll let you know," he said, and stepped toward her, stopping when he heard the doorbell ring.

THIRTEEN

King County Jail
Seattle, Washington
The walls seeped the dull malaise of institutionalization — muted grays, opaque yellow lighting, and spartan furnishings.

The feeling of institutionalization and claustrophobia increased as Sloane ventured farther into the jail. When he stepped from the elevator onto the seventh floor, the Psych Unit for those never before incarcerated, he covered his mouth and nose, the pungent smell a cross between the rot of food and the smell of urine in a public bathroom poorly masked by disinfectant and deodorant cakes. Though he stood in a glass foyer, it did little to mute the incoherent screams and shouts of the inmates milling about in red jumpsuits.

He hated the thought that Barclay was among them.

An hour earlier, when Sloane had pulled

open his front door, Detectives Rowe and Crosswhite had flashed their identifications as if they'd never met. Whereas Rowe had previously entered Sloane's home polite, even a bit apologetic, this time he looked like a man who had been hard at a task and cocksure he was about to accomplish his mission.

When Barclay walked from the kitchen into the living room, holding the wooden spoon above the pot of spaghetti sauce, Rowe wasted no time advising Reid she was under arrest for the murder of Filyp Vasiliev.

After the initial shock, Sloane had stepped forward. "Wait a minute."

But Rowe would have none of it, warning Sloane not to interfere or he would arrest him for obstruction. Rowe was not to be reasoned or argued with; the time for debate had long since passed. Rowe had already moved to action.

Crosswhite read Reid her Miranda rights and accompanied her upstairs to change clothes. When Reid emerged, she wore the blue-gray pin-striped suit. She had removed her contacts and put on glasses. Rowe asked her to turn around and applied handcuffs.

After Rowe and Crosswhite escorted Reid to their car, Sloane called Carolyn at home,

251

instructing her to find John Kannin. Then he threw a change of clothes in his gym bag, locked the house, and left for downtown, uncertain when he might be back.

If I had known he was going to walk, I would have just put a bullet in him and been done with it.

Sloane hadn't believed Barclay capable when she'd made the statement and still didn't, but he hoped he never had to tell Rowe or a prosecutor she had said it.

Sloane pushed a button on another call box and informed the guards in a raised circular tower that he was there to visit Barclay Reid. A guard directed Sloane to a booth with thick glass separation.

"I want a visit face-to-face," Sloane said, continuing to follow Pendergrass's instructions. He'd called Tom Pendergrass on the drive to the jail. A military lawyer before joining Sloane's practice, Pendergrass had handled several small criminal cases and gave Sloane as much assistance as he could over the phone. He'd offered to come to the jail, but Sloane had declined, telling Pendergrass he would call later.

A guard led Sloane to a windowless room no bigger than a broom closet with battleship-gray walls, a square table, and two plastic chairs.

"Leave the door open," the guard said.

"How long can I stay?"

"How much money did you put in the parking meter?" When Sloane didn't respond, the guard said, "As long as you want; we're open twenty-four/seven."

After several minutes, he heard footsteps. Barclay shuffled in between two officers, her hands cuffed to a chain belt around her waist. She wore slippers, a red jumpsuit, and her black-framed glasses.

"Can those be removed?" Sloane asked, referring to the handcuffs.

The officers said no, then departed, leaving the door open.

Sloane struggled to project calm though he continued to feel lost in a system with which he had no prior experience. "Are you all right?" It sounded feeble and stupid under the circumstances.

Reid's gaze shifted to one of the walls. She sighed audibly. "I have to know." She looked at him. "I have to know that you believe me, David. I have to know that you have no doubt, because right now I need someone to believe in me. Otherwise, I am going to go stark raving mad."

Sloane knew she felt as he did, a person used to being in control suddenly without any.

"I told you, I believe you." Sloane took one of her hands, which was cold to the touch and they sat knees to knees. She looked pale, but it could have been the lighting. "You didn't talk to anyone?"

She shook her head. "Who could have taken it, David? Who would —"

"Barclay, stop." Her brow furrowed. "You can't tell me anything," he said. "Not anything that could be evidence."

"What? Why not?"

"There's no privilege." He didn't need to explain that the law accorded a privilege to communications between certain relationships: lawyer and client, physician and patient, husband and wife, even clergy and penitent. Sloane did not fit any of those. "If they subpoena me, I'd have to tell them anything you say."

"No . . ."

"Barclay —"

"No. I want you, David."

"And I'll be here."

"No. I want you to represent me."

Sloane straightened and released her hand. The thought had never occurred to him. "Barclay, I'm not a criminal lawyer; this is way out of my expertise. We can find someone . . . the best. I already called Carolyn to get ahold of —"

She shook her head, emphatic. "No, I want you." She retook his hand. "You have to represent me, David. I don't want anyone else."

He pulled back. "You have to under-stand . . . you need a criminal defense lawyer; you need the very best lawyer out there."

"You're the very best lawyer out there."

"I'm a civil lawyer."

"I've watched you in court. I know what you can do. I saw it. I've talked to people who've gone up against you, who said they never had a chance. You can't be beat. You never lose." She drew out the final words. "They say what you do to a jury is some-thing that can't be explained, cases that you should have lost, cases —"

"Civil cases." He pushed back his chair and stood. "All civil cases. Your life is on the line here."

"Don't you think I know that!"

For a moment neither spoke.

"At some point it is going to come down to what a jury, twelve people, believe and don't believe," she said. "That's why I have to know that you believe me, so that when you stand up in front of them —"

Sloane wheeled, turning his back, finding only a wall. He rubbed his forehead, thoughts coming from all different directions. He felt the press of her hand at the small of his back.

"When you get up and tell them that I did not do this, they'll believe you. I know it. But I need you to believe me. I want you to represent me without any doubt."

The voice of reason shouted at him to tell her this was not a good idea. It was a crazy, irrational, horrible idea. It was the product of her feeling vulnerable and alone and scared. He needed to tell her she shouldn't rush to any decisions, that she could decide on her representation later, after the initial shock of her arrest and her surroundings faded.

Her hand gently turned him. She stood, head cocked, as she had the night they played pool at the Arctic Club, her jade-green eyes sparkling, a thin smile. "I don't trust anyone but you. These past weeks, I've never let anyone so close . . ." A tear leaked, running down her cheek. "You know me, David. You know my heart, my soul . . . better than anyone ever has. I love you."

The three words stunned him, not because she'd said them but because he had been certain, or at least had convinced himself, that they would never again mean anything to him. But hearing them sent an electric pulse through his body, touching a part of him he had believed dead, incapable of ever feeling again, a part that Barclay had brought back to life.

FOURTEEN

Friday, September 9, 2011
King County Courthouse
Seattle, Washington

"Déjà vu all over again," Rick Cerrabone said, as he walked into the conference room on the fifth floor of the King County courthouse, which housed the offices of Cerrabone's boss, King County prosecutor, Amanda Pinkett.

Rowe knew enough baseball to suspect Cerrabone's malaprop had been intentional, one likely uttered by the Yankees' legendary catcher and even more legendary butcher of the English language, Yogi Berra. Rowe would have smiled had he not been so tired. Crosswhite's dull expression indicated she felt the same. After the high of arresting Barclay Reid and escorting her to jail, Rowe had crashed. He could feel the fatigue tingling in his joints. His eyelids drooped, begging to close.

Cerrabone asked Rowe and Crosswhite to meet with him to discuss the evidence before his meeting with Pinkett. With the media already generating local and national stories, Pinkett had scheduled a news conference to issue a statement on Barclay Reid's arrest. She wanted all of them, including the chief of police, Sandy Clarridge, present. The invitation wasn't to applaud Rowe's and Crosswhite's efforts. That would come after the trial, and only if they obtained a conviction. This invitation, they knew, was to hold them accountable, and there was no better way to do that than to have them stand before the cameras and let the world know who was responsible for Reid's arrest.

"You feel comfortable about it," Cerrabone said, taking a seat across the table and flipping through his file. "You feel comfortable with this kid Joshua Blume?"

Rowe sipped coffee. "Hey, I'd prefer the kid was a Harvard graduate with twenty/ fifteen vision, but you get what you get."

"What kind of impression does he make?"

"He's a sixteen-year-old kid, Rick. He mumbles, doesn't make great eye contact, has a limp handshake. But he's certain about what he saw, and he signed a statement."

"He picked her out without hesitation," Crosswhite added. "First chance. Boom, 'That's her.'"

"When can I talk to him?" Cerrabone asked.

"I'd give him a day. The defense won't have the report for a while, and the father is squirrelly, one of those guys who keeps talking about his attorney. He was worried about liability."

Worry lines creased Cerrabone's forehead. "Liability for what?"

"Not coming forward sooner."

"Why? Was the kid impaired?"

"He admitted to drinking a couple of beers," Crosswhite said. "And I believe he was telling the truth about that. The father is just one of those control-freak, paranoid types."

"We've got the names of his friends with him that night," Rowe said. "We'll follow up."

Cerrabone sat back. "But we still can't explain the other footprints."

That was the turd Rowe and Crosswhite were now dumping in Cerrabone's pocket, and they all knew Pinkett would smell it immediately. It would be the piece of evidence the defense targeted to create reasonable doubt unless Cerrabone could explain it. At the moment they had no good explanation.

"Maybe we no longer have to," Rowe said. "It could have been two people sleeping on a boat who heard the gunshot, went to check it out, but didn't want to get involved. We don't know. What we do know is that the shooter's footprints are size seven, the same size and same brand of running shoe Reid wears." Kaylee Wright had confirmed that the brand of shoe was a Nike AS300 cross-trainer. "The bullet was a thirty-eight. Reid is the registered owner of a thirty-eight and her gun is conveniently missing. We found ball-round ammunition in her home. The shooter, according to ballistics, was between five feet and five feet four inches tall. Reid is five-two. Blume puts her at the public easement where she would have entered and exited the water. He'll testify Reid looked to have gotten out of the water after a swim and got onto a bike. Reid is a triathlete. She has no alibi for the night of the murder, and she certainly had a motive. She told her ex-husband she would kill Vasiliev in exactly the manner he was killed."

"Yeah, about that — why would she do that?" Cerrabone asked. "It isn't the smartest thing to do if she was actually considering it."

"It might be exactly why she did it," Rowe said. "Just like she went to an attorney and inquired about filing a wrongful-death lawsuit the afternoon before she intended to shoot Vasiliev."

"A reverse alibi," Cerrabone said, following Rowe's reasoning but not sounding convinced. "That's a hell of a risk." He pressed wisps of hair flat on his head. "Does she have a lawyer yet?"

"Sloane."

Cerrabone cocked his head. "I meant her criminal lawyer."

"Sloane was at the jail all last night," Rowe said.

"Really?" Cerrabone asked.

"Why? What's wrong?" Crosswhite asked.

"Nothing. It's just that I did some checking. Sloane has a bit of a reputation," Cerrabone said. "A law-school classmate says Sloane wins cases he has no business winning."

Crosswhite sat forward. "Implying what? He cheats somehow?"

"No." Cerrabone seemed to be searching for words. "Apparently, he's just that good." He rocked back in his chair, seeming to further consider it. "Still . . . a civil lawyer . . ."

A hell of a risk, Rowe thought but did not say.

Law Offices of David Sloane
One Union Square
Seattle, Washington

Sloane fought through the cobwebs, his mind slow and his thinking blurred. A copy of the *Seattle Times* lay on the conference room table, the banner headline screaming at him.

Prominent Seattle Attorney
Arrested in Drug Dealer's Murder

Positioned beneath it was a four-by-six-inch photograph of Sloane trying to shield his face from the cameras as he left the jail, looking foolish doing so. He used to wonder why people bothered; it only made them look all the more guilty. Now Sloane knew. He had reacted instinctively to the bright light and to the intrusion on his personal space, the camera like a punk kid challenging him to a fight. He looked ridiculous, definitely not the first impression he wanted to convey about the guilt or innocence of his client.

Sloane hadn't slept, going directly from the jail to the Washington Athletic Club,

263

where he showered and changed clothes before getting to the office. Based on Jenkins's greeting when he had entered the conference room — "You look like shit" — the fatigue showed on Sloane's face. Now seated at the far end of the table, Jenkins stretched his arms and yawned. Pendergrass sat across from Sloane with a notepad and a cup of coffee, his hair still damp, the red a darker shade.

Jenkins had been Sloane's first call upon retrieving his cell phone from the gun vault converted to safe deposit boxes at the jail. Sloane hadn't bothered to call the prior night, there being nothing Jenkins could do. His second call had been to Carolyn. She hadn't even said hello: "At this hour of the morning, somebody better have died, or somebody is going to."

God love her, she was in the office within the hour, coffee made and answering the phones, which were ringing off the hook. In addition to the local news stations, she fielded calls from national shows: CNN, MS-NBC, *The O'Reilly Factor, Anderson Cooper 360, 48 Hours, Dateline,* even a representative of Larry King. They all wanted to find out if Sloane would be representing Barclay Reid. In between fielding the inquiries and telling them nothing,

Carolyn continued her efforts to contact John Kannin. Without Kannin, the task of giving Sloane a crash course on criminal law continued to fall to Pendergrass.

"The first appearance will be a probable-cause hearing in district court, which is inside the jail," Pendergrass said. "They're held every day between two and two-thirty. I've made some calls to find out who the prosecutor will be, but no one is saying much. Reading between the lines, we can anticipate this won't be a typical hearing, where the prosecutor of the day handles whatever cases came in the prior night. On the more serious crimes, the senior prosecutors work directly with the detectives from the initial call. So you can expect a heavyweight, and whoever that is, he or she will have been intimately involved from the get-go and prepared right out of the chute."

"Any chance the judge will set bail?"

"Not likely. It's strictly to determine if the police have sufficient probable cause to charge. If not, they have to release her within seventy-two hours. Bail usually comes up at the arraignment. I'm told a million dollars per murder is the going rate."

"I'll need to know everything the judge will consider. See if you can find other cases with similar charges and whether the judge did or did not grant bail."

Pendergrass nodded but looked pained. "I'll look, but . . . we might be up against it."

"What do you mean?"

"A case of this notoriety . . . Judges are elected officials. The King County prosecutor and chief of police will be fully engaged. No judge wants to take a chance of looking bad if something goes wrong, a suspect flees."

"She's not going to flee; she runs a two-hundred-person law firm."

"All I'm saying is the notoriety may work against her. And she has money and . . . her only child — her only family — is dead. The prosecution will argue she's a flight risk. With a murder-one charge — and we have to anticipate that will be the charge — I can see the judge going either way."

"Get me what I need to know," Sloane said. He slid Jenkins a packet. "The U.S. attorney's office filed these after the raid on Vasiliev's used-car lot. I had Carolyn pull them off the Internet this morning. We can use these as support that Vasiliev was recently the subject of an investigation, a significant heroin dealer suspected to have ties to the Russian mafia. You understand what I'm saying?"

Jenkins nodded.

"Dangerous profession. Any number of people out there who might have wanted to kill him."

"Can we get it into evidence?" Pendergrass asked.

Sloane had already considered the question. "The prosecutor has to argue Barclay's motivation for killing Vasiliev was revenge — that she blamed him for supplying the drugs that overdosed her daughter. When he does, it's fair game." Turning back to Jenkins, he said, "See what you can find out about the organization Vasiliev worked for, his associates, rivals."

Jenkins nodded. "I'll make some calls, but if you want someone with some contacts and knows their way around a computer, I'd suggest Alex."

"What about CJ?"

"My mother's overdue for a visit. Alex wants to help."

Sloane was not about to turn down an offer of help from someone who had worked years for the Defense Department. "Which brings us back to probable cause," he said. "We know Rowe didn't have the gun, because he came looking for mine."

"Maybe they found it," Jenkins said.

"Maybe, and the gun would go a long way

to establishing probable cause, but not far enough."

Pendergrass agreed. "Barclay is a very big fish. They aren't going to go after her with just the gun."

"So Rowe has to have something more," Jenkins said. He stood and poured a glass of water.

"Who could have taken the gun?" Pendergrass asked.

"She doesn't know, but she said a couple of weeks ago she got home from work and had a feeling someone had been in the house."

"You said there was an alarm," Jenkins said.

"There is, and she's religious about setting it."

"Religious before or after this incident?" Jenkins asked.

Sloane made a note to ask Barclay and to find out more about the security system, whether they could determine if and when it had gone off.

"Was anything stolen?" Jenkins asked.

"She didn't think so, but she never checked to see if the gun was still there. She was thinking jewelry or money, valuables."

"Any ideas?" Jenkins probed.

Sloane shrugged. "Maybe someone in Vasiliev's organization."

Jenkins shook his head. "I don't see it. These guys are cowboys. They would have just killed her and been done with it."

"Not with the U.S. attorney going after Vasiliev," Sloane said. "The feds would have been all over Vasiliev and anyone associated with him. When I spoke to Vasiliev, he was more worried that I might sue him. He said he wanted Barclay to let the matter go. Maybe someone in the organization was worried she wouldn't and what it might lead to."

"Maybe I'm dense, or maybe I'm tired, but I'm still not following," Jenkins said.

"I'm saying that maybe they decide to kill two birds with one stone. They get rid of Vasiliev to end the inquiries and they get Barclay off their back."

"Then why not leave the gun for the police to find?"

"Too obvious."

Jenkins frowned, unconvinced. "It sounds like Vasiliev was moving a lot of product, which means a lot of money for the organization. If he was also laundering the proceeds, he was a valuable asset."

"*Was*," Sloane said. "Rebecca Han said that all stopped with his arrest, that the organization wasn't going to take a chance with the feds watching. And the civil suit would have made his suppliers really uncomfortable. In a civil suit I can go after all of Vasiliev's financial records, including his business records."

Carolyn pushed open the door and stepped in, her eyes finding Sloane. "The King County prosecutor's office is on the phone."

Seventh Floor North
King County Jail
Seattle, Washington

Sloane stood in the broom closet he had left just hours before. Barclay entered, this time wearing a white jumpsuit with ULTRA-HIGH SECURITY stenciled in black on the back. Her hands remained handcuffed to the belly belt. She looked even more tired.

"The King County prosecutor wants to cut a deal," he said.

Reid shook her head. "No —"

"Not to the charges."

"Then what?"

Sloane had been on a conference call with Rick Cerrabone and Amanda Pinkett, the King County prosecutor. "Given the media circus, Pinkett saw no reason to put you through both a probable-cause hearing *and* an arraignment. She wants us to stipulate to

270

probable cause." Sloane held out the police certification Pinkett had faxed to his office. "They have a witness who puts you at the scene the morning of Vasiliev's murder."

"What?" She took the certification, reading it.

"They also say that you told your ex-husband you intended to shoot Vasiliev in the head."

"Are you kidding me? My ex-husband hates me, David. He'd say just about anything to hurt me."

"Did you say that to him?"

Her voice rose. "Of course not."

"You said something similar to me."

"I did?" She sat back. "I don't know. Maybe a figure of speech. Why would I say something like that if I intended to do it?" Her voice lowered, an exhausted whisper. "That's ridiculous." She considered the report again. "Who is the witness?"

"We don't know yet. Pinkett said the statement will be in the police file. She'll expedite it after the arraignment."

"Why not before?"

"The name isn't important. The contents are. The witness claims to have seen you that morning running up an easement from the water about a half mile from Vasiliev's home, pulling a bike from the bushes, and riding off. I know this is hard to hear, but I don't see any reason not to stipulate. I can't imagine a judge not finding probable cause. And if we don't agree, you'll definitely have to spend the weekend in jail. The arraignment won't occur until Monday, and you'll go through a media circus twice. We agree and they do the arraignment today; they have a judge and a courtroom for late this afternoon."

She considered for a moment. "What do you think?"

"I'd like the weekend to prepare, but I'd also like to try to get you out of here today."

"Will they stipulate to bail?"

"No. Pinkett says they intend to oppose any bail, but they were never going to agree. We're going to have to fight about it whether the arraignment is today or Monday."

"What are the chances the judge grants it?"

"I have someone in my office looking into it, but I'd say they're reasonable, given who you are in the community. If the judge grants bail, it's going to be a million dollars minimum."

"I can get it," she said. "Talk to my assistant, Nina. She has all of my financial information."

He pulled another document and a pen

from his briefcase and handed both to her. "I prepared a limited power of attorney giving me authority to have your bank release the money into the court registry."

Reid nodded and signed it.

"There's something else we should discuss," he said. "We don't have to decide now, but I think we need to consider not waiving your right to a speedy trial."

"If I get out on bail, why not push the trial out as far as possible?"

"Because you won't have a life until this is behind you. The media will hound you daily."

"How bad is it?"

"The *Times* ran the story across the front page and national news agencies are picking up on it. We're getting dozens of phone calls from newspapers and magazines from all over the country. The paparazzi won't be far behind. The pundits are already discussing things like vigilante justice and the advantages and disadvantages of drug dealer liability acts."

She shook her head. "I guess I got my publicity, huh?"

"I'm going to ask Nina to set up a meeting after the hearing so I can talk to your partners. I'll tell them you're innocent of these charges and will be vindicated, and not to talk to the media or to the prosecutors without me or someone working for me present. Rowe and Crosswhite have already issued subpoenas for all of your e-mails, calendars, and phone records."

"There's nothing there, David."

He held up the police certification. "I'll know more after I have the file, but in my opinion, this is thin. It's all circumstantial."

"Except the witness who says he saw me there."

"In the dark, on a stormy night, at three-thirty in the morning? It's thin. They moved too quickly, in my opinion. Maybe it was the media coverage from the leak. I don't know, but I'm thinking they want to play chicken, let's play chicken . . . and we'll see who flinches first."

FIFTEEN

King County Courthouse
Seattle, Washington

That afternoon, when he turned the corner onto Third Avenue, Sloane saw white news vans, more than half a dozen, satellite dishes protruding high above the vehicle roofs. Reporters holding microphones jockeyed for space on the sidewalk, angling for live shots with the courthouse behind them. Though Sloane had arrived early and a light rain fell, a long line had already formed outside the glass door into the courthouse, people dressed in rain gear waiting to weave their way along the stanchions and belts, like tourists waiting for an amusement-park ride.

Sloane detoured up the hill to the county administrative building on Fourth Avenue. Inside the building, King County sheriffs monitored a metal detector. Most of the people entering were dressed in business attire. A stark white tunnel beneath the street led to the courthouse. Most of the public didn't know about it.

Court Operations had called Sloane at his office to advise that the arraignment had been moved from the traditional courtroom on the twelfth floor to room 854E to accommodate the expected crowd.

When he stepped off the elevator onto the eighth floor, reporters, including several camera crews, had gathered in the hallway. They wasted no time asking Sloane questions, which he declined to answer before ducking inside the courtroom. The five pews in the gallery running the width of the room, perhaps thirty feet, were filled. A King County sheriff in a hunter-green shirt and light brown pants put up a hand to stop Sloane, then lowered it with an acknowledgment.

Sloane made his way to the table closest to the jury box, keenly aware that pens and pencils had materialized and the reporters sitting in the gallery had begun scratching on notepads.

Counsel tables were arranged in an L. In civil cases, the plaintiffs took the table closest to the jury box — that was the table parallel to the judge's bench. No railing separated counsel's table from the first pew and several reporters approached but Sloane dismissed them. Then he sat.

The dull fluorescent lighting, the only illumination in the windowless room, brought a perpetual feeling of dusk. Only the clock on the wall kept time. The judge's elevated desk was centered beneath a wood carving of the seal of the state of Washington, a United States flag on one side and the green flag of Washington State on the other. The slatted wooden witness chair to its right — elevated and without any railing — looked naked. Undoubtedly, those who sat in it would feel the same. To its right, close enough that a witness could reach over and shake hands with the closest juror, was the jury box and its empty leather swivel chairs.

The State of Washington vs. *Barclay Alison Reid* had been assigned to Judge Virginia Dugaw. Pendergrass had tried two criminal cases before Judge Dugaw, though nothing of the magnitude of a murder trial. He described her as fair and efficient. That was apparently the good and the bad news, since the judge who handled the arraignment could not be the trial judge. Earlier that morning, Pendergrass had mused that Dugaw's gender would be a plus, but Sloane cautioned against any such assumption when it came time to choose a jury.

"Some women may sympathize with her," he had said, meaning Barclay. "But there will be others jealous and spiteful." He knew that sitting on a jury was, for some, their lone opportunity to wield power, let alone power over someone of Barclay's stature, and they would relish it.

As Sloane set out his materials, the crowd stirred again. Seconds later, a heavyset man in a light brown suit, cream-colored shirt, and tan tie stopped at the edge of the table.

"Mr. Sloane," he said. "Rick Cerrabone."

Pendergrass had also provided Sloane with the rundown on Cerrabone, which, he said, rhymed with "baloney." He'd never had a case against Cerrabone, but he knew others who had. "He's the best they got," Pendergrass related. "Efficient, thorough, and well respected. Jurors love him. He's not in it for the ego or the glory. He completely buys in to the notion that he's a servant of the people, and he is very, very good."

That wasn't the conclusion one would reach upon a visual inspection. Perhaps in his late forties, Cerrabone had thinning black hair, wisps of which stood as if electrified, a heavy five o'clock shadow, bushy eyebrows, and the thick features of a man who looked to have boxed and used his face to stop most of the punches. A pair of cheater reading glasses dangled from a chain just beneath his chin.

After introducing himself, Cerrabone pulled a box on a handheld cart to the well in front of the bench. The judge's bailiff smiled. "I saw you in the Red Sox hat," she said.

"Don't remind me," Cerrabone answered. "How'd your son's baseball game go the other night?"

"The umpire killed us. But Jack had three hits."

The court reporter joined the revelry. Sloane was an experienced civil lawyer, but this was Cerrabone's home court.

Commotion in the hall drew everyone's attention. Three correctional officers in navy blue uniforms, one a woman, escorted Barclay into the room. Hands behind her back, she remained in the white prison jumpsuit, white socks, and slippers.

Barclay entered as Sloane had instructed: head held high and a neutral expression. She did not shy from looking at those in the audience when she turned to allow the sheriff to remove the handcuffs. Sloane wanted her to become the victim, a mother who had suffered one tragedy and was now suffering another because of her determination to bring to justice those responsible. He wanted her to be viewed not as a vigilante but as a citizen who refused to accept that young people should have to dodge drug dealers on their way to class, in the same way Mothers Against Drunk Driving had lobbied to change the cultural assumption that it was acceptable to have a few cocktails before getting behind the wheel of a car.

The bailiff, an elegant-looking Indian woman who had left the courtroom when Reid arrived, reentered from the door to the left of the bench, followed by Virginia Dugaw. The judge wasted no time taking her seat and getting down to business. "Good afternoon, Counsel. Mr. Cerrabone, let's get started."

Cerrabone stepped around the table so as not to be stuck in the corner of the room, the reading glasses now perched on the bridge of his nose. "Number twenty-seven on the arraignment calendar, Judge, *State of Washington* vs. *Barclay Alison Reid* —"

Sloane approached the bench. "Good afternoon, Your Honor, David Sloane appearing on behalf of the defendant."

As Dugaw greeted him, Sloane handed the clerk a notice of appearance.

"The clerk will enter the notice of appearance of Mr. Sloane," Dugaw instructed.

Cerrabone took another step forward, remaining on script. "Defendant is present in custody —"

Pendergrass had advised that arraignments were cattle calls, with the prosecutor running the show and the defense attorney often ignored. Sloane was not about to be treated as some vestigial organ, knowing full well the subtle battle for control inside a courtroom.

"Your Honor, the defense acknowledges receipt of a copy of the charging document and agrees to accept service and to waive a formal reading of those charges. The defendant is Barclay Alison Reid, a citizen of the United States. The treaties of other countries do not apply here and need not be read. We would request that the court enter a plea of not guilty."

The room froze, silent, as if all of the oxygen had been sucked from it, which had been Sloane's intent by entering the plea quickly and without fanfare. After a moment, there was movement and mumbling in the gallery.

"A plea of not guilty will be entered," Dugaw said.

Sloane continued, "Your Honor, we would like to discuss the issue of bail."

Cerrabone took another step toward the center of the room; he now stood just below the bench and directly beside Sloane. He placed his file on the railing near the court clerk. "The state objects to bail. This is a first-degree-murder case." Sloane noticed an East Coast accent, likely one of the boroughs of New York, Brooklyn or Queens.

Sloane moved so that he and Cerrabone stood elbow to elbow. "To the contrary, Your Honor, there is no *case* yet. We are here for a murder *charge,* and that is all it is, a charge. Ms. Reid has not been convicted of any crime, let alone the charge of murder. She is innocent until proven guilty, and that presumption of innocence applies here. The prosecutor is also well aware that every person in the state of Washington is entitled to bail. The only relevant issues are Ms. Reid's ties to the community, of which she has many, and whether she is a flight risk or a risk to the community, which she is not." Though Pendergrass had done his best to educate him, Sloane was, to a certain extent, winging it, his depth of knowledge as shallow as a puddle. If Cerrabone dove deeper, Sloane would quickly hit bottom.

Cerrabone responded. "The crime of which the defendant is accused is premeditated murder. The victim was shot in the back of the head with a caliber of bullet that matches the caliber of a weapon registered to the defendant; that gun remains missing; and there is evidence the defendant was lying in wait. The defendant also has substantial resources and no familial ties to the community. She is divorced, and her only child is deceased. She has no other immediate family."

Sloane knew Cerrabone had purposefully advised the people sitting behind them of the charges Sloane had sought to avoid having read out loud, as well as some of the evidence to substantiate that charge. Since Cerrabone had opened that door, Sloane decided to blow through it.

"Your Honor, with all due respect, the prosecutor is incorrect on a number of counts. While the caliber of bullet may be of interest, there is no evidence that it came from a weapon registered to Barclay or that she fired any weapon of that caliber or any other caliber. Similarly, while the killer may have been lying in wait, there is no evidence that Barclay was lying in wait." Just as it appeared Dugaw was about to cut him off, Sloane moved on. "As for the pertinent issues regarding bail, it's specious for the state to argue that Barclay has no ties to the community. She has been a respected member of the bar for twenty years. She is the managing partner of a law firm of more than two hundred attorneys, as the court well knows, and is involved in many charitable and civic causes. Moreover, she has no prior criminal record of any kind that would make her a risk to the community. As for her resources, she should not be penalized simply because she is successful. She has surrendered her passport. Not only is she not a flight risk, she is eager to appear in court and defend against this charge and clear her name. The court must honor her presumption of innocence."

If Dugaw was disturbed by the attorneys' banter over Reid's guilt or innocence, she did not display it. She listened patiently. When they had finished she ruled. "I am going to grant the defense's request for bail. Bail will be set at one million dollars . . . to be deposited in the court registry."

Sloane felt relief. "Your Honor, we will have that sum deposited in the court's registry within the hour."

"Very well. Thank you, Mr. Sloane. Anything else, Mr. Prosecutor?"

"No, Your Honor." Cerrabone turned from the bench.

Sloane, however, was not finished. Pendergrass had advised Sloane that the presiding judge, Mathew Thompkins, had recently mandated a fast-track system to expedite matters and reduce the backlog of those in custody.

"Your Honor, we note for the record that Ms. Reid does not waive her right to a speedy trial and requests that the court immediately set a case-scheduling hearing within the next seventy-two hours."

Cerrabone wheeled. "Your Honor," he started, then, perhaps perceiving the game of chicken, said, "The state has no objection."

SIXTEEN

Tuesday, September 13, 2011
Law Offices of David Sloane
One Union Square
Seattle, Washington

Over the weekend, Sloane and Barclay had taken refuge by day at his office and by night at her home. The gated fence served as an impediment to the media scrutiny. Sloane initially thought it best they not be seen entering and exiting her home together late at night or early in the morning, but the news of their relationship had already broken, and trying to hide it was like trying to camouflage an elephant with a dish towel.

The stress and anxiety of the impending trial could have separated them but instead it drew them closer together. At night they released that tension in intense and pro-longed lovemaking. Afterward, they would lie in bed, sometimes facing the sliding-glass door, or lying head to foot so they could look at each other as they talked — not about the law but about themselves, their pasts and their future.

In the office, Sloane turned the big conference room into a "war room" where they would all meet to discuss trial strategy and keep the accumulating documents. He, Barclay, and Tom Pendergrass spent long days planning her defense, making reams of notes on witnesses they needed to talk with, experts they would need, legal issues to be researched, and motions to be written.

The media frenzy reignited the following Tuesday. The reporters returned for the case setting and preliminary hearing conference, but with no chance of a plea deal and neither Sloane nor Cerrabone willing to flinch on Reid's refusal to waive her right to a speedy trial, there wasn't much of a show. Judge Dugaw set the case for trial seventy-five days out — merry Christmas to all — and advised Sloane and Cerrabone that they would trail on the court's calendar until a trial judge became available. Show over, Sloane left with a promise from Cerrabone that the police file would be delivered to his office that afternoon, a promise the prosecutor made good on, but only to a certain extent.

As Sloane pored over the file, he began to

suspect it was incomplete. He did not find statements for Felix Oberman or Joshua Blume. Neither Alex nor Carolyn had been able to contact Felix Oberman. His receptionist had offered a myriad of excuses for his unavailability, and it was becoming increasingly clear the doctor had no interest in helping his ex-wife. Oberman's reticence did not come as a surprise, but the lack of any statement in the file did.

"They'll do that," Pendergrass explained while they sat around the conference room table, "to make it more difficult to prepare for cross-examination, or if they're concerned that the witness might say something that could be used to impeach him at trial."

"Something like he hates the defendant's guts and would very much like to get even with her for every perceived ill that has ruined his life?" Barclay said.

Oberman was important, but Sloane considered Joshua Blume the state's most important witness and the reason Barclay was in custody. Everything else Rowe and Crosswhite had — the footprints, the fact that Vasiliev was killed with a .38, Reid's gun mysteriously missing, her alleged statement to Oberman — was not enough to get a conviction. Blume's statement did not just refute Reid's alibi, it placed her down the road from the shooting and it supported the prosecution's theory of how Reid, a triathlete, had committed the crime. The state would argue Barclay had biked into the neighborhood so that a car would not be heard or seen, and accessed Vasiliev's property by swimming half a mile to his backyard.

Alex had reached Blume's father but he refused to make his son available. Unlike Oberman's receptionist, Richard Blume offered no excuses for his reticence. It wasn't going to happen. Cerrabone said he would do what he could to arrange the meeting, but Sloane knew he'd have to get a court order and depose Blume under oath.

As Sloane sipped cold tea and reviewed the police file, Pendergrass entered the conference room holding a sheet of paper and looking puzzled. "Did you see this?"

Sloane reviewed the document. Pendergrass had highlighted a name. Julio Cruz. "They found his fingerprint on the sliding-glass door. The report from the latents unit confirmed a ten-point hit when the print was run through AFIS," he said, meaning that the fingerprint had ten characteristic points that matched a fingerprint in the system. "I cross-checked the name with the list of people who signed in at the scene —

uniformed officers, detectives, CSI, people from the medical examiner's office. Julio Cruz is not on the list. He's also not on the witness statement list I made."

Sloane looked up from the document. "Maybe an associate of Vasiliev?"

"Maybe, but if he was, and he was in the system, one would expect him to have a criminal record, right?"

"One would think," Sloane agreed.

"Which is why I had a friend at Fort Lewis run a criminal history for me," Pendergrass said, referring to the military base where he had been a JAG officer. "He didn't find anything."

"No criminal record?"

"Not even an outstanding parking ticket."

"Then why would he be in the system?"

"I don't know. I know that AFIS includes civilians who have submitted to background checks for their employment, and federal and state law enforcement, but like I said, he's not on the sign-in sheets. You want me to ask Cerrabone about it?" Pendergrass asked.

Sloane considered it. "No," he said. "Get it to Alex. See what she can pull up on the guy."

Alex had set up in one of the unused associate offices down the hall from the war room. She and Charlie had moved to the Washington Athletic Club during the weekdays, cutting their commute from an hour and a half to five minutes. For the time being, Jenkins's mother had flown out from the East Coast to take care of CJ and the dogs. Given Alex's proficiency on the computer, and her connections in the cyber world that even Charlie professed to not fully know, Sloane had tasked her with finding and talking to the witnesses who provided police statements. Hers was a gentler voice on the phone, and her physical appearance didn't immediately evoke fright and intimidation, as Jenkins's did.

As Jenkins walked into her office, Alex was finishing a phone conversation. He waited for her to hang up. "I'm sure Carolyn could come up with a poster or something for you to look at," he said. The walls were unblemished by even a nail hole.

She looked to the rectangular-shaped window. "Million-dollar view is enough for me. That was the alarm company. My phone charm didn't get me far. They need a subpoena to produce any records."

"Let Pendergrass know, that's his territory."

Jenkins smiled at the considerable amount

of paper Alex had already managed to accumulate. It overflowed her L-shaped desk to stacks on the floor. "Didn't take you long to jump back in."

"Did you doubt me?" she asked.

"Never."

"Where are you off to?"

"King County jail. David wants to talk to the guy who sold Barclay's daughter the heroin, see if he knows anything about Vasiliev's organization."

"Give these to David for me." She handed Jenkins a series of articles printed from the Internet. The headlines gave him a good idea of the content — statements from the U.S. attorney's office after the raid on Vasiliev's used-car business.

"What's the matter?" she asked.

He looked up from the documents. "I didn't say anything."

"No, but you just did that thing when you're frustrated. You blew out like a whale spouting."

He closed the office door and lowered his voice. "SODDI?" he said, referring to the acronym for "Some other dude did it."

"Every street punk in America knows that defense, Alex. 'I didn't do it. It was some other dude.'"

Alex walked around to the front of the

desk and leaned against it, arms folded. "Do you think she did it?"

"I don't know, but it seems like a real coincidence that she makes plans to go to that dinner that very day, then just happens to run into him."

Alex shrugged. "That kind of thing happens all the time."

"You know I don't believe in coincidences."

"How could it have been anything but?"

"He was the speaker. The organization promoted the event."

"And she's a lawyer," Alex said.

"Which means she likely gets all the legal publications and, given her stature, all of these kinds of invites. She would have known he was going to be the speaker . . ."

"But your theory assumes she knew all along she was going to kill Vasiliev. Now, *that* would take a lot of foresight, don't you think?"

"All I'm saying is we both know that ninety percent of all homicides are solved because they were committed by family members or someone with a motivation to kill. She had the motivation, the opportunity, and the weapon. And now the weapon is missing."

"David's convinced she didn't do it."

"David is too emotionally invested to know how he feels."

"What do you want to do?"

"She says she bumped into her husband at the symphony benefit."

"You want me to look into it?"

"It's like the dinner at the Rainier Club, right? I mean, there has to have been a registration list, people who signed up, paid to attend? So if she signed up months ago, paid for the tickets, maybe I'll start believing in coincidences again."

"And if she didn't?"

"Then it's something else to consider, isn't it?"

King County Jail
Seattle, Washington

Sloane and Jenkins sat shoulder to shoulder in one of the attorney rooms of the King County jail. With a phone call to the public defender's office, Sloane had learned that Scott Parker, nineteen, was a high school dropout with a long history of drug use and arrests, including his arrest for selling the heroin that killed Carly Oberman. Parker had fired the public defender assigned to him and was, at present, representing himself. His former public defender said Parker had been uncooperative with the police and with her, and he was just as unlikely to talk to Sloane, though since Parker was representing himself, Sloane was free to try.

The kid who shuffled into the broom closet wearing baggy red jail scrubs slumped into a chair with the bored indifference of a high school letterman to a poetry class. His dirty-blond hair hadn't seen a comb in years, and red acne scars and whiteheads pocked his skin beneath wispy blond facial hair. Multiple tattoos colored his forearms, weird images of a naked woman with flowing hair, the head of a lion, and some celestial planet. Three Asian letters ran vertically down his neck from his left earlobe. All he needed was the baseball cap twisted sideways on his head and the large silver chain around his neck. Jake referred to kids like Parker as "wangsters," slang for "white gangsters."

"Mr. Parker, I'm David Sloane."

Parker made eye contact long enough to smirk. "I know who you are."

"Yeah, how's that?"

"What, you think I live in a deprivation chamber here? I know Vasiliev is dead, and I know that girl's mother killed him. And I know you're representing her. It's on the freaking news, dude." He raised his shackled hands and shook them like Marley in *A*

Christmas Carol rattling his chains. "You're the attorney who doesn't lose. Ooooooh!"

Sloane bit his tongue. "I'm told you don't have an attorney."

"Don't need one."

"Seems like you do."

Parker grinned, his teeth yellowed and crooked. "I'll be out of here in no time."

Sloane couldn't fathom the source of the bravado. This kid was not going anywhere. Not for a very long time. Maybe not ever. It made him recall the public defender's statement that Parker wouldn't cut any deals, that he had some fantasy the charges were going to be dismissed and he was going to walk.

Sloane turned to Jenkins. "What do you think? Old Scotty here getting out any time soon?"

Jenkins stared at the kid with the menacing glare that made grown men cross the street. "I'd say that a typical drug bust, nobody gets too worked up about. A guy like Scotty here is back out on the street doing probation after promising to do better. Not this time. This time somebody died." Parker looked up from under his bangs. "And not just anybody — the daughter of a well-known and well-connected attorney. And this woman is seriously pissed.

She's on a crusade to shut down guys like Vasiliev and old Scotty here."

Parker put his forearms on the table and leaned forward, talking slowly. "And Vasiliev still walked." He sat back in the slump, a fingernail between his teeth, grinning. "So will I."

"Let me know when you do," Jenkins said. "I'll send flowers to your funeral."

Parker's eyes narrowed, but he otherwise didn't respond.

Sloane spelled it out for him. "Let's assume for a minute, Scott, that my client didn't kill Vasiliev." The grin disappeared. Scott apparently hadn't considered that possibility. "Let's assume that, if the feds made their case, Vasiliev was looking at going away for a very long time."

"Just like you," Jenkins said.

"So while ordinarily, guys like Vasiliev wouldn't be inclined to cut a deal . . ." Sloane let the thought hang.

"So?" Parker clearly wasn't the sharpest tool in the shed.

Jenkins picked up the ball. "So? So maybe the organization thinks that this time Vasiliev might just try to save his own butt, and not wanting to take that chance, they send someone to put a bullet in the back of his head before he can even think about talking. So when pigs fly and you do get out of here — and I'm not betting on either happening in the next thirty to forty — I'd watch your back."

"I'm not making any deals," Parker said, the bravado absent from his voice.

"Neither was Vasiliev." Sloane shrugged. "So I wonder why they killed him."

Parker fidgeted in his chair, gnawing on a fingernail.

Jenkins tapped Sloane's arm. "Let's go. I told you he'd be too stupid to figure it out."

Parker thrust out his chin. "You think so, King Kong? You think I'm stupid? So let's say I do know something. What's in it for me?"

"Depends on what you know," Sloane said.

"Oh, I know something. Something good."

"If that turns out to be true, then I go to the assistant U.S. attorney and tell her you might be willing to help with her investigation, and she starts talking to the prosecutor about a deal, maybe getting you in a witness protection program, give you a new identity and a new chance at life." Sloane didn't bother to tell Parker that with Vasiliev dead, there wasn't going to be any further investigation.

Parker sat back, legs extended in front of

him. "I want you to represent me."

Sloane laughed. "Think about it, Scott. I represent the mother of the girl you're accused of killing."

"I didn't kill nobody."

"It's a conflict of interest. I can't represent you."

He sat up. "But you probably have friends who could, friends who are as good as you, better than that freaking PD bitch."

Jenkins tapped Sloane on the shoulder. "He doesn't know anything. Let's go."

They stood.

"Wait. Look, I don't know anything about Vasiliev's organization. I got my stuff from one of the car guys that worked for him. That was it. That was the only guy I ever met."

"Then I can't help you," Sloane said.

They made it as far as the door.

"Wait."

Sloane turned. "This is getting monotonous, Scott."

"You have to get the prosecutor to make a deal first."

Jenkins asked, "If your informant is so good, why didn't you have your attorney cut a deal?"

"Get the wax out of your ears. She don't

know nothing. That's why she's a fucking PD."

"You got to give me something to whet the prosecutor's appetite," Sloane said.

Parker shook his head like a defiant kid. "I want to know what they're offering first."

Jenkins grabbed Sloane's shoulder. "Told you he's full of shit."

Sloane thought so, too. Another dead end.

"Am I?" Parker yelled. "Am I really, you big son of a bitch? Then why don't you tell the fucking U.S. attorney that I know how they keep getting off."

Sloane got two steps into the hall when he remembered his first meeting with Rebecca Han. She said Judge Kozlowski had been flat-out wrong in his ruling. When he walked back into the room, Parker sat grinning as if he'd just laid the girl tattooed on his arm.

"Hell, yeah . . . you tell them that, Mr. Attorney who does not lose."

Law Offices of David Sloane
One Union Square Building
Seattle, Washington

Back at his office, Sloane relayed the information aloud to those sitting around the conference table eating the box lunches Carolyn had ordered.

"He said he knew how Vasiliev got off?"

Barclay asked.

"Not just Vasiliev," Sloane said. "He said *they.* He said he knew how *they* keep getting off."

"Who are 'they'?" Barclay asked.

"You think he's just blowing smoke?" Pendergrass asked between bites of a turkey sandwich.

"He was smiling like the Cheshire Cat," Jenkins said.

"The public defender said Parker wouldn't cut a deal, that he had some fantasy he was going to walk." Sloane walked to the white chart hanging on the wall with the names of Vasiliev's crime organization partially filled in. Han's office had sent it over.

"He knew he was going to walk," Reid said, which drew the attention of everyone at the table. She put down her sandwich. "That day in federal court, after Kozlowski granted the motion to suppress . . . Vasiliev looked at his lawyer and said, 'I told you. No worries.' "

"That doesn't necessarily mean he knew anything," Pendergrass said. "A lot of guys are cocky after the fact."

"No," she said. "You had to be there. He was smug. He knew."

For a moment no one spoke. Then Sloane said, "Maybe he had someone on the inside, a cop . . . someone in the courthouse feeding him information."

"Or maybe" — Pendergrass put down his sandwich and looked at Alex — "a federal agent."

Alex handed Sloane a document. "Julio Cruz is a former DEA agent." Sloane read as she spoke. "Apparently, he worked out of Miami in the 1980s. I called Rebecca Han. She did not recognize the name; said he was not one of the agents she worked with. I called the local DEA and got the SAC. Guess what he said?"

Sloane shook his head.

" 'No comment,' " Alex said. "Which means Rowe and Crosswhite probably already raised the same questions we're asking, and this guy doesn't have the answers."

"Like what was he doing at Vasiliev's home," Jenkins said.

Alex said, "I got someone looking into it. I asked him to try to find out what this guy worked on, why he might be out here in the Northwest."

"Last known address?" Sloane asked.

"His federal pension is a direct deposit. Mail goes to a P.O. box in Miami."

Sloane stared up at the chart. "See what else you can find out about anyone else on this chart," he said, pointing to names in the rectangular boxes. "See if any of them have been arrested recently, whether there's any common denominator — same prosecutor or arresting officer, anything."

SEVENTEEN

Friday, September 16, 2011
Law Offices of David Sloane
One Union Square
Seattle, Washington

Three days later, late in the afternoon, Sloane walked into the war room to find Jenkins and Alex smiling. Multiple white cartons sat open on the table, napkins and chopsticks beside them, along with several green bottles of Tsingtao beer. Sloane had spent much of his time out of the office lining up and meeting with potential expert witnesses. Today he had met a man who at one time had been a part of the King County sheriff's special operations unit before going into business for himself providing professional tracking services.

Sloane draped his sport coat over the back of a chair and dropped his briefcase with a thud. "Either the two of you just had a quickie, and I'm hoping not on the table, or you have something good to tell me. I hope it's the latter, because while the former might have put the smiles on your faces, it won't do much for me."

"If it was the former, I probably wouldn't be smiling this much," Alex said, maneuvering chopsticks through one of the cartons. "And he'd still be fighting for oxygen."

"As Jake would say, TMI." Sloane picked up a carton — P. F. Chang's spicy beef — and split apart a pair of fresh chopsticks.

"What do you want first? The good news or the good news?" Alex said.

Sloane spoke as he chewed. "Best offer I've had all week."

She put down her carton. "According to my source, Julio Cruz worked on a drug task force in the 1980s called Centac."

"Which was what?"

"Heavily classified."

"But not for someone as skilled at getting information as you?" Sloane prodded, knowing Alex had more.

"It was run out of the special action section of the Drug Enforcement Administration but had nearly complete autonomy, which I can tell you is highly unusual. In Washington you can't fart without asking someone's permission."

"Do you see why I love her?" Jenkins said.

"Is she a classy broad or what?"

Sloane put down the box and used a bottle opener to pry off the cap of a beer, taking a sip. "So why would this Centac be an exception to the norm?"

Alex looked to Charlie. They had clearly discussed the same question. "Probably so no politician could be held accountable if the shit hit the fan and something went wrong."

Jenkins snapped apart a fortune cookie, munching on half while unfolding the small white slip of paper. "That would be Washington. Take all the credit but never the blame." He read the strip of paper. " 'You will receive a fortune cookie.' Brilliant."

Sloane exchanged the beer for the carton and continued eating. "So what did your contact know about it?"

"The guy in charge was named Micheal Hurley. Bit of a wild card, according to my source, but some serious credentials in drug-task-force stuff — Afghanistan, Cyprus, Greece, Turkey. He was the real deal, a guy on the front lines of Reagan's war on drugs. At any given time, he had fifty agents around the world working directly for him —"

"Including Julio Cruz?" Sloane asked.

"Looks like it. They worked with other

agencies: the Internal Revenue Service, customs, foreign police agencies in about a dozen countries, many of which had no idea Centac even existed. When a case broke and the arrests were made, Centac quietly withdrew, leaving the headlines to the local officers and their politicos. Hurley wasn't looking for photo ops, medals, or Christmas bonuses."

Sloane left the sticks in the box. "Was he successful?"

"Centac took down the biggest marijuana dealer in North America, the largest cocaine and hashish supplier in the East, and about ten others over a four-year period."

Sloane said, "Let me guess. Four years. Change in administrations."

Alex nodded. "We went from the Reagan and Bush years of fighting the war on drugs to the Clinton years pacifying it. Centac got shut down."

"Does your source know what happened to Cruz?"

She shrugged. "Records show Cruz went back to the DEA's office in Miami, worked until he vested, and retired. Last known address the P.O. box."

Sloane thought about the information, continuing to pick through the carton. "Did your source know what Cruz worked on while he was with Centac?"

Alex popped the other half of Jenkins's fortune cookie into her mouth, chewing it. "Thought you might want to know that."

"That's bad luck, you know, to eat another person's cookie. Now my fortune won't come true," Jenkins said.

She shook her head. "As successful as Centac was, one of the biggest fish eluded them. And drug agents are a lot like fishermen."

"It's the fish that get away that bothers them most," Jenkins said, reaching for a beer and using his hand to twist off the cap.

"So who was the big fish?" Sloane asked.

"A man named Petyr Sakorov. You might know him as the Russian billionaire who owns a dozen or so hotels and casinos around the world, at least one resort, and has his name on hospitals and civic buildings from Moscow to Siberia. He's a heroin dealer, David. He went from being one of the proletariat to trafficking in heroin."

Sloane put down the carton and the chopsticks. "And Cruz was working on that investigation."

"Bingo," Jenkins said, drinking a third of the bottle.

Sloane considered them both, then moved aside the cartons and lifted his briefcase onto the table to retrieve his notes from his meeting with the tracking expert and a copy of Kaylee Wright's report at Vasiliev's home. He handed both to Alex and walked behind her chair. "Wright reports the presence of multiple shoe prints at the site that she has eliminated as being made by police officers. But look at the bottom line of the third paragraph," he said.

Alex read it out loud. " 'Two sets of prints, sizes ten and a half and twelve, of unknown origin.' "

"Likely two men," Jenkins said.

Sloane went to the white board and used a red dry-erase pen to draw a crude house and a lawn sloping to a rock wall. He made squiggly lines to represent the water.

"I hope you didn't major in art," Jenkins said.

Sloane exchanged the red pen for black and drew a line on the right from the water to the house, then to a stand of trees and back to the water. "This is the track for the size-seven prints." He drew two lines on the left leading from the beach to the back of the house. "She tracked these prints from the water to the patio and back, but on the opposite side of the lawn."

Jenkins asked, "Could one of them have been the shooter?"

"That was my question. Wright's report says these two sets of prints were made *after* the size-seven prints."

"How the hell can she tell that?" Jenkins said.

"It has to do with the way the blades of grass lay over the top of one another. My point is that both she and the ballistics expert eliminate them as the possible shooter."

"The trajectory?" Alex guessed.

Sloane drew the sliding-glass door at the back of the house and put two X's on the left side of the patio. "According to the ballistics expert, the angle from where these two people stood on the patio would have been wrong based on the trajectory of the bullet." He drew a line on the right through the sliding-glass door to indicate the actual trajectory of the bullet. "It would not have been possible for either person to have taken the shot. I have someone looking into it, but he appears right."

"So what were they doing there?" Jenkins asked.

"That would be the next logical question, wouldn't it? According to my expert, they left multiple prints in the sandy area below the rock wall." Sloane circled the area. "And his guess is they were exiting and entering some sort of boat."

"So we assume one of those two shoe prints belongs to Cruz," Jenkins said, "which would account for his fingerprint on the sliding-glass-door handle."

"Which brings us to the sixty-four-thousand-dollar question," Sloane said, putting down the pen.

"Why was he there?" Alex asked.

"Maybe Cruz is dirty, like Pendergrass said," Jenkins said. "Maybe he made some contacts back in the eighties, and now, retired, he's working them."

"Or maybe Centac isn't completely gone," Alex said. "Maybe it's like that fish that got away."

"They had Vasiliev under surveillance?" Jenkins asked.

"It would explain why the Seattle DEA office claims ignorance," Alex said. "They didn't know."

"Okay," Jenkins said. "But that's a double-edged sword."

"I know." Sloane picked up the carton and his chopsticks. "It doesn't explain the size-seven shoe prints, but it certainly allows me a good reason to intimate why Vasiliev is dead. Maybe that ruse we played with Scotty Parker was a premonition. Maybe Vasiliev had cut a deal."

311

"Speaking of which," Jenkins said, "you're going to love this. Looks like old Scotty Parker is sitting on a keg of dynamite."

Alex smiled. "I found that connection you were looking for."

"How they keep getting off," Jenkins said. "Four of them."

"Five, if you count Vasiliev," Alex said.

Sloane put both hands on the table, palms flat. He leaned forward, head cocked, disbelieving. "Kozlowski was the judge on *every* case?"

"Every . . . one," Alex said, rocking back in her chair.

"And there's more." Jenkins smiled.

"I talked with Rebecca Han," Alex continued. "Kozlowski wasn't originally assigned the Vasiliev matter. She's going to look into how that came about, and she's looking into the other four cases as well, whether they were originally assigned to him."

Sloane straightened, not sure what to make of the information and, more important, what to do with it.

"A couple years back, Kozlowski went through a very public and nasty divorce," Alex said. "It cost him a bundle in lawyers' fees, over a million dollars." She handed Sloane a document. "He stiffed his lawyers.

They were creditors on his personal bank-ruptcy."

"Desperate people do desperate things," Jenkins said, reaching for the final fortune cookie. "And you can never discount the allure of pure, unadulterated greed."

Sloane flipped through the bankruptcy petition. "What happened with the bankruptcy? Did you check?"

"It was withdrawn," Alex said.

Sloane looked up from his reading. "Which means he somehow satisfied his creditors. Can we get any of his financial records? Determine if he suddenly had an influx of cash?"

"I'm already working on it," Alex said. "Federal judges are required to file financial reports every year. It should be simple accounting to determine how much reported income the judge had coming in and how much went out to satisfy his creditors."

Sloane put down the report. "How the hell do I prove Vasiliev bribed a federal judge?"

Jenkins cracked another cookie and read the fortune. " 'Help! I'm being held prisoner in a Chinese bakery.' These guys are a riot." He munched half. "I'll tell you how. You get the prosecutor to cut a deal with Scotty Parker and have him testify."

"A drug dealer's accusation against a

313

federal district court judge?"

"It's not just his word. You have the circumstantial evidence — the four recent drug busts, all in Vasiliev's organization; Kozlowski somehow manages to end up with all four, and all four walk on technicalities."

"Maybe," Sloane said, already thinking about the bigger problem. "But even if I can prove it, how do I get it in? What's the relevance to Vasiliev's murder?"

No one had an answer.

Sloane ran his hand through his hair, frustrated. "We need to find Julio Cruz, and sooner rather than later."

EIGHTEEN

Thursday, November 24, 2011
Three Tree Point
Burien, Washington
It would not be sooner. As the weeks passed, Julio Cruz remained a mystery.

The crisp blue skies of September gave way to the cold, gray days of October, and the leaves on the trees changed color to autumn's array in November. He and Barclay were driving home from Camano Island after celebrating Thanksgiving dinner with Alex and Charlie, CJ, and Charlie's mother. It had been their first formal dinner together, and Sloane thought it had gone well, though he sensed some reticence from Alex, which he had expected. She and Tina had been close.

They had settled into a routine, he and Barclay, much like a married couple, though they no longer spent every night together or made love at every opportunity. Despite taking a leave of absence, Barclay could not stay away from her firm. She went in several times a week to "mind the store," as she put it. When not at her firm, she was busy performing research and working on her own defense. Sloane traveled to meet experts, to talk with witnesses, and even occasionally to attend to his other cases, though he had brought in another attorney to handle much of that workload. Outside of the office, they tried hard not to discuss the impending trial, but it lurked, like a distant train hurtling full speed and headlong down the tracks, and kept getting closer by the day.

It was that train that had awakened Sloane in a cold sweat and sent him downstairs to his office. He sat at his desk with just a circle of light in the otherwise dark house, uncertain how long he had been at work when he heard the old house creak and moan — Barclay getting up from bed, searching for him. He heard her descend the stairs.

The French door cracked open. "You okay?" she whispered, her voice hoarse from sleep. She walked behind him and slid her hands to his chest, resting her head on his shoulder. Her breath felt warm against his neck.

Outside, the leafless branches of the cottonwood tree danced and swayed like anorexic arms and bony fingers as gusts of wind shook the house.

"Storm's coming," Sloane said. "The weatherman's predicting a bad winter."

"They always think the worst. But they never really know until it arrives, do they?"

"None of us do."

He reached up and squeezed her forearm. Across the blackened waters of the Puget Sound, Sloane found the distant white light on Vashon Island, the one that he had been staring at before she came downstairs, the one that made him think again of that approaching train.

Monday, November 28, 2011
King County Courthouse
Judge Reuben Underwood's Chambers

A week before trial, the court administrator had called to advise Sloane they had a trial judge, Reuben Underwood, and that they would remain in courtroom 854E to accommodate the anticipated public interest. Underwood wasted little time jumping in, sending out an order he wanted to meet with counsel for a pretrial conference at eleven in the morning two days before the trial date.

Sloane knew little of Underwood and had set Pendergrass to the task of gathering information, which he delivered the morning of the pretrial meeting. "He's bright," Pendergrass said. "Harvard undergrad, Yale Law School."

African-American, Underwood had grown up the son of two doctors in Atherton, an affluent neighborhood in Northern California. His parents had impressed on him, at an early age, the value of education. Though he was a swimmer and a tennis player who garnered interest from local colleges, sports were not in the game plan. Upon graduation from Yale, Underwood clerked for a federal district court judge in Alabama, where he met his wife, a native of Seattle, who, like most Seattle natives, had no desire to live anywhere else on the planet. Marriage and Seattle became a package deal. In Seattle, he forsook hundred-thousand-dollar-a-year offers from half a dozen law firms for the opportunity to immediately try cases with the King County prosecutor's office. After fifteen years, and perhaps because he had five kids and the oldest was close to considering colleges, Underwood jumped sides and joined a prominent criminal defense firm where he gained a reputation as one of the best criminal defense lawyers in the state. After his children were grown, several prominent black businessmen and -women convinced him to seek election to the bench at the age of fifty-five. He had presided for the past five years.

As Sloane and Cerrabone entered the judge's chambers, Sloane noticed a large glass chessboard in the corner of the room beneath shelves stocked with books, framed family photographs, and plaques and trophies that indicated the judge still played in chess tournaments, as well as participating in competitive tennis and masters' swimming meets, and was proud of it. Beside Underwood's desk was an empty chair and, in front of it, a stenographer's machine.

Cerrabone and Underwood talked as if acquainted — inevitable, given that Cerrabone was not only a fixture in the prosecutor's office, but his wife, Sloane had learned, worked in the clerk's office.

The judge wore thick black-framed glasses that he somehow made look stylish, with hair that had grayed along the sides. But he also filled out a starched blue shirt and had the lean features of someone who had earned the trophies on the shelf.

"Thank you for accommodating my

schedule," Underwood said to both men. They took chairs across from his desk. "I like to get as much settled as we can before we start trial, any last-minute details, complaints, objections. I don't like to keep my juries waiting." He raised a hand, long delicate fingers and manicured nails. "Now, I know from experience that things come up during a trial that cannot be avoided, but I have found that most of those things are disputes that, with foresight on the part of the attorneys, could have been anticipated ahead of time." He sounded like a man who very much likened a trial to a chess match. "I will therefore be reluctant to punish a jury by keeping them waiting in the jury room while we haggle over issues that should have been resolved. So you might consider this meeting like that moment when the minister looks out at a wedding crowd and says that if you have any objections, you should speak now or forever hold your peace."

Neither Cerrabone nor Sloane spoke.

"Good. Let's start with the media. It will be a circus. But not in my courtroom." The judge eyed them both. "The media has a right to be present, according to my learned colleagues on the Supreme Court." To Sloane, it didn't sound as if Underwood agreed. "And I will accommodate that right, but I have discretion to limit that presence so as not to prejudice the defendant's right to a fair trial. While I can't limit the number of reporters, I can limit the number of cameras. There will be one in the back of the court on the far left that will provide a live feed for all of the networks. I do not want this trial played out in the media by either side. I am not imposing a gag order, but I am appealing to your sense of integrity and respect for the judicial system." He paused again to give that glare. "Is that clear enough?"

Sloane and Cerrabone answered in unison that it was.

"Good. Then let me get my court reporter in here and we'll get started."

Moments after Underwood hung up the phone, a red-haired man took the seat alongside the judge's desk, his fingers moving as soon as the judge opened his mouth to note for the record the caption and case number, date and time. Underwood also noted they were present in his chambers to discuss the pretrial motions filed by both sides as well as other matters. Then he asked both Cerrabone and Sloane to state their appearances.

He shuffled a set of papers. "Okay, let's

get started with the state's motion to limit the evidence to be introduced about the victim's involvement in drug trafficking."

Cerrabone sat up. "Your Honor, the state is concerned that the defense is going to try to poison the jury with evidence that Mr. Vasiliev was part of a criminal enterprise — the Russian mafia, if you will — to somehow justify his death. It is highly prejudicial and of limited probative value."

With a flick of his eyes, Underwood looked to Sloane, who said, "Judge, Mr. Vasiliev was under indictment for drug trafficking by the U.S. attorney's office."

"But never convicted of anything," Underwood said.

"Never convicted," Sloane agreed.

"So what's the relevance?"

"Your Honor, the state's own papers, starting with the police certification of probable cause, have consistently argued that my client's motivation for this killing was that Mr. Vasiliev provided the heroin that resulted in the overdose death of her daughter. If the state is willing to stipulate that it will not raise that argument" — Sloane knew Cerrabone had no intention of giving up Barclay's motive for committing the crime — "I would be happy not to mention Mr. Vasiliev's occupation."

Sloane's intuition was right. "Let me clarify," Cerrabone said. "The state's concern is the defense's listing an assistant United States attorney, Rebecca Han, as a witness." Both sides had been obligated to exchange a list of known witnesses and their anticipated testimony. "The only potential relevance Ms. Han could have is that she prosecuted Mr. Vasiliev on the federal-drug-trafficking charge."

Underwood, well versed in both sides' pleadings, raised his hand again. "And you're concerned that the jury will see Ms. Han's testimony as somehow a tacit statement that the government is on the side of the defense. All right, gentlemen, here's what we're going to do. If the state is willing to stipulate that Mr. Vasiliev was under a federal indictment for drug trafficking in heroin, then I see no reason for Ms. Han's testimony."

"The state is willing to so stipulate," Cerrabone said.

"Then we'll leave it at that. But under no circumstances, Mr. Sloane, do I want to hear the words 'Russian mafia' in my courtroom. Is that understood?"

"It is," Sloane said, taking the first blow but a glancing one.

Underwood turned to the next motion.

"The state wants to exclude a fingerprint of a Drug Enforcement agent?"

Cerrabone nodded. "Your Honor, it's the state's position that the fingerprint is a false positive, which the court knows does happen. We have looked into this matter in great detail, and there is no evidence that the agent, Julio Cruz, was present at the crime scene. Mr. Cruz was a DEA agent who worked out of Miami in the 1980s and has long since retired, with no known ties to Seattle."

Sloane had refrained in his written opposition to the motion from bringing up anything about Centac; he did not want to give up the information until he knew its significance.

"What does Mr. Cruz have to say?" Underwood asked.

"Neither side has been able to locate him," Cerrabone said, answering for them both.

"The latents unit identified the fingerprint," Sloane said. "There's no indication in their report that it is not a good fingerprint, that it could be some sort of false positive, which is extremely rare. In fact, they note it's a ten-point confirmation. The defense has the right to bring this evidence to the jury's attention, just as the jury has the right to know that the state has no explanation for the two other sets of shoe prints running along the left side of the property to the patio at the back of the house. The state can call whomever it deems fit to explain that Mr. Cruz should have had no interest in this case and that it therefore believes the print to be a false positive. But the evidence is what it is. The weight is for the jury to decide."

Underwood's eyes flickered to Cerrabone, but not for comment. "I agree with Mr. Sloane. The evidence is what it is. If you believe the print to have been in error, you can have a witness explain that to the jury and let them weigh the evidence."

On they went for the next two hours. Underwood was efficient but did not rush either side, allowing them to make their arguments, though once and only once. This was a man who understood the adage that saying something twice did not give the argument more weight. It usually detracted from it.

As they neared completion, Sloane said, "Your Honor, the defense has been waiting nearly sixty days for the contents of the defendant's computers, financial records, and cell phone records. We were promised the information some time ago by the state and —"

"Where are they, Mr. Cerrabone?"

"It took time to get the records, Your Honor, and the number of documents is substantial, more than twenty-five thousand." Cerrabone got as far as saying that the documents were in the process of being Bates-stamped, meaning sequentially numbered so that both sides could be certain that nothing could be mysteriously slipped in or removed, but Underwood cut him off.

"And the state has had plenty of time to do that. I want them delivered no later than tomorrow."

"I'll try, Your Honor."

"You'll do better than try. It will happen, or I will impose penalties."

It was, for Sloane, a hollow victory. There was no way on God's green earth he and Pendergrass could get through twenty-five thousand documents with the laundry list of things that needed to be done in the next day and a half. But there was also nothing Sloane could say that was about to change that. Underwood had already pushed back his chair and stood to shake their hands.

"I'll see you both Wednesday morning," he said.

Outside the courthouse, Sloane slipped on

his long wool coat and gloves before calling the office. Pendergrass said he was sitting in the conference room with Barclay, and put Sloane's call on speakerphone. Sloane told them they would be getting a substantial care package from the prosecutor's office and advised them on the outcome of the motions. "Won some, lost some" was how he put it, with a promise to fill them in further when he returned. That was the way it went with most pretrial conferences. With experience, the good lawyers learned they were never always right. Sometimes motions were brought not to win but to test the waters, determine how far a judge would allow the lawyer to go, or to flush out the other side's argument. Sloane hadn't expected Han to be able to testify when he listed her as a witness, but by putting her on the list, he had forced Cerrabone to bring the motion and expose his position, which allowed Sloane to educate the judge about Vasiliev.

"Are you on your way back?" Pendergrass asked.

"Not just yet. I have an appointment to speak to Felix Oberman."

"You finally reached him?" Barclay asked, her voice anxious.

"No. But he's going to have to tell me no

327

to my face. I'm out of time and patience."

Late afternoon, Jenkins walked into Alex's office with two cups of coffee in paper cups with lids. He set them on the desk and rubbed his hands to get feeling back into his fingers.

"Temperature's dropping again," he said. "I called my mother and told her to turn up the thermostat until I could get up there this weekend and wrap the pipes."

"Which one is mine?" Alex asked. She drank lattes. Jenkins drank black coffee, though with three packs of sugar.

"The one on the left." He wore blue jeans, boots, and his black leather car coat. He had been out on a boat, taking photographs of the back of Vasiliev's house, as well as the public easement.

"I take it you had another uneventful morning?" She had not seen him since he left at five A.M.

He picked up his cup and let it further warm his hands. He'd spent several hours every evening and early morning watching Judge Myron Kozlowski's apartment building on Capitol Hill. He stayed until he was

328

certain the judge had gone to bed, then returned to follow him to the federal courthouse garage. So far, the most exciting thing Kozlowski had done was go to the supermarket.

"You could set your watch by the guy: lights go on at six on the dot, out the door to walk the poodle by six-fifteen, back by six-forty-five with a doggie poop bag that he deposits in the blue bin at the back of the building. He leaves for work by seven-thirty, works through lunch, and leaves the office at six. Home by six-twenty. Out the door with the pooch and another poop bag, home by seven-twenty." He sipped his coffee, which remained scalding-hot, then fingered the roof of his mouth, knowing he'd just burned it. "What did you find out?"

"She purchased a ticket to the benefit that day. She used a credit card."

Jenkins put down his coffee.

"I also found out Oberman is a season ticket holder, has been for fifteen years."

"So he had the tickets when they were married."

Alex nodded. "And it would have been simple enough for her to get on the Internet and find the date and time of every performance or a benefit."

Jenkins thought about it. "She says she bumped into him, just like she bumped into David that night."

"And she very well might have. Think about it. Why would she purposefully bump into her ex-husband and tell him she wanted to shoot Vasiliev? If we're assuming this was a calculated act by a calculating person, wouldn't that person, weighing the positives and negatives, have concluded it was better not to have the statement out there?"

"One would think," Jenkins agreed. "But one of them is lying, and if she didn't say it, then Oberman is more than a vindictive ex-husband; he's a sick son of a bitch."

"She says he is."

"I know." He pulled out his gloves from his jacket pocket.

"Where are you headed?"

"I'm going to see if I can speed things up. I'm too old to be staying out this late freezing my ass off."

Overlake Medical Park
Bellevue, Washington

Sloane had put Carolyn to a task for which she was particularly well suited — getting information out of other assistants. She didn't let him down. As he grabbed a bite to eat and waited at a restaurant in the Lincoln Plaza, Carolyn called to confirm that the receptionist at Dr. Felix Oberman's office, Shawn Cortes, had informed her that Oberman's schedule had not changed, and the doctor would be in appointments until five P.M. Cortes said that if Carolyn's problem was an emergency, she should call the hospital hotline. Otherwise, Oberman could fit her in tomorrow.

Oberman's office was located in a single-story complex in Bellevue, not far from Overlake Hospital, where he maintained medical privileges. The exterior of the wood-sided buildings looked in need of a paint job, and the pavement had been patched with tar, though there remained several significant cracks. Surrounding the complex, multistory buildings were in various stages of construction, including a new Seattle Children's Hospital surgery center across the street. Sloane deduced that the owner of Oberman's complex was using the property as a land bank, spending the minimum on upkeep until the economy turned and he could sell the entire site to a developer looking to construct another highrise. That meant the tenants were likely on short leases at reduced rents to accommodate tight budgets. Oberman's psychiatry practice was not booming, as Barclay had deduced it.

At just after five, Sloane watched a diminutive man who fit the physical description Barclay had provided exit the building carrying a leather satchel. Her ex-husband was ten years older and looked to be mid-fifties with curly soot-colored hair and a matching unkempt beard. Oberman wore round, frameless glasses, though reading glasses dangled by a chain around his neck and bounced against a plaid shirt tucked neatly into brown corduroys. A heavy winter coat with a hood hung to his knees.

Sloane intercepted Oberman as the doctor stepped to the driver's side of an older-model blue Toyota Corolla retrieving keys from a worn suede satchel.

"Dr. Oberman?"

Oberman dropped the keys. Turning, he didn't bother to ask Sloane's name or offer his hand. His eyes confirmed that he either recognized Sloane or had known from the series of phone calls to his office that this meeting was inevitable. "I'm not going to talk to you," he said, bending to recover his keys.

"Can I ask why not?"

"Because I don't have to." He lowered one knee to the pavement and reached beneath the car.

332

"Actually, that's not true, Dr. Oberman. You'll have to talk to me in court, on the witness stand."

Oberman stood again and turned his back, inserting the key in the door lock. "The prosecutor told me to call him if you showed up."

"You could do that. I have his cell phone number programmed into my phone. But why would you? I'm just trying to get the same information you provided him; I'm doing my job, like he is."

Oberman pulled open the car door. "I'll think about it. Leave a card with my receptionist."

"I've left a dozen messages with your receptionist, Dr. Oberman. Frankly, I'm out of time. I have to give an opening statement day after tomorrow."

"Then perhaps you should use your time preparing for that."

"Do you hate her that much?"

Oberman wheeled and took a hostile step toward Sloane. "Hate? . . . Hate has nothing to do with this," Oberman said.

At least Sloane had the man's attention. "Doesn't it? Then why are you punishing her?"

"I'm not punishing her. I simply told the detectives and the attorney what she said."

333

"Then why are you punishing me? You talked to the prosecutor. All I'm asking for is the same professional courtesy. I don't have an ax to grind, but I have a document from the prosecutor saying you are going to testify that Barclay told you she was going to kill Vasiliev." Sloane held up the prosecution's witness list.

"She didn't use the word 'kill.' "

Sloane shrugged. "That's all I'm trying to do — clarify what she did and did not say."

Oberman's lips pursed. Worry lines formed between his eyebrows. "The prosecutor said I should call."

"You can do that. But I have to do this today, and I'll tell him that, and it will just take longer while we wait for him to get here. Look, if you don't like a question, you can tell me to pound sand."

Oberman's breath marked the cold air. "What do you want to know?"

What Sloane wanted was to get Oberman away from the car and the prospect of easily fleeing. He rubbed his hands together, then crossed his arms. "Is there a warm place we can talk?"

Oberman seemed to consider the question — not whether there was a place but, again, whether he wanted to talk. "I'll give you fifteen minutes," he said, and shut the car door with a thud.

Sloane followed Oberman inside the building and down a hallway of worn carpet and poor lighting. Oberman unlocked and pushed open a cheap door, his name on a plastic plaque, the kind that could be easily and inexpensively removed at the end of a lease. Oberman did not sit behind the desk in the office. He dropped his satchel beside a high-back leather chair and plopped into it, his coat still on. Sloane took one of two upholstered seats. With the shade drawn on a narrow sidelight, a muted desk lamp offered the only light. A framed print of the earth taken from space hung on the wall behind the desk, below it the word IMAGINE. Two bookshelves took up a corner of the room, a potted plant in need of watering at the intersection.

Before Sloane could say a word, Oberman's voice became harsh. "Tell me, has she only hired you, or is she also fucking you?"

The vulgarity, coming from an educated man in an office environment, set Sloane on his heels; he wasn't quite sure how to respond. It sounded almost as if Oberman wanted to add the word "over" to the end of his question.

"She hired me to file a civil action for

335

wrongful death against Vasiliev. After her arrest, she asked me to represent her in the criminal matter."

Oberman closed his eyes, seeming to take a moment to calm himself. "I'm sorry. When it comes to matters regarding my former wife, I'm not always at my best. I apologize. I suppose I should ask, how is she holding up?"

The question sounded sincere, but coming so soon after the outburst, Sloane wasn't sure what to think of it. When it came to his ex-wife, Oberman clearly remained conflicted, and Sloane assumed that to be the reason the man had reacted so strongly to the word "hate" when Sloane used it in the parking lot. Oberman might not hate his ex-wife, but neither was he ambivalent about her, as some divorced couples became — live and let live. Barclay still provoked deep-seated emotions.

"She's strong, but obviously, this hasn't been easy. It's taken its toll," Sloane said.

"Yeah, she's strong."

Again, Sloane detected a hint of what — sarcasm, bitterness? "I understand that your divorce wasn't amicable?"

Oberman scoffed. "That's an understatement."

"Hard feelings?"

"Many."

Might as well get it out on the table, Sloane thought. "Barclay indicated you believed she was responsible for your daughter's death. She said you accused her of not being a good mother."

Oberman gave Sloane a cold, hard stare, and Sloane expected the man to exercise his right to tell Sloane to get out, but then Oberman diverted his eyes as if resigned that he'd have to answer the question eventually. He reclined in the chair and tilted his chin. "I was upset. My daughter was dead, and I was in pain. Maybe I said things I shouldn't have."

"We're all guilty of that at times," Sloane said, hoping to plant the seed.

"My wife tended to put her career — maybe I should say herself — ahead of everything, Mr. Sloane, including me and Carly. I'm not surprised she didn't realize Carly had started using again."

Barclay had said it was Oberman who put his career first, and he'd sacrificed a relationship with his daughter in the process.

"Can you tell me the circumstances that led to your meeting with the detectives?"

"I called them."

"Why?"

"Because when I saw the news on the

television that Vasiliev had been killed, my first thought was that my lovely ex-wife shot him."

"Why did you conclude that?"

"Isn't it in the statement?"

"There isn't much in the statement, Dr. Oberman, and I'd like to hear it from you, if you don't mind."

"Because several weeks before — I believe it was a Thursday night, the symphony plays on Thursday nights — I was surprised to run into her."

"At the symphony."

"In the parking lot, actually. It was purely happenstance. I locked my car door, turned to leave, and there she stood. I was taken aback at first, as I'm sure she was."

"Why were you taken aback?"

"Because the symphony was always my love, and Barclay had never been particularly fond of attending when we were married. I always had the impression she did it more for the stature, for the people she was likely to meet there, client contacts for her practice. She even joined the board of directors at one point."

"So maybe she was there for that reason," Sloane said.

Oberman shrugged. "She said she was meeting a friend."

"What did you say to each other?"

"We exchanged . . ." Oberman rocked in his chair, legs straight, brown loafers crossed. "My ex-wife and I aren't on the best of terms. She's probably told you that. We don't have a lot to say to each other, but with Leenie's death . . . We were cordial. I said something like 'I've seen your name in the paper quite a bit.' She'd been lobbying the legislature for tougher laws against drug dealers. I asked if she thought it would make a difference. She said she hoped it would. And then I asked her how the trial was going."

"What trial?"

"I'm not great with legal terms. Barclay had convinced the U.S. attorney to prosecute Mr. Vasiliev."

"And you were asking about the status of that case."

"Honestly, I was just making conversation, Mr. Sloane. Frankly, it was very awkward."

"After all these years?"

He didn't answer. "She said the defense had brought a motion to have the case thrown out, something to that effect. It upset her. I could hear it in her voice. She said she was going to the hearing. And then she said it."

"What exactly did she say? Do you remember her words?"

Oberman tilted his head back and looked up at the ceiling. His beard was darker beneath his chin. When he spoke, the position of his head gave his voice a froglike quality. "I believe her exact words were 'If I had known it was going to be this much trouble, I would have just put a bullet in the back of his head.' "

"Did you take her seriously?"

This brought a burst of laughter. "Oh, I learned long ago to *always* take my ex-wife seriously."

"Why is that?" Sloane asked.

Oberman smoothed the hair around his mouth and chin, still smiling, but this time it appeared more irony than amusement. "Answer me this first: *Are* you sleeping with her?"

Sloane wanted to tell Oberman it was not germane to the issue, but he also wanted to keep the conversation alive. "Yes. Barclay and I are dating."

"Where do I begin . . ." The doctor smirked. "When I sought the divorce, my wife told me she would take everything from me. She succeeded. She told me she would take my daughter from me, and at that she succeeded. She told me she would ruin my

340

practice, a threat she also fulfilled."

Sloane had assumed from his conversations with Barclay, and now, from seeing Oberman, who was less than physically impressive, that she had sought the divorce, but it did not sound that way. "Who filed for divorce?"

"I did. You see, Mr. Sloane, I came to the conclusion that my ex-wife is narcissistic and sociopathic."

"That's a pretty serious thing to say," Sloane said.

"Perhaps, but I think twenty-five years of practice and ten years of marriage qualify me to make that diagnosis. My ex-wife hates to lose . . . at anything. That's an admirable quality for an attorney but not necessarily conducive to a healthy marriage. Everything became a competition to Barclay and everyone either a rival or a pawn, including me — and Carly, for that matter. When we disagreed on anything, mostly how to raise our daughter, she couldn't compromise."

"You said she ruined your relationship with Carly?"

"She poisoned her against me." Oberman seemed reluctant to continue. "For the longest time, I blamed myself for being weak, but I've come to realize there was no reasoning with her."

"I'm not following. I'm sorry."

"That's because I'm trying to condense two years of hell into a single sentence. That's how long it took her to destroy me — two years. I found out that the house I thought we had purchased together was in her name only, as were nearly all of what I understood to be mutual investments. I hadn't paid much attention to any of that. Since it was her professional forte, I was happy to leave it in her domain. My attorney said that given the manner in which the accounts were set up — including the prenuptial agreement stating that all of our finances would remain separate property, a document I don't ever recall seeing or signing but which had my signature — I would have a very difficult time even arguing that the investments or real estate were community property. He also indicated that, while he could not prove it, it seemed that a significant amount of our accumulated wealth was nowhere to be found. I barely had enough to rent an apartment, but when you're going through a divorce, you just want it done. I always figured I had my practice to sustain me."

Oberman swiveled his chair to reach a glass of water on the edge of his desk. "I wasn't happy to be fleeced, mind you, but money was never a huge concern of mine." He drank the water and put the glass back on the desk. "I turned my attention to my daughter. When I sought joint custody of Carly, I learned that Barclay had hired a private investigator to follow me. One of my clients, Mr. Sloane, was a transvestite with suicidal tendencies. I had talked him out of killing himself on several occasions, and since the call service at the time was under a legal obligation to call us at home when such circumstances presented themselves, Barclay was aware of this particular patient. She hired a private investigator and this man photographed me in the parking lot of a known homosexual establishment when I responded to a telephone call that my patient was contemplating mixing his next drink with a dozen sleeping pills. If the implications were not clear enough, her attorney presented me with a signed affidavit from the patient that we had been engaged in an affair. My license was suspended pending a very expensive investigation and inquiry that cost me a fortune in legal bills. I ultimately prevailed when the patient failed to appear at the hearing."

Oberman's nostrils expanded. Sloane could hear the intake and outtake of air. "Seeking a truce, I asked Barclay to meet me one evening for a private conversation. No lawyers. No investigators. Just the two of us having a civil conversation. Perhaps I am an optimist — or an idiot. Perhaps I underestimated the extent of her disorders . . . I don't know. But she agreed. We had a civil discussion. Later that evening, two police officers arrived at my apartment and fitted me with a pair of handcuffs."

"What for?" Sloane asked, though he already knew the answer. He had obtained a copy of the file from the police.

"Domestic violence. I told them it was preposterous but I spent the night in jail anyway. The next day, at my arraignment, I was astonished when she walked in with her eye swollen shut, lip split, abrasions along her cheek."

"You're suggesting what, that she did it to herself?"

"I wouldn't know. All I know is that I did not strike her. Nor have I ever struck a woman. You're a lawyer. You know the drill. I spent sixty days in jail and was ordered to undergo a psychiatric evaluation and to enter anger-management classes as part of my five-year probation. A restraining order prohibited me from having any contact with Barclay or my daughter. Of course, all of this made the newspapers, which was the further ruination of my professional practice."

Oberman tilted his head and lifted his palms in the air. "As I said, the woman hates to lose."

Outside the building Sloane watched in his rearview mirror as Oberman drove off. He didn't know what to think. He had read the divorce file and the domestic-violence report, and Barclay had told him that Oberman was bitter, that he blamed her for just about every failing in his life and . . . Come on, did Oberman really expect the court to believe . . . what? That she'd let someone punch her in the face in order to bring a domestic charge against him? She'd have to be certifiable.

He thinks she is.

Yes, but Oberman is a psychiatrist and would know exactly what to say and what type of behavior to allege to support his diagnosis. Barclay had been president of the Washington Bar Association, sat on numerous legal and charitable boards, and remained the managing partner of a successful law firm. And, Sloane had spent 24/7 with the woman for three months and not seen any of the behavior Oberman said made her a closet Ted Bundy.

Sloane was no psychiatrist, but after meeting Oberman and witnessing his mood swings, he thought it Oberman who needed psychiatric help. The man had a persecution complex and appeared obsessive and emotionally troubled when it came to anything regarding his ex-wife. He concluded it wasn't Barclay who hated to lose, it was Oberman, and what he had lost, and clearly had still not come to grips with, was Barclay. Sloane wondered if the loss of Carly had set Oberman off again, bringing with it the intense feelings of abandonment that he had projected on Barclay ten years earlier, whether that could be the motivation for the man to go to such extremes to hurt her now. Whatever the answer, Sloane no longer questioned why Barclay had installed a security system at her home.

NINETEEN

Capitol Hill
Seattle, Washington

Judge Myron Kozlowski waited until the metal security gate to his building's underground garage clattered closed before turning off the car engine. The headlights reflecting off the cement wall extinguished, and he sat in a yellow-tinted light. Winter darkness came just after four in the evening, and the lights in the cement bunker of his apartment building were not what they should be, though better after his complaint. A complaint from a federal district court judge tended to provoke the building owner to action.

Kozlowski exited and squeezed between his car and the one in the adjacent stall, stopping at the rear bumper to assess his surroundings. Seeing no one, he walked to the elevator lobby, ran his passkey over the sensor pad, and pulled open the door.

He would have preferred a secure building with a guard at the front desk, but you got what you paid for in life, and since he continued to pay for his ex-wife to live in the luxury that he had afforded her when they were married, this was going to be it for a while. His choices had been further limited because of Berta.

As soon as he inserted the key in the deadbolt of his apartment, Berta begin her routine, barking and panting, paws digging at the carpet. When he opened the door, her black nose inched through the crack, sniffing, but it wasn't until he stepped in that the real histrionics began.

"Back up now, Berta. Back up," he said. "Be a good girl."

His wife had kept Gertie, Berta's companion, mostly out of spite. She didn't much care for the animals, but it was another way to hurt him, and the woman's vengeance seemingly knew no bounds. She would make him pay dearly for his tryst with his former legal secretary, and if that meant splitting up Berta and Gertie, two white standard poodles, well, that was just more guilt on his conscience.

Berta circled the center of the room as if chasing an imaginary tail, whining and whimpering. She would not stop until he took her out, and who could blame her after being kept up inside for nearly twelve hours.

"Give me a chance to get changed." She followed him into his room and found her chew toy — a large rubber bone — shaking her head back and forth. Kozlowski draped his tie over the tie rack in the closet and hung up his suit jacket. He smelled the armpits of his shirt and examined the collar before placing it on a hanger rather than depositing it in the dry-clean pile. He could stretch another day out of it. He exchanged the suit pants for a pair of sweats, pulled on his fleece and a pair of tennis shoes, and made his way to the door, where he slipped on his heavy winter coat and gloves and took the leash off the peg. By now Berta's entire back end was swinging from side to side like a streetwalker's. It was all he could do to get her to stand still long enough to clip the leash to the metal ring on her collar.

"All right, girl. Come on, now."

Outside, he turned left, taking their normal route east on Thomas Street to Fifteenth Avenue. Just over a mile and a half, the walk satisfied both Berta and him. Turning right on Roy, he began to weave his way back west. Berta found her usual spot just past the cherry tree and stopped to do her business. Kozlowski waited, his breath white puffs. When Berta had finished, he reached into his pockets to retrieve the plastic newspaper bag he brought each day for this occasion and realized he had, in his haste, forgotten to grab it off the kitchen counter. About to look around to determine whether he and Berta might sneak off without cleaning up her mess, he felt the presence of someone approaching from behind.

"Good evening, Judge. It is nice evening for walk, no?"

Queen Anne Hill
Seattle, Washington

Sloane had intended to return to the office to prepare his jury voir dire questions, but Barclay had called and asked that he meet her at her home. He heard a sense of urgency and vulnerability that was unlike her. He picked up Italian food from Maggiano's in the Lincoln Center before crossing the I-90 bridge and fighting the traffic on I-5 North.

When he arrived, she opened the door with an apology. "I'm sorry," she said. "I think with everything coming to a head, I had an anxiety attack. I went for a run, and I feel better."

He held her close. "You don't have anything to be sorry for. I'm glad you told me."

Just as quickly, she regained her confidence. "I'll be all right."

"It's okay if you're not, you know."

She sighed and nodded.

"Are you hungry?" he asked.

In the kitchen, she put plates and silverware on the counter as he removed the lids from tinfoil pans. "I hope it's still hot."

Conversation at dinner was limited. Barclay seemed lost in thought and, perhaps knowing what it was like for a trial attorney on the eve of any trial, let alone a murder trial, she let him alone with his thoughts. People complained that attorneys overbilled them, but anyone who had practiced law, or lived with someone who did, knew that, when in trial, good lawyers could bill every waking moment of the day and a few hours during the night when they awoke to make notes or because they could not get the next day's cross-examination questions out of their head.

Reid stood. "I have something for you." She left the room and returned with one hand behind her back. "Close your eyes and hold out your hand."

When he opened his eyes, she had placed a gift-wrapped box about three inches wide and eight inches long in his hand.

Sloane weighed it. "Well, I don't think it's that new Ferrari I've been eyeing. Maybe the key?"

She punched his arm. "Open it."

He slipped off the bow and undid the wrapping, revealing a gold-leafed box. He slid the top off. "Oh my." He looked up at her, then back at the watch, a silver and black Rolex.

She smiled. "Do you like it?"

"I don't know what to say."

"Read the back."

Sloane removed the watch and turned it over.

All my love,
Barclay

"I thought you could wear it at trial . . . sort of a good-luck charm."

He remained dumbstruck.

"Try it on," she said. She helped fasten it to his wrist. "When you look at it, you can think of me and know I'm always with you."

"You didn't have to do this," he said. "You're already always with me."

They made love on the rug in the living room. Afterward, Reid's head rested on Sloane's chest until he could not put off any longer the realities of starting a trial in twelve hours.

"Okay," he said. "Time for this cowboy to get some work done."

"Maybe I shouldn't have bought you that watch," she said, getting up.

Sloane stood. "It's beautiful, but it won't tell me much about the jurors."

She walked into the kitchen. "I'll make some tea."

They had not spoken about his conversation with Felix Oberman, and, sensing that it had been the source of her earlier anxiety, Sloane decided to get it out in the open. "Do you want to know about my conversation with your ex-husband?"

She pulled the box of tea from the cabinet and turned and looked at him, stone-faced. "Let's see. Did he tell you how I set him up with his transvestite patient? Or about how I ran my face into a wall repeatedly to accuse him of beating me up?"

Sloane nodded. "Both."

"And how I poisoned our daughter against him?"

"That too."

Her voice became more satiric. "Let's see . . . oh, yes, he likes to tell people that I'm a sociopath. Did he tell you that as well?"

"Yes, he did."

"And?"

"And I think he has some deep-seated emotional problems."

She exhaled, and with it went the hostility. She took the teakettle and filled it at the sink. "I don't know what was more ridiculous, that I would set him up with one of his patients or that I would repeatedly bang my face against the wall."

"I'd say they're about equal on the ridiculous scale," Sloane said, trying unsuccessfully to lighten her mood.

"He's an intellectual bully." She put the kettle on the stove. "But don't underestimate him. He's very bright . . . brilliant, in fact. That's what initially attracted me. He was more refined and interesting than the idiots I'd meet in the bars or who would hit on me in depositions. He was interested in what I had to say, my opinions on things. And he seemed gentle, kind."

Sloane didn't stop her. He'd need everything he could get to cross-examine Oberman.

She walked back into the living room. "I knew he drank, but I didn't know how much. It turned out to be vodka, and a lot of it. He was very good at hiding it, which made it even more difficult to detect. I also began to suspect that he was gay, or at least bisexual. Our sex life became virtually non-existent, and if I confronted him, he blamed my career, said I was never home, that I was 'wed to the law' and always too tired. I *was* wed to the law. I had no choice. I had no husband."

He let her go on, sensing it to also be cathartic.

"I began to realize that I had been something to further his career. When we met, he was on the University of Washington faculty. He wanted to be chief of the psychiatry department. He sat on national boards. He needed the appearance of stability and normalcy, and he needed my income. Whenever I confronted him on things like where he'd been or how much he'd drunk, he would bully me, tell me I didn't know what I was talking about, then he'd begin to play intellectual chess games with me, turn it around, say I was the one with the problems. I discovered large cash withdrawals, and so I began to hide income from him, to protect me and Carly."

She walked back into the kitchen and pulled mugs and the sugar bowl from the cabinet.

Sloane followed, leaning against the counter. "He said he filed for divorce."

"Of course he did." She shrugged. "I threw him out, and he saw the writing on the wall. After dozens of phone calls, he realized I wasn't going to capitulate. It infuriated him. So he went on the offensive and filed for divorce. He thought he was going to get a huge chunk of money." She pulled open the refrigerator in search of the cream. "Then he began a systematic campaign to prove I was unfit to be a mother. He knew exactly what symptoms and behavior to tell the attorneys and the child-custody evaluators to convince them I was mentally unstable." She closed the door. "Did I fight back? Did I hire a private investigator? You bet I did. Wouldn't you? Wouldn't you when the well-being of your child is at stake?"

Sloane thought of his fight with Tina's parents in the battle for custody over Jake after her death. He had fought back, and he had been willing to do just about anything for Jake, including giving custody to his biological father so as not to hurt him further.

"Leenie was everything to me. I wasn't going to give her to a man who drank and had shown little interest in actually being a father. Did I set him up?" She frowned. "Please. He set himself up. He was having a relationship with one of his patients. I had to get tested for venereal diseases. Do you know . . ." She shook her head. The emotions finally caught up with her. She pinched tea into a strainer, but tears leaked down her cheeks. "It was humiliating."

"I'm sorry you're going through this again." He held her. "But this is not all bad, you know. It shows a bias. It creates serious doubt as to his credibility."

"It's a part of my life I had hoped was behind me forever. To have it come back now, and in a public arena, is just . . . It brings back a lot of bad memories. I want to move forward."

"You will," he said, knowing whether she actually would or not was squarely in his hands.

Capitol Hill
Seattle, Washington

Kozlowski flinched, heart hammering in his chest. He recognized the accent but not the voice. A large dark-skinned man stood with his hands thrust in the pockets of a black leather car coat, the collar turned up, a black knit hat pulled low on his forehead.

"Who are you?" Kozlowski felt out of breath from the cold and the adrenaline rush.

"Just a man who enjoys a nice evening."

"How do you know me?"

The man pointed to Berta. "I think your dog is finished."

Berta tugged on the leash, ready to move on. The man reached inside his coat, and it caused Kozlowski to take a precautionary step backward. The man removed several plastic bags, the kind used for groceries at the local supermarkets. "You look to be in need of assistance."

Kozlowski hesitated, but when the man shook the bag, he took it and slowly stooped to clean up Berta's mess.

The man sighed, his breath marking the cold air. "Such is life, Judge, is it not, that we are always cleaning up someone else's shit."

Kozlowski wound the top of the bag into a knot. "What is it you want?"

"Just to walk." The man pointed at Berta. "Is never good to keep a woman waiting, no? Especially one who is kept inside so many hours a day."

Kozlowski felt his stomach grip. He looked about, hoping to see . . . whom? What could he do? Cry out for help? Even if a police officer appeared at that very moment, as in some predictable movie scene, what would he say? No. He'd built this pile of shit. No one else could clean it up.

He walked west on Aloha. Ordinarily, he turned on Federal, but Broadway, one block farther to the west, was a much busier street and likely to have more foot traffic. If the man meant him harm, the presence of others might dissuade him. But the man stopped at the corner of Aloha and Federal. "Is this not your normal way, Judge?"

Resigned, Kozlowski turned. "Why don't you tell me what it is you think you want?"

The man smiled. "I think I want your help."

"I can't help you."

"Don't be so quick to decide. I want only as you helped Vladimir Kurkov, Ivan Alekseev, and of course, Filyp, God rest his soul."

Kozlowski felt a wave of panic. "I don't know what you're talking about."

The man stopped. Though Kozlowski stood three inches over six feet, he had to look up at him. "I will call on you again, Judge. And when I do, you will help — or it will be much more than your dog's shit that you are cleaning up."

He stepped from the curb into the street and disappeared around the corner.

Sloane slid from the bed, careful not to wake her, slipped on a robe, and went back downstairs, where he had left his briefcase. He turned on the light over the dining room table and pulled out his notes for his voir dire — questions he would ask the jurors to try to determine their predispositions, anything from what they read to how they felt about certain topics in the news. He had always been able to sense each juror's predilections, never felt the need for help, but this time he had hired a jury consultant and spent several hours with her earlier in the week, going over possible lines of inquiry. It would be dicey. If he asked questions concerning people taking matters into their own hands, it could very well leave the impression that Barclay had done just that. But since that was exactly the seed Cerrabone would attempt to plant in their minds, Sloane needed to know how strongly they felt about the subject. Their feelings on Carly's drug use were also significant. Many in the general public would have little sympathy for a heroin addict. It wasn't as if she'd been hit by a drunk driver.

Feeling overwhelmed and in need of fresh air, he unlocked the glass door and slid it open. When he did, it triggered the alarm, a persistent beep. He rushed across the room to the control panel at the right of the front door, but it took him a moment to enter the corresponding numbers for the letters LEENIE. When he had, the alarm silenced.

Barclay made her way down the stairs, slipping on her robe. "Is everything okay?"

The telephone rang. She moved to the alcove near the kitchen and answered it. "The password is Leenie. This is the owner, Barclay Reid. Thank you for calling."

She walked back into the living room.

"Sorry," he said. "I got up to do some work and felt the need for some fresh air. I forgot about the alarm."

"Are you all right?" He didn't know what to say.

"David?"

"I can't guarantee you I'm going to win."

She took his hand. "Come back to bed," she said. "You're ready. You know you are. Just trust your ability. I've seen it. I know what you can do."

TWENTY

Judge Reuben Underwood proved a man of his word. Sloane had been in trials where the jury selection slogged on for days. Not this trial. Despite the large number of people automatically disqualified because they claimed to have read newspaper accounts or seen television reports on Barclay Reid's arrest — some lying to avoid their civic duty — by the end of the day they had more or less selected a pool of fourteen jurors. Twelve would decide Barclay's fate, with two alternates, though which two would not be determined until a random draw just before Underwood sent them to deliberate. The procedure prevented any claim that the alternates had paid less attention to the evidence than the selected twelve.

Underwood's efficiency was the proverbial good news and bad news for Sloane — the bad news being the Bekins boxes of documents the state had dumped, as promised, at Sloane's office that morning. Because Pendergrass would try the case with Sloane, he had been in the courtroom during the jury selection. That meant they would have to go through the documents at night, while trying to otherwise prepare for trial. Sloane could have objected and sought a continuance, but he sensed Underwood had been the type of attorney who never sought an indulgence from the court or from opposing counsel and hadn't changed his demeanor — or his view of attorneys who did — since winning election to the bench. Trials were a bitch. Suck it up and deal with it. Sloane would lose points even for asking.

So Sloane was not exactly eager when Jenkins came into the war room early that evening and told him they needed to take a drive. But when Jenkins used the word "need," he meant it, and Sloane didn't argue. Jenkins had been out late most nights and then again early mornings, watching Kozlowski.

"Go," Barclay said to him. "I can go through the documents; I know them better than anyone, anyway."

Inside Jenkins's Buick, Sloane asked, "How can you be sure? You've been following him for weeks. Why tonight?"

Jenkins adjusted one of the vents as the heat kicked in. Sloane felt it flutter his suit pants and warm his shins. "Let's just say I think the judge has a little more motivation tonight than in the past."

"Do I want to ask how you know that?"

"Nope."

Sloane looked around the neighborhood. "I thought he lived in an apartment on Thomas."

"He does. But tonight he's on the move, and he didn't even give his poor dog a chance to relieve herself. I hope she leaves him a present on his pillow." Jenkins inserted the earpiece that had been dangling over the back of his ear. "You have a bead on our pigeon?"

"Alex?" Sloane asked.

Jenkins raised a hand to silence him, listened a moment longer, then said, "On our way. Let me know if he moves."

"She's following the judge?"

"She's not following him. He's landed. She's watching him. And apparently, he's not alone."

"Why is *she* watching him?"

"Because he might recognize me."

Sloane started to ask why, then decided against it. "I don't want to know," he said.

Fuel Coffee
Capitol Hill

Julio Cruz took a seat at a table near the window and had only begun to sip his coffee when he saw the champagne-colored Lexus attempt to parallel-park across the street. That Judge Myron Kozlowski had driven the four blocks from his apartment rather than walk the poodle was a further indication something had him spooked, though the judge would not discuss what when he had called Cruz, sounding panicked, and asked for a meeting. Cruz had heard the sound of city traffic, indicating that the judge had left his office to make the call on his cell. Familiar with the area from his prior visits, Cruz suggested the small coffee shop close to the judge's apartment. The windows faced the tree-lined street, allowing Cruz to keep an eye on who else might be around.

The decor was coffee brown — the floor, walls, ceiling. Newspapers lay scattered about, mostly the weekly papers with advertising in the back for "massages" and other paid services. Books flopped to the side on a shelf along one wall, and the tables and

365

chairs, a hodgepodge mix, looked like somebody had picked them up individually at a flea market. Together, they gave the place that grunge feel Cruz had read about Seattle. But the coffee was strong, and the burnt-bitter smell of roasted coffee beans reminded him of warmer climates. Cruz thought it was bad enough that Seattle got rain in the summer, but the cold was killing him. Cold in Miami meant putting on a T-shirt. Tonight he had left his hotel dressed like he was going skiing, wearing a knit hat, gloves, and a thick jacket, all of which rested on the chair beside him, not to mention the waterproof boots and long johns beneath his blue jeans and flannel shirt. He looked like a freaking lumberjack.

Kozlowski finally parked the car on his third attempt, though the back end still stuck out farther from the sidewalk than the front. As he walked across the street, he caught sight of Cruz in the window and quickened his pace, gaze so fixed that he nearly T-boned the woman walking down the sidewalk. She paused, apparently realizing the judge was not about to slow his pace, and allowed him to enter in front of her. The man had to be seriously spooked to not notice a creature like her. With flowing black hair, a navy blue peacoat, and blue jeans sprayed over legs that could wrap around a man's head twice, she would have been something special even in Miami, which specialized in gorgeous chiquitas. In Seattle she was like a winter goddess, so hot she'd melt the snow. Cruz couldn't help but stare as she followed the judge into the coffee shop and walked to the counter holding a novel in a leather-gloved hand.

Kozlowski had apparently come straight from his chambers, still wearing a suit and tie, though he had tugged the knot down and undone the top button of his shirt. The man looked sickly, more so than normal. His skin had the yellow-gray tone that reminded Cruz of his father's complexion from the chemotherapy treatments. Dark bags sagged beneath his eyes, and his shock of white hair looked as if he had recently wrung his hands through it.

Kozlowski removed his overcoat, fumbled with the scarf, and finally threw both over the back of a chair before sitting.

"Evening, Judge." Cruz turned to admire the vision with the heart-shaped butt at the counter.

Kozlowski looked quickly about the interior and leaned forward, speaking in a hushed tone. "How many times have I told you not to use my title or my name?"

His sour, acidic-smelling breath over-whelmed even the aroma of the coffee. Cruz pulled back. Pathetic, really, to see a man who wielded so much power from the bench, and seemed to relish doing so, act like a beaten dog — cowering in fear. "Relax, Judge. This place isn't exactly hopping at the moment."

"Are you responsible for Vasiliev's death?"

Cruz stroked the beginnings of the black beard he'd decided to grow for the winter, but with the itching, he was now rethinking. "Let me ask you, Judge, why would I go to so much trouble to keep Vasiliev on the street if I was intent on killing him?"

The tufts of eyebrows protruded forward. "Then who did?"

The woman took her book and an espresso to a table by the window. She gave Cruz a quick glance and a hint of a smile. She was toying with him, but it still made his heart flutter. He was not the man he had been in his youth, when the smile would have been an invitation to join her. Now it served as a warning: "You can't touch this no more, old man." Sad but true. Cruz would likely die of a heart attack before he got his pants unbuttoned.

He shifted his eyes to Kozlowski. "If you believe everything you read in the papers, it was the attorney."

Kozlowski sat back and let out a held breath. "I did what I was asked to do."

Cruz shook his head, reached inside the pocket of his jacket on the chair, and tossed an envelope on the table. The flap opened, revealing the edges of several hundred-dollar bills.

Kozlowski shoved the envelope inside his suit jacket, eyes wide.

"This is the end of it. I'm finished."

"Who says you're not?"

"The man who followed me last night?"

That got Cruz's attention. "What are you talking about? What man? Are you being paranoid, Judge?"

"If I am, I think I have a pretty good god-damn reason to be."

"Calm down. Tell me what happened."

"I was out walking Bertie. He appeared out of the dark is what happened."

"What did he say? Did he give you a name?"

Kozlowski remained irritated. "I don't think he was carrying any business cards, Julio."

"Easy, Judge, don't be casting no stones from that glass house of yours. Tell me what this man wanted?"

The judge ran a hand over his face, like

someone trying to wipe away the fatigue.

"He said he wanted me to help him — like I helped Kurkov, Alekseev, and Vasiliev."

Cruz leaned forward. "He used their names?"

"He had an accent, Russian, and he was big. Very big." Cruz thought of Chelyakov, but that was before the judge added, "And he was dark-skinned."

"He was black?"

"I couldn't tell. He was wearing a ski hat, jacket, gloves. All I could see was his face. And it was dark."

"His face was dark or it was dark out?"

"Both. He could have been Hispanic."

"But he had an accent."

"Yes, he had an accent."

Cruz didn't know any Hispanic or black Russians, and he certainly didn't know the man the judge had described. But if he used the three names, it was a problem.

Cruz stood.

"Where are you going?"

"I'll be in touch. But you might want to find another place to walk Bertie."

Charles Jenkins pressed his finger to his ear. "Speak to me." He sat up and put his hand on the key, which he had left in the ignition. His eyes remained fixed through the windshield on the front entrance to the coffee shop. "I got him."

The short man exiting the coffee shop did so in a hurry, carrying a thick ski jacket. He had a beard. "I'm assuming that's not Kozlowski," Sloane said.

Jenkins started the engine and pulled from the curb as the man got into a car and quickly headed south on Nineteenth Avenue. "Alex has Kozlowski. He's likely headed home to clean up a pile of shit on the carpet."

"Who's this guy?" Sloane asked.

Jenkins glanced at him. "You mean if I were a betting man? If I were a betting man, I'd bet this is Julio Cruz."

International District
Seattle, Washington

Following Cruz without being noticed with the man's senses likely on heightened alert would not be easy, but on a weeknight, Jenkins could use the other commuters for cover. Cruz worked his way to Madison Avenue, a major artery that traveled east to west, and turned west toward downtown. When he got there, he turned left on Second Avenue South, then made a right on Jackson Street and a few more random turns, though Jenkins thought it was to avoid pockets of traffic and not to determine if he was being followed.

When Cruz turned down an alley, Jenkins pulled the car to the curb.

"Get out. I'll circle the block. If he drives out the other side, I'll call you and let you know. If he doesn't, find out where he's going."

Sloane exited the vehicle and hurried down the alley, staying near the building walls, though it was dark, and he would not readily be seen. He found the car parked near the back entrance to a restaurant, which he deduced from stacked empty wooden crates that once held produce, and a blue garbage bin. He watched Cruz climb a wooden staircase attached to the original stucco structure. Sloane slipped into the shadows and called Jenkins on his cell as Cruz used a key to open an exterior door on the second story and disappeared inside.

When Jenkins approached, Sloane gave him the lay of the land. "The door's locked. He used a key."

"Were the lights on?" Jenkins asked, referring to light emanating from two aluminum-framed windows facing the alley.

"Yeah," Sloane said. "What do we do now?"

"We go see what's on the menu."

Jenkins led Sloane down the alley to the front entrance of the Golden Dragon restaurant. The tables were full, most everyone of Asian descent.

"I'll have to bring Alex here," Jenkins said. "It must be good."

The hostess advised them the wait would be five minutes, which Sloane thought unlikely but didn't really care. As soon as she left, Jenkins walked toward a hallway with a sign for the bathrooms and motioned for Sloane to follow. The interior staircase led to a second-floor, poorly lit, narrow hall with shabby carpet and cheap wood paneling that smelled of grease and fried food. Jenkins had his gun out, barrel pointed at the floor, as they crept forward.

Nearing the door at the end that led to the outside landing, Jenkins stopped beside an interior door and raised a hand. Sloane heard voices from inside a room. They pressed their backs against the wall. Jenkins gripped the door handle and turned it, giving a nod to Sloane to convey that the door was not locked. With a second nod he pushed open the door and entered.

Two men stood near a large desk. A third man sat in a chair behind it. He gripped the chair arms as if he might try to stand.

"Uh-uh, partner. Everyone remain calm," Jenkins said. He stepped farther into the room. Sloane followed, about to speak, when a voice also came from behind.

"It would be wise for you to take the same advice."

In his peripheral vision, Sloane saw a gunmetal-gray barrel pointed at Jenkins's head. Then Sloane heard a second voice, this one familiar and without any accent. "Same for you, big fella."

The man seated behind the desk spoke first. "We're federal agents."

"And we're Seattle police officers," Rowe said.

"I'm a licensed private investigator," Jenkins added.

"Well, if we're playing Texas Hold'em, I fold. I'm just an attorney," Sloane said. That brought a glimmer of a smile to the barrel-chested man behind the desk. He had broad shoulders and a snow-white goatee.

Rowe said, "I want everyone to lower their guns and let them fall to the floor, then we'll all step into the room and sort this out."

Sloane heard three thuds. As they stepped farther into the room, Detective Crosswhite moved in and stood over the guns, her own gun still in her hand.

"Let's start with you," Rowe said to the man behind the desk. He identified himself as Micheal Hurley and said he worked for the DE A. He then identified the Latino man as Julio Cruz, one of his agents, and the second man, with reddish hair, as Jerry Willins, another agent.

"And who are you, big boy?" Rowe directed the question to the man who had held a gun to the back of Jenkins's head. His bald pate nearly skimmed the ceiling tiles and might have scraped the protruding sprinkler heads if he wasn't careful. Standing in front of the window, he blocked the artificial light from the street lamp.

"Sunyat Chelyakov."

"And what's your role in what we're all doing here?" Rowe asked.

"He works for me," Hurley said.

"And what exactly do you do, Mr. Hurley?"

Hurley stroked his goatee. "I'm afraid I can't tell you that. But if you call the number I'm about to provide, you will have enough information to convince you that you need to walk out of here."

"Then I don't think I want that number," Rowe said.

Sloane was developing a liking for Rowe. "Mr. Hurley runs an organization called

375

Centac."

Hurley looked at Sloane with unrevealing coal-black eyes, but Cruz was not as good a poker player. When his eyes shifted to Hurley, Sloane knew Alex had been right on track. "You had Vasiliev under surveillance. That's why Judge Kozlowski let him out of jail. You put Vasiliev back on the street so you could continue the surveillance. Am I close?"

Rowe looked to Sloane. "What are you talking about?"

Sloane laid out Centac's role in fighting the war on drugs, as Alex had previously advised. "From what I can piece together, Centac has been after Petyr Sakorov for decades. So I'm guessing that the shipment of heroin to Vasiliev was part of an elaborate undercover operation that Mr. Chelyakov here arranged." He looked at Hurley. "Chime in whenever you want."

Hurley's face remained a blank mask. "But when the police officer doing a routine traffic stop stumbled onto the shipment in the tires, it put a huge wrinkle in the operation. The local DEA and the U.S. attorney's office — neither of which knows anything about the resurrection of Centac — got involved. Vasiliev was looking at significant time, and Centac would have lost its best lead to Sakorov in decades. So you went to Kozlowski." Sloane looked to Rowe. "But I don't have to tell you that part, because you wouldn't be here unless you also spoke to Scott Parker and he told you the same thing he told me about knowing how Vasiliev and the others were beating the charges. You figured out Kozlowski was the unifying factor and you've had the judge under surveillance."

Rowe nodded to Cruz. "Tell me how your fingerprint got on Vasiliev's sliding-glass door?"

Cruz looked to Hurley. This time he nodded his consent.

Wednesday, September 7, 2011
Union Bay
Seattle, Washington

Jerry Willins set the headphones on the polished walnut table and rubbed his ears, inflamed and sore despite the cushioned padding. Standing, he stretched and rotated at the waist, hearing his vertebrae pop like a string of firecrackers as he took in the view out the rain-spotted windows. The storm had made the night ink-black, no hint of stars or moon.

The light from the sliding-glass door at the back of the house — no bigger than a postage stamp from where they had anchored the boat — stood out like a lighthouse beacon.

"It must be nice." Julio Cruz exited the bathroom zipping his fly. "The fixtures in there are nicer than my home."

When Willins learned he and Cruz would be conducting surveillance from a seventy-two-foot Northwest Trawler, his mind had conjured up the image of a hollow metal fishing drum with the two of them freezing in the hull like two large salmon. Thank God he'd been wrong. The mahogany paneling, leather upholstery, and incandescent lights made the boat far more yacht than trawler.

"Might as well be your home," Willins said, "the amount of time you spend in there."

"What, are you timing my bowel movements now?"

"Make sure the door latches; the chemical smell is like sitting in the back row of an airplane."

Cruz pushed shut the door until it clicked, then pointed to the earphones on the table. "What's our boy doing?"

Willins held one of the earpieces near his ear and looked to the shore. Even at this distance, without the binoculars, he could see the flickering colors of the flat-screen TV mounted on the wall. "Still watching the hockey game."

"Who plays hockey in September, anyway?"

"It's Detroit and Pittsburgh, from the Stanley Cup a few years back. He must have recorded it. Go do a visual from up top."

The rain continued to beat on the upper deck. "Screw that. What's with the rain? It's summer, man."

"It's Seattle. It rains nine months of the year here."

"Yeah, and I thought this was supposed to be one of the months it didn't rain. Good thing we're in a boat, or I'd be building one." Cruz walked to the fridge and pulled out a soda, popping the lid. "In Miami we'd be out dancing in the streets."

"And sweating in one hundred percent humidity."

"Maybe so, but that means the chiquitas would be sweating, too, and the more they sweat, the less they wear." Cruz held up the can and swayed as if to some silent samba music.

"Like they'd want your sorry old butt."

Cruz walked to the window and looked in the direction of the light from the house.

"Who won?"

"Won what?"

"The Stanley Cup. Who won?"

At close to three in the morning, after a week together, they were running out of things to talk about. "I don't know. Pittsburgh, I think. You follow hockey in Florida?"

"I wouldn't know which end of the hockey stick to hit the puck with." Cruz drank in gulps, then crushed the can. "Could be worse, right?"

"How's that?"

"Our boy could be watching another porno."

"Thank God for small favors." Willins eased the headphones back on.

"Maybe he'll go to bed before the sun comes up."

Willins pulled one of the earphones away. "What's that?"

"Nothing. I just said maybe he'll go to bed —"

Willins put up a hand. "No. I mean, did you hear that?"

"Hear what?"

He set the padding back to his ear. Then pulled it away, head cocked. "You didn't hear anything?"

"Like what?"

"Thunder. Did you just hear thunder?"

"I didn't hear nothing, man. I think you been on this boat too —"

Willins grabbed a pair of binoculars hanging by the strap from a dowel on the wall as he hurried up the staircase to the deck.

"Man's going crazy . . . hearing things now." Cruz picked up the headset and pressed it to his ear. "I don't hear anything," he said before following Willins up the stairs.

Willins stood under the cover of the overhead deck, binoculars aimed at the shore, thigh pressed against the railing to keep his balance. The boat pitched and rolled. Cruz joined him at the railing, talking over the storm. "What did you hear?"

"A bang, like thunder." Willins shook the water dripping from his forehead and adjusted the focus. "I don't see him."

Cruz looked to the shore, the rain hitting him in the face. "Maybe God answered our prayers and he went to bed."

"He left the TV on. He's never left the TV on."

"So he got up to get another drink or take a leak."

"I don't — Oh no."

"What?"

Willins shoved the binoculars at Cruz and hurried to the back of the boat. Cruz grabbed the strap just before the binoculars fell over the railing into the water. He pressed the lenses to his eyes, shouting over the rain. "What am I looking for?"

Willins manually cranked the winch to lift the Zodiac from its spot at the end of the boat and swung it over the water. "Just to the right of the sofa. The floor."

Cruz adjusted his focus. "Oh, shit."

He dropped the binoculars on the deck and rushed to help position the Zodiac as Willins lowered it into the water, then held the boat until Willins had climbed in and started the engine. Jumping in, he disengaged the winch and Willins hit the gas hard. The rubber boat bounced and skimmed across the whitecaps, the rain and foam from the waves spraying them. As they approached the shore, Willins cut the engine and let their momentum and the waves propel them to the strip of sand at the rock wall. Cruz jumped out into ankle-deep water with the nylon rope, stepped onto the sandy strip, lifted himself up the four-foot-high wall, and tied the rope through an eye hook cemented in the mortar. Willins didn't wait, abandoning the boat and rushing up the sloped lawn, feet slipping in the wet grass. He slowed as he neared the concrete patio, realizing in his haste that he had not brought his firearm. Cruz caught up to him, also unarmed. Together they crept toward the sliding door, their eyes scanning the yard, both men wiping away the water, Willins having to take off his glasses.

Blood splattered the inside of the glass door, and tendrils spread like a spiderweb from a concave hole. Their target remained on the sofa but had pitched forward and to the right, head slumped on the sofa arm. Blood leaked down the leather, pooling on the hardwood where the Persian throw rug did not reach.

Willins heard another sound, turned, and took two steps toward the water, shielding his eyes.

"What is it?" Cruz asked.

"I thought I heard something."

Cruz slapped the side of his head like a swimmer trying to knock water free. "Man, I haven't heard shit all night; I'm going to get my damn hearing checked."

Willins took two more steps toward the water, Cruz at his side. Then he turned and looked again at the sliding-glass door.

"What do we do now?" Cruz asked.

Willins no longer bothered to shield his face or wipe away the water. They were all getting too old — and running out of time.

TWENTY-ONE

Wednesday, November 30, 2011
King County Courthouse
Judge Reuben Underwood's Chambers

The discussion in Judge Reuben Underwood's chambers the following morning sounded like a family feud — each participant with his own agenda, talking over one another, offering counterarguments to arguments and shouting soliloquies until the court reporter threw up his hands in frustration and disgust. Underwood put an end to it with a raised hand and voice. He dismissed the court reporter; then, already perturbed that he had impaneled a jury and realized there was no way in hell they were going to start promptly at nine, he scowled, silently fuming.

Micheal Hurley sat on the leather sofa between two attorneys from the Justice Department. The fact that the two suits had managed to fly across the country from

Washington, D.C. for an early-morning meeting impressed upon Sloane what Hurley had said. People in power had his back. The two suits had informed them that neither Willins nor Cruz nor Hurley, for that matter, could be compelled to testify in a public forum.

"We can't allow that, Judge. And we have a court order signed by a federal district court judge of the District of Columbia as well as a letter from the United States attorney. It would jeopardize an ongoing investigation, not to mention endanger the lives of well-placed informants."

Cerrabone countered that he either wanted the court to compel Cruz or Willins to testify, or he wanted an order that no one be allowed to make any reference to their footprints or to Cruz's fingerprint.

"It's irrelevant, Your Honor. We now know it has nothing to do with who shot Mr. Vasiliev. It will greatly prejudice the state if it is introduced without explanation, and it will confuse the jury."

Sloane, just as adamant that the evidence be allowed, interrupted the argument with his own. "The state was prepared to go forward when they had no idea who'd made the footprints or how Mr. Cruz's fingerprint ended up on the slider," he said. "For them to now argue prejudice because they can't explain something for which they had no explanation in the first place is ridiculous."

But Sloane knew he was treading water. Now that they could identify the two people responsible for the shoe prints, and they were not the assassins he had hoped for, there was no way Underwood would allow him to imply that to be the case to the jury. Having deduced this, he had already mentally moved to plan B, which was to try to at least be allowed to argue that federal officers were keeping Vasiliev under twenty-four-hour surveillance.

"What inferences the jury draws from that is fair game," he said. What he was hoping, of course, was the jury would infer other potential reasons Vasiliev had been shot, such as someone within Vasiliev's organization having learned of the surveillance and had decided it was time for Vasiliev to go. It was thin, Sloane knew, and Underwood didn't look to be buying it, though at the moment the judge didn't appear to be buying anything. He brooded behind his desk, glasses off, elbows propped on the calendar pad, hands clasped beneath his nostrils. His eyes shot daggers at everyone in the room.

The debate continued until Underwood put an end to it a second time and called for his court reporter to reenter. The red-haired man took his seat, hands on the stenographer's machine.

"Here's what we're going to do," Underwood said. "First of all, the fact that a federal district court judge may or may not be guilty of serious misconduct is not relevant to the case I have before me . . . which we were supposed to begin this morning." He did not try to conceal his irritation. "There will be no mention of Judge Kozlowski or what he did or did not do in this proceeding. That will be a matter for the Justice Department, I presume, at some later date. As for the presence of the other two sets of footprints, Mr. Cruz will testify."

One of the suits began to object, but Underwood cut him off with a glare and a raised hand. "He will testify in chambers and outside the presence of the jury. His testimony will be solicited by one of you gentlemen, and Mr. Cerrabone and Mr. Sloane, you will be free to ask whatever questions you desire. The testimony will thereafter be sealed and not made a part of the official court record, but it will be available to any appellate tribunal should that become necessary to substantiate my ruling, which is as follows: there is to be no mention of these second and third sets of shoe prints. That being the case, I don't see how I can allow introduction of the presence of Mr. Cruz's fingerprint on the sliding-glass door. Based upon what I have heard this morning, and the testimony I anticipate to follow, neither the footprints not the fingerprint relate to the issue that is germane to this case — namely the guilt or innocence of Ms. Reid. Were I to allow the introduction of this evidence, the jury would certainly expect the state to explain it, and would perceive the state's inability to do so as a tacit admission of its relevance and substance. Accordingly, I find that the prejudicial impact of the evidence and the further potential that it might reasonably be expected to cause juror confusion outweighs its probative value. Mr. Cerrabone, Mr. Sloane, you are to advise your witnesses that there is to be no mention of that evidence. And it is to be stricken from any documents to be admitted and shown to the jury."

Underwood turned to Sloane. "Mr. Sloane, I am not unmindful that you must feel as if you just had the rug pulled out from beneath you. You have lost a significant piece of potentially exculpating evidence. At the same time, we now know it is not exculpating evidence, and to argue that it is, knowing that it is not, would violate your duty as an officer of the court not to mislead this tribunal. While this may require that you reshape your arguments, it does not prevent you from representing your client to the fullest extent of the law. I am also not unmindful that your client declined to waive her right to a speedy trial, and therefore, we are here in part because of that declination. Had she done so, this evidence might well have come to light before we impaneled a jury. But we are where we are, and my intent is to move forward. You would be well within your right to seek a continuance, if for no other reason than to preserve your client's rights on appeal."

In judge-speak, Underwood was advising Sloane that he could bring the motion to continue the trial, but the judge was not about to grant it. Still, Sloane would file the motion to preserve the record. Mindful of the judge's attitude toward attorneys whom he perceived to be unprepared, however, Sloane took a different tack in chambers.

"Your Honor, this is an unfortunate development, but it does not change the fact that my client is innocent of the charges being brought by the state. We have maintained and continue to maintain that the jury will find not only a reasonable doubt but a significant one. That being said, I do wish to confer with my client before advising the court of my intentions."

Sloane had put up the brave front, but inside, he knew he had suffered a tremendous blow. On the eve of his biggest trial, with the most to lose, he had lost his best chance to create a reasonable doubt.

Law Offices of David Sloane
One Union Square
Seattle, Washington

That afternoon, Sloane assembled the troops in the war room to discuss the outcome of the morning hearing and testimony. Neither Reid nor Pendergrass had been allowed into the hearing, the suits from the Justice Department wanting to limit the number of people privy to the information. Jenkins and Alex joined them at the table. Carolyn stood near the door, a spot she favored, arms crossed like a sentry.

Sloane did his best to keep from acting like the ship was sinking. It was taking on water, for certain; he couldn't hide that fact, but the job now was not to panic and jump overboard. He had no alternative explanation for who else had both the motivation and opportunity to kill Vasiliev, or who could have had access to Reid's home, left size-seven prints on the lawn, and fit the description of the person Joshua Blume claimed to have seen. It left him little choice but to go back to playing defense, attacking the state's witnesses one by one and trying to create reasonable doubt at every opportunity on cross-examination. That wasn't his first choice, but it was what it was.

"I agree with David," Reid said, remaining philosophical. "I see little value in seeking a continuance. We go forward."

"We're going to have to shift focus." Pendergrass, clearly the most forlorn, flipped through a stack of pleadings on the table. "I mean, many of our arguments are premised on the other sets of footprints and the fingerprint — our cross-examinations . . . experts . . . I don't know what we have left to argue."

"I take it neither Cruz nor Willins actually saw the killer?" Jenkins asked.

It had been the first question Sloane had asked. "No. Willins said he heard something like a splash, but with the storm, he couldn't be certain."

"Which fits the state's theory that the killer swam to and from the property," Pendergrass said.

"Doesn't matter. What Willins heard isn't coming in," Sloane said. "How much progress have we made on the documents?"

Pendergrass put down the pleadings, changing focus. "Not much. I went through another couple hundred this morning, but with all of this, I haven't made a dent. I guess the good news is that I have the rest of the day and all night to continue."

Sloane shook his head. "I need you to go through our motions and briefs and determine what we can salvage."

"I'll continue," Barclay said. "I can go through them."

"All right, then. Let's try to put this time to good use." That was as much of a pep talk as Sloane had in him. He went into his office, shutting the door. A few seconds after he did, it opened. He didn't need to turn to know who had entered.

"You okay?" she asked.

He forced a smile. "Shouldn't I be asking you that question?"

She shrugged. "What's done is done."

Sloane knew the stoicism was for his benefit. He also knew Barclay understood, perhaps better than anyone, the seriousness of the blow they had suffered.

Alex had the divorce file open on her desk, paging through it, when Jenkins entered.

"What do you know?" he asked.

"I know that I'm tired and my husband is

an insensitive boob."

"Yes, but we both already knew that." He smiled. "Sorry. How are you holding up?"

"Too late." She handed him a slip of paper. "You have a meeting at three-thirty."

"Did you speak to Rowe?"

"They work in the same building. Same floor. He said he'd be there."

The Justice Center
Seattle, Washington

Rowe met Jenkins in the lobby of the Justice Center, and they rode the elevator to the seventh floor.

"Tell me again why I'm doing this?" Rowe asked.

"You're humoring me."

"I'm a bit out of humor after last night. I'm tired."

"Have you been talking to my wife?" That got a smile. "You see, you do have some humor left."

On the seventh floor, they entered an interior office where a dark-haired man sat talking on the phone. "I got to go. They're here," he said.

Rowe made the introductions. "This is Bernie Hamilton. He runs our cold-cases unit. This is Charles Jenkins. He works for Sloane."

393

Hamilton grinned. "Knock knock."

Jenkins looked at Rowe.

"We're in a bit of a hurry, Bernie, anything?"

Hamilton flipped open a file. "Zach Bergman. Killed January twelfth, 2001."

"How did he die?" Rowe asked.

"Shot in the head," Hamilton said.

Rowe glanced at Jenkins, then back to Hamilton. "Do we know the caliber bullet?"

"A thirty-eight."

"Suicide ruled out?"

"Given that they never found the gun, and the location of the bullet was the back of his head, yeah, suicide was ruled out."

"Any suspects?"

"One, but nothing ever came of it. This case is as cold as the queen of England in bed."

Rowe turned to Jenkins. "Okay, Mr. Jenkins, you've piqued my curiosity. So tell me who this guy is — or was."

"He was a private investigator on a very acrimonious divorce."

"And do I know either of the unhappy couple?"

"Both. He worked for Barclay Reid."

Rowe turned his attention back to Hamilton. "Who was the suspect?"

"Some guy named Oberman. A doctor."

TWENTY-TWO

The media returned with a vengeance, having assembled the previous morning only to be turned away. Rumors had begun to circulate, as they do when something unusual is left unexplained. Sloane had heard everything from he and Cerrabone were discussing a plea deal, to Barclay was pregnant.

So it was no surprise that an even bigger crowd assembled on the sidewalk outside the front entrance to the Administration Building on Fourth Avenue. Sloane had known that Yamaguchi's trick, like any trick, would work only so many times before the media figured it out, and they had. They didn't recognize the car, but as soon as Jenkins eased to the curb, they figured it out quickly enough and converged.

395

"You okay?" Sloane asked Barclay.

She nodded, wearing her game face, and Sloane pushed open the door.

The cameras clicked and flashed from the moment they exited. Sloane and Pendergrass — who looked a bit shell-shocked — flanked Reid like two bodyguards as they worked through the group to the front entrance, ignoring the shouted questions.

Two sheriffs designated by Court Operations waited at the glass doors to assist them in entering the building, being processed, and running the media gauntlet that filled the underground tunnel leading to the courthouse. Men with handheld cameras perched on their shoulders and reporters with notepads followed them in lockstep. The swarm increased on the eighth floor and followed until they stepped through the double doors into the sanctity of the courtroom. Men and women sat shoulder to shoulder while two King County sheriffs directed those still seeking admittance to the room next door. To accommodate the media and public interest, Court Operations had opened the courtroom immediately adjacent to 854E and set up a television to receive a live feed of the proceedings.

Seated at the counsel table, Sloane did

not feel the sense of comfort that usually came with the familiar surroundings. As the number of cases he tried mounted, he had come to find the structure of a trial relaxing. He developed a rhythm, and he knew for that day he had just one case to concentrate on, one witness at a time. But this morning he felt like a man who had asked a woman to marry him, and now, standing at the altar, the guests assembled behind them and the minister about to appear at any minute, he was having serious second thoughts.

Perhaps sensing his unease, Barclay leaned to her left to shorten the distance. "I like the watch, counselor."

He turned his wrist to admire it and returned her whisper. "So do I."

She squeezed his hand, then allowed hers to retreat back beneath the table.

Cerrabone and Rowe had draped their suit jackets over the backs of their chairs. At the moment they were wheeling a large flat-screen television on a stand so that it would be visible to the members of the jury. Satisfied, Cerrabone continued to walk about the room like a stagehand arranging his props for the show's performance — brown paper bags sealed with blue painter's tape containing the evidence to be introduced and an easel for the series of blowups he would use. In the corner of the room, the sliding-glass door — replete with the single concave hole and the spiderweb of cracks — stood upright on a dolly. The blood on the interior of the glass had dried to a rust color.

At nine A.M. sharp, Underwood's bailiff, the attractive, dark-skinned woman of Indian descent, stepped into the courtroom with Judge Reuben Underwood hot on her heels. He ascended to the bench before she had finished her instruction for all those present to rise.

"The People of the State of Washington versus Barclay Alison Reid. Judge Reuben Underwood presiding."

"Are there any preliminary matters before we bring in the jury?" Underwood's tone clearly intended to convey "And God help the attorney who says there are." There being none, he instructed his bailiff to bring in the jury.

Trials unfold much like theater productions, with the spectators getting to see both the actors onstage with the curtain up, as well as what transpires backstage, when the jurors leave for the jury room. The eight men and six women had an inkling of the nature of the case from the questions Sloane and Cerrabone had asked during the voir dire selection. As they took their seats, picking up the spiral notepads they would use throughout the trial, several looked over at Barclay.

Underwood's face had transformed, and he sat looking like a proud father — or in the case of some youthful jurors, a grandfather — smiling down at his children. When he spoke, it was in a benevolent tone, and he wasted little time before thanking the jurors for their service. He then provided them with the basic allegations of the case they were about to hear. Finished with the stipulated statement to the jury, Underwood turned to Cerrabone. "Mr. Cerrabone, you may give your opening statement."

Cerrabone approached the jury box holding a yellow notepad. He maintained the appearance of the everyman in an off-the-rack brown suit a little too wide in the shoulders, a little too long in the cuffs, and bunched at his loafers. He put his pad on the railing beneath the bench, and it promptly slid over into the well and onto the clerk's desk, bringing nervous laughter from the jury and those seated behind them in the gallery. "Butterfingers," Cerrabone said.

Sloane wondered if the act had been purposeful.

Recovering with a shrug, Cerrabone gave a slight bow to Underwood, to Sloane, and finally, to the jury. "May it please the court, respected counsel, ladies and gentlemen of the jury, I am Rick Cerrabone, and I represent the people of the state of Washington." He paused as if to gather his thoughts. Someone coughed. "A moment ago Judge Underwood read to you a stipulated statement of the *allegations* the state has brought here today against the defendant, Barclay Reid." Cerrabone pointed and looked at Reid, as all good prosecutors were trained to do, the belief being that if the prosecutor couldn't be certain, then neither could the jurors. "The statement read to you did not contain any facts, because there are no facts before you. That's my job, to present to you the facts of this case through the evidence that I will solicit from persons seated in that chair — police officers, detectives, the medical examiner, and forensic specialists, which is a fancy term for people with expertise in certain fields such as bullets and guns."

A few jurors smiled. Cerrabone seemed to find his stride after the initial jitters. "You will find the facts to be uncomplicated, and when I am finished, I believe you will have no doubt of the charge brought here today, that Barclay Reid" — this time he moved to within inches of the front of their table — "with premeditation and forethought, shot and killed Filyp Vasiliev."

Cerrabone paused again. This time Sloane knew it was for effect.

"This is a tragedy, ladies and gentlemen," he said, which was argument and not fact, but Sloane was loath to object during another attorney's opening or closing statement. A jury could perceive an objection as Sloane trying to keep information away from them. Besides, he thought it was a good line and he could now use it himself.

"The evidence introduced will be that just over a year ago, Ms. Reid's daughter died from an accidental overdose of heroin. That is the conclusion of the county medical examiner. The medical examiner will testify that an autopsy of Carly Oberman revealed that she had ingested a lethal combination of heroin and crushed amphetamines, a concoction known on the street as 'cheese.' Now, there is no such thing as good heroin, but the heroin that Carly Oberman ingested was more pure than normal. It stopped her heart, and she died."

From his peripheral vision, Sloane noticed Reid drop her head, the first time she had done so since entering the courtroom.

"Any time a young person dies, it is a tragedy. The police arrested the man who supplied Carly Oberman those drugs, and he is incarcerated here in the King County jail, awaiting trial for his crimes. Witnesses will testify, however, that following her daughter's death, Ms. Reid became a crusader against drug dealers, and as part of that crusade, she pushed the United States attorney's office and federal agents with the Drug Enforcement Administration —"

This time Sloane stood. "Objection. Your Honor, I apologize for the interruption, but I object to the prosecutor's use of the word 'pushed' to describe a nearly yearlong investigation by the U.S. attorney's office against Mr. Vasiliev after which the U.S. attorney, not Ms. Reid, filed charges."

"Sustained. Pick a different word, Mr. Cerrabone."

Cerrabone acted nonplussed. "Ms. Reid was intimately involved in the U.S. attorney's investigation to bring charges against Mr. Vasiliev for drug trafficking, including trafficking in heroin. Witnesses will testify that Ms. Reid told them she held Mr. Vasiliev responsible for the chain of distribution that supplied the drugs that killed her daughter. Now, as I mentioned, the U.S. attorney's office brought charges against Mr. Vasiliev. However, a federal district court judge decided that certain evidence obtained in that investigation could not be admitted in court. The evidence will show that as a result of that ruling, Mr. Vasiliev, while *charged* with drug trafficking, was never convicted. What does this have to do with the case I will present to you? Let me explain.

"After Mr. Vasiliev walked out of that federal courtroom Barclay Reid would go before the television cameras and proclaim her fight was not over, that she would continue to pursue those who supply drugs that kill. You will hear her say on that tape, 'I will avenge my daughter's death.' "

Cerrabone looked to his notes, another calculated moment to let the jurors ruminate on Barclay's words.

"Witnesses will testify that Ms. Reid was upset at the outcome, and one of those witnesses, Dr. Felix Oberman, Ms. Reid's former husband, will testify that she expressed frustration with the federal case and specifically told him, 'If I had known it was going to be this much trouble, I would have put a bullet in the back of his head and been done with him.' "

Two of the female jurors sitting in the

front row and a male juror in the back row glanced at Reid.

Cerrabone continued, systematically laying out the evidence he would introduce to prove Barclay's guilt. Sloane took notes, but only a few; he'd tasked Pendergrass with that responsibility, and the young lawyer scribbled furiously as Cerrabone continued for another twenty minutes.

Using aerial blowups showing the location of Vasiliev's home on the easel, Cerrabone re-created the crime scene as Rowe encountered it. He advised that the evidence would show that Reid owned a .38-caliber Smith & Wesson handgun but could not account for the whereabouts of that gun; a ballistics expert would testify that based upon the trajectory of the bullet, it was fired by a person of a certain height range into which Barclay fell. He discussed that Reid was a triathlete and what that meant, and how it fit with the state's theory of how the crime was committed. He discussed the size-seven shoe prints and what the tracker, Kaylee Wright, would say they revealed. He left the most damaging evidence for last, advising the jury that Barclay had no alibi for the morning of the shooting, that she had told Detective Rowe she was home in bed, asleep.

Cerrabone changed the blowup on the easel. "In fact, a witness, a young man coming home after a late night with friends who lived in this house, half a mile down the street, will testify to the contrary." Cerra bone used the aerial photograph to orient the jury to the location of Vasiliev's home, the public easement, and where Joshua Blume claimed to have seen Barclay. "And what this young man will testify is that he saw the defendant, Barclay Reid, jog up this path in a dark Lycra suit and pull a bike from the bushes. Mr. Blume will testify that although it was dark, there is a nearby street lamp." Cerrabone identified it on the photograph. "And that he had enough light to identify Ms. Reid beyond any doubt."

With that pronouncement, Sloane noticed several other jurors turn their heads and glance at Barclay.

Cerrabone was as billed — workmanlike. His opening took just over forty-five minutes: efficient, with enough detail to arouse the jurors' curiosity and suspicions without boring them. He had laid out a highly plausible scenario that included a motive, a weapon, opportunity, and perhaps most important, a seemingly false alibi that would cause the jurors to immediately question what Sloane was about to stand and tell them.

As defense counsel, Sloane had the choice of making an opening statement immediately following Cerrabone's or waiting until the state had presented all of its witnesses and rested its case. Sloane didn't think that was much of a choice. He wasn't about to let the jurors sit for days and nights considering Cerrabone's words without giving them something to consider in rebuttal. Cerrabone had called Barclay a crusader, but he had implied she was actually a vigilante, an argument he would surely make in his closing argument — that citizens cannot take the law into their own hands. He would argue that the rule of law did not change simply because Filyp Vasiliev was a drug dealer; that a judicial system for the people, by the people, and of the people meant *all* the people, including low-life scumbags like Vasiliev.

Sloane approached the jurors without notes and, like Cerrabone, addressed the court and his opposing counsel. About to begin, his eyes swept across the jurors, but unlike his other trials, he could not feel them, could not assess their thoughts and predilections. They sat alert and attentive, but it felt as if an invisible pane of glass had been erected in front of them. He could see through it, but his words would not penetrate.

"This *is* a tragedy," he started. It was not how he had intended to begin, but those words came to him. "The tragedy is that a mother who has lost her only child to drugs, and who Mr. Cerrabone told you has since devoted her life to not only bringing that drug dealer to justice but to empower every citizen to bring drug dealers to justice, now sits before you accused of murder."

Cerrabone could have objected, since the statement was argument, but Sloane had used the prosecutor's words, and Cerrabone could not be heard to object without losing some credibility with the jurors.

"The evidence will prove that Filyp Vasiliev *was* a drug dealer. The investigation to which Mr. Cerrabone made mention resulted in the confiscation of ten kilos of heroin, which the DEA estimated to have a street value of between one and a half and two million dollars, drugs smuggled into this country in the tires of cars Vasiliev sold at his car dealership in Renton." Sloane paced but did not wander. "Federal agents involved in that investigation will testify that Vasiliev used couriers through a sophisticated and complicated network of employees to dispense these drugs onto the streets, then used his car businesses to launder the proceeds of the sale of those drugs. On this there should also be no dispute."

He waited as if to give Cerrabone every opportunity to challenge him, hoping the jurors would take the silence as a tacit admission.

"Those agents will explain to you, ladies and gentlemen, that the drug business is not unlike the purchase and sale of other commodities — like used cars, for instance. The buyer often purchases the drugs on credit at a wholesale price, sells them at a retail price on the street, pays his supplier, and uses the profit to reinvest in more drugs. They will tell you that when the drugs are confiscated, the seller has a problem. He has no product to sell on the street, no income, and thus no ability to pay the supplier.

"Yes, Mr. Vasiliev walked out of a federal courtroom, but those federal agents involved in the investigation will tell you Vasiliev was far from out of the woods with the people who supplied him the drugs."

At this Cerrabone stood, and rightly so. "Objection, Your Honor. Counsel is getting more into speculation and argument than fact."

Underwood, who had sat listening with his hand at his mouth, one finger pointed toward his temple, agreed. "Sustained. I will remind the jury that opening statements, any statements by the attorneys, are not evidence. They are statements of what counsel believes the evidence will show. Mr. Sloane, stick to what the evidence will show, without speculation."

Sloane simply nodded. He had crossed the line, but he had done so on purpose. He had goaded Cerrabone to object in order to make his next point, and the judge, in dressing him down, had actually aided his cause.

"Now, the prosecutor has told you his version of what he believes the facts will prove transpired. He has offered the *circumstantial evidence* he believes is sufficient beyond a reasonable doubt to convict Barclay Reid. Circumstantial evidence, ladies and gentlemen, is a bit like speculation — it requires you to make a deduction, to conclude from one piece of evidence that something else must have occurred. Circumstantial evidence is not direct evidence. Let me explain the difference. Direct evidence would be a witness who sits in that chair telling you, 'I saw Barclay Reid shoot Filyp Vasiliev.' There will be no such witness. The prosecution also will not produce a gun with Barclay Reid's fingerprints on it. The prosecution wants you to *deduce* from the *circumstantial evidence* that Barclay's gun is missing, that *she* must have used it to kill Mr. Vasiliev, then thrown it away. But there will be no direct evidence that she did this.

"Yes, the prosecution has evidence of shoe prints in Mr. Vasiliev's backyard, a size-seven women's running shoe. And from this they will ask you to deduce that, because Barclay wears the same size shoe, she must have made the shoe prints. But the prosecution will produce no witness who saw Barclay's feet in those shoes, let alone in Mr. Vasiliev's backyard." This brought a few poorly concealed smiles.

Sloane shrugged. "The best *direct* evidence the prosecution has to offer, ladies and gentlemen, is the testimony of a young man sneaking home at three-thirty in the morning, after a night partying at an underground club, who claims that on a dark and stormy night, as he hid in some bushes, he could make out the face of a person twenty-six and a half feet away." He shook his head in doubt.

"The prosecutor called Barclay a

'crusader.' That was a term used to describe her efforts to rid the streets of Seattle of drugs. She *is* a crusader." He let that statement hang, knowing again that Cerrabone would be hard-pressed to object. "She is not a vigilante. The evidence will not prove that she killed Filyp Vasiliev. What the evidence will reveal is that because of her efforts, Barclay received threats — threats that she reported to the police. The evidence will reveal that she was followed, which she also reported to the police.

"So, who did kill Mr. Vasiliev?"

Sloane had heard other attorneys in civil cases argue that the opposing side had the burden of proof and had failed to meet that burden. He had always thought that argument to be a cop out, tantamount to a kid in a playground accused of doing something wrong responding, "Prove it."

Instead, he looked at each of the jurors, gave a simple shrug, and said, "But I am confident, after you hear all of the evidence, that you will conclude it was not Barclay Reid."

They were under way.

Underwood instructed Cerrabone to call his first witness, and the prosecutor obliged, calling the county medical examiner Stuart

411

Funk. He retrieved Funk from the hall outside the courtroom. Witnesses could not sit in the proceedings until after testifying.

Funk entered looking like a slightly off high school science professor in a brownish-orange tweed jacket complete with elbow patches, a pale green shirt, and a brown tie. Tall and gangly, with thick gray hair and glasses, Funk carried a file under his arm, the pages sticking out one end. But he knew his way to the witness chair, having testified more than four hundred times. He did not remain seated for long. After soliciting Funk's considerable education and work history, as well as the inner workings of the King County medical examiner's office, Cerrabone sought Underwood's permission that Funk be permitted to testify from the area between his easel and the jury box.

Using an antenna pointer, Funk educated the jury on how he was called to Vasiliev's home, waited until CSI had completed its investigation, then proceeded to process the body, which took a little under thirty minutes. His direct examination had been well orchestrated and rehearsed offstage, Cerrabone smooth at introducing the testimony and the evidence. Funk gave Sloane few reasons to object.

As Funk testified, Cerrabone used the

television to display documents and photographs taken at the crime scene and during the autopsy. Several jurors winced at a photograph showing the back of Vasiliev's head, a portion of the skull blown away. This was the moment when reality hit, after the initial excitement and anticipation of serving as a juror in a murder trial subsided. The brutality of the wound clarified that this was not a television show and the people before them were not actors. This was real. It was a crime of violence intentionally inflicted and with the single purpose of taking another human being's life.

Funk's testimony continued for nearly two hours before Cerrabone arrived at the single reason he had come to the courtroom that day — to offer his opinion on the cause of death.

"And did you reach a conclusion of whether the death was accidental, a suicide, natural, or a homicide?" Cerrabone asked, again duty-bound.

"It was a homicide," Funk said.

Sloane had interviewed Funk prior to the trial, with Cerrabone present, and found him to be forthright. There was not much Sloane could do on cross-examination concerning the cause of death, but experience had taught him that jurors expected counsel to ask questions, especially of the first witness. So when Cerrabone passed Funk, Sloane stood and obliged.

On cross-examination, Sloane wanted to be center stage and asked Funk to return to his seat while Sloane stood directly in front of the jury.

"Dr. Funk, you have no interest in the crime scene, do you?"

"No," Funk said. "Our concern is only the condition of the body."

"And based upon your testimony and the photographs, you examined that body in great detail from head to toes to fingertips, correct?"

"That is our practice, regardless of the cause of death."

"And looking at the notes you made during your examination, you noted the presence of multiple wounds on the body, did you not?"

Funk retrieved his report from the file in his lap and flipped it open. "I did."

"Now, to be clear, these were not wounds that, in your opinion, contributed to Mr. Vasiliev's death, correct?"

"That's correct. The cause of death was the single gunshot wound to the back of the head."

"But this is not the only gunshot wound

on the body?"

Cerrabone looked like he might stand, then thought better of it and remained seated. An objection could draw more attention to a question, and a good attorney had to pick his spots, for that reason. He also likely had confidence in Funk.

"No, it is not. There is evidence of a healed gunshot wound just above the right pectoral muscle."

"Could you show this bullet wound to the jury on one of the photographs or diagrams Mr. Cerrabone used today?" Sloane walked back to his table, grabbing the stack of photographs, though he already knew the answer. When Funk did not respond, Sloane turned and waited, the jurors watching him. "Dr. Funk?"

"I don't think we showed any photographs or diagrams depicting that wound to the jury. It's not our practice —"

"I think Mr. Cerrabone already went into great detail with you concerning your practice, Dr. Funk. What I want is a photograph used by Mr. Cerrabone that depicts that wound."

"He didn't use any," Funk said.

"So I'm clear, that wound is not depicted on any of your diagrams or any of the photographs Mr. Cerrabone showed the jurors, is it?"

"No, it is not."

"Did you note any *other* wounds on the body?"

An intelligent man, Funk knew Sloane's direction. "Yes, there is a scar just below the rib cage on the left side."

"And did you reach a conclusion as to the cause of that scar?"

"It is a healed knife wound."

"And that also has not been depicted on any diagrams or in any photographs displayed for the jurors today, has it?"

"No."

"Any other wounds?"

"I found evidence of healed lacerations — multiple lacerations on the victim's forearms — as well as scarring of tissue on the knuckles of the right hand."

"Again, do you have any opinions as to what caused the lacerations?"

"They are also healed knife wounds."

"More knife wounds," Sloane said. "And the injuries to the knuckles on the right hand?"

"I can't definitively say."

"Do you have a hypothesis based on your training, education, and expertise?"

Funk adjusted his glasses. "They are consistent with the type of injuries one would associate with blows administered by fists, like a boxer, someone who used his hands to inflict blows."

"Was Mr. Vasiliev a boxer, Doctor?"

"I have no idea."

"Did your direct examination introduce any photographs or diagrams to show the jury these injuries?"

"No."

After Sloane sat, Cerrabone spent twenty minutes on redirect, but Sloane asked no further questions. He'd accomplished what he intended. He'd established that Vasiliev was a violent man who had lived a violent life and had nearly been killed before. In the process, he'd implied that the prosecutor had kept that information from the jury. It wasn't a home run, not by any means, but it was a sharp single, and on cross-examination, that was often as good as it got.

When they returned from their lunch break, Cerrabone called his next witness, Officer Darius Adderley, the first responding officer to the crime scene. A good-looking black man, Adderley entered the courtroom in full-dress blue uniform, complete with body armor beneath his shirt and a utility belt strapped about his waist containing a gun, pepper spray, handcuffs, and radio. Keys on a key ring jingled as he made his way to the witness stand and sat.

After Cerrabone solicited Adderley's education and training, which included a tour in the Gulf War as an Army Ranger, and which Adderley recounted in a commanding baritone voice, Cerrabone got down to the business at hand. Adderley advised that he had received a 3:03 A.M. call from dispatch the morning of September 7 of a possible prowler at an address in Laurelhurst. He had arrived at the residence ahead of other units and waited for backup.

Using a diagram of the house, Adderley relayed how he mentally labeled the front of the house side A and proceeded in a clockwise direction, the south side being B, the rear C, and the north D. He explained that side C included a sliding-glass door, through which he and the second officer to arrive first viewed the victim.

"And what did you do?" Cerrabone asked.

"I called it in as a person down and held for more resources."

"How'd you call it in?"

"Cell phone."

"Why a cell phone?"

"Media can't monitor it."

That brought a few chuckles from the gallery, and Cerrabone, relaxed in his delivery, acknowledged them with a smile of his own.

"Did you attempt to enter?"

Adderley shook his head. "No reason," he said. He noted that the door was shut, pierced by a single concave hole that caused a spiderweb of cracks, though the door had not shattered and the glass had not crystallized.

With Rowe's assistance, Cerrabone had the door wheeled front and center for Adderley to identify. He then used one of the crime-scene diagrams for Adderley to explain the physical location of the body on the sofa, head slumped on the arm, a pool of blood on the hardwood floor.

As Sloane listened to the testimony, something bothered him, though he could not determine what. Still, having learned to trust his gut, he opened his file and pulled out Adderley's report, studying it yet again, wondering what he might be missing. What didn't quite make sense?

Barclay picked up her pen and scribbled a note on the yellow pad. *Everything all right?*

Sloane nodded but remained unsure what had caused his visceral reaction to the testimony. He'd had similar experiences, when the cause for his concern would suddenly come to him later, at an odd moment

— driving, exercising, or in the middle of the night.

Cerrabone asked Adderley whether he and the second officer attempted to enter through the sliding-glass door, but again Adderley said that they had concluded the victim was dead, so they did not even touch the door.

"What did you do next?" Cerrabone asked.

Adderley described how he stationed himself at the back of the house while the second officer waited at the front for SWAT.

"When SWAT arrived, we cleared the house . . . looked to make sure no one else was inside," Adderley explained.

"And did you find anyone else inside?"

"No. Just the victim."

"You didn't disturb anything inside?"

"Tried not to. Once we cleared the residence, we taped it off, secured the perimeter, and waited for the detectives."

"Did you do anything else? Talk with anyone? Go anywhere else on the property?"

Adderley shook his head. "When Detective Rowe arrived, I turned over the site to him."

When Cerrabone sat, Underwood looked at the clock. There were just fifteen minutes remaining in the day, and Sloane would

420

have preferred to have the evening to let the unknown thought that Adderley's testimony had summoned percolate further, but that wasn't an option. Underwood was not about to waste a minute. "Mr. Sloane, cross?"

Sloane remained seated. "Officer Adderley, you testified that when you arrived at the back of the house, you considered the sliding-glass door and it was closed, correct?"

"That's correct."

"Closed all the way, as it is displayed here in court, with no opening at all between the edge of the door and the vinyl doorjamb?"

Adderley looked at his report. "I didn't note that, but that is what I recall."

"You didn't attempt to slide the door open?"

"No."

"So you don't know if it was locked."

"I don't."

Sloane stood and approached. "Now, you testified that you received a call from dispatch of a suspected prowler, correct?"

"That's right."

"It wasn't 'shots fired'?"

"No."

"In your line of work, you get reports of shots fired fairly frequently, do you not?"

Cerrabone objected to the use of the

words "fairly frequently" as vague, and Underwood sustained it.

"You receive those calls, do you not?" Sloane asked. He knew the answer from conversations with two retired King County police officers.

"Yes," Adderley said, then, apparently feeling in the mood to educate, offered, "They are more common than the average person might suspect."

Sloane silently thanked the officer. "Why is that, Officer Adderley?"

"Most of the time the calls turn out to be false alarms — maybe a car backfiring or a firecracker or something. I had one when a tree branch cracked and two neighbors called it in as a gunshot."

"Would it be fair to say, given that most of these calls turn out to be false alarms, that you and your fellow officers have become a bit desensitized to them?"

Adderley became cautious. "We treat all calls seriously."

"I'm sure you do. But would it be fair to say that a report of a suspected prowler would generate, let's say, greater interest?"

"It's fair to say that a report of a prowler is less common."

"And generates a quicker response?"

Adderley had figured out where Sloane

was headed. "We respond as quickly as we can to every call."

"Officer, isn't it true that because you get calls of shots fired more frequently, and because many of those turn out to be false, that a call of a suspected prowler causes you and your fellow officers to react more earnestly?"

"It's possible."

"And police officers recognize this, correct?"

"I suppose we do, yes."

"Who else would know that a call of a suspected prowler would generate a quicker police response?"

"I don't know what you're asking me."

"What about experienced criminals?"

Cerrabone was up. "Objection. He's asking the witness to speculate."

"I'm asking, based upon his education, training, and experience as a King County police officer for more than ten years, whether experienced criminals become savvy in police procedure — that sometimes they can know the law better than even us lawyers?"

Several jurors smiled at that comment.

"The witness can answer," Underwood said.

"Some are pretty savvy, yeah," Adderley said.

"Was there a prowler?"

"We didn't find one, no."

"Police officers interviewed the neighbors, did they not?"

"Yes."

"You are familiar with the reports?"

"Yes."

"None of Mr. Vasiliev's neighbors called in shots fired?"

"No."

Sloane looked at the clock on the wall as the big hand ticked to the twelve. Four o'clock straight up. He made sure Underwood noticed. The judge sat up, about to call the proceedings to a close for the day. Perfect timing.

"One last question. Which one of them called in the prowler, Officer Adderley?"

TWENTY-THREE

Law Offices of David Sloane
One Union Square
Seattle, Washington

Sloane walked into the conference room to find Pendergrass, jacket off and tie pulled loose, recounting for those who had not been present in court — Carolyn, Alex, and Charlie — how Officer Adderley had sat on the witness chair dumbfounded. Sloane hadn't rescued him with any further comment but had allowed the silence to punctuate his question and Adderley's inability to answer it.

Cerrabone had sat with his foot angled around the leg of the counsel table as if contemplating standing to object, but he pulled back the foot.

"None of them," Adderley had finally said, the words sounding more like a question than an answer. Better than Sloane could have hoped for.

Adderley had not been privy to the conversation in Judge Underwood's chambers and likely had not been told about Willins and Cruz, there being no reason for him to know about them or Centac. The obvious question Sloane left the jury to ponder overnight was, if the caller wasn't one of the neighbors, then who was it? Barclay wasn't a sensible option. If she had been intent on killing Vasiliev and getting away with it, why would she have called in the crime after the fact? The implication was that the caller must have been the experienced criminal to which Sloane had made reference.

Sloane interrupted Pendergrass. "Let's not get too full of ourselves." He knew they could expect an equal number of bad days ahead. He directed Carolyn to order in dinner and retreated to his office to prepare for the next day. He did not notice that Barclay had followed until she shut the door and kicked off her shoes. She slipped silently between his arms and placed her cheek against his chest. As experienced in the courtroom as Sloane, she was fully aware she was a long way from feeling secure.

Jenkins and Alex retreated to her office and shut the door. It smelled of popcorn. Jenkins picked up the microwave bag and shoveled

426

a handful into his mouth as Alex pulled back her curls, manipulating them into a bun on the top of her head, which she somehow held in place with a pencil. With a pair of cheaters on the bridge of her nose, she looked like one of those women in a music video, the high school teacher about to whip off the glasses, let down her hair, and transform into a luscious vixen. Jenkins shook away the thought. He was on his way out again and likely until late in the evening or early in the morning. He hoped to talk to the owner of the underground nightclub where Joshua Blume and his friends had partied the night of the murder. The man had been avoiding Jenkins, apparently not eager to have a discussion that included his allowing underage patrons into a club that sold alcohol. But that was not what Jenkins wanted to discuss with Alex.

"Anything on the transvestite?" he asked.

Andrew Lorin appeared to have dropped off the face of the earth shortly after he signed a statement that he and Felix Oberman had a personal relationship.

"Nothing." She sipped from a can of Diet Coke. "No job history, no bank accounts, no medical records. He hasn't filed a personal tax return since 2001, hasn't registered a car, and I found nothing in the King

County assessors' records. It's like the guy just disappeared."

"Maybe like the private investigator disappeared?"

She took the popcorn bag and ate several pieces. "Maybe, except then there would at least be a death certificate, or maybe an obituary. There's nothing."

Jenkins twirled the car keys around a finger, and bent to kiss her. "Wish me luck. I'm off to crash an underground bar."

She considered his attire. Black jeans, black T-shirt, black jacket. "At least you're dressed for the occasion."

Late in the evening, Sloane stood to stretch his legs, hoping that increased circulation and additional food might get the synapses of his brain firing again. Adderley's testimony continued to bother him, though he still didn't know why. He had asked Pendergrass to get him a copy of the transcript from the court reporter so he could review the testimony in greater detail and without the stress of having to listen and consider objections. With computers, a witness's testimony could be transcribed nearly instantaneously. He hoped reviewing it might spur his subconscious.

Barclay sat alone at the conference room

table, surrounded by several piles of paper from the boxes of documents the prosecutor's office had delivered. Light blue Post-its with handwritten notes stuck out of the piles from all four sides. Going through the materials — records of her financial transactions, phone calls, and computer searches — had to be like a flashback of the prior three years of her life. The prosecution was hoping, of course, for some tidbit of evidence, like how Barclay used MapQuest to determine the best path from her home to Vasiliev's backyard, or perhaps a Google search on how to keep a .38 revolver from getting wet while swimming.

"Are we making progress?" He picked up one of the white cartons and considered its contents, put it down, and searched another. He had insisted they all take a half-hour break to eat dinner together rather than fill their plates and dash back to their respective offices. He felt it important they remain connected, part of a team with one goal. He also found the input from others on areas of potential cross-examination and trial strategy insightful.

Barclay did not answer. She held a document in her hand but stared past it, out the windows, her gaze so intense Sloane shifted focus to see if something or someone stood in one of the rectangular lighted cubes of the nearby office building.

"Barclay?"

She looked up at him. "Do you have Rowe's report of what they took from my house when they came with the search warrant?"

"The inventory? Yeah, it's in my office." Carolyn had put a copy in Rowe's witness binder. "Why, what is it?" he asked.

He followed her to his office where she surveyed the dozen or so black binders on the carpet. He stepped past her, checked the spines, and handed her Rowe's binder. She placed it on his desk and flipped the tabs, stopping when she came to the inventory from the Washington State Patrol evidence facility. She ran her finger down the list, flipped the page, and continued on the second page. Her finger came to a stop halfway down. Her focus shifted from the list to the documents in her hand, a series of credit-card transactions. She flipped through those pages, lips moving silently. She reconsidered the inventory, then looked at Sloane. Her expression appeared indecisive, like she wanted to smile but refrained, not yet certain.

"I think I might have something you can use," she said.

The Paragon
Pioneer Square, Seattle

Located in an alley surrounded by the three-story brick buildings that made up Seattle's Pioneer Square, the Paragon wasn't actually underground, though it was close. Jenkins had to descend a flight of stairs from ground level to get to the door. Alex had been correct — black was the preferred color of clothing — but it didn't help Jenkins to blend. People his size didn't blend, and even if he tried, there wasn't much room for him to do so in the forty-foot-square club. A raised platform, with a set of drums, speakers, microphones, a keyboard, and sound equipment took up one corner. A navy blue curtain draped from the ceiling hung behind the stage. Though the walls were painted black, flyers and scraps of colored paper covered much of the space. The club smelled like clove cigarettes.

As Jenkins walked toward the bar at the end farthest from the stage the few patrons seated at the dozen or so round tables watched him with curiosity, no doubt certain they had spotted an undercover cop. The woman behind the bar, however, gave Jenkins only a tacit acknowledgment. She continued to laugh and chatter with a smitten young man at the other end of the slab of wood. She was obviously the young man's type. Hell, she was everyone's type, and in this place, that meant men and women.

And she knew it. She had cropped her jet-black hair short and folded it behind her ears. Silver balls pierced her right brow and lower lip. Brightly colored tattoos adorned both shoulders, covered only by the lace straps of a black camisole that stopped short of her navel, also pierced. Despite the accoutrements, or perhaps because of them, Jenkins found her strangely attractive. It could also have been that, unlike the others in the club, some of whom had subtly made their way to the door, she didn't seem the least bit intimidated by his presence. To the contrary, when she turned to greet him, she smiled with teeth so white and straight she had to be an orthodontist's daughter, and had eyes so blue he finally understood the saying about Irish eyes smiling. He couldn't help but smile back.

The kid at the other end of the bar left.

"Sorry if I'm causing you to lose business," Jenkins said. "I'll refrain from flashing my badge, if that helps."

She propped her forearms on the counter and leaned forward, displaying a hint of cleavage, eyes fixed as if in a staring contest. The smile morphed into a flirtatious grin. If she was twenty-one, it wasn't by much; "cute" was still a word that could be used to describe her. "You want to show me your gun instead?"

"I don't carry a gun," he said.

"So you're not a cop."

She was good. "Nope. I work for an attorney."

She stood up, animated. "I used to work for an attorney."

"Paralegal?"

"Receptionist." The eyebrow without the piercing arched, daring him to ask the obvious question.

"Okay, I'll bite. How did you get the job working at a law firm?"

"When I interviewed, I removed all the jewelry and wore a shirt that covered the tattoos."

"The old bait and switch, huh? Let me guess. Then you put the jewelry back in and slipped on the camisole, and you didn't fit the corporate image they were trying to impress upon their clientele, and you got sacked because you refused to compromise your principles."

She slapped the counter. "Wrong." Her voice rose with pride. "I put in the jewelry, and the attorney found it a turn-on. When I wouldn't sleep with him, he fired me."

Jenkins chuckled because he knew the story was completely honest.

She lowered back to her forearms. "So, what *do* you do?" she asked.

"Private investigator."

"Oooh. Are you any good?"

"Sometimes I am."

"You want a drink?"

"Can't. I'm working."

"That was a test."

"Did I pass?"

"So far."

He smiled. "Have you worked here long?"

"Do you come here often?" she said. Then, "About six months."

"Weeknights or weekends?"

"I'm here, aren't I?"

"And it being a weeknight, I will take that as a yes to the first part of my question."

She touched her finger to the tip of her nose and winked. "Ding, ding, ding, ding, ding. Give that man a cee-gar."

"How could I get a copy of the bartenders' schedule?"

"Are you hitting on me, Mr. Private Investigator . . . with the wedding band?"

"I'm too old for you. I meant a copy of the past work schedule."

"What night are you interested in?"

"Tuesday, September sixth."

"Wow, that's specific. What happened that night?"

"Were you here?"

"It was a Tuesday night in September?" she asked.

"The sixth."

She pulled out a black calendar from beneath the bar and flipped the pages backward. "Yep, I was here that night." She pointed to the date in the calendar. There was an X in the box that corresponded with the name Anastasia. Other names filled other dates.

"You're Anastasia?"

"Wow, you are good." From anyone else, it would have sounded sarcastic, but she made it sound cute.

Jenkins realized his attraction to the girl. With longer hair and a lot less jewelry, she'd look vaguely like Alex. Though she had a little more attitude, she had Alex's confidence and spunk. From his pocket, he pulled the pictures of Joshua Blume that Alex had somehow downloaded from Facebook, pictures of Blume holding an electric guitar, playing in a band. She had also provided pictures of Blume's friends.

Anastasia leaned forward, inching closer.

"Is this where you show me pictures of the perp?"

He arched his eyebrows. "The perp?"

"Isn't that what you guys call the suspect? I saw it on a TV show — the perp."

"I don't watch TV, it depresses me; nothing good on anymore."

"I hear you, brother." She gave him a mock frown. Dear God, where was she when he was twenty-one?

"You remember seeing this kid in here."

"That night? That's awfully specific."

"Any night. Maybe you served him and his friends?"

She considered the pictures. "Is there a reward?"

"If there was, I would split it with you."

"Liar." She stuck out her tongue and gave him a raspberry, then continued through the photographs before slapping them down. "Nope."

"I think he plays in a band," Jenkins said.

She rolled her eyes. "Everyone in here plays in a band. They're all going to be the next Nirvana. See that stage?" She pointed. "We get three or four bands every night. They come in here to play for an hour, then the next one gets a chance. They have battles."

"Battles?"

"Battle of the bands," she said. "The people cheer. The band getting the loudest cheer wins."

"What do they win?"

"The undying applause of their fans . . . and a beer."

"But you don't remember this kid in particular?"

"Can't say he's that memorable."

"And you were the only one on duty that night."

She gestured to the narrow area behind the bar. "Where are you going to put anyone else?"

He gathered the photographs and slipped them back in his pocket. "I like your tattoo," he said. "What does it say?"

She shrugged one shoulder. "Just something I read somewhere. I don't even remember."

Jenkins stood. "Well, Anastasia, I'll be leaving now."

She clutched her hands over her heart, tilted her head to the ceiling, and touched the back of her left hand to her forehead. "Romeo, Romeo, parting is such sweet sorrow."

"Ah, you're an actress."

"I used to be." She raised the eyebrow again and held her finger near her nose, tempting him.

"But the director fired you because you wouldn't sleep with him," Jenkins said.

TWENTY-FOUR

Friday, December 2, 2011
King County Courthouse
Seattle, Washington

The following morning, Underwood asked if there were any matters to be discussed before the bailiff brought in the jury. Sloane was surprised to see the same shoe Cerrabone had inched around the leg of the table the prior afternoon, only this time Cerrabone did not pull it back. He rose.

"There is, Your Honor. And I would suggest we meet in chambers."

Cerrabone approached and handed the clerk a document, a pleading she dutifully handed to the judge. Cerrabone gave a copy to Sloane. The motion requested that Underwood instruct the jury to disregard the late-afternoon testimony of Officer Adderley concerning the anonymous telephone call from the crime scene.

Taking a moment to read the first few

paragraphs, Underwood rapped his gavel and swiveled to the side, standing. "The court will be in recess."

In the judge's chambers, Cerrabone verbalized the written motion, arguing that Sloane's solicitation of information concerning the phone call violated the intent of the judge's order that there be no mention of Cruz or Willins, their footprints, or Cruz's fingerprint. He said it implied there had been a third party at the site who could have shot Vasiliev when in fact it was Willins who had made the anonymous call.

"The potential confusion of the jurors is obvious, Your Honor."

Sloane fought to control his anger. "To the contrary, counsel raised the subject in his direct examination when he asked Officer Adderley to describe how it was that he came to the crime scene. He solicited the response from Officer Adderley that he was responding to a call of a prowler."

Cerrabone said, "But I did not go further because of the court's order. Counsel's line of questions implies to the jury either that the shooter called it in, which would make no sense whatsoever, or there had to be an 'experienced criminal' at the scene who called it in, when we are all aware there exist no facts to support such a theory. I can't do anything about it on redirect to explain Jerry Willins made the call without violating the court's order that we not discuss Willins or Cruz. It was disingenuous of counsel to put the witness in the position of violating the court's order."

Underwood nodded. "I agree. Mr. Sloane, I don't think you did it deliberately, but I do think, as any good attorney would, that you exploited a crack in my prior order. Since Mr. Cerrabone cannot explain the evidence without violating that order, it is my intention to advise the jury that it has since been determined that the call reporting a prowler was made by a person who is not a suspect in this case."

Sloane could not help but consider that Cerrabone had sandbagged him, that when he had pulled back his foot the prior day, it was not because he thought it best not to try to save Adderley in front of the jury, but because he planned instead to have the judge do it for him. Ordinarily that might have been a risk for an attorney not known to be a risk taker, but given the judge's prior order and the fact that Cerrabone's objection would have looked like he and Adderley were hiding evidence, the decision not to object was a smart one. Cerrabone must have gone back to his office and immediately prepared the motion.

"Your Honor, Mr. Cerrabone had enough time yesterday to object to my line of questioning as I cross-examined Officer Adderley, and he did not do so. This is not his first rodeo, and I would suggest that what is disingenuous, given that the state offered *no* objections to *any* of my questions that it now finds so offensive, is to come into this court the following morning and request that you instruct the jury. It implies wrongdoing on the part of the defense — that I was trying to mislead the jury, pull a fast one, and that was not the case."

Underwood raised a hand to cut off any response by Cerrabone. "I will advise the jury that defense counsel did nothing underhanded and that there was no impropriety, that if anyone is to blame, it is me for failing to properly instruct counsel on the matter."

Sloane thought it a hollow concession, but with it already five minutes past the hour, he knew Underwood was not about to listen to further argument. Even if he did, nothing Sloane said was going to change the judge's mind.

When the jurors entered the courtroom, Officer Adderley had already retaken his seat on the witness chair, part of the facade that everything was as it had been when they recessed the prior afternoon. After they settled, Underwood instructed them as he had advised, and Cerrabone proceeded with his redirect.

Just like that, everything good about the prior day felt as if it had been erased, making Sloane's statement to Pendergrass that they not get ahead of themselves prophetic.

After a brief redirect of Adderley, Cerrabone dismissed him and called the CSI detective, Kathy Stafford. An attractive blonde, Stafford dressed in tight blue jeans, boots, and a suede jacket. In case a juror had any doubt of her occupation, she clipped her badge to her belt, and a shoulder holster and gun could be seen beneath her jacket. Sloane anticipated that Cerrabone would follow Stafford with Barry Dilliard, the ballistics expert, then tracker Kaylee Wright before hitting him with Joshua Blume and Felix Oberman. That would leave a series of witnesses to discuss Barclay's motivation after Carly died of a drug overdose, with Detective Rowe to bat cleanup, summarizing the evidence that proved Barclay's guilt just before Sloane put on his defense witnesses.

Stafford spent the morning testifying

about the condition of the crime scene as she and the resources at her disposal encountered it. She and Cerrabone used crime-scene sketches and photographs to describe for the jury the precise location of the body, what she called the "defect" in the sliding-glass door, and the location and caliber of the bullet embedded in the floor. She testified that they did not locate a spent shell casing, which was consistent with the police's theory that the killer had used a revolver, and of course, she testified that they did not find the gun, which she said was not unusual. As part of her detailed report, she noted that she and Rowe had agreed to call out both Kaylee Wright and Barry Dilliard.

"And why did you do that?" Cerrabone asked.

"During the course of my walk-around with Detective Rowe, we noted footprints in the backyard on the lawn. We discussed the possibility that the perpetrator had used the lake to gain access to the property."

It confirmed for Sloane the likely order of witnesses.

Cerrabone didn't leave him much to work with on cross-examination, but again Sloane set to the task.

"Detective Stafford, you testified about

calling out fingerprint technicians from the Washington State Patrol crime lab. Is that unusual at a crime scene such as this?"

"It's a bit unusual, yes."

"Why was it done in this instance?" Sloane knew the answer. He asked an open-ended question hoping Stafford would provide a narrative response.

A savvy witness, she did not oblige him. "Detective Rowe asked that it be done."

"And did Detective Rowe tell you why he wanted it done in this instance?"

"He said he wanted the interior of the house dusted for fingerprints," she said, not answering his question.

"And dusting an entire house for finger-prints requires a significant amount of manpower, or at least more than what you initially brought to the site, correct?"

"It does, yes."

"So again, I ask." Sloane wanted the jury to understand Stafford had not answered his prior question. "Did Detective Rowe explain to you the reason he wanted it done in this instance?"

She paused as if considering how to phrase her answer. "Given the condition of the crime scene, the lack of a weapon or a suspect, he said this could be a difficult case."

"But you just testified it was not unusual to not find the weapon at the crime scene, didn't you?"

"I did."

"So surely Detective Rowe must have given you some other reason to justify his request for this significant increase in manpower?"

"Detective Rowe informed me that he had been advised by one of the responding officers that the victim had recently been a suspect in a federal investigation," she said.

"Let's not mince words, Detective. Mr. Vasiliev had been suspected of being a significant trafficker of heroin, had he not?"

"Yes, that's what I was told."

"And that is what you wrote in your report, correct?"

"I did, yes," she said, knowing the contents without looking.

"And didn't you also note in your report that Detective Rowe sought the additional manpower because, given Mr. Vasiliev's reputed line of work — trafficking in heroin — Detective Rowe wanted to determine Mr. Vasiliev's associates?"

"He did express that to me."

"Because dealing large quantities of heroin can be a dangerous profession?"

Cerrabone was up. "Objection, Your

446

Honor, this goes far afield. Mr. Vasiliev was suspected, not convicted."

Underwood shook his head. Perhaps he sought to even the playing field following his morning statement to the jury, like an umpire's makeup call. Or perhaps it was because judges were far less likely to rescue someone who was part of the judicial system — such as a detective — but he overruled the objection.

Stafford looked up at the judge. "You may answer, Detective."

"I don't know if that was part of Detective Rowe's thinking or not."

"That's not what I asked. You are a detective, are you not?"

"I am."

"And based upon your education, training, and experience as a detective, is the dealing of large quantities of heroin a dangerous profession?"

"I suppose it could be, yes."

"Could be? Let's start with the fact that it's against the law, is it not?"

"It is."

"And it can involve millions of dollars, can it not?"

"It can."

"Did you not process three crime scenes this past year that were determined to be

447

homicides as a result of rival gangs fighting over their drug turf?"

"I don't know the number, but I do recall one."

Sloane refreshed her recollection with three reports Alex had obtained. Stafford conceded there had been three such homicides. Sloane moved on.

"Now, you did not find Barclay's fingerprints anywhere in the house or the backyard, did you?"

"No, we did not."

"You did not find any traces of her DNA anywhere inside or outside the house."

"We did not."

"However, you did obtain four fingerprints at the crime scene that, when run through the AFIS computer system you and Mr. Cerrabone earlier discussed, did produce positive identifications, correct?"

"That is correct."

Underwood had previously ruled admissible the identity of the four individuals and the crimes for which they had been arrested. Sloane had Stafford identify on one of her charts where the first of the four fingerprints had been located, in the den where Vasiliev's body had been found. "And that fingerprint belonged to Vladimir Kurkov, who has a criminal record for selling heroin, correct?"

"Correct."

"Didn't Mr. Kurkov also work as a used-car salesman for Mr. Vasiliev?"

"I don't know."

Sloane went through the second fingerprint, also belonging to a person of Russian descent with a criminal history of drug trafficking. That fingerprint also had been lifted from a counter in the den. The other two fingerprints belonged to Russian women who worked as "dancers" at a club in Renton. Each had a criminal record of prostitution.

Underwood had ruled that Sloane could not use the term "Russian mafia," and he would not. But that didn't prevent him from using the evidence to imply that Vasiliev associated with known criminals.

Turning to the gun, Sloane said, "No weapon was ever found, correct?"

"No weapon was found at the crime scene," she said.

"So your unit was unable to match the bullet found at the crime scene with any particular gun, correct?"

"We have not, no."

"The bullet you located was subsequently identified by the Washington State Patrol crime lab as a thirty-eight Special, correct?"

"That's correct."

"That's one of the most popular bullets produced, is it not?"

"I don't know."

Sloane didn't care. The answer was implied. "But you do know there are several different handguns on the market that are capable of firing a thirty-eight Special bullet, correct?"

"I would assume that to be the case. Barry Dilliard would be better able to answer that question."

"In fact, isn't it the case that even guns that aren't thirty-eight-caliber, such as the three-fifty-seven Magnum revolver, are capable of firing a thirty-eight Special bullet?"

"Again, I would defer to Barry on that," she said.

Again, Sloane didn't care. "Isn't it also true that some guns that aren't even revolvers — semiautomatic pistols, for instance — are capable of firing the thirty-eight Special bullet?"

"Again, I don't know for certain. But I can say that we did not find any spent cartridges at the crime scene."

"Which led you to believe a revolver was used?"

"It is another piece of evidence factored in."

"And did you factor in the possibility that the shooter could have used a semi-automatic and simply picked up the spent casing?"

"We don't come to conclusions at the crime scene," she said. "Our job is to process the information and provide it to the homicide detectives."

"Is that why I don't see any note in your report that the lack of a shell casing at the site could be due to the shooter picking it up from the ground after shooting a semi-automatic?"

"Again, that would be a conclusion, and that is not my job."

And again, Sloane didn't care. "How many registered owners of thirty-eight-caliber handguns live in the state of Washington, Detective?"

"I don't know."

"How about in King County?"

"I don't know."

"We could probably get those records, could we not?"

She smiled, indicating she knew what was coming next. "I'm sure you have."

"Two hundred and thirty-six thousand, six hundred and nineteen registered thirty-eight-caliber handguns," Sloane said, knowing he was testifying. It drew an objection from Cerrabone, which Underwood overruled. "And that wouldn't include unregistered handguns, would it?" Sloane went on.

"Not as you have phrased it, it wouldn't."

"Nor would it include weapons that are capable of firing a thirty-eight-caliber round such as the three-fifty-seven Magnum, would it?"

"Again, not as you have phrased the question."

"So, would it be fair for me to say that since you don't have the gun that fired the thirty-eight-caliber bullet found at the crime scene, that gun could have been any of those two hundred and thirty-six thousand, six hundred and nineteen registered thirty-eight-caliber handguns, one of the unknown number of unregistered thirty-eight-caliber handguns, or one of the registered or unregistered handguns capable of firing a thirty-eight-caliber bullet? Would that be fair?"

Cerrabone was on his feet before Sloane finished the question. "Objection, Your Honor. Counsel is speculating and testifying again."

"Sustained."

Sloane looked at Stafford. "You can't say for certain what caliber of gun was used, can you, Detective?"

"Not without the gun," she conceded.

When they broke for lunch, Pendergrass, Sloane, and Barclay ate in the food court in the basement of a building near the courthouse. They took a table once satisfied that no jurors or courthouse personnel sat nearby. Sloane didn't each much, splitting a pastrami sandwich with Pendergrass and leaving half of that unfinished. Barclay didn't order, and to Sloane, she looked to be losing weight, but she kept telling him she was fine and that she hadn't lost a pound.

"Stafford went well," Pendergrass said.

It had gone well, but mentally, Sloane had already moved on. He had retained his own ballistics expert to review the evidence and the report prepared by Barry Dilliard, the head forensic scientist of the firearms section of the Washington State Patrol crime lab.

"You don't want to match wits with this guy in his arena," Sloane's expert had warned. "This is the Doogie Howser of ballistics."

Sloane watched a woman behind a cash register at an establishment selling Mexican food reach behind her and slide open a glass door to retrieve two cans of soda. When she turned to put them on the counter, the sliding-glass door slid closed, but not completely, leaving a two-inch opening.

And the nagging thought that had bothered Sloane for two days finally crystallized.

"David?"

Sloane looked to Reid, knowing he had missed whatever question had been posed.

"Excuse me." He walked away to make a call on his cell phone.

When Jenkins answered, Sloane said, "I need you to find Micheal Hurley."

Though Barry Dilliard's curriculum vitae said he was forty-six years old, nobody in the courtroom would have believed it. Sloane watched at least one juror mentally add the years as Dilliard recounted for Cerrabone how long he had been with the forensic unit. With an easy style, Dilliard told how he had received an MFA in English literature from a school on the East Coast, but when he moved back home to Seattle, he had been unable to find the teaching job he craved and took a low-level job in the crime lab to pay the bills and student loans. He joked that maybe if he had studied forensic science he'd be teaching James Joyce to college students. Once at the crime lab, Dilliard found he had a natural aptitude for determining things like the trajectory of bullets. During his subsequent twenty-three years, he had been rapidly promoted and had developed innovative methods and equipment to re-create crime scenes that were being employed by crime labs throughout the country.

He didn't look like Doogie Howser, the boy-genius doctor on the television show of the same name. He looked more like the actor Ron Howard when Howard played Richie Cunningham on the television show *Happy Days* — before he lost his reddish-blond hair. The hair swept across Dilliard's forehead, and with clear blue eyes and boyish features he looked like he would have been more comfortable wearing long shorts and flip-flops instead of the hunter green suit, white shirt, and tie.

Dilliard said he viewed each crime scene much the way he considered jigsaw puzzles, one of his passions. "The pieces are all there but scattered. They need to be fitted together to see the full picture."

Good at making the mundane interesting, when Cerrabone asked him about the use of a .38 revolver and whether it had enough power to shoot through the double-paned sliding-glass door, Dilliard related how Jack

Ruby had used a .38 Special, a Colt Cobra, to kill Lee Harvey Oswald. "It has plenty of power, and it's a reliable weapon."

Dilliard became downright gleeful when asked to talk about his latest forensic toy — the $140,000 Leica ScanStation C10, which he called a "crime-scene time machine." The machine took a 360-degree photo of the crime scene, then used lasers to scan it. The result was a 3D image that could be computer-manipulated "to re-create what the evidence and science indicate happened," Dilliard said.

For the next hour and a half, the jury was treated to a simulation showing the crime scene in a 3D image, beginning with Vasiliev slumped on the sofa. Then the image changed to a 3D aerial view of the outside of the home, with the image of an androgynous-looking mannequin sitting and watching a flat-screen television mounted on the opposite wall.

"The image matches Mr. Vasiliev's exact measurements," Dilliard said. As the image rotated, an equally androgynous-looking figure appeared outside the back door, raised a gun, and fired a shot, a blue line showing the trajectory of the bullet through the glass, striking the back of Vasiliev's head, and deflecting off course before becoming wedged in the baseboard.

"Were you able to draw any conclusions concerning the height of the shooter, based upon your simulation?" Cerrabone asked.

"Based upon the trajectory of the bullet, which the ScanStation duplicated and which we confirmed the old-fashioned way through photographs and measurements and a scanner on a tripod, I concluded that the shooter was between five feet two and five feet five inches tall," Dilliard said.

Cerrabone continued for another twenty minutes before concluding what had been the most entertaining witness to date.

Sloane stood. "Mr. Dilliard, how tall am I?"

Dilliard considered Sloane. "I don't know."

"Give me an estimate."

"Maybe six-two or three . . ."

Sloane put his hands in front of him, as if holding a handgun the way the mannequin had held it in the video. Then he spread his feet, bent his knees, and lowered. "How tall am I now?"

"I don't know."

"Your simulation shows the figure outside the sliding-glass door standing erect. What if the person were taller, like me, but spread their feet and squatted, as I just did.

Wouldn't that result in the same trajectory?"

"We used the information provided by Kaylee Wright, the tracker, concerning the location of the foot impressions on the concrete patio in relation to the sliding-glass door and to one another. You will note that in the simulation, the shooter stood with the right foot positioned sixteen inches in front of the left, measuring from heel to heel, and the width is eight inches. That is typical of someone who has taken a shooter's stance, knees flexed, upper torso turned at an angle. That evidence was the basis for my providing the three-inch differential for the range in height."

"But if they flexed their knees more than the simulation, they could have been taller than five feet five inches, correct?"

"Could have been." He shrugged, letting both Sloane and the jury know he wasn't buying the argument.

"And the stance you mentioned, right foot in front of the left" — Sloane stood as Dilliard had described, even angling his body — "would that not be a stance more commonly associated with someone shooting with the left hand?"

"It usually would, yes."

It was a significant concession. Reid was right-handed.

"You also assumed, did you not, that the sliding-glass door was closed when the shot was fired?"

"The door was closed when I arrived, and I reviewed Officer Adderley's report as the first responding officer, which confirmed that to have been the case."

"Both of which still require that you make the assumption that the door was closed when the shot was fired, don't they?"

Dilliard's eyes narrowed. "I'm aware of no evidence that the door was open and then closed, if that is what you're postulating. The measurements would not make sense. Based upon the distance the person stood from the sliding-glass door, the position of their feet, the height and location of the bullet hole, the angle and trajectory of the bullet to its target on the sofa, the glass door was closed. If it had been opened, the measurements would not have worked, the angle would be off."

With the day drawing to a close, Sloane had one last line of inquiry and wanted to leave the jurors with something to ponder over the weekend.

"Did you draw any significance from the fact that just one bullet was found at the scene?" Nothing in Dilliard's report indicated that he had, but Pendergrass had

459

found a report Dillard had authored in another case in which he had drawn a significant conclusion from that piece of evidence.

"Nothing that I noted in my report."

"I didn't ask you what you noted in your report. I asked if you drew any significance from the fact that there was only a single hole in the glass."

Dilliard smiled. "That just one bullet was fired?"

The jury laughed, and Sloane joined them. Then he said, "Mr. Dilliard, do you remember a case entitled *State of Washington* vs. *Allan Green?*"

Dilliard nodded. "I do, though not in a lot of detail."

"You authored a report in that case." Sloane handed Dilliard a copy of his report, had him authenticate it, and gave him the chance to read it while providing a copy to Cerrabone and to the judge's clerk. After introducing the report, Sloane read from it. " 'The fact that we have located five spent cartridges is also consistent with an act of rage or vengeance.' " Sloane looked up. "Did I read that correctly?"

"Unfortunately you did, though I think my English-lit teachers would cringe that I wrote that." This brought more smiles from the jury. "Can I explain?"

Sloane wasn't about to cut off a witness who had cultivated such a good rapport with the jury. Besides, Pendergrass had also obtained a copy of the file for which Dilliard had written the report, and Sloane had familiarized himself with the facts of that case. Confident Dilliard could wiggle but not free himself of what he'd written, he let him go on.

"When I wrote this report, I did not have the experience or the technology we have available today. A husband came home from work after learning that his wife was having an affair and shot her five times. The detective wanted me to note that evidence of multiple shots fired was consistent with a crime of passion or anger. With experience, I have learned that not only are such statements speculative, I have no business making them. My job is simply to evaluate the physical evidence at the crime scene and let you lawyers argue about its significance."

"A crime of passion," Sloane said. "Sort of like a mother accused of killing the drug dealer who overdosed her daughter would be a crime of passion?"

Cerrabone stood. "Objection. Speculation," he said.

Underwood looked at Sloane over the

black frames of his glasses to convey that he was not pleased. "Sustained," he said. Sloane had expected the objection and thought it a tactical mistake by Cerrabone. Sloane wasn't the least bit interested in Dilliard's answer, concerned that Dilliard would take the opportunity to contend the two cases were not comparable given that Carly had been killed seven months earlier. Now there was no reason for Dilliard to explain.

"Thank you," Sloane said, leaving the unanswered question for the jury to ponder for the weekend.

Outside the courthouse, Sloane, Barclay, and Pendergrass ditched the media and found a corner to talk. They agreed to take the night off and start in again Saturday morning.

"I need to meet with an expert," Sloane said. "He can't meet over the weekend."

"You want me to take the meeting?" Pendergrass asked.

"No. Go home and drink a beer. I mean it. I don't want you even reading the newspaper accounts. We still have a lot of long days and nights ahead." Sloane turned to Barclay. "My meeting is down south. I'll stay at Three Tree and meet you at the office tomorrow morning."

He watched as she and Pendergrass walked up the street together. When they turned the corner, he pulled out his cell phone.

"What do you have?" he asked.

Golden Dragon Restaurant
International District
Seattle, Washington

Micheal Hurley was not a man Sloane ever wanted to play poker with. The dark eyes — black, really — remained expressionless, as did the rest of his facial features. Hurley sat smoothing the snow-white goatee with his right hand, not the slightest hesitation when Sloane explained his theory. Sloane knew he was right, whether Hurley wanted to acknowledge the truth or not, and he had come prepared to explain why he was right, if Hurley denied it. Then it would be a matter of whether Hurley cared — the placid expression not of a poker player bluffing but of a poker player holding four aces, an unbeatable hand, and knowing there wasn't a damn thing Sloane could say that would change that.

"Tell me why?" Hurley said. "Based upon the judge's ruling, you can't use it even if you're right."

463

Sloane couldn't. Not in a court of law.

But before Sloane could respond, before he could tell Hurley that what had set the wheels spinning was when Cerrabone asked Officer Adderley whether he had tried to open the sliding-glass door and Adderley had responded, "No reason to," a glimmer of light flickered in the black eyes, and the corner of Hurley's mouth twitched beneath the facial hair. It was not a smile or even a grin but it served as a tacit acknowledgment that Sloane was right and that Hurley knew Sloane's interest wasn't about getting evidence admitted in a court of law.

Sloane just needed to know.

Three Tree Point
Burien, Washington

Just after eight in the evening it was not too late for Sloane to drive to Barclay's house, but he had felt the need to be alone, to process the information Micheal Hurley had confirmed: that the reason Julio Cruz's fingerprints were on the slider was because, as Sloane had deduced, Cruz had slid open the door. Unlike Adderley, Cruz *had* a reason to open the door. He needed to go inside to retrieve the bug they had planted in Vasiliev's den, which they couldn't very well have left for the CSI team to discover.

What it meant, Sloane was not yet sure.

When Sloane turned the corner, he was surprised to see Barclay's BMW parked perpendicular to the laurel hedge. He pushed through the gate to the side yard. The interior of the house remained dark, not a light on in any window, not even the lights on the timer.

He looked for her along the beach, but saw no one out walking.

Back at the house, Sloane pushed through the back door but kept his keys in hand rather than place them on the hook protruding from the life-size Larry Bird cardboard cutout. He put his briefcase on the kitchen counter, about to call her name, when he felt the presence of others. The floor creaked unnaturally. A movement in the dark. The lights burst in a flash.

"Surprise!"

Two voices.

When the black spots faded, Sloane saw Barclay. Beside her, wearing an uncertain smile, stood Jake.

"I didn't want to say anything to you after court," Barclay said. "I wanted it to be a surprise."

After the initial shock, Sloane had held Jake in a fierce embrace. At sixteen, Jake was nearly as tall as Sloane, though still thin as a rail. "How did you do this?" Sloane asked.

"Ms. Reid — Barclay called me a few days ago. She said she thought it would be a nice surprise," Jake said. "She said you needed something to perk you up."

Sloane had not mentioned his and Barclay's relationship to Jake, not sure the boy was ready to hear it. He was uncertain how he felt about Barclay doing so.

"What happened to Italy?" he asked.

"The project ended early. And you can tell Charlie he was right. I'm sick of oil and vinegar."

"Okay," Barclay said. "I'm going to leave you two men to catch up."

"Stay," Sloane said.

She waved him off. "Not on your life."

"Really, you don't have to leave," Jake agreed, but it sounded half-hearted.

She smiled. "You're a polite young man. I can see that your mother did a wonderful job raising you. But a girl knows when men need their bonding time. I've taken enough of your father's time these past months, and I'll be seeing him a good deal more."

Sloane walked her outside to the easement. "I don't know what to say."

"I really debated this," she said. "I hope it

466

wasn't too bold of me. If it was, I apologize."

"No, it was a very kind gesture."

"You seemed down the last couple of days. I thought maybe you needed something to remind you of the good things in your life."

"More than the watch?"

She looked up at the house as the light in Jake's room came on.

"What did you tell him?" Sloane asked.

"I told him I was one of your clients, but he already knew all about it. He's followed the story on the Internet. He didn't say anything, but I'm sure he read the reports about us. Even if he hadn't, he seems like a bright kid."

"I didn't mean to imply that I thought it was something we should hide —"

"He's sixteen," she said. "Carly wasn't thrilled when I dated. I know it will take time, but I'm not in a rush. I'm hoping the three of us will have a lot of time to get to know one another."

Back inside the house, Sloane found Jake with his head in the refrigerator. His hair had grown well past his ears and touched the hood of his 49ers sweatshirt.

"You hungry?" Sloane asked — a dumb question of a teenager with the metabolism of a jackrabbit.

Jake pulled out a tomato that had rotted and mildewed. "Not anymore. How are you still alive?"

"The life of a trial lawyer. I've been working late and eating at the office. Come on, we'll go up to the Tin Room."

Jake shook his head. "I think I'd like to stay home."

Sloane detected melancholy in the comment. "How about my famous grilled cheese?"

"You mean the cardiac-arrest sandwich? Sure."

As Sloane pulled the cheese, mayonnaise, and butter out of the fridge, Jake retrieved the cast-iron skillet, then jumped up and sat on the counter. Tina would have swatted him with a towel.

"She's pretty cool," Jake said.

Sloane kept his focus on the refrigerator. "Barclay? Yeah, she's a good person."

"So she's innocent?"

Sloane closed the fridge and pulled open drawers, looking for the cheese slicer. "Yes, she's innocent."

"Really? Or it's your job to defend her even if she isn't?"

They'd had conversations about Sloane's job, defending clients to the best of his abilities no matter his personal feelings about their innocence or guilt. "Really." Sloane spread mayonnaise on one side of the bread, then added the cheese.

"So are you guys, like, dating?"

Sloane handed Jake a slice of cheese. "How would you feel about that?"

"The newspapers said you were."

"Yes," Sloane said. "We're dating. You okay with that?"

"Kind of hard, you know?"

Sloane stopped making the sandwich. "Yeah, I know. It has been hard," he said. "I miss your mom every day. I'll miss her every day for the rest of my life. No one will ever take her place. But you get to the point" — how to say it? — "you don't want to feel bad every morning you wake up. You just want to smile and mean it . . . laugh, feel good, and not feel guilty because you do. You know?"

Another nod.

"So what do you think of her?"

Jake stared at the floor. Then he looked up at Sloane. "What if she's convicted?"

TWENTY-FIVE

Monday, December 5, 2011
King County Courthouse
Seattle, Washington

Sloane entered the courtroom Monday morning not as prepared as he would have liked but a great deal more refreshed than how he had felt Friday afternoon. Jake spent Saturday morning at the office doing his homework, studying for a calculus test, and hanging out with Alex and Charlie. Barclay had not come in, telling Sloane she had taken a box of documents home and would continue to go through them. Jake and Sloane left early and took the boat out trolling for salmon, without any luck. They ate dinner at a restaurant in Burien and watched a screening of *The Girl with the Dragon Tattoo* at the Tin Room's new movie theater adjacent to the restaurant.

When Sloane took Jake to the airport Sunday morning, the boy's hug lingered.

"I'll see you soon," Sloane said.

Jake entered the line for preboarding screening without a response but teary-eyed. Sloane waited until he reached the conveyor belt, about to leave, when Jake turned. "It's how we heal, you know."

"What's that?"

"The pain."

"What about it?"

"Feeling it every day . . . it's not a bad thing. That's how we heal," he said. Then he slipped through the detector and did not look back.

Sloane had considered the comment much of Sunday. He knew Jake had been in counseling for over a year, and he deduced the comment to be something his counselor had told him — that it was better to feel the pain and deal with it than to bury it. Given the trauma Sloane had endured as a result of burying the recollection of his mother's murder when he was a boy, he agreed. Still, it seemed an odd comment, and Sloane wondered why Jake had chosen to bring it up just then.

Cerrabone began Monday morning with additional witnesses to confirm Carly had died of an overdose of heroin, that Reid had been upset that the police had not done more to find and charge the dealers who supplied Scott Parker, and that she had begun training for and participated in triathlons. The witnesses were largely uneventful, and Pendergrass handled the cross-examinations. That left Sloane to concentrate on the next witness, Earl Perkins, one of the King County sheriffs who worked with Freddy, the Belgian Malinois brought to the crime scene.

A small-framed man with a Scandinavian accent, Perkins testified that Freddy's olfactory gland was the size of a walnut — as opposed to a human's gland, which was no bigger than the tip of an eraser. He explained that this allowed the dog to track the fifty thousand skin cells humans shed every hour, cells that contained trace scents from the person's eccrine gland — the human sweat gland — and the apocrine gland, which was activated by stress, fear, or anxiety and was sometimes referred to as a person's "fear scent."

Using the diagram of the property, Perkins explained that Freddy had picked up a scent at the water's edge, trailed it to the back of the house, then followed it from the patio to a stand of trees before it continued back to the water.

"And is that where the scent ended?" Cerrabone asked.

Perkins used the diagram to explain his testimony. "Freddy continued to track the scent south along the beach until he reached this wall of the adjacent property and couldn't go any farther."

"What was Freddy scenting in the water?"

Perkins advised the jury that the dog continued to track the person's skin cells, those that had floated to the shore on plant material and other debris. The jury looked duly impressed.

"And what conclusion can you draw from the evidence that the scent trail continued along the beach, though you found no further footprints in the sand?" Cerrabone asked.

"That the person entered the water and swam south, parallel to the shoreline."

The information set up the testimony of Detective Kaylee Wright, who followed Perkins to the stand.

Wright had the healthy look of someone who spent much of her time outdoors, which most people in the Pacific Northwest would equate to pleasure activities such as hiking and mountain climbing, or snow skiing in the winter. And though Wright may have participated in some or all of those activities, it became quickly apparent, as she recounted her employment history and training, that her muscular build and tan complexion had little to do with how she spent her leisure time. Wright spent her time outdoors searching for bodies, like some of the bodies Gary Ridgway, the Green River Killer, and other psychopaths, dumped in ravines, wooded areas, and other places not easily accessible.

"And how many officers work for you at present?" Cerrabone asked from his customary spot at the end of the jury box farthest from the witness chair.

"Fourteen duty officers." She explained that the King County special operations unit consisted of multiple units with particular specialties — hazmat, bombs, marine, mountain climbing, and others.

"And what is it that your unit specializes in?"

"We're sign cutters," she said.

"What does it mean to have achieved the ranking of a sign cutter?"

"A sign cutter is someone who has spent a minimum of twelve hundred hours and ten years studying and training to see the physical evidence that a person leaves when they enter or exit a particular environment."

"Can you explain the principle behind that?" Cerrabone asked.

Wright discussed the science of Locard's

principle — how a person cannot move around his environment without taking evidence of where he has been and transferring it to where he goes. Cerrabone eventually progressed to the morning Wright was called to Vasiliev's home.

"And what were you looking for?" he asked.

"Signs of someone doing something different than the investigators at the crime scene — footprints positioned in such a way to indicate a person making ingress or egress, lying in wait, trying to gain entry into the house through a window or a door."

"Did you find any such signs?"

"I did," she said. With prompting from Cerrabone, Wright left the witness chair and used diagrams, photographs, and charts to explain that she had located footprints that corresponded with the scent trail Freddy had traced from the water to the patio and back. She explained that the footprints had "flagged" the grass, meaning the blades had been flattened where the person had walked and lay with the tips pointing in the same direction.

Using her hand to demonstrate, Wright said, "Over time, the blades, if not broken, will begin to rise. Based upon my examination of the blades, these footprints were made within four hours of my arrival at the site."

"And you arrived at roughly six in the morning?"

"Correct."

"Did you find any similarities in the footprints?"

"The footprints were of the same size, shape, and tread pattern," she said. "The distance between each print was also consistent."

Cerrabone asked that his paralegal post a photograph on the television depicting a series of yellow flags leading from the beach to the patio. "Did you draw any inferences from this particular path of footprints?"

"The person who made those footprints was walking with a purpose and intent."

Sloane stood. "Objection, Your Honor, speculation and lack of foundation."

Underwood sat at an angle, listening to Wright with his index finger just beneath his nose, hand covering his mouth. "Explain your objection, please."

"Purpose and intent necessarily relates to a person's state of mind. While Detective Wright is within her expertise to explain to the jury the physical evidence — what she saw and her conclusions from what she saw — with all due respect, there has been no testimony she is a mind reader."

A few of the jurors smiled.

Underwood nodded but said, "I'm going to withhold my ruling. Mr. Cerrabone, please lay a foundation for Detective Wright's prior answer."

Cerrabone asked, "Detective Wright, how is it that you can conclude the person walked with a purpose or intent?"

Wright suggested that certain photographs would assist her testimony. Cerrabone obliged her by displaying another photograph of the lawn leading from the water to the back of the house, taken from an angle low to the ground. She said, "You can see that the stride intervals between the prints are consistent. They don't veer off course or meander. I measured the distance between each print and found that distance to be consistently twelve inches."

"What does that tell you?" Cerrabone asked.

"It tells me several things — the person's stride did not deviate in direction or pace. Also, the person who made these prints impacted the ground consistently with more of a toe dig than a heel dig, indicating the person was walking."

"And all of these physical signs allow you to conclude what?"

"That the person moved with a purpose — in this case, to get to the back of the house."

Underwood looked at Sloane. "The objection is overruled."

Cerrabone had Wright discuss the particular footprints that she studied, measured, and photographed. She explained that each footprint equated to a size-seven shoe. After returning to her office, she used several resource materials, including the website called Zappos, which allowed her to access and view hundreds of different shoe treads.

"Did you find the make and model of the shoe that made the imprints leading from the water to the back of the house?" Cerrabone asked.

"The tread pattern is consistent with the tread pattern for a Nike AS300 cross-trainer," she said.

"And does the manufacturer market that type of shoe for a particular purpose?"

"It's marketed as a woman's athletic shoe," she said.

Cerrabone then solicited, and Wright explained, how the person who made the footprints had "stood on the patio for some time before the right leg extended forward, the heel sixteen inches to the front, weight distributed on the ball of the foot."

"And what evidence is there that allowed you to make that deduction?" Cerrabone asked.

"The footprints on the patio include grains of sand and bits of lawn, and the imprint is wider than the other imprints measured."

"What does that tell you?"

"That the shoe was saturated with water, and when the person transferred their weight to the ball of their foot — pressed down — water oozed onto the patio, increasing the dimensions of the print."

Again, the testimony supported that provided earlier by Barry Dilliard — that the person on the patio had assumed a shooter's stance.

Cerrabone then asked Wright about the footprints she marked with red flags that ultimately led back to the rock wall. Wright said those prints differed from the yellow-flagged prints in that her examination revealed more of a heel strike and a longer stride.

"A pronounced heel strike is indicative of a person running," she said.

"Where do those prints end?"

"The last print was two inches from the rock wall."

"And did you note a pronounced heel

strike in that print as well?"

"Actually, that print had a pronounced toe dig."

"Were you able to draw any conclusions from that physical evidence?"

"That the person pressed down in order to push off with that foot."

"To do what?" Cerrabone asked.

"The logical assumption is the person dove or jumped into the water."

Just ask Freddy, Sloane thought. Cerrabone finished up and Sloane made his way to the witness chair.

"Detective Wright, you testified that your measurements equate to a size-seven shoe print, correct?"

"That's correct."

"But you can't tell us if the person who made the print has a size-seven foot, can you?"

"I cannot."

"The person making the prints could very well have been wearing a shoe too big or too small for their feet, right?"

"It's possible."

"And you can't tell us if the person was a man or a woman, can you?"

"I cannot."

"It could have been a man wearing a woman's athletic shoe."

"It could have been."

"You were asked to compare the make and model of the shoe you identified with the shoes taken from Barclay Reid's home. Do you remember that testimony?"

"Yes, I do."

"And you testified that the shoe tread of the five pairs taken from the home were all consistent with the shoe tread of the prints you identified at the scene, correct?"

"Yes."

"But you cannot say with certainty that the person who made the prints at the back of the house wore any of those five pairs of shoes, can you?"

"I cannot."

"There was no anomaly in the shoe tread of the prints you studied, for instance, that allowed you to say it was a particular shoe; only that it was a particular brand of shoe, correct?"

"That's correct."

"And you didn't find any of the physical evidence you talked about — evidence you said we all take with us when we pass through our environment — on any of the five pairs of shoes, did you?"

"I didn't examine them for that purpose."

"What I asked was, on your examination of each of the five pairs of shoes, you didn't find any grains of sand or blades of grass or lake soil, anything like that, on any of those ten individual shoes, did you?"

"I didn't note the presence of anything, no."

"Were any of the five pairs saturated with water?"

"Not that I noted."

"Did any smell like they had been wet?"

Another smile. "I didn't note that to be the case."

"You do know what a tennis shoe that gets wet can smell like?"

"Unfortunately."

The jurors smiled again.

"You testified that the person who made the shoe prints leading from the water to the back of the house was walking with an intent and purpose."

"I did."

"That purpose being to get to the back of the house?"

"That's the logical conclusion."

"Beyond that, you have no way of knowing what the person was thinking, do you?"

"I do not."

"It could have been a person who heard a gunshot and ran to the back of the house out of curiosity."

"I don't agree with that hypothesis," she

482

said, and before Sloane could move on, she explained. "If it had been, then I would have expected to find two sets of prints, one by the person you've suggested, and a second by the shooter, who preceded that person."

"*If* the shooter came out of the water and up the lawn, as you've suggested, and did not gain access to the back of the house by some other means, correct?"

"I found no evidence to suggest that a person came by any other path."

Cerrabone looked ready to stand, as if he suspected Sloane was about to violate the judge's order and ask about the other two sets of shoe prints.

"But isn't it true that your focus when you arrived was the back of the house?"

"Not initially, no."

"It wasn't?" Sloane asked, his voice rising. "So you and Detective Rowe discussed that the killer could have gained access to the property other than by water?"

She recognized the trap. "We did not have a set theory when I started."

"But it seems so obvious now that you've testified; wouldn't you at least say that the backyard was your primary focus?"

"No, I wouldn't say that."

"So it's not as obvious as you've made it seem, is it?"

Growing frustrated, Wright said, "When I started my investigation, I walked the entire property with Detective Rowe. It was not until after we walked the entire property that I focused on the continuous lines I noted in the backyard."

"But you did find footprints throughout the property, did you not, on all four sides?"

"Yes, but I was able to eliminate almost all of those prints as belonging to law enforcement officers who responded to the scene."

"Almost all, but not all."

"Not all, but I also did not find a continuous line of footprints such as the prints on the lawn, to suggest ingress and egress to the patio."

Sloane wasn't going to get anything better and moved on. "The make and model of the shoe to which you referred, that's a very popular brand and model of shoe, isn't it?"

"I don't know."

"You're not aware that it is one of the most popular brands of shoe sold in the Pacific Northwest?"

"No. That is not important to my analysis."

"It's common."

"I don't know."

"You testified that the shoe prints on the

484

concrete patio were wider than the other prints you measured, and you attributed that to the person standing in that location, water oozing from the saturated shoes onto the patio."

"Yes."

Using a photograph taken from the water looking at the back of the house, Sloane asked, "By the way, you found no physical evidence that a person sat down on the beach or the rock wall, did you?"

"I did not."

"So your theory requires that we presume the person who came out of the water did so wearing the shoes, right?"

"It does."

"Can you think of any logical reason why a person would wear running shoes in the water?"

"You're assuming the person acted logically."

Sloane's eyebrows arched. "Aren't you?"

"Not necessarily."

"No?" He glanced at the jury. "You are, after all, hypothesizing that the person walked with a 'determined' gait and with a 'purpose' and 'intent' to the back door. Doesn't that require some logic on the person's part?"

"It's what the evidence dictates."

"So you never bothered to question why the person would wear the shoes while swimming?"

"No, I did not."

"And there's the problem of the gun, isn't there?"

"I don't understand your question."

"Well, your hypothesis also presumes that the shooter swimming in the water while wearing shoes also brought the gun with him, doesn't it?"

"I didn't offer a hypothesis, I only testified as to the physical evidence."

"You said the person walked with a determined gait, with purpose and intent, to the patio, correct?"

"I did."

"You found nowhere along that path that the person deviated in another direction, stopped, or otherwise paused, did you?"

"Not on the path to the house."

"So you found no evidence that the person stopped to, for instance, take a gun out of a backpack or pouch, did you?"

"They could have been doing that on the patio."

"And risk being seen? That wouldn't be very bright, would it?"

"I don't know."

"Then let's stick to what you do know.

You found no evidence that the person deviated to a location where they might have previously placed the gun, did you?"

"I did not."

"So the evidence dictates that the person brought the gun with them, correct?"

"That would appear to be the case," she conceded.

"So, again, I ask, is it logical that a person who arrived at the scene with such purpose and intent would not have planned ahead and had a method to keep the gun dry?"

Flustered, Wright said, "I don't know that they didn't."

"Are you questioning the physical evidence, Detective?"

"No."

"Because if they had brought some sort of waterproof pouch, as you now suggest, to keep the gun dry, why wouldn't they have also put the shoes in it?"

"Is there a question you want me to answer?" Wright asked.

"The question is, if the person had some means to keep the gun dry, like a waterproof backpack of some sort, wouldn't you have expected the physical evidence to reveal that the person stopped somewhere other than the patio to remove the gun, and if they had, then why wouldn't they have kept the shoes in the same pack?"

"Again, you're assuming that the person was acting logically or rationally."

"How about practically? Have you ever tried to swim in shoes, Detective?"

"No, I haven't."

"But you would have this jury believe that someone who had intricately planned a murder — who had planned it so that they knew they were going to swim to the property with the forethought that they had to have some means of keeping dry the weapon they intended to use to kill their victim — didn't also have the foresight to think about how to keep their shoes dry?"

Wright shrugged. "I can only testify about the physical evidence."

"Tell me, Detective, when you and Detective Rowe walked the property and discussed the evidence, was it then that you decided to just throw common sense out the window?"

Cerrabone was up. "Objection, Your Honor, it misstates the testimony, and it's argumentative."

Sloane didn't wait for a ruling. "You're darn right it's argumentative."

"Hang on," Underwood said. "The objection is overruled. Mr. Sloane, you'll direct your comments to me. Now, did you want

Detective Wright to answer your last question?"

Sloane looked at Wright. "I think we all do."

"I followed the evidence," she said.

"Even if the evidence led to illogical conclusions?"

"I followed the evidence," she repeated.

"The shoe prints on the patio, as you have described them, were aligned so that the right foot was positioned about sixteen inches in front of the left foot, was it not?"

"Yes, it was."

"And if that person was the shooter, as you indicate, would the position of the feet" — Sloane demonstrated — "be indicative of someone shooting left-handed?"

"I can't speculate."

"I'm just asking you to follow the evidence, Detective. Wouldn't the physical evidence dictate that the shooter was more likely than not left-handed?"

"One could draw that conclusion," she said, "but I can't say with certainty."

The Paragon
Pioneer Square
Seattle, Washington
She saw him enter, though she tried to hide it. Her eyes shifted to the crowd, but her

489

voice betrayed her, a tiny hesitation that caused the next note to be flat. No one else in the club seemed to notice or care. The young men and a few of the women sitting at the mismatched tables in the standing-room-only crowd gazed up at her with unbridled lust. She had that intangible quality — that charisma, an aura. She had "it."

He waited at the back until she finished her set. The crowd gave him only brief consideration, another testament to her appeal. He had expected the music to be deafening, especially in the small confines, but her voice was not the hard-edged screeching he had anticipated. Melodic and sultry, it was deeper than her normal speaking voice.

Finished, she gave a furtive glance to the doorway to the right of the bar leading to the alley in back — he'd walked the perimeter after his prior visit. Then, resigned, she stepped from the platform, walking among her admirers in tight-fitting black jeans and a blood-red camisole to match the spiked pumps. The other members of the band looked like stagehands at a play, dressed in black clothing — including long black coats — a sharp contrast to their pale white makeup. Everyone still trying to cash in on the vampire craze, he guessed.

Eyes watched as she approached with a sheepish grin. "You're a better detective than you let on."

"And you're a better singer."

"I didn't let on I was a singer."

He put his finger up near his nose.

She smiled at the irony and rolled her eyes. "The tattoo?"

Jenkins touched the tip of his nose. The tattoo — GOD'S NAILS, written in Gothic script across her shoulder — had also been on the flyers posted on the bar walls announcing the band and its lead singer, Anastasia. The same script adorned the front of a set of drums in the background of a Facebook picture depicting Joshua Blume playing his guitar.

"So, Claire," Jenkins said, the use of her given name a subtle hint that he had done his homework and wasn't the gullible ox she thought him to be, "how long have you known Joshua?"

She looked at her admirers at the tables, who continued watching her. "Do you smoke?"

"Bad for your health," he said, "and your voice." But he gestured to the door leading to the alley.

Outside, she bummed a cigarette and a light from a young man and Jenkins followed her down the alley. It smelled of clove cigarettes and marijuana. Others acknowledged her, telling her she sounded great, that they liked the new song. They gave Jenkins sidelong glances. She stood with one arm draped across her midsection, the other arm perpendicular, a trail of smoke wafting up from the cigarette between her fingers.

"Are you cold?" Jenkins said, indicating a willingness to give her his jacket.

She smiled. "Smart and a gentleman. Wow. We don't get that in here too much. That ring on your finger wouldn't be just a prop, would it?"

"If it is, it comes with a wife and a son."

She blew smoke out of the corner of her mouth. "Bummer." Then she said, "He's played with us for about six months."

"Why'd you lie?"

She shrugged her shoulders. "To see if I could get away with it."

He shook his head to let her know that she hadn't and still wasn't.

"He's what, sixteen?" she said. "That was a problem. He's not supposed to be in there. But he can play. I mean, he can *really* play — the best guitar player I've ever heard. Believe it or not, some people used to come just to hear him."

"Then he must be really good," Jenkins

said, and she smiled at the compliment.

"But his father's a bit of a fuck. I figured he sent you to scare us again; he sent his attorney once, another fuck . . . not that you are. I mean, he said he'd sue us because Joshua is underage."

"What did Joshua say when you called him?" Jenkins guessed they had spoken after his visit.

She drew on the cigarette, causing the end to flare red, then blew another stream of blue-gray smoke skyward. "He said I shouldn't talk to you. He said his father told him not to. He said his father had him locked down nights, that he'd put in a security system so Joshua couldn't sneak out." Something about it amused her, and she glanced at him with the flirtatious eyes that seemed to captivate every person she met. Then she lost the smile. "The asshole busted his guitar, too."

"But that's not all Joshua told you, was it?"

She took another drag on the cigarette, dropped what remained on the damp pavement, and crushed the butt with the ball of her pump. She curled her hair behind her ear — which, he was surprised to find, had just one piercing — then, as if she couldn't help herself, she grinned and touched the tip of her nose.

TWENTY-SIX

Tuesday, December 6, 2011
King County Courthouse
Seattle, Washington

Cerrabone began the following day with Blume. The young man who entered the courtroom only faintly resembled the Joshua pictured on the Facebook page of the underage lead guitarist for the band God's Nails. It was not a Madison Avenue business cut, but Joshua Blume no longer hid from the world behind a clump of brown hair. And while they hadn't adorned him in a suit and tie — Cerrabone no doubt cautioning against making him too much of a choirboy — he did wear a pressed polo shirt and gray slacks, more color than in all of his Facebook pictures combined.

Joshua looked apprehensive, which would give what he had to say even greater credibility with the jurors. His mother and father sat in the front row behind the counsel table, not far from Detective Rowe. The jury noticed their presence and certainly had determined their roles in this production. Sloane would have to tread all the more carefully. No one liked to see a grown man picking on a kid, especially not with his parents watching.

Cerrabone walked Joshua through the preliminaries, where he lived, where he went to school, and where he had been the night in question. The young man had a tendency to mumble, a universal condition for nearly every sixteen-year-old boy Sloane knew, Jake included. Cerrabone reminded Blume several times to keep his voice up and at one point moved the microphone closer to compensate for his soft-spokenness. It caused several of the jurors to lean toward Blume, a few of the women with placid smiles — mothers who, Sloane knew from voir dire, had children about the same age. The kid's nerves lent credibility; he did not want to be there.

Cerrabone didn't hold back, clearly deciding it was prudent to take the wind out of Sloane's cross-examination and ask Joshua how he got away with being in a club.

Joshua admitted he had a fake ID. "I had one," he said. "I mean, until my dad took it away."

That brought a few more smiles and approving nods from several jurors. Richard Blume appeared to sit a little taller in the pew.

"What were you doing in that nightclub?" Cerrabone asked.

"I play in a band. I play guitar," Blume said.

"And were you playing in that nightclub on Tuesday night, September sixth?"

"Yeah," Blume said. He cleared his throat. "Yes."

"What time was your performance?"

"We had the late set that night, so it was eleven to one."

"Eleven at night until one in the morning?" Cerrabone asked.

"Yeah. Normally, bands only get to play one set, but we get two because people like us . . . I mean they did."

"And what time did you leave the club?"

"Not until maybe two-forty-five, about then."

"What did you do from one o'clock in the morning until you left?"

"We listened to this other band, and then we talked about band stuff. We were trying to raise enough money to record an album. There's a recording studio in Belltown . . . if we got the money."

"Did you drink any alcoholic beverages while you listened to the other band?"

Blume nodded. "I had a couple of beers."

"How many is a couple?"

"Two or three. I don't remember, exactly."

"You don't remember? Could it have been more than three?"

He shook his head. "No. I'm pretty sure it was two. I'm not much of a drinker."

"Did you drink anything else?"

"No."

"Did you ingest any other drug of any kind?"

"No."

"And did you drive home?"

Blume related that another member of the band who lived on the east side with his parents had driven him home. Jenkins had confirmed all of this.

"And did he drop you off in your driveway?"

"No, he dropped me down the street; there's an easement that leads to my backyard."

Cerrabone moved the easel into place and displayed the aerial photograph for the jurors. "Can you point out the easement on the photograph?"

Blume did, and Cerrabone marked it with a red dot. "And why did you have your friend drop you there?"

" 'Cause I wasn't supposed to be out," Blume said. "The path leads to my backyard, and I can sneak into my room." He had a sudden look of alarm, and his eyes flickered to the front row. "But not anymore."

Cerrabone established that Blume had been dropped off at about three-thirty in the morning. "And on the morning of Wednesday, September seventh, did you walk immediately down the easement to your room?" Cerrabone asked, getting to it.

"Not right away."

"Why not?"

"I heard something, so I hid in the bushes."

"What did you hear?"

"I heard someone running, footsteps. And then I saw someone coming up the path across the street."

"Let's mark that on the photograph."

Blume did so with a blue line so it was clear to the jurors that the path led to the water. Getting back into the witness chair, he said, "It's a public easement. It's not like it's anybody's backyard."

"What did you see this person do?"

"She stopped at the top of the path, and she looked around, like maybe she heard something. Maybe the car. I don't know. Then she walked over to the bushes and pulled out a bike that was in there and got on it, and rode off."

"Did she ride off right away?"

"Not right away. She put on a helmet."

"And during this period of time before the person rode off, as you watched her run up the path, pull out the bike, and then slip on a helmet, did you get a good look at this person?"

"Pretty good," Blume said.

"Just pretty good?"

"That means good, you know."

"Wasn't it dark?"

"There's a street lamp not that far away. So there was some light, not great, but good enough that I could see her."

Cerrabone established the street lamp on the aerial photo. "Is the person you saw here in this courtroom?"

"Yes, she is."

"Can you point to the person you saw?"

"I saw her." Blume pointed as Cerrabone had no doubt instructed him. But the young man could not keep Barclay's gaze. After a quick glance, he lowered his hand and retreated to the safety of Cerrabone.

In preparing for his cross-examinations, Sloane had to make several decisions but none more important than how he would handle Blume. Blume was the most damaging witness, and the jury would expect Sloane to challenge the young man's testimony. It would be an uphill battle. They would have a hard time believing that a sixteen-year-old kid, especially one with Joshua's demeanor, would lie about something so important; most sixteen-year-old boys didn't even want to get out of bed, let alone get involved in a murder case. There had seemed no winning, until Jenkins had reported back on his conversation with Anastasia the night before.

Now it was up to Sloane.

"You must be a very good guitar player, Joshua," Sloane said as he approached.

Blume looked a bit perplexed. "I'm okay."

"Sixteen years old, playing in a group in which the average age of the other band members is twenty-two, you must be better than okay?"

"I'm pretty good." He tried to hide a smile.

"Is that what you'd like to do, play guitar in a band?"

"I guess so. I don't know."

"Well, it must be pretty important to you."

"I guess so."

"How many times had you sneaked out

before that night when you say you saw Barclay?"

"I don't know."

"Quite a few?"

Joshua looked past Sloane to his parents. "Not that many."

"More than twenty?"

"Like I said . . . I don't remember."

"How long were you the lead guitarist for God's Nails?"

"About six months."

"And how often did the band play at the club in Pioneer Square?"

"Couple times a week, I guess."

"And I'm assuming you had other performances besides playing at that club?"

He shrugged. "Some."

"So that would equate to what, fifty or so times that you had sneaked out to play?"

The eyes darted again, the voice hesitant. "I don't think it was that many."

"You said that your father took away your fake ID. When did he do that?"

"That day."

"What day?"

"When I got home."

"September seventh?"

"Yeah."

"And is that also the last time that you played with God's Nails?"

"Uh-huh."

"Are you playing in any other bands?"

Blume shook his head.

"Is that a no?"

"No."

"And why not?"

Blume looked again to the front row. "I can't."

"Your father won't allow it?"

Blume shook his head. "No."

"Your father doesn't approve of your playing in a band?"

Cerrabone was up, and Sloane was surprised it had taken him this long. "Objection, Your Honor. Relevance. I think this is getting pretty far afield."

Underwood considered Sloane. He knew Blume was the prosecution's most damaging witness, so he would cut Sloane some slack, but only so much. "Mr. Sloane, I'll give you some leeway, but I want to see some connection here, and sooner rather than later."

Sloane turned back. "Joshua, I think my question was how your father felt about you playing in a band."

Joshua lowered his eyes. "He hates it."

"Mr. Cerrabone asked you why it took you nearly two full days to tell someone that you saw something, and you said because you were afraid of getting in trouble for sneaking out without permission, do you remember saying that?"

"Yeah."

"This person you saw . . . you didn't see them commit any crime, did you?"

"No."

"You said they ran up this path, got on a bike, and rode off, right?"

"That's all they did."

"So you didn't tell your mother or father about it the following morning, right?"

"Right."

"And you didn't call any of your friends, did you?"

He shook his head. "No."

"And no one called you up and said, 'Hey, Joshua, did you hear about the guy who got shot down the street?' and you said, 'I saw someone that night,' or anything like that, right? That didn't happen either, did it?"

"No. Nothing like that."

"You didn't tell anyone right away."

"No one."

"So how, then, Joshua, did your father find out that you sneaked out and took away your fake ID?"

"I told you . . . I told them that I saw this person . . ." He stopped and looked at his parents, realizing the inconsistency.

Sloane waited for the jurors to realize it also. Gently, he asked, "How did your father find out that you sneaked out if you didn't tell anyone about this person you saw, Joshua?"

The boy paused, quickly realizing he was on an island with no one to save him. He took a deep breath. His lower lip quivered. "He caught me sneaking back in. He was awake."

"And he punished you that night."

Joshua nodded.

"You have to answer out loud, son."

"Yes."

"He took your fake ID."

"Yes."

"And he forbade you to play with the band anymore?"

"Yes."

"And he did more than that so you wouldn't play, didn't he?"

Blume looked up at Sloane, eyes wide. Then his gaze darted past. Sloane didn't need to turn to find out where. Cerrabone was up. "Again, Your Honor, I think this inquiry is not relevant —"

"Your objection, Mr. Cerrabone?"

"Irrelevant."

This time Underwood did not hesitate. "Overruled."

Sloane took a step closer to the witness chair to cut off the line of sight to the Blumes in the front row. "What else did your father do?"

The young man looked on the verge of tears. "He broke my guitar. He threw it out." The first tear leaked from the corner of his eye.

"And that's what you loved the most, isn't it, playing your guitar and playing with God's Nails?"

Blume wiped the back of his hand beneath his nose. "Yes."

"And you'd do just about anything to play the guitar with God's Nails and be onstage with Anastasia again, wouldn't you, Joshua?"

He shrugged. "I don't know."

A couple of the female jurors blotted their eyes.

"But you did tell her that you thought if you testified, your dad might buy you another guitar and let you play in the band again, didn't you?"

He shrugged.

"You have to answer verbally," Sloane said.

"I don't know. I guess I did."

Sloane walked back to the counsel table and returned carrying a copy of the *Seattle Times*. "So you got out of bed on Thursday,

506

already grounded and forbidden to play in the band, and you read the article in the newspaper about the murder just down the street, didn't you?" He held up the newspaper that had the article on the front page but, more important, had Barclay's picture.

"Yeah."

"And you saw Barclay's picture in the paper that morning, didn't you?"

"Yes."

"And you read that the police questioned her."

"Yes."

"And that was before Detectives Rowe and Crosswhite came and showed you the photograph of Barclay that you picked out of the group, isn't it?"

Blume sighed audibly. "Yes."

Sloane held up the montage photograph near the photograph in the newspaper, the two remarkably similar. "And you thought that if you testified here, being the star witness, maybe your father would let you play in the band again, didn't you?"

Joshua had checked out. He shrugged. "I don't know."

From behind, Sloane heard Mary Beth Blume sigh, "Oh Joshua." Underwood heard it also. So did the members of the jury.

Some turned their head to look.

"Didn't you also tell Anastasia that your father had talked to his attorney, that he thought this was a big case; that someone might even write a book about it, maybe even make a movie, and if they did, you'd get a lot of money to tell your story and maybe God's Nails could record an album?"

When Joshua didn't immediately respond, what was left to fill the silence were the stifled sobs of a mother. His head down, Joshua had retreated, this time without the bangs to hide him from the rest of the world and, more important, the disapproving eyes of his father.

After Joshua answered in the affirmative, Underwood took a recess.

Outside the courtroom, Sloane retreated to a corner at the far end of the hallway with Pendergrass and Barclay. Pendergrass looked like a kid trying to suppress the greatest surprise in the world. Barclay looked as though she'd already seen the surprise and still couldn't believe it. She stared, her jaw slightly open, speechless. The obvious cross-examination would have been to take on Joshua Blume's senses, to question and cast doubt that he could have been so sure of what he saw so late on a dark and stormy night, while likely intoxicated. Then

Sloane could have held up the newspaper with the picture of Barclay that looked remarkably like the picture that had been part of the montage Rowe and Crosswhite had shown to Blume. Sloane had even retained an expert to testify about the power of suggestion and how Blume would have been predisposed to pick Barclay's picture — not because he had seen her that night but because he was familiar with her face. But that would have left unanswered the question for which Sloane had no answer and thus no way to discredit Blume. Even if it had been dark and stormy, even if the closest street lamp had been twenty yards away, even if Joshua had drunk a couple of beers, that only cast doubt on the specifics of what he saw, it did not change the fact that he had seen *someone.* Sloane had no way to combat that underlying fact until Jenkins had advised Sloane on what he had learned and deduced from his second trip to the club in Pioneer Square.

"He loves this girl," Jenkins had said.

"How can you be sure?"

"Because every sixteen-year-old boy in the world loves this girl; she's the fantasy, the proverbial wet dream, what they all want to have and wouldn't have the slightest clue what to do with if they did. Marilyn Monroe to me, Angelina Jolie to you, Megan Fox to Jake. Adam would eat the forbidden fruit ten times out of ten for a girl like this. Hell, I'm not so sure I wouldn't. And the father took her from him. Doesn't matter that it was a fantasy, that the kid didn't have a chance. He loves her, and his only goal was to play with her again, be close to her, in the band."

That was when Sloane tore up his cross-examination and started over. He knew he couldn't convince a jury that Blume had hallucinated the whole thing. The better course was to challenge the boy's heart, and thus his motivation, and hope the jurors remembered what it was like to be young and hopelessly, painfully in love for the first time, that you would do or say almost anything to be near that person, to be a part of his or her life. It was better left to the jury to infer that the boy had made up the whole story, made it up to appease a father he could never appease, with the hope that he might get back his guitar and another chance to be near Anastasia. Cerrabone would attempt to rehabilitate Blume after their break, but the damage had been done, the boy's motivation undermined and crumbling, his testimony like the wall of a house built on a damaged foundation, standing, perhaps, but its integrity severely in question.

Sloane had heard the analogy, even used it himself a few times, the one about trials being like climbing mountains, a test of not only stamina but will power. Those who finished the climb were those who refused even the slightest rationalization that to quit the climb was acceptable.

So although every muscle and joint of his body burned and his mind felt as tired and clouded as it had that day when he reached the thin air atop Mount Rainier, Sloane couldn't quit. Joshua Blume was behind them, but looming directly ahead was Felix Oberman. Unlike Blume, Oberman would not be a slap fight in the grammar school playground. Sloane needed to turn his cross-examination into a good old-fashioned brawl. He needed to take Oberman apart, to take shot after shot at him until, hopefully, Oberman displayed the temper and cruelty Barclay said lurked within the man.

The problem with that course of action, however, manifested when Dr. Felix Oberman entered the courtroom looking too old and too small to be the oppressive ogre he had been during his marriage. The reading glasses remained tethered on a chain around his neck despite the round wire-rimmed glasses. Both gave him a studious, professorial appearance. He'd tamed his curls with water, but the beard remained an afterthought, an untended brown and gray patchwork that started high on his cheekbones and disappeared beneath the collar of his forest-green shirt.

After the preliminaries, Cerrabone asked, "How often do you go to the symphony, Dr. Oberman?"

Oberman spoke in a quiet, measured tone. "The season runs throughout the year, so it varies. I could go every night of the week, but I have neither the time nor the finances to do so. I usually go more frequently during the summer months."

"Do you have any favorites?"

"I'm partial to Beethoven and Mozart, but my love is Beethoven's Symphony No. 8, *Allegro vivace e con brio,* which is why I was going that night."

"What night was that?"

Oberman provided the date.

"And is your ex-wife aware of your fondness for that particular symphony?" Cerrabone asked.

"She certainly . . . Well, she certainly was. I played it often in our home, and we heard it together at least twice."

"When was the last time you saw your ex-wife at the symphony?"

"Not since our divorce. Ten years."

"Ten years? It must have come as quite a surprise, then, for you to see her there."

Sloane contemplated objecting, as the question implied Reid never went to the symphony, but he decided to let it go and made a note to attack it on cross-examination.

" 'Shock' might be a better way to put it."

"You were alone?" Cerrabone asked.

"At that moment I was, yes. I was meeting someone there."

"And what happened?"

"As I exited my car, I turned, and there stood Barclay engaged in conversation. I initially contemplated acting as if I hadn't seen her, but she turned and . . . as I said, it came as a bit of a shock . . ."

"What was her reaction when she saw you?"

"Surprisingly, she smiled and walked over."

"Why did you contemplate ignoring her?"

"Our marriage did not end well."

"You had an acrimonious divorce?"

"That would be an understatement. But we had seen each other at our daughter's funeral, and I think it had a sobering effect on us both, you know; made us realize life is too short."

"And so you spoke?"

"We did. I expressed surprise to see her."

"And what was her response?"

"She said she needed to get a little more culture in her life, that she was tired of sitting at home watching mind-numbing movies . . . words to that effect."

"You mentioned she was engaged in conversation when you first saw her. Did you have an impression this person was a date or escort for the evening?"

"No. It was a couple. They departed when Barclay came to speak to me."

"So she was alone when you spoke to her."

"She was."

"Did she say whether she was meeting anyone?"

"She did not."

"And did the conversation eventually turn to Mr. Vasiliev?"

"It did. I brought him up, actually."

"You brought him up?"

Oberman nodded, looking chagrined. "It was uncomfortable . . . there was little to talk about, and so I said that I'd seen the article in the paper, the one about the U.S. attorney bringing charges against Mr. Vasiliev. I knew she had been heavily involved in fighting drugs since our daughter's death, and I asked her if she knew what was to come of it."

"And what was her response?"

"She sighed a bit, you know, wistful. She seemed tired. Perhaps 'resigned' is a better word."

"And you recall that specifically?"

"If you knew my ex-wife . . . she is rarely resigned to anything."

"Then what happened?"

"The fire came, the one I became all too familiar with during our marriage, when her eyes change color from green to a dull gray. That's when she said it."

"And what did she say?"

"She said, 'You know, if I had known it would take this kind of effort, I would have just put a bullet in the back of his head and been done with him.' "

Cerrabone waited a beat. Then he asked, "And did you have any reaction?"

"No, not particularly."

Several jurors looked confused, as if they had misheard the testimony. Cerrabone too looked and sounded curious but his was no act. "Why not?"

"Because during ten years of marriage, I'd seen Barclay say things like that before. She cannot help herself."

"So you did not take her seriously?"

A small laugh. "To the contrary, I've learned to always take my ex-wife seriously, Mr. Cerrabone. Yes, I thought she meant it, if that is the intent of your question. And yes, I thought she was capable."

Sloane shot from his chair. "Objection, Your Honor, speculation. No foundation."

"Sustained. The jury will disregard the witness's last remark."

In theory, perhaps, but practically, Sloane knew the jurors would not be able to do so. Apparently recognizing this, Cerrabone was content to leave the jury to consider those stricken but not forgotten words.

Sloane rested an arm on the railing of the well near the court reporter. "You said you learned to take your ex-wife seriously. So I imagine you called the police to tell them of this statement and your concern that she might actually do it."

"No, I did not."

"You told your date for that evening."

"I saw no reason to do that."

"So you told no one?"

"I told the police."

"Two weeks after the fact and after Mr. Vasiliev was dead, correct?"

"Correct."

"Prior to that, you did nothing."

Oberman looked as though he were about to say something, then cleared his throat. "I did nothing prior to that."

"You didn't say why you had learned to take your ex-wife seriously. Why was that?"

"Because my ex-wife is a person who follows through on what she says she will do."

"Like getting a restraining order from the Superior Court against you after your separation?"

Oberman pinched his lips. "Including that."

Sloane positioned himself at the corner of the counsel table so that to look at him, Oberman would also have to look at his ex-wife. "Let's not dance around the pink elephant in the room, Dr. Oberman; your divorce was far more than acrimonious. It was vicious, wasn't it?"

"I certainly thought so."

"It even became violent, did it not?"

Oberman shook his head. "I tried to keep things civil."

Sloane raised his voice, disbelieving. "You were arrested for assaulting her." He pulled a sheet of paper from the file he had set on the table and approached. "You blackened her eye, split her lip, fractured one of her cheekbones. Do you call that keeping things civil?"

Oberman's jaw clenched. "I never touched her," he said.

Sloane held up the police report. "So the police report is what . . . a fantasy?"

"She lied. I never touched her."

"Did she make up the injuries in this report? Were those also a fantasy?"

"I don't know how she obtained her injuries, but I was not responsible."

Sloane was amazed that even now, after ten years, under oath and on the witness stand, the man could be so adamant. "You were arrested for assault, were you not?"

"I was."

"You spent time in jail."

"I did."

"So we know the court didn't consider it a fantasy."

Cerrabone rose. "Objection, Your Honor."

"Sustained."

"And as part of your release, Judge Corliss issued a restraining order against you."

"He had no choice under the circumstances. He had to respect the allegations. I was never convicted of any crime, and I maintain my innocence."

"You were never convicted because Barclay convinced the prosecutor to drop the charges against you. Isn't that true?"

"She dropped them after I agreed to give

up my custody battle for Leenie; she used our daughter as a bargaining chip."

"What are you suggesting, Dr. Oberman, that Barclay rammed her face into a meat tenderizer to gain leverage in the divorce?"

Oberman's voice rose. His eyes became animated. "She wanted full custody of Carly. She told me if she didn't get full custody, she would destroy me. She succeeded. As I said, my ex-wife usually does what she says."

"And you had no part in your own demise?"

He clenched his jaw. "She ruined my business, my ability to make a living."

"I was under the impression that your business was ruined because you chose to have a relationship with one of your psychiatric patients, something the State of Washington Medical Board frowned upon and which resulted in the suspension of your license to practice. Isn't that true?"

Oberman pointed at him. "I did not have an affair with any of my patients, and the medical board's inquiry never held such to be the case."

Sloane nodded as if accepting Oberman's explanation, then held up a document. "Never held that to be the case because the medical board *also* dropped the charges when the patient failed to appear and testify against you, isn't that correct?"

"It was one of the reasons. It was not the only reason."

"Another condition of your parole was that you refrain from the use of alcohol and that you attend Alcoholics Anonymous meetings; isn't that also true?"

"That is true."

"But alcohol played no part in your demise, either, did it, Dr. Oberman?"

"I acknowledged my drinking."

Sloane let it go. "Now you indicated that your daughter's death had a — how did you put it . . ." He walked to the table, and Pendergrass handed him his notes. " 'A sobering effect on us both, you know; made us realize life is too short.' Is that accurate?"

Oberman calmed. "I believe so, yes."

"Isn't it true, Dr. Oberman, that after your daughter's death, you began to leave Barclay messages accusing her of being an absentee mother and blaming her for not being more diligent, that if she had been more diligent, she would have seen the signs that Carly was using drugs?"

Reid had recorded the messages and phone calls. Sloane had the tape if Oberman denied it.

Oberman took a breath, gathering himself.

"I was angry and upset when I received the news of my daughter's death, as any father would be. I said some things that I regret, I said them in the heat of the moment," Oberman blurted, anger seeping into his response.

"Sort of like 'I would have just put a bullet in the back of his head and been done with it' could be said in the heat of the moment?"

"No, it's not the same."

"I'm sure it's not," Sloane said. He turned his back, walking to the counsel table.

"You don't understand," Oberman said. Sloane wheeled and looked to Underwood to admonish Oberman and to strike his unsolicited comment. Underwood had already raised his hand, but before the judge could speak, Oberman looked at Sloane, his brown eyes hooded and tired.

"But you will," he said.

The Justice Center
Seattle, Washington
Rowe reached for the phone on his desk. He had a few minutes to change into more comfortable clothes, grab his materials, check his messages, and call home to reacquaint himself with his wife's voice. Then he would head back to the courthouse to

meet with Cerrabone for what would likely be a very long evening. Sloane had lived up to the hype. He seemed to have an innate sense of the best way to attack each witness. With Joshua Blume, he had been compassionate and sensitive, and it was clear from the expressions on the jurors' faces that they had appreciated it. With Oberman, that compassion was nowhere to be found. Sloane took the man head-on, provoked him, and again his style seemed to resonate with the jurors. And yet — to Rowe, anyway — Sloane seemed to be holding back, perhaps saving his best shot for last, and that last shot was Rowe. He would have to be better prepared than he had ever been.

After speaking to his wife and each of his three sons — his oldest had a baseball game that evening — Rowe grabbed his materials and headed for the elevator but heard someone call his name.

"Sparrow. Hey, Sparrow?" Bernie Hamilton chased after him, a document in hand.

"What's up, Bernie?"

"Where are you off to?"

"Meeting with Cerrabone. I'm on the stand tomorrow first thing." Rowe looked down at the document. "I'm late."

"Not for this. Ballistics are back from the cold case that big PI told us to pull. Zach

Bergman."

Half a turkey sandwich grew stale on a piece of white butcher paper, and the tea Carolyn had made for him had long since grown cold. The door pushed open and Reid walked in, looking exhausted. "How much longer do you have?" she asked.

"More than I have time for," he said.

"Isn't it always that way."

"Rowe's their last witness," he said. "I want to make sure we finish strong before we begin our case in chief."

"Where's Tom?"

"Drafting our motion for a directed verdict."

The motion was routine, brought by the defense at the end of the prosecution's evidence — a request that the judge dismiss the case because the state had failed in its burden to prove beyond a reasonable doubt that Reid was guilty. Judges were reluctant not to allow a case to go to a jury. Sloane and Pendergrass gave the motion no chance.

"I won't get my hopes up," Reid said.

"Why don't you go home?" Sloane said. "I'll get in a few more hours and grab a

523

room at the Club."

"You're not coming home?"

Home. Sloane hadn't thought of Barclay's house as his home, but he supposed it had become that. Many of his clothes now hung in her closet, and she had cleared space in the top two drawers of a dresser for him. He'd spent far more time at her house recently than at Three Tree Point.

"If I did, it would be very late and I'd just wake you, or you'd wait up for me, and you need a good night's sleep." He smiled. "I'll bill the room to the client."

"Then get a good room," she said. Her kiss lingered. When their lips parted, she did not pull back. Eye to eye, she asked, "Is everything okay?" He nodded, but she didn't buy it. "Sorry, but you don't get off that easy. Something is bothering you. I sensed it over the weekend. What is it?"

"Nothing."

"David, tell me."

"I'm worried," he said.

Her brow furrowed, but her voice was light. "The lawyer who does not lose, worried?"

"I'm not getting an impression from the jury; what they're thinking and feeling."

She put her hands on his shoulders, remaining close. "You've been brilliant, just as I knew you would be."

They kissed again before she departed. When the door closed, he turned and looked out his office window. In his head, he heard his conversation with Jake as the boy left for the airport.

It's how we heal, you know?

What's that?

The pain.

What about it?

Feeling it every day . . . it's not a bad thing. That's how we heal.

TWENTY-SEVEN

Wednesday, December 7, 2011
King County Courthouse
Seattle, Washington

Cerrabone spent the morning doing cleanup, putting on additional members of the CSI team as well as witnesses to testify that Reid was intimately involved in Vasiliev's federal prosecution. It set the stage for Rowe.

That afternoon the detective took the stand in a pin-striped suit, blue shirt, and silver tie. Rowe testified that he received the telephone call from Felix Oberman after returning to his office following the daylong investigation of the crime scene. "The first thing I did was run a data check to determine if Ms. Reid owned a handgun, as her ex-husband claimed."

"And what did you determine?"

"I determined that Ms. Reid had purchased and registered a handgun."

"Of what caliber?"

"A thirty-eight. A Smith and Wesson revolver."

"What did you do next?"

Rowe related how he and Crosswhite had gone to Reid's home and asked to see the weapon, and how the gun was not in the safe on the floor of her closet.

"Did Ms. Reid have any explanation?"

Rowe shook his head. "She said she hadn't seen it, hadn't opened the box since taking shooting lessons some time after her daughter's death. She said she had no idea why it wasn't in the box."

"She didn't know where it was?"

"She did not."

Rowe discussed the search warrants and what they had removed from Reid's home, including the five pairs of running shoes. Cerrabone had him identify and authenticate each pair so they could be admitted into evidence.

"What size are the shoes?" Cerrabone asked.

Rowe dutifully pulled out the tongue of each of the pairs as if considering them for the first time. "Seven," he repeated five times, like a bell tolling.

"What is the brand of each pair?"

"Nike AS300," he repeated.

"Did you interview Ms. Reid about her collection of shoes?"

"I did."

"Why so many pairs?"

"She said she was training, that she did triathlons, and that included running long distances."

"Did she say what else triathlons included besides running?"

"Swimming and riding a bike."

Cerrabone asked about Reid's training, how far she swam, ran, biked. Then he had Rowe tell the jury the distance from the public easement where Joshua Blume claimed he saw Barclay to the back of Vasiliev's house, as well as the distance from her home to the public easement. Both distances were well within what Reid had told Rowe to be her regular training regimens.

Despite his best efforts with Blume and with Oberman, Sloane could see some of the jurors nodding as Cerrabone and Rowe methodically laid out the evidence that had led Rowe to arrest Reid. No matter how good Sloane's cross-examinations had been to that point, there remained the unspoken question — if Barclay had not killed Vasiliev, then who had? It was not his burden, but human nature being what it was, several jurors would be asking that question in the jury room.

Sloane approached. Ordinarily, he did not ask open-ended questions on cross-examination, but felt comfortable if he knew the answers. "Detective Rowe, did Barclay advise you when she began to train for triathlons?"

"She said it was shortly after her daughter's death."

"Did she say why she took up triathlons?"

"She called it her therapy."

"Did she explain that further?"

"She said that after her daughter's death, she was depressed, and rather than go on prescription medication, as the doctors had recommended, she began to exercise and eventually began to do triathlons."

"She didn't say she began training so she would be in shape to bike, swim, and run far enough to go and shoot Filyp Vasiliev a year after the fact, did she?"

Rowe couldn't hide a smirk. "No. She didn't."

"You asked Ms. Reid how she heard of Mr. Vasiliev's death, did you not?"

"I did."

"And she told you that I had informed her, didn't she?"

"That's what she said."

"She told you that she had sought to

retain me the day before Mr. Vasiliev was shot; that she wanted to file a wrongful-death civil action against Mr. Vasiliev to recover monetary damages against him, didn't she?"

"She said that, yes."

Sloane would leave it for his closing argument to point out the inconsistency of someone intent on killing Vasiliev also hiring an attorney to sue him for money the prior day.

"Let's talk about the shoes you took from Barclay's home," Sloane said. "You took every pair of athletic shoes in the house, did you not?"

"Every one we could find."

"You searched her office and car as well, I presume?"

"We did."

"You're confident you have every pair of athletic shoes from her house, car, or office?"

"Reasonably confident."

"You and Detective Cerrabone were present when each of the search warrants were executed, were you not?"

"We were."

"It was a very thorough search, was it not?"

"It was thorough, Mr. Sloane. We took

every athletic shoe we found."

"And so we have these five pairs, correct?" Sloane placed each of the five pairs on a table.

"That's correct."

"As part of a separate subpoena, you also sought Barclay's financial records — records of her credit-card and debit-card purchases — correct?"

"That's correct."

"And you went through those financial records carefully?"

"I went through them, as did my partner, Detective Crosswhite."

"Did you note credit-card purchases of athletic shoes?" Sloane knew they had.

"I believe we did."

"In fact, you highlighted each of the purchases on a copy of the documents produced in this litigation, did you not?"

"Yes, we did."

"You highlighted six purchases of running shoes?"

Rowe didn't immediately answer. "I'm not sure."

"Well, let's be sure, Detective." Sloane handed Rowe a stack of the records, the same documents Reid had found in his office and said, *I think we may have something.*

Rowe went through them, hesitant. "There

are five purchases."

"On the credit card statements, yes. But there is also a receipt for a cash purchase, isn't there?"

Rowe flipped the pages and reconsidered the documents. Though the jury likely did not detect the brief moment Rowe's eyes closed, Sloane did. "Yes, there is," Rowe said.

"So the total would not be five."

"The total would be six."

"I suppose that, as an experienced investigator, you could infer from that evidence that Barclay, as the perpetrator of this crime, disposed of the pair of shoes she wore the night when she biked and swam all the way from her house to Vasiliev's house to shoot him."

"I accounted for five pairs of shoes. But to answer your question, yes, a sixth pair could have been worn and disposed of."

"Just as you would like the jury to infer that Barclay disposed of the gun she used to kill Mr. Vasiliev, right?"

"I'm just here to testify about the evidence."

"And the inferences you made from that evidence that led you to arrest Barclay, correct? I mean, you wouldn't have arrested her unless you inferred that she had biked to the easement, run to the water, swum to the house, shot Vasiliev, and returned home, disposing of the weapon somewhere along the way, right?"

"As an investigator, I do make inferences from the evidence."

"But you also keep an open mind, don't you? You don't rush to conclusions, right?"

"You consider all the evidence."

"Just like you considered me a suspect at one time, didn't you?"

"We thought it prudent to talk with you."

"Because I had been in Ms. Reid's home the morning before Mr. Vasiliev was shot, correct?"

"Ms. Reid told us that you had been present."

"And so you contemplated the *possibility* that I might have taken her gun and used it to kill Vasiliev, didn't you?"

"We followed up on several leads."

"I'm sure you did, including the possibility that someone other than Barclay, perhaps even me, somehow got ahold of her gun and used it to kill Vasiliev?"

"We had no such evidence that was the case."

"And yet you interviewed me about it for two hours in my home, didn't you?"

"We did."

"So you had to have at least thought that a possibility, right?"

Rowe shrugged. "As I said, we try to follow up on every lead."

"Did you suspect anyone else besides me could have taken the gun and used it to kill Mr. Vasiliev?"

"No, we did not."

"But if someone had taken and used the gun to kill Vasiliev, couldn't that same person have taken the sixth pair of athletic shoes that cannot be accounted for?"

"I wasn't aware of the sixth pair of shoes."

"So you didn't have all the evidence when you decided to arrest Ms. Reid?"

"We believed we had sufficient evidence to warrant Ms. Reid's arrest."

Sloane held up the financial records. "But not all the evidence."

Rowe tilted his head, a tacit acknowledgment.

Cerrabone's redirect took up the rest of the afternoon. When he had finished and Underwood asked him to call his next witness, Cerrabone stepped forward. "The state rests, Your Honor."

Underwood dismissed the jury with a warning that the weathermen were predicting snow flurries that could persist throughout the night. He advised them to give themselves plenty of time in the morning to arrive by nine and to not leave for the night without his bailiff's cell phone number in case they had difficulty. After the jury departed, Underwood heard Sloane's motion to dismiss and promptly denied it.

In the morning Sloane would begin his case in chief.

Pendergrass walked into Sloane's office looking perplexed. He explained that he had been reviewing the stack of documents from the state.

"There's a gap in the Bates-stamp numbers." Pendergrass showed Sloane the numbers stamped in the lower right corner of the documents. "The number jumps from P-six-nine-eight-seven to P-six-nine-nine-five." Pendergrass also said he found other, smaller gaps.

"Could they have gotten out of order? There've been a few of us looking through them."

"I checked. The pages aren't here. We don't have them."

Sloane didn't have the time or inclination to get into a fight with Cerrabone about it. "Determine what pages we're missing, call up Cerrabone's paralegal and ask her to send them over. Better also prepare a motion to compel, just in case."

As Pendergrass left his office, Carolyn walked in carrying three piles of documents, each secured with a rubber band.

"What are those?" Sloane asked.

"The documents you subpoenaed. Do you want me to give them to Tom?"

"Yes," he said, not believing he'd have time to go through them, then realizing he'd just tasked Pendergrass with another motion. "No."

Carolyn spun. "I don't care what you decide so long as I can put these down sometime tonight."

"Leave them here. I'll have to look at them later."

Just after nine in the evening, Sloane slipped the rubber band from the largest pile, documents from the home-security company that installed and monitored the alarm in Barclay's home. He'd gotten the idea to subpoena the documents the night he had accidentally set off the alarm by opening the sliding-glass door. He flipped the pages to the date that most interested him and saw what he had expected, then something he had not. He reread the information, then read it a third time. He considered his watch, hurried down the hall, and pushed open the door to the office at the end.

Jenkins and Alex looked to have been engaged in an intense conversation when Sloane interrupted.

"I'm going to need you to serve two more subpoenas, and I need the witnesses in court first thing tomorrow morning."

TWENTY-EIGHT

Thursday, December 8, 2011
King County Courthouse
Seattle, Washington

Thursday morning it was Sloane's turn to test Judge Underwood's patience. Cerrabone stood, red-faced, and advised that the state had a matter to take up with the court before the jury entered. Sloane had faxed a revised list of witnesses to Cerrabone's office at seven o'clock that morning, and the list included the names of two witnesses not on any prior list. To make matters worse, Sloane advised that he intended to call the two witnesses first thing that morning.

Cerrabone did not try to hide his annoyance. Voice animated, he argued that the "surprise" witnesses prevented the state from adequately preparing for cross-examination. He called it a sandbagging.

Sloane fell on the sword, apologizing profusely, but he also had decided it was time to get even with the state for dumping thousands of documents on his doorstep on the eve of trial. He advised Underwood that he had not known he would need to call the witnesses until late the prior evening, when he came across certain documents. He added that it now appeared the state had unilaterally withheld certain documents, the sequence of numbers for which Pendergrass had listed on a short motion to compel. Sloane knew Underwood would be reluctant to issue any ruling that could be construed as preventing Barclay Reid from putting on a complete defense. This was, after all, a first-degree-murder trial. No judge liked to be reversed on appeal, especially on a case that continued to generate daily headlines. After asking Sloane the nature of the two witnesses and their testimony, he issued his ruling.

"I'm going to allow the two witnesses to testify. Mr. Cerrabone, if you determine that you need additional time to prepare to cross-examine these witnesses, you may defer and recall them."

With that, the bailiff brought in the jury, and Sloane called his first witness.

Damon Russo looked apprehensive when Sloane greeted him in the austere hallway outside the courtroom and quickly introduced himself. He apologized for the short notice and thanked Russo for being there — not that he had a choice, once Jenkins handed him the subpoena. Sloane told Russo to just answer the questions he asked, and things would be fine.

Russo took the witness stand in black polyester pants and a white long-sleeved shirt that looked to have been purchased when he was ten pounds lighter and worn to every occasion that required something more formal than jeans and a T-shirt. The cuffs and collar were threadbare. Russo parted his prematurely gray hair in the middle and pulled it back in a ponytail that extended to his shoulders.

Sloane walked him through the preliminaries, hoping they would give Russo time to relax.

"You and I have never spoken before, have we, Damon?"

"Not until just now in the hallway."

"And before I introduced myself in the hallway, we'd never met, had we?"

"No."

"In fact, my investigator, Mr. Jenkins, served you with a subpoena this morning when you walked in the door to work, didn't he?"

Jenkins sat in the back row of the courtroom, head and shoulders above the rest of the crowd.

Russo nodded and gave a nervous laugh. "Yeah. He . . . Not exactly how I intended to start the day."

"I'm sure it isn't," Sloane said. "Where do you work?"

"I'm head of the technical and customer-support division of American Security Systems."

"And what type of business is American Security Systems?"

"We're the largest residential home-security company in the world," Russo said. "We provide systems that monitor the home in case of burglaries, fires, floods, carbon monoxide poisoning . . ."

Russo sounded so proud Sloane thought the man might take out a brochure and solicit the closest juror. "And how long have you been working for American Security?"

"I've been with the company eight years, the last five in my current position."

"What do you do on a daily basis as head of the technical and customer-support division?"

"I oversee our monitoring centers."

"Does that include the monitoring center for your Seattle region?"

"It does."

"And what does the monitoring center monitor?"

"We monitor our clients' security systems twenty-four/seven. Anytime there is an alarm, for any reason, it triggers a dedicated cellular connection to one of our interconnected customer-monitoring systems. We also provide technical service to our customers, such as if they can't get the alarm to reset — any number of things."

"When you describe an alarm triggering a dedicated cellular connection to one of your interconnected monitoring systems, is that a fancy way of saying that when an alarm is triggered, your center gets a call?"

"That's a good way to put it."

"Does your department keep records of when the security system of a particular residence is tripped and an alarm is activated?"

"The date and time are automatically recorded by the computer and supplemented by the technician."

"And how does the technician supplement the record?"

"The technician calls the residence to determine the nature of the alarm — whether it requires a police or emergency personnel response or if it is a false alarm."

"How can the technician tell the difference?"

"If no one answers the telephone at the
residence the technician is trained to immediately dispatch the call to the local
police or emergency personnel. If the telephone is answered, then the technician asks
the person to provide a password for their
system. If the person provides the password,
the technician does not act further. If they
cannot, we dispatch the call."

"The subpoena served on you today
requested that you bring certain records
with you. Did you do that?"

Russo held up the file from his lap and
confirmed he had brought records for the
security system installed at Barclay Reid's
home on Queen Anne Hill.

"And do those records include August
twenty-third of this year?"

Russo nodded. "Yes, I brought it."

"Can you tell the jury what that record
shows?"

"It shows that the alarm was tripped that
day at twelve-fifty-four in the afternoon."

"And was that call dispatched to police or
to emergency personnel?"

Russo studied the record. "No, it was not."

"Does the record indicate why not?"

"The technician noted that she called the

residence and spoke to a person who provided the password for the system."

"And what was that password?"

Russo spelled it. "L-E-E-N-I-E."

Sloane paused for a moment. "Did the technician note the identity of the person she spoke with?"

"Yes. They're trained to get the name of the person."

"And what name is reflected on the record for August twenty-third at twelve-fifty-four in the afternoon?"

"The person identified themselves as the residence owner, Barclay Reid."

Cerrabone deferred his cross-examination. He looked perplexed by the testimony. So did some of the jurors. After Russo departed, Sloane called Nina Terry, Barclay's assistant. She was the first person to enter the courtroom and smile when she looked at Barclay. It wasn't a big-toothed grin, just a thin-lipped statement that conveyed Terry believed Reid innocent.

"How long have you worked as Barclay's assistant?" Sloane asked.

"We've been together nearly fifteen years," she said.

"How many hours a day are you at the office?"

Perhaps in her midforties, Terry smiled and folded her shoulder-length, auburn-tinted hair behind an ear. In a cream-colored turtleneck sweater and champagne slacks, she looked like the CEO of her own company. "Well, I don't think I need to tell you that the hours can fluctuate. Normally, I work eight to five, five days a week. But I'm usually at my desk by seven-forty-five, don't leave until six, and sometimes work Saturday and Sunday, when we're in trial or especially busy."

Sloane would have paid to have Carolyn sitting in the gallery for that answer. "As Barclay's assistant, you keep her professional calendar of appointments?"

"I keep her professional and her personal calendars," Terry said. "It just made sense for me to keep both to avoid unnecessary conflicts or mixups."

"Do you keep it on the computer, or do you keep an actual physical calendar?"

"I use both," she said. "The computer allows Barclay to access her calendar remotely, and the hard copy gives me something at my fingertips when I need it."

"And did you bring the physical copy of that calendar with you today, as I requested?"

"I did."

"Before we get to it, let me ask you this. I would imagine, spending so many hours in Barclay's company over the years, that you have come to experience just about every one of her moods."

Terry responded with another poorly concealed smile. "Oh, yeah," she said in a tone that drew chuckles from the jury. "Practicing law lends itself to mood swings. I've yet to work for an attorney immune to it."

Sloane let the jury enjoy the answer. "You've seen her angry?"

"Yes."

"And sad?"

"Yes."

"Happy, depressed, contemplative?"

"All of those things," Terry said.

"Have you ever seen her violent?"

Terry shook her head. "No."

"Never?"

"Never."

"Has she ever raised her voice at you in anger?"

"She's raised her voice, but I wouldn't call it in anger — more like frustration at something that has happened. She's not a robot, though given the amount of work she generates, sometimes I wonder."

The jurors again chuckled.

"Have you ever felt threatened by Barclay?"

"Never."

"Let's take a look at her calendar. Were you working Wednesday, September seventh of this year?"

Terry looked at the calendar. "Yes, I was."

"And do you recall if Barclay was in the office that day?"

"She had a meeting at eight that morning and another at one. She also had a court appearance late that afternoon. I do remember the morning meeting because I set up the conference room."

"Do you recall what time she got to work that morning?"

"I recall that she was already at her desk when I arrived at seven-forty-five. That's when I go in and we discuss what is on her calendar for the day and any changes."

"So you spoke to her that morning?"

"Yes."

"You observed her demeanor?"

"Yes."

"Can you tell us how she seemed to you?"

Terry shrugged. "She seemed like she always does. She seemed fine."

"You didn't notice anything different about her demeanor than any other typical morning?"

"Nothing at all."

"She didn't look exhausted?"

"No."

"Nervous, anxious?"

"No."

"And did she make it through all of her appointments that day?"

"She did."

"Anything out of the ordinary happen that day?"

"You came that day."

"Explain that to the jury."

Terry related how Sloane had called and asked to speak to Barclay, then appeared in the lobby and asked again, which resulted in a short meeting in the conference room.

"And after I left, did you speak to Barclay?"

"She told me that you told her that Mr. Vasiliev was dead; that someone had shot him."

"Again, based on your fifteen years and thousands of hours working with Barclay, can you describe her demeanor when she gave you that news?"

"She seemed . . . I don't know." Terry looked across the courtroom at Reid. "Honestly, she seemed sort of saddened by it. After she told me, she sort of shrugged and shook her head. Then she went into her office and closed the door. 'Depressed' might be the best way to describe her mood."

Sloane asked Terry to open Barclay's calendar to August 23. "Can you tell me what was on her schedule that day?"

"That's an easy one. That was the Bergstrom mediation with Judge Peters."

"How is it you remember that mediation?"

"It was a significant case in the office, and we were trying to get it settled before trial. If a case doesn't settle, then it's Katie-bar-the-door, and that makes my life a lot more challenging. We go into trial mode."

"Where was the mediation held?"

"In our offices. I commandeered three conference rooms to accommodate all the sides. I wasn't the most popular person in the office that day."

"What time did the mediation start and finish?"

"I recall that we went from nine in the morning and didn't get the final paperwork signed until after nine o'clock that night. I know because Barclay asked me to stay and type it up."

"Did they break for lunch?"

"They did, but I ordered in sandwiches for Barclay and our clients."

"She didn't leave the office?"

"Not for a minute. Not until after nine

that night."

Sloane let that piece of information sit with the jury as he flipped through his notes — the obvious question being how Barclay could have answered the security company's telephone call to her home and provide the password if she was in the office all day.

Cerrabone kept his cross-examination brief. "During all of the hours that you've spent with Ms. Reid, have you ever seen her hide her emotions?"

"I don't understand the question."

"There must have been occasions when you knew Ms. Reid was angry or upset or saddened by something but didn't want to show others, like a client or staff, and so she hid or suppressed those emotions."

"Yes, there have been those occasions."

"Would January fourteenth be one of those occasions?"

Terry flipped through her calendar. "I don't know."

"Ms. Reid was in the office that day, wasn't she?"

Terry considered the calendar. "She had appointments."

"Is there anything to indicate she canceled those appointments or rescheduled them?"

Terry flipped through the pages. "Not that I recall or see."

"Nothing to indicate she left work early that day or otherwise didn't keep her appointments."

"No. Nothing."

"And yet that was the day after her daughter's funeral, wasn't it?"

Terry looked stricken. She glanced at Barclay, then back at Cerrabone.

"It was, wasn't it?"

"Yes," she said. "It was."

Cerrabone paced before the jury. "Has Ms. Reid ever forgotten something at home and asked you to get it for her?"

Terry considered this. "I can recall one occasion."

"How did you get in the house?"

"She gave me the key."

"What about the code?"

"She gave me the password."

Cerrabone looked to the bench. "I have no further questions at this time."

When Cerrabone sat, Sloane stood for redirect. "Were you surprised to see Barclay the day after Carly's funeral?"

"Not particularly."

"Why not?"

"Because she told me at the reception that she would be in."

"She told you at the reception following her daughter's funeral that she intended to go to work the next day?" Sloane raised his voice to sound incredulous. "Did she say anything further?"

"She said she had to . . . she had to keep herself busy, keep her mind occupied, that if she didn't, she'd go crazy." Terry shrugged.

"And on August twenty-third, the day of the Bergstrom mediation, did Barclay send you to her home at twelve-fifty-four in the afternoon to get anything that she forgot?"

"No."

"Are you aware whether she sent anyone to her home at twelve-fifty-four that day?"

"I'm not."

After Underwood excused Terry, Sloane called Shawn Cortes to the stand, Cortes being the second of the two added witnesses. In her early twenties, Cortes had a purple streak in her dyed red hair. A small diamond stud pierced her right nostril. She wore black boots into which she'd stuffed green cargo pants, and a black T-shirt with the image of Jimi Hendrix, who had likely been dead nearly two decades before she was born. Cortes explained that for the past six months she had been employed as a receptionist for a group of doctors at a building in Bellevue.

"Is Dr. Felix Oberman one of the doctors in the group for which you serve as receptionist?" Sloane asked.

"Yes."

"What are your duties as a receptionist?"

"Uh, I answer the phone?"

The jurors chuckled.

"And do you advise the person who has called whether the particular doctor is available or not available?"

Cortes continued to grin as if she had walked into the easiest pop quiz in history. "Uh, yeah."

"So if a doctor is on his phone, you tell the caller that the doctor is unavailable, right?"

She shrugged. "Or I ask if they want to hold or be put into the doctor's voice mail. It's really not that complicated."

"What if the doctor is out of the office, what do you tell the caller?"

The sardonic smile returned. "That he's out of the office?"

More chuckles from the jurors.

"How do you know that a particular doctor is out of the office at that particular time and not just in the bathroom or down the hall getting a cup of coffee or glass of water?"

"They're supposed to tell me when they

553

leave and when they come back."

"Do you note this somewhere?"

"I note it on a sheet at the desk."

"You note when a doctor leaves the building and when he returns?"

"There's a box next to the doctor's name. You just write in the times."

"What are those sheets called?"

"Daily records?" She made it sound like a question.

"And you keep one of these daily records every day that you're the receptionist?"

She nodded. "That's why they're called *daily* records." She was enjoying her time in the spotlight and was playing to the jury.

"Are they dated?"

"You write in the date in the upper-left-hand corner."

"What do you do with the sheet at the end of the day?"

"File it in a drawer behind the desk."

"How long are they kept?"

She shrugged. "I don't know."

"Did you bring the file of daily records with you today?"

Her eyebrows peaked, and she held up the file in her lap.

"Would you open the file and find the sheet for August twenty-third of this year?"

Cortes took some time to flip through the

554

sheets. Sloane was glad she did. The jurors watched intently, wondering what was to come. She pulled out a sheet, considered the date at the top, and held it up.

"Did you find the daily record for August twenty-third?"

"Uh-huh."

"And do you recognize the handwriting on that document as yours?"

"Yep, it's mine."

Sloane further authenticated the document, asked the clerk to mark it, and moved to introduce it into evidence. Cerrabone did not object.

"Now, would you please look at the line next to the name Dr. Felix Oberman for that date and tell me if Dr. Oberman left the office that day and at what time?"

"He left at twelve-fifteen."

"And what time did he return?"

"It was two-thirty."

"You wrote something else by the numbers two-thirty. What did you write?"

"I wrote 'LATE!' "

"Why did you write that?"

"Because he *was* late, and because there was a patient waiting for him, and the guy was not happy and he was taking it out on me every five minutes."

"Did you talk to Dr. Oberman when he

returned from being late?"

"He doesn't really talk to me except to say if he's leaving or when he's back. I remember, though, because when he walked in and saw the patient, he acted all surprised and stuff and made up some bullsh —" She looked up at Underwood. "He said he didn't have it on his calendar."

Cerrabone objected that Cortes was speculating as to Oberman's state of mind but Underwood overruled him.

Sloane stepped closer to the rail. "Do you have any idea where Dr. Oberman was from twelve-fifteen until two-thirty in the afternoon on August twenty-third, Shawn?"

She shook her head. "Nope. That's not my job."

After Cerrabone's cross-examination of Cortes, Underwood dismissed the jury for the day with the same warning about the weather. The minute the jury room door closed, the people in the gallery began to buzz, and the media filed out into the hallway, opening cell phones and laptops.

Sloane found Jenkins at the back of the courtroom. They moved to a corner. "Any luck?"

Jenkins shook his head. "The receptionist said he hasn't been in all day. He's not answering his cell or his apartment phone. I went by earlier. If he's home, he isn't answering the door."

Cerrabone and Rowe talked at the prosecution table, obviously perplexed by the turn of events.

"Oberman's gone," Sloane said to Cerrabone. "My investigator has tried to get ahold of him all day. He isn't answering his cell phone or the phone at his apartment, and the receptionist at his office says he hasn't been in all day. I want him back on the stand tomorrow morning."

"He's still under subpoena," Cerrabone said, sounding as disinterested in Oberman's whereabouts as Cortes had been. He was clearly not happy about the two surprise witnesses.

"At the moment, that isn't helping," Sloane said. "If I have to get a continuance, I will."

Cerrabone looked to Rowe. "Why don't you drive out and see if he answers the door."

Sloane told Barclay he would meet her back at the office. She told him she was going home, that she had a vicious headache and would try to sleep it off. Jenkins offered to come with him, but Sloane told him to drive

Barclay home, then go back to the office and see what Alex had learned. She had a contact monitoring Oberman's bank accounts and credit cards in an effort to determine if he had fled.

On the elevator to the lobby, Rowe and Sloane found themselves alone. Rowe had a cynical, disbelieving smile. "So Oberman breaks in to her house, takes her gun, and kills Vasiliev. Is that your theory?"

"He knew the password, Detective. They used it on all of their bank accounts and computers."

"Come on, Sloane. You saw that guy. He couldn't swim ten yards. And he doesn't wear a size seven."

"Maybe he didn't make the swim."

"What, he hired somebody? Who?"

Sloane shrugged.

As they stepped outside, the snow the weathermen had predicted had begun to fall, large heavy flakes that indicated it would be more than a flurry. Rowe turned to Sloane. "With the snow, traffic will be shit this time of day. Come on."

Terra Creek Apartment Complex
Bellevue, Washington
The Terra Creek apartment complex had been built across the street from the Belle-

vue Library, within walking distance of the Lincoln Town Center with its bars and restaurants, shopping, cinema complex, and business tower. But Terra Creek wasn't one of the fancy condominium complexes built to house the residents the city planners hoped would support those establishments. It had a couple of ground-floor businesses — a Subway sandwich shop and an Italian pasta restaurant, along with a dry cleaner and, next to it, an empty storefront.

Felix Oberman's apartment was located on the second floor. The hallway smelled of Indian food and was so narrow Sloane wondered how anyone could possibly move in any furniture. When Rowe knocked, the door shook in its jamb but no one answered. They left and returned with the supervisor. The man unlocked the door without question and stepped back, no doubt believing that when a police detective flashes his badge and asks you to open the door to one of the residents' apartments, it is not a precursor of good things to come.

With the blinds drawn, the snow falling, and the early-winter sunset, the only light in the room came from the hallway. Rowe flipped a light switch that illuminated a kitchen not wide enough to accommodate two people and separated from the living space by a four-foot-high pony wall and granite counter. Two plates and a fork lay in the sink. Otherwise, the counter was clean. The living area consisted of a sofa, a recliner with a back massager, a reading lamp, and a small television. Rowe knocked on a door to their right, presumably the bedroom, and called out Oberman's name. When he got no answer, he pushed it open, ran his hand along the wall, and flipped another light switch.

Stepping in, he said, "What the Sam Hill?"

TWENTY-NINE

Law Offices of David Sloane
One Union Square
Seattle, Washington

Jenkins and Pendergrass continued the conversation as they stepped from the elevator into the lobby. They began the discussion on the car ride back to the office after driving Reid home.

"What are you talking about? She was in a mediation. No way she could have set off the alarm and provided the password," Pendergrass said.

"It doesn't explain the size-seven shoe prints or how Oberman could have done it."

"Oberman took the missing pair of shoes when he took the gun," Pendergrass said, pulling open the door to the office and letting Jenkins slip through ahead of him.

"Maybe. And maybe he even fits his foot into a size seven, but tell me how he makes the swim."

"He could have had a boat tied up, or a raft or kickboard."

"Could have, but that doesn't explain how Joshua Blume could mistake a bearded man for a woman."

"Blume's testimony is discredited," Pendergrass said.

"With the jury."

"Well, isn't that who we're concerned with?" Pendergrass asked. "What, you think he actually saw something? He made it up to appease his dad and the girl."

"Maybe," Jenkins said.

"Maybe? You interviewed her."

Alex stepped into the hall from her office holding several sheets of paper.

"What canary did you swallow?" Jenkins asked.

She handed him sheets of paper. "Guess who's left-handed?"

Terra Creek Apartment Complex
Bellevue, Washington

The corners of some of the photographs, tacked to the wall with a single pushpin, had curled. The newspaper clippings had yellowed. Together, they stretched nearly the entire bedroom wall.

"Do not touch anything," Rowe said to

Sloane. He flipped open his cell phone and stepped into the living room. Sloane heard him talking to Crosswhite, telling her to get ahold of Cerrabone, prepare a search warrant, and dispatch a CSI unit to the address.

The collage was sick in its detail, a chronology of Barclay Reid with various hair lengths and engaged in different activities. Supplementing the photographs, Oberman had collected what must have been every *Bar Journal,* magazine, and newspaper article ever written about his ex-wife, along with articles mentioning her name in the cases she had tried.

Sloane stepped forward and considered a cluttered desk of unopened mail, psychiatric journals, and scraps of paper with handwritten notes. He turned the switch to a metal desk lamp. It illuminated an aerial photograph in the center of the pile with which Sloane had become intimately familiar.

Rowe reentered the room carrying a black case, opened it, and pulled out two pairs of blue gloves. "Put these on," he said. Then he took out a camera.

Sloane nodded to the photograph. "Vasiliev's home and backyard."

Rowe shook his head and began to snap photos.

"Look at this." Sloane lifted the aerial

photograph to further examine the document beneath it. "It's a lunar chart showing the days of the month the moon would provide the least amount of light. He circled September seventh."

"The thunderstorm must have been an added bonus." Rowe continued to take photographs. He lowered the camera. "So who did he get? No way he did it himself. I'm not buying it, and the evidence doesn't support it. Neither does common sense."

"Common sense just went out the window, Detective. Someone this obsessed, he finds a way to get it done." Sloane continued looking through the materials, though careful not to disturb them. He pulled open the top drawer of a gray filing cabinet against the wall separating the bedroom and living area and flipped through the manila tabs. As he did, his cell phone rang.

"We found him," Jenkins said.

"I'm at his apartment right now. Where is he?"

"You're at his apartment?"

"Yeah, in Bellevue. I'm with Rowe. You're not going to believe —"

"Not Oberman. Andrew Lorin."

"Who?" Sloane asked.

"The transvestite. Only he isn't a he anymore. He's a she. That's why Alex couldn't find him. That's why he had no further employment records or bank accounts. That's why the DMV had nothing and Alex couldn't find any medical records. Andrew Lorin no longer exists. Andrew Lorin is now Lori Andrews. And guess who's left-handed?" Jenkins asked. "You still there?"

"I'm here," Sloane said, a thought coming to him. He pushed the files to the right and stepped to his left so that he could see the initial files in the drawer. He did not see the tab, fingering past the A's to the D's.

"And guess what hobby Lori Andrews competes in?" Jenkins didn't wait for Sloane to answer. "Triathlons. She competed in four this past year."

Sloane closed the top drawer and opened the lower drawer, flipping through the L's. "It's not here," he said.

"What's not there?" Jenkins asked.

"Oberman has a filing cabinet with patient files but no file for an Andrew Lorin or a Lori Andrews."

"He might have it at the office. Or in storage. It's been ten years."

Sloane closed the bottom drawer and slid open the top again.

"Alex has an address and phone number," Jenkins said. "Andrews lives in an apartment in Madison Park. It's one of the brick apartment buildings at the point. You can see it as you drive across the 520 floating bridge."

"I know it," Sloane said. He and Tina had considered the complex when they moved to Seattle and couldn't find a house, but the apartments, built in 1939, had the box feel of military housing — each exactly the same. Tina nixed the idea when she learned the units had neither a dishwasher nor a washing machine.

Sloane flipped through the tabs again, noticing a pattern. Oberman put a single manila file, no matter how thin or thick, in its own separate hanging green folder. He flipped quickly through the files to names beginning with the letter L. Just after the name Jason Locker, he found the green hanging folder immediately following it empty.

Edgewater Apartment Complex
Madison Park, Seattle

Rowe left Crosswhite and Cerrabone to process Oberman's apartment. He and Sloane slogged through traffic north on the 405 out of Bellevue, then east on the 520. A flood of workers trying to beat the already falling snow added to the usual heavy Mi-

crosoft reverse commute, turning the freeway into a parking lot. Rowe finally hit the
siren and used the commuter lanes to weave
in and out of the stream of cars. As they
reached the west side of the bridge, they
could see the lights for the Edgewater on
the shore of the lake. Rowe took the Lake
Washington Boulevard exit and drove
through the residential streets. The windshield wipers slapped at the flakes of snow,
which had become larger as the temperature
fell and were accumulating on the windshield.

Rowe told Sloane that the Washington
State Patrol crime lab had confirmed that
the gun that fired the bullet that killed Vasiliev had also been used in a murder ten
years earlier of a PI named Zach Bergman.

Sloane knew the name. "Barclay's private
investigator," he said. "He took the photographs of Oberman with Andrew Lorin."

"I know. And the detectives questioned
Oberman about it."

"How did you even know to check?"

Rowe gave him a glance. "Your PI asked
me."

"Charlie asked you to do it?"

Rowe looked and sounded surprised that
Sloane didn't know. "He said he had a
hunch. I thought you asked him to find out."

Sloane hadn't.

In addition to the half-dozen two-story red brick buildings at the point of land abutting Lake Washington, the apartment complex extended several blocks, at least another dozen buildings, not including the pool and office complex.

The darkness and accumulating snow on the windshield made it difficult to identify building numbers. Rowe's GPS, of little help, kept repeating "You have arrived." Rowe finally switched it off.

Rowe turned right on East Edgewater Place, then made a right onto Forty-second Avenue East. When they passed between two familiar brick pillars, Sloane told Rowe to park. "I know where the office is. We can move faster on foot."

Sloane turned up the collar of his overcoat, shoved his hands in his pockets, and lowered his head. Wet snow blew in his face as he cut across a square patch of lawn blanketed with snow. He felt the moisture seeping through the bottom of his leather shoes, soaking his socks. Kids dressed in snowsuits, knit hats, and gloves threw snowballs, their laughs the only detectable sound in the snow-deadened air. He got turned around once, then saw the familiar rental office.

He reached for the glass door, but the office interior was dark, and he knew before he pulled on the door it would be locked.

Rowe blew into his cupped hands and turned 360 degrees, considering the buildings. Melting snow had matted his hair. Flakes stuck to the shoulders of his suit jacket. After a few moments he seemed to pick up something, like a dog to a scent, and began to jog with a pronounced limp through the complex, considering the buildings.

The address Jenkins had provided for Lori Andrews turned out to be one of the buildings abutting the lake. Rowe removed his gun, put it in his left hand, and flexed the cold from his right hand and fingers. He held the gun straight down at his side as they approached Andrews's unit. He had called for backup on the drive, but with the snow and traffic his backup was likely also fighting both the traffic and the elements. Rowe didn't seem inclined to wait. The cold had reddened his cheeks. When he spoke, his breath marked the air. "You wait here."

"Not a chance." Sloane blew into his own hands.

"That's right. I'm not taking a chance of getting you killed."

"We're wasting time, Detective, and we

may not have time to waste. Plus, we're both freezing out here."

Rowe grunted, in obvious pain, but moved to the edge of the door to a ground-floor unit. He reached out and banged on the wood. "Seattle Police, Ms. Andrews. Open the door."

Sloane heard sounds inside, but no one came to the door.

Rowe reached out and banged again. "Seattle Police, Ms. Andrews. Open the door."

When he still got no response, Rowe stepped out and thrust his black wingtip against the lock. The door flexed but did not give. Rowe kicked again, and the door flung inward but Rowe collapsed, grimacing in pain. "Shit. My hip." Sloane entered to the left of the door frame then swung around a wall into a living area. The television was on. A wedge of light marked the carpet from a porch light above a back door to the unit, which was ajar.

Sloane pulled open the door and cautiously looked out. Footprints marked the snow-covered porch. Sloane remembered Kaylee Wright's testimony about a continuous line and followed what appeared to be a set of prints.

With the snow now above his ankles, his

feet became so numb they stung. He used a hand to shield his face from the swirling flakes and turned the corner of the building. A man hurried away, slipping and sliding as he approached the well-lit parking lot.

Sloane shouted, "Oberman!"

Felix Oberman looked over his shoulder but trudged on.

"Dr. Oberman. Stop."

Oberman stumbled and fell. Sloane closed ground. When Oberman tried to get up, his legs came out from under him and he collapsed in the snow. Sloane stopped just short of the man. "Dr. Oberman, stop."

When Oberman turned, he pointed the revolver at Sloane. "You don't understand." The snow had coated his hair and clung to his beard. Beads of water spotted his glasses, but Sloane could still see the tears.

"I do understand," Sloane said.

Oberman shook his head. Face red, he struggled to catch his breath. "No. I tried . . . I tried to warn you, but you wouldn't listen."

Sloane kept his hands raised. "I understand," he said. "You still love her. I know that. I know you love her."

The wall-length collage had only confirmed what Sloane deduced from their initial meeting, when the doctor snapped, "Hate has nothing to do with this." Though he clearly had serious issues with his ex-wife, Oberman's obsession with her had never ended.

"I wanted to stop her. I wanted to keep her from doing it."

"I know," Sloane said. "Just put the gun down."

"She said she had the gun. She said she was going to kill him. I just wanted to stop her. But then the alarm went off and the company called and . . ."

His words choked in his throat.

"Drop it, Oberman. Drop the weapon," Rowe shouted as he limped forward, clearly in pain. Gun extended, Rowe assumed a shooter's stance.

"Hang on," Sloane yelled.

"Drop it, Oberman."

"You don't understand," Oberman said.

"Calm down. Everyone calm down," Sloane shouted.

"Drop the gun, Oberman."

"I tried to warn you."

"Felix," Sloane said, drawing Oberman's attention. "Please. Put down the gun. Put it down."

THIRTY

The Justice Center
Seattle, Washington

Sloane stared through the plate-glass window at the pathetic figure slumped in a chair in the interrogation room. Oberman's beard lay flat against his chest, gaze fixed on the floor. Andrews was currently seated in the soft interrogation room next door with Crosswhite.

The gun Oberman had pointed at Sloane was a .38 Smith & Wesson revolver. Rowe ran the serial number through Data and learned within minutes that the gun was registered to Barclay Reid. After several tense moments, Oberman had let the gun slip from his hand into the snow. When he did, Rowe wasted no time flipping him facedown and handcuffing him. He and Sloane found Lori Andrews hiding in her apartment bedroom, saying Oberman had surprised her. After obtaining a search warrant, Rowe went through Andrews's apartment and found a pair of size-seven Nike AS 300 athletic shoes.

Rowe pushed open the door and entered the darkened room. "I don't think he's going to say anything." He sat, pulled a bottle of Ibuprofen from his jacket, and popped two pills into his mouth, chewing them.

"He never asked for an attorney?" Cerrabone asked.

Rowe shook his head, grimacing at the aftertaste. "Hasn't said a word." He looked to Sloane. "What did he say to you?"

Sloane shook his head. It didn't matter what Oberman had said. "He said he took the gun to stop her."

Cerrabone looked at his watch. "I have a meeting," he said, sounding none too happy about it. The brass band would be gathering again. It would be another long night. "I'll call you later, he said to Sloane. "I suspect we'll have something to discuss in the morning."

Queen Anne Hill
Seattle, Washington

Barclay threw her arms around Sloane's neck, holding him tight. "Thank God you're all right." Sloane had called her from the Justice Center to explain what had hap-

574

pened. She pulled him inside, started to turn the deadbolt, stopped. "I'm not even going to lock it." She shook her head. "I feel liberated. For the first time since Leenie's death, I feel safe. Are you okay? You must be freezing. Let me get you a drink."

"I'm fine."

"I can't believe this." She moved to the living room. "It's like a bad dream, a nightmare that won't end . . . only it has. It's over. It's finally over." Reid pulled the bottle of Scotch from the liquor cabinet, taking it into the kitchen. "What did he say? What did he tell the police?"

"He hasn't said anything. Not a word."

She pulled a glass from a cabinet and opened the freezer. Sloane heard the clink of ice cubes dropping in the glass. "And the transvestite? Has he said anything?"

"She," Sloane said.

She stopped the Scotch in midpour. "What?"

"Andrew Lorin is now Lori Andrews. Has been for ten years."

"Whatever. What did she say?"

"She denies any involvement. She has no idea how your shoes ended up in her closet."

Reid scoffed. "And I suppose Felix has no idea how the gun ended up in his hand." She handed him the Scotch.

"Left hand," Sloane said.

She took her drink into the living room. Sloane followed.

"Oberman is left-handed," he said.

"You're right, he is. I'd forgotten."

"Lori Andrews is also left-handed." Sloane took a sip of Scotch, feeling it warm his throat and radiate across his chest. The evidence fit with Barry Dilliard's and Kaylee Wright's testimony that the shooter's stance indicated someone left-handed. "How's your headache?"

"What? . . . Oh, it's fine. I just needed a couple hours of sleep."

"I feel sorry for him," Sloane said.

Her brow furrowed. "You feel sorry for him? That man has put me through hell."

He moved to the sliding-glass door and watched the snow continue to blanket the streets and sidewalks, piling on the edge of the wooden fence and street lamp crossbars. "He still loves you after all these years, after everything. He still loves you."

"He's obsessed. There's a huge difference between love and obsession, especially when obsessive love becomes obsessive hate."

Sloane faced her. "That's why he went to your house that day — to get the gun. He didn't want you to do it. He didn't want you to kill Vasiliev. It was his way of protecting you."

"He said that?"

Sloane took another drink. "That's what he said. But you already knew that, didn't you?"

"Knew he would what?"

"You knew he was obsessed with you; that was the power you held over him."

She crossed her arms. "What are you talking about?"

He put the glass on the dining room table. "That's why you went to the symphony that night . . . to tell him you still had the gun and you were going to blow Vasiliev's head off."

"What? I never said that."

"You wanted him to think you couldn't help yourself. But you could. You knew exactly what you were saying and you knew what he would do."

"Did he tell you this? He's lying."

"Then he wouldn't have gone to your house to take the gun, would he?" The logic was so simple, he wondered how he could have missed it for so long. "If you hadn't said it, he never would have set off the alarm. The security company would have never called."

"He came on his own," she said. "He planned this from the start. The two of them planned to frame me. He needed my gun to do that and he knew I owned it."

"But he had no reason to believe you intended to kill Vasiliev until you told him."

She threw up her hands, then pressed them together as if in prayer. "Have you gone crazy? What did he tell you to make you say these things to me?"

"He didn't have to say anything. I told you, he held the gun with his left hand."

"You're not making any sense. So what if he's left-handed? He didn't even shoot the gun. Andrew Lorin shot it."

"But the shooter shot with her right hand."

She shook her head. "What? All of the evidence is that the shooter was left-handed. The tracker, Barry Dilliard . . . they all said it." She approached. "What is this about?" He stepped back from her. "David, you're starting to freak me out."

"The shooter took a left-handed stance, but she wasn't left-handed. That's why the foot impressions show she stood there before she moved her right foot forward. She had to think about it. It didn't come naturally."

"It doesn't change the evidence; the shooter still took a left-handed stance. The trajectory of the bullet confirms it."

"Except Dilliard didn't have a critical piece of evidence when he performed his analysis."

"Which is what?"

"The door wasn't closed when the shooter shot through it. It was open two to three inches, maybe to allow a breeze."

"How the hell do you know that? There's no evidence the door was open."

"The only way Julio Cruz could have left a fingerprint on the sliding-glass-door handle would be because he touched the door. And the only reason he would have touched the door would have been to slide it open to go inside."

"He didn't say he went inside. Nobody said that."

"Micheal Hurley did. Centac had a bug planted inside Vasiliev's family room. In the rush to get out of there, neither Cruz nor Willins paid attention to or remembered the door was open a few inches. When Cruz closed it flush with the jamb the bullet hole moved to the right, which lined the hole up damn near perfect if the shooter shot with her left hand. Only the shooter couldn't have shot with her left hand, because her left hand was heavily bandaged to protect the stitches needed to close the cut from the glass she broke two days before."

Pendergrass held the door open as Jenkins, Alex, and Carolyn returned to gather their coats and purses. Sloane had called in updates about the amazing turn of events. After his final call from the Justice Center to tell them he was going to Barclay's they walked across the street to have dinner and drinks at the Hilton.

It saddened Jenkins that Sloane was not with them to celebrate. He knew it was likely a precursor of things to come. Charlie and Alex had a personal connection with Tina and Jake. They did not share the same connection with Barclay Reid, and Charlie suspected his and Sloane's relationship would weaken. On the other hand, he was happy for his friend, happy he and Alex had been wrong. They'd doubted Barclay, but only because they cared so much about Sloane and didn't want to see him hurt. Sloane had endured so much pain in his life, so much angst. He didn't need any more. Jenkins decided he would never tell Sloane they had looked into Reid's alibis, and he would never again say he didn't believe in coincidences. Barclay's meeting Sloane had not been part of any elaborate plan. It had been, as Alex had said, a chance encounter, the kind that happens all the time — a meeting that leads to a date that leads to another, and before they know it, the couple is telling the story of how they met to their children. Jenkins hoped that was how it would be for Sloane and Barclay. He hoped she would give Sloane another lease on life, another chance to find happiness. Still, he would miss him.

Inside the office, Carolyn set to the task of shutting things down for the night. She and Pendergrass would need to be back early in the morning. Sloane and Pendergrass would have to appear in court when Cerrabone formally dismissed the charges. Afterward, there would be a press conference. Jenkins wasn't about to miss it for the world, but Alex had another, greater interest. She was headed home to Camano Island, and snow was not going to prevent this East Coast native from seeing her baby boy.

As Pendergrass emerged from his office, raincoat draped over his arm, briefcase in hand, Carolyn stopped him. "Hold on there, Red." She handed him an eight-and-a-half-by-eleven-inch orange envelope. The return address indicated it had been hand-delivered by the prosecutor's office.

"Probably the missing documents," Pendergrass said, making it sound eerie. "The smoking guns." He put down his briefcase and opened the envelope flap, considering the contents.

Alex said her goodbyes.

"Come back soon," Carolyn said. "We can use another woman around here to balance out the testosterone."

Alex smiled. "You never know. I just might."

Jenkins held the door as Alex stepped through it.

"Huh?" Pendergrass said, drawing Jenkins's attention.

"What is it?"

Pendergrass shook his head. "Nothing . . ." He smiled. "Absolutely nothing. I guess I just thought it would be something more interesting, you know?" He shrugged. "It's just a Google search and more credit-card transactions."

"Well, not every case can be like *Perry Mason*," Jenkins said.

Pendergrass thrust the document at Carolyn. "And isn't it true that you performed a Google search on September third, 2011?"

Carolyn scowled at him. "If you're Perry Mason, I'm Marilyn Monroe."

Jenkins laughed and exited, hearing Pendergrass continue the charade as the door swung shut. "Answer the question," he said. "Isn't it true . . . that on September third, 2011, you did a Google search for Cadillac Coupe de Villes."

Jenkins looked at Alex, who had stopped in the hallway. He pulled back open the door and snatched the documents from Pendergrass's hand.

Queen Anne Hill
Seattle, Washington

The eyes had faded from the beautiful jade green to a dull gray. The smile, which had started small, spread across her face into a thin-lipped grin. She laughed, clapping her hands — once, then again and again.

You don't undertand . . . but you will.

"Excellent, counselor. Excellent."

The transformation alarmed him. Her features becoming hard and ugly.

"Too bad you're not going to be using any of that in your closing argument. But tell me, when did you figure it out?"

"I think I knew all along," he said.

She shook her head, sneered. "Bullshit. You had no fucking clue. You, the lawyer who does not lose. You had no idea."

"Not at first," Sloane admitted, "but it bothered me that no one had ever explained why Cruz's fingerprint was on the door; there was no need to explain it after Underwood ruled it inadmissible. Cruz had to have had a reason to touch the door and Hurley confirmed what that was. Cruz went inside to retrieve the bug so the police wouldn't find it."

She picked up his glass and sipped the Scotch, her voice rough. "You're lying. If you knew, why didn't you say anything?"

"Because I didn't want it to be true. Because there was a part of me that was willing to accept that you killed Vasiliev to avenge your daughter's death." He walked away from her, his anger building. "There was a part of me that could have accepted that, could have forgiven you."

"Forgiven me?" She laughed, mocking him. "What makes you think I ever wanted your forgiveness? And don't you dare judge me. You and I are exactly alike. I just had the guts to pull the trigger. You didn't."

His voice rose, and he took a step toward her. "Don't . . ."

She lifted her chin. "Don't what?"

"Don't you dare equate the two; this was never about avenging your daughter's death. This was never about justice. If it had been, you could have killed Vasiliev any time you wanted. This had nothing to do with your daughter. This was all about you getting even after Vasiliev walked . . . after he won and you lost."

She raised her voice, pointed. "He never won."

"What did he do, Barclay? What did he say? What set you off?"

The sickened smile returned. "He grinned," she said, her voice almost a whisper. "The son of a bitch nodded and grinned. Well, he's not grinning anymore, is he?" She took a drink. Then she screamed, *"Is he?"* She wheeled and threw the glass at the fireplace, shattering it. The anger and rage seeped from her, bringing a feral smell. He'd seen it that brief moment at Kells, but this time she could not control it. It boiled over, her eyes wild, her face a mask of ugliness. She was a foot smaller and a hundred pounds lighter than he, but she snarled and hissed like an animal backed into a corner, prepared for a fight.

"He didn't realize the game wasn't over. Neither did you. Oh no, I hadn't forgotten about you, either."

"What are you talking about?"

She took a step closer. "Please. Don't pretend like you never cared."

"Cared about what?" he asked, though the answer began to dawn on him.

She hates to lose at anything.

"Kendall Toys. Or did you think I'd forgotten all about that?"

In his mind, he saw her standing beside the pool table, head cocked, watching him. She hadn't distracted him to seduce him, though that was a part of it. She couldn't help herself. She'd distracted him to win.

"I beat you," she said, then reemphasized each word. "I . . . beat . . . you. The lawyer who does not lose. I outsmarted you every step of the way. I got even with you, Vasiliev, and that ex-husband of mine. I got even with you all. So don't you dare stand here and tell me you had it figured out. Don't you dare."

"Why Oberman? Hadn't you punished him enough?"

She shook her head, emphatic. "Oh, no. No, no, no. I was not done with him. He humiliated me, asking *me* for a divorce? Are you kidding me? I was a gift. He was never going to find anyone close to my league." She stepped toward him. "Do you know what it was like going to work every day, having people stare at me, wondering what had to be wrong with me for someone like that to divorce *me?* And then I had to read about it in the newspapers. Well, I humiliated him, didn't I?" Her voice wavered

586

between anger and tears. "Then, after Carly died, he started in again, calling me on the phone, swearing, telling me it was my fault. My fault? How dare he. How dare he! So I decided to put an end to him once and for all. You're wrong about this being spur-of-the-moment. I planned it for months, since Carly's death. I planned every minute detail. It was perfect, all the way down to flying Jake up here to distract you and give me time to plant the gun in Felix's apartment and the shoes in Lori Andrews's closet."

"How?" Sloane asked.

"Shit. Do you know how easy it is to get a superintendent to open a door? So don't tell me you figured it out."

But he had. "Someone called the security company three nights before, as well as the night that Oberman set off the alarm," he said. "There would have been no reason for you to make those calls if you had never suspected Oberman might set off the alarm. And you shouldn't have known the alarm went off, because Oberman was able to provide the password. The only reason for you to call the security company was to find out if your scheme worked, if he'd come looking for the gun."

She laughed, but it was hesitant, uncertain. "That doesn't mean anything. It doesn't mean you knew anything."

"Not by itself. But as Detective Rowe likes to say, I followed the evidence. I began to question why Cruz would have left his fingerprint on the sliding-glass door, why the killer who walked with purpose and intent would have hesitated when she reached the patio, why the trajectory of the bullet wasn't just right. I needed to find out if I was right, whether you had set the whole thing up from the start."

She grinned. "Let me answer that question, darling. I bought the dress the day of your speech, after I read about it in the *Law Journal.* I got my hair done, put on the makeup and jewelry, and waited for that moment to accidentally stumble into you. The whole speech about my father and his Cadillac and how I loved to smell his after-shave? Most men would have done me in the backseat of the car after a story like that, and I would have let you. Oh yeah. You could have banged my brains out. But no, not you. You're too much of a gentleman. I had to take my time with you."

"You didn't count on cutting your hand, though, did you? You couldn't help yourself, couldn't control the anger, just like Oberman said."

She shrugged. "No plan is perfect. I didn't plan on that little shit sneaking home at three in the morning and seeing me, either. But every good attorney knows you have to adapt. So I gave Yamaguchi the anonymous tip that you and I were both being questioned. I knew they'd run a picture with the story. What paper wouldn't? And that would at least give you grounds to argue that the montage was tainted. But you did so much better than that." She chuckled. "You destroyed that little shit. I mean, I knew you were good — I thought I might have to lead you to certain evidence — but . . ." She smiled at him, eyes brimming with interest, biting her lower lip. "But forget all of that. Tell me, because I've been dying to ask . . . how does it feel to lose?"

"Winning isn't as rewarding as you think, Barclay."

"David," she said, "we both know that winning is the only thing."

"No. Sometimes it comes at too high a cost."

"Spoken like someone who just lost."

"Did I?"

She laughed again. "At least be man enough to admit it." She walked closer, nearly touching him. "Come on, let's not hold grudges. I think Jake likes me."

He grabbed her just under the chin. She stuck out her tongue, licking her lips, whispering. "Go ahead, hit me. I like it like that."

He released his grip, stepping back and turning for the door.

Her voice became melodic, nearly a hum. "Don't be a sore loser. Be a good sport and admit that I beat you and we can go upstairs. There's no reason to waste a perfectly good opportunity to celebrate." Sloane pulled open the front door. She called out to him, "I'll see you in court tomorrow, counselor. And remember, this is all a privileged conversation."

Sloane pushed open the wooden gate and stepped onto the sidewalk. Jenkins leaned against the hood of the Cadillac, the collar of his leather jacket pulled up. He wore gloves and a knit ski cap. "You all right?"

Sloane struggled to catch his breath, the adrenaline still pulsing. "How'd you know?"

Jenkins held up the manila packet. "She googled Cadillac Coupe de Ville the day of your speech. I was debating whether to ring the doorbell, but something told me you already had it all figured out."

"Nobody has it all figured out, Charlie."

"What are you going to do?"

Sloane shrugged. "I'm an officer of the court; I'm going to do my job."

"You're going to let her get away with this?"

Sloane looked up at the house. Part of him expected to see her in the window, but the window was dark. "Nobody gets away with anything. We all have to pay for our mistakes."

"Maybe, but I'd like to be there when that happens."

Sloane turned from the window. "Tell me what you know about Zach Bergman."

THIRTY-ONE

Friday, December 9, 2011
United States Federal District Court
Seattle, Washington

Rebecca Han caught Judge Myron Kozlowski by surprise. He lifted his gaze from the papers on his desk, pleadings in cases he would decide that morning.

"Ms. Han? What is the meaning of entering my office without an invitation?" She closed the door. "What exactly do you think you're doing?"

"I'm closing the door. Unless you want your entire staff to hear our conversation."

Kozlowski reached for the phone. "I'm going to call security before you do or say anything that might further destroy what you have left of your career."

"I am fully aware of what an act such as this could potentially mean to an ambitious young lawyer," she said. "But a United States attorney must be above the sway of the media, which is why I'm here and not down at the *Seattle Times* talking to my friend Ian Yamaguchi."

"What are you babbling about?"

"I'm babbling about an investigation that would be front-page news in this city for days, and likely across the country — a story of a federal district court judge accepting bribes in exchange for rulings that put drug traffickers back on the streets. An investigation of something like that could really mean something to a young U.S. attorney's career, couldn't it? Or would that be self-aggrandizing?"

Kozlowski hung up the phone.

King County Courthouse
Seattle, Washington

The news conference took place in a room at the courthouse. King County prosecutor Amanda Pinkett stood at the podium answering questions. She did not hang Cerrabone out to dry. Chief of Police Sandy Clarridge also stood present to support Rowe and Crosswhite. Both acknowledged they agreed with Cerrabone's decision to dismiss the charges against Barclay Reid, a motion Judge Underwood had granted in his courtroom earlier that morning. The press had received wind of what was to transpire, and the numbers present had quadrupled to a sea of cameramen, reporters, and photographers. They snapped Reid's picture from the moment she stepped off the elevator on the eighth floor until she reached the courtroom doors.

At the moment, Reid stood between Sloane and Pendergrass, to the right of Detectives Rowe and Crosswhite.

"Will the police reopen the investigation into Vasiliev's murder?" a reporter asked.

"We are in the process of evaluating whether there is sufficient evidence to bring any further charges against any other persons," Pinkett said, though Sloane knew that, practically, that could never happen.

One of the problems with a high-profile prosecution was the prosecutor had to stand before not just a jury but the entire community, point his finger, and say that a particular person was guilty of the crime. When that same prosecutor had to stand up in court and admit he had been wrong, it raised considerable credibility concerns for the prosecutor to stand up a second time, point the same finger, and say, "Okay, this time I really mean it. This time this person did it."

Oberman would never be charged; nor would Lori Andrews.

Not that it mattered.

Oberman had been injured once too often. He could never fully recover. He was leaving Seattle, likely someplace far from his ex-wife and the insanity he had been forced to endure because he loved someone who was mentally ill.

After several more questions, Pinkett gave way to Sloane. He stepped to the podium with Reid at his side.

Sloane said, "I want to thank the prosecutor and Mr. Cerrabone for having the courage to make this decision. It is never easy bringing charges against a person of Ms. Reid's stature, and I know that it was not done lightly in this instance. We are pleased the matter has resolved itself."

A reporter in the audience shouted above the other voices. "Would you have preferred to go to a jury and receive a not-guilty verdict to prove Ms. Reid's innocence?"

"We believe that a dismissal by the prosecutor is tantamount to a finding of —"

Reid interrupted. "Every good lawyer wants to win," she said, beaming in front of the cameras. "It's what we do. It's what gets us out of bed in the morning and gets our adrenaline rushing — the competition, the desire to be the best, to win. I know that's how David feels. But I consider this to have been a complete victory." She turned to Sloane, wrapped her arm through his. "I was blessed to have the very best legal counsel not only in this city but, in my opinion, the United States. David Sloane has proved again why he is so often referred to as the attorney who does not lose."

The words sent a chill through him. "All I can say is it would take one hell of a lawyer to beat him."

"Will you handle more criminal cases?" another reporter asked Sloane.

"I don't know," Sloane said. "This case took an emotional toll."

"Will you continue to push the legislature for a drug dealer liability act?" another asked Reid.

"I think that is best left to the politicians," Reid said. "I'm eager to get back to my practice and to move on with my life. Leenie's death was tragic, but it is in the past, and I realize now I must look to the future."

The news conference lasted little over an hour. Sloane, Pendergrass, and Reid left the building and stopped at the corner of Third and James. The snow had not stuck to the ground downtown, though the streets and sidewalks were wet, and it remained cold. Heavy gray clouds blanketed the Emerald City.

"You coming back to the office?" Pendergrass asked Sloane, his tone cautionary. Sloane had not had time to explain the situation to Pendergrass in any detail, nor had Jenkins, who had shot out of the office the night before without explanation about what the documents meant. But Pendergrass seemed to have some sense that things were not as they seemed.

Sloane said, "Barclay and I have some unfinished business. Tell Carolyn to shut down the office. Then head home. Take a few days or a week."

"Better alert the police," Pendergrass said, trying to lighten the mood. "She's liable to trample me getting out the door."

Sloane thanked him for all he had done and watched him depart.

"Is this where you tell me what a horrible person I am, that I've thrown away the best thing I was ever going to have in my life, then walk off, leaving me to pine for a love lost?" The corner of her mouth and left eyebrow raised, mocking him.

"Happy endings are only in the movies, Barclay. You know that."

"Really?" She smiled wide. "Because I'm feeling pretty happy right now. Come on. Don't be sore. We could be a great team, you and I. We'd be tough to beat, and I have

597

to admit you are really good in bed. I only had to fake it once."

"What is it you said about games?" he asked.

"What?"

He looked past her, causing her to turn.

"Ms. Reid?" Detectives Rowe and Crosswhite, and a third person Sloane had never met but whose name he suspected he knew, approached. Rowe leaned on a cane.

Reid gave Sloane a quick, hesitant glance, then turned and nodded. "Detectives. No apologies are necessary. I understand you were only doing your jobs, and I admit this did look bad. But I'm not a person to hold a grudge."

"We appreciate that," Rowe said. "But we'd like to talk to you about another matter."

"Another matter?" Uncertainty crept into her voice.

"Do you know the name Zach Bergman? I believe he worked as a private investigator for you during your divorce."

Reid's eyes found Sloane's, but her recovery was remarkable. "Yes, he did. What about him?"

"Well, you see, he's dead."

She chuckled. "I'm well aware of that, Detective. I believe he died ten years ago, and I think it's rather obvious now that my ex-husband must have killed Mr. Bergman because of the investigation into his sordid lifestyle. He was very bitter and angry at the time."

"That is a theory," Rowe said, "but you see, one thing I've learned from this case is that sometimes the evidence is not what it seems."

"Really? And what makes you say that?"

"I was considering the police report in your divorce file, and it notes that you had bruises and contusions on the side of your face."

"It was a severe beating."

"That's what the report says. It says those bruises were definitely the result of someone hitting you with a fist multiple times."

"So what exactly is it you wanted to talk to me about?"

Rowe scratched his head. "I'm curious, because the medical report indicates that the person who delivered those blows had to have been right-handed."

The color drained from Reid's face.

"And of course we all now know that your ex-husband is left-handed," Rowe said.

Reid looked to Sloane. The jade-green eyes had turned gray again. The smile faded.

"Oh yeah," Sloane said, drawing Reid's

attention. "Now I remember. You said, 'You never know who's won until the game ends.' "

The third detective stepped forward. "Ms. Reid, I'm Bernie Hamilton. I'm the detective in charge of the unit's cold cases. Knock knock."

Reid shifted her gaze from Sloane to Hamilton. "What?" she said, looking and sounding annoyed.

"You're supposed to say, 'Who's there?' "

She shook her head in disgust. "Is this some kind of a joke?"

"Actually, it is," Sloane said. "Let me show you how it's done." He indicated for Hamilton to start over.

"Knock knock."

"Who's there, Detective?"

Hamilton's eyes fixed on Reid. "Remember a long time ago . . ."

EPILOGUE

Three Tree Point
Burien, Washington

Sloane finished another beer and embedded the bottle in the pebbles near the other empties. Between his shoes, the shaft of his fishing rod, also embedded in the rocks, twitched and bent with the ebb and flow of the tide. He sat on one of the many driftwood logs the tide had washed onto the beach, wrapped in a thick jacket and wearing a knit hat and gloves. With the tide in, he could cast while seated. Jake would have been aghast. *You never put your fishing pole in the rocks, and you never stop reeling in the lure.*

Sloane knew it to be wise advice. The minute you stopped reeling, the lure sank to the bottom of the Sound to become snagged on any number of things and likely lost forever. He didn't care. He'd never caught a single fish from the shore in all his years at Three Tree. He'd seen Jake do it, a big king salmon, too, but Sloane never had.

A hundred yards offshore, the parade of boats trolled north to south and back — fishing poles bowed over their sterns like the bent spines of old men. Behind them, the winter light had mottled the clouds pink and red, the sun continuing its descent behind the Olympic mountain range. Tina had loved the view this time of year. They used to walk the beach or sit on the porch and watch Jake cast his line in the water until his image faded into the darkness.

"I better be getting home," Jenkins said, finishing his only beer.

It was the first time the two men had seen each other in three weeks. Sloane left the day after the trial for the beach house in Zihuatanejo. Jake joined him for two of those weeks, his Christmas vacation. They spent much of the time fishing, bodysurfing, and eating more than they should. Sloane told Jake that it hadn't worked out with Reid, and the boy had accepted the explanation, though Sloane knew he was smart enough to understand there was more to the story. This time Sloane didn't stay in Zihuatanejo nearly as long as his retreat following Tina's death. He left Seattle to escape the insanity he knew would follow Reid's second arrest, for the murder of her private investigator, Zach Bergman. As Sloane had warned, the game wasn't over, and no one was perfect. Everyone made mistakes. She'd made a big one. Bergman had beat her, as she had paid him to do, so she could blame Felix Oberman.

But Oberman was left-handed, and the blows were clearly delivered by someone with a dominant right hand. No one had paid that close attention ten years ago, during a bitter divorce proceeding. But Hamilton took the lead and uncovered evidence of cash withdrawals from Reid's account that could not be accounted for, sums of money that identically matched sums Bergman had deposited in his checking account.

As for Oberman shooting Bergman, he already had an airtight alibi ten years ago. He had fled on a cruise ship to get away from his ex-wife at the time Bergman was shot and killed.

Lori Andrews had also confessed, saying it felt cathartic to rid herself of the guilt. She told Crosswhite that ten years earlier she had agreed to set up Oberman in exchange for enough money to pay for her sex change. The money was delivered by Zach Bergman, but Andrews knew where it had come from. Barclay Reid. She said

Bergman had brought the money along with a message: "Don't think there's any more here. This is a onetime payment."

Bergman should have heeded his own words.

A friend with Bergman in a bar the night he was shot provided a statement that Bergman had been bragging about a client who kept on giving while throwing around a lot of cash.

There being no statute of limitations, Reid would again stand accused of murder in the first degree, and Seattle would have another sensational trial. She would never plea. She would never admit defeat. The media wanted to know if Sloane would defend her, but he left word with Carolyn to advise anyone who asked that he believed representing Reid would be a conflict of interest, given their prior personal relationship.

Reid remained incarcerated in the King County jail, her bail denied. Trial was set for the spring. She had called Sloane from the jail. The first two messages, she sounded like the woman he had met and fallen in love with, pleading with Sloane to help her. The third call, he barely recognized her voice. She called him vile names, and told him when she got out, she would find him and get even.

Before leaving town, this time for good, Oberman advised Rowe and Crosswhite he considered Reid a sociopath and likely schizophrenic. Sloane hoped, at the very least, she would receive the treatment she had long needed.

"You going to be okay?" Jenkins asked.

"Aren't I always?" Sloane twisted the cap off another bottle of beer.

"Quite a collection," Jenkins said.

"I'm just getting started."

"And I'm leaving before the neighbors start talking about the two of us watching sunsets together. You need anything before I go?"

Sloane shook his head.

The log shifted when Jenkins stood. Sloane listened to the fading sound of his friend's shoes sinking into the rocks.

"Charlie?"

Jenkins turned back.

"Thanks."

The big man nodded, turned, and walked off.

Sloane slipped his hands under his armpits to keep them warm and watched the sky continue to change color. Tina had said the colors reminded her that there was beauty in the world, and that it was important to stop every once in a while and acknowledge that beauty. Sloane saw it as the end of another day, one more he had survived since her death. He was unsure what the future would have held with Barclay Reid, but while in Zihuatanejo, he had also come to realize that it was that uncertainty that had made him feel alive again from the moment he first stumbled into her, not knowing what each new day might bring. In some strange way, he believed that was why Reid had entered his life, at a time when he was so vulnerable, to serve as a vivid reminder that things were never as good or as bad as they seemed.

They just were what they were.

He wasn't prepared to say it had all been a part of some divine plan, as Father Allen had intimated during a recent chat. Sloane didn't really believe God worked that way, controlling everyone's life like moving pieces on a chessboard. But he felt a sense of strength he hadn't expected. The loss of another woman he had grown to love could have devastated him, but he didn't feel that way. He saw it as a step forward in his grieving process, and he knew now what Jake had meant about the pain being part of the healing.

He also knew he could love again.

And that he could survive anything the

world had yet to throw at him.

Unlike after Tina's death, he no longer feared the unknown. He'd come to realize it was not knowing the future — the unexpected — that made life worth living.

He picked up his fishing pole and reeled, not getting far before the line snapped taut and the tip of the pole bent forward. In his head, Sloane could hear Jake's voice.

I told you so.

Then the line darted right across the surface of the water, the tip of the pole dancing, the reel buzzing — the big fish making a determined run.

ACKNOWLEDGMENTS

Last spring, I had the unfortunate and fortunate experience to sit in on a capital murder case in King County Superior Court. Knowing that I would soon force my protagonist David Sloane into the criminal justice system, I thought it prudent that I educate myself, a civil attorney, on as many of the nuances of that system as I could. The case received publicity nationwide; the defendant, in his midtwenties, was accused of walking across the street and brutally murdering two women and two children he did not know, then setting the bodies and the house on fire in an attempt to conceal his crimes. I quickly realized that while the physical courtroom looked the same as those I had entered many times while practicing law — the two counsel tables facing the elevated bench, jury box to the right, the gallery behind — that was where the similarities ended.

Each day, before trial, the presiding judge took the bench, the lawyers took their seats at the counsel tables, and the defendant entered escorted by sheriff's deputies and wearing handcuffs. The courtroom had very much the feel of the greenroom backstage of a theater production, where the actors and directors discuss their performances and upcoming scenes. Upon completing this daily routine the bailiff would seat the jury and the curtain would rise on another day. Unfortunately, what I was watching was not theater, but the aftermath of a horrific crime. I spent much of the day focusing my attention on King County Senior Prosecutor Scott O'Toole and his innate ability to interact with the jurors through his opening statement and the dozens of witnesses he would call on behalf of the state. While Scott would not talk to me about the case, he would answer general questions about criminal proceedings. I learned a tremendous amount, including that if I ever were to commit a crime, and I don't intend to, I would not want Scott prosecuting me. Excellence does not quite describe how good he is. The trial would last months, but he entered each day looking fresh and energized, and his direct and cross-examinations rarely strayed from perfect.

While I did not talk to the attorneys representing the defendant I did have three months to observe them and their demeanor. In addition, I asked questions of attorneys Russell H. Dawson and John Kannin, both of whom have spent years navigating the criminal justice system on behalf of their clients and who have developed well-deserved reputations as proactive advocates. I am grateful for their assistance.

I am also grateful to Kelly Heafy Rosa, investigator, Criminal Division, King County Prosecutor's Office, and good friend. Kelly helped to put me in touch with many of the specialists who generously gave their time so that I could try to get the police procedure accurate and include cool things like man-tracking, dog-scenting, and forensic ballistics. Thanks for coming through, Kell.

The first person Kelly put me in touch with was King County sheriff detective Scott Tompkins, Major Crimes Unit/Cold Case Homicides. Despite his busy schedule, Scott spent the better part of half a day discussing the idea for this novel, how he would investigate the crime as I presented it to him, and gave me ideas on how I could make it even more intriguing.

Scott, in turn, put me in touch with

Detective Jennifer Southworth of the Seattle Police Department Crime Scene Investigations Unit. That's CSI for you TV folks. Detective Southworth not only provided me with a tour of the King County Evidence Center, but also spent her time discussing how a CSI unit would respond to the crime scene I proposed. In addition, she spent time discussing with me what it is like being a female detective in what remains a predominantly male profession.

Detective Southworth put me in touch with Detective Dana Duffy, Seattle Police Department Homicide/Assault Unit. Detective Duffy is Seattle's only female homicide detective. Again, I was grateful for her willingness to answer questions, her suggestions such as the polygraph test, and her insight on being the only woman on the homicide team. Both detectives helped me to create what I hope to be a realistic portrait of a female homicide detective. I'm grateful for their time and honesty.

I am also grateful to Kathy Decker, King County Sheriff's Office search and rescue coordinator and instructor/sign cutter, otherwise known as a "man-tracker." Detective Decker helped me to understand how a tracker can follow signs that most of us would never see to track where a human being has been, or where they might currently be. It is a fascinating science and I hope my brief explanation in the book does it justice. It was Kathy who suggested I get in touch with and speak to King County sheriff's deputies Randy Houser and Zbig Kasprzyk, K-9 Unit. They explained the science behind training a dog to scent a human being. As good as Kathy and her compatriots are at their jobs, man's best friend was blessed with a sense of smell we can't come close to, and it allows them to do remarkable things in the hands of their trainers. I'm grateful to both men for meeting me and answering all my questions.

Along my research journey I was also placed in touch with Washington State Patrol supervising forensic scientist, Firearm/Toolmark Section, Rick Wyant. Rick, I was told, is the "boy wonder" of forensic science, and he did not let me down. His motto is "Why speculate when you can simulate," and he gets to do for a living things that make most men salivate — shooting and blowing up things to help him determine the trajectory of bullets and how a crime unfolded at the crime scene. I hope I did his profession justice and thank him for his time.

As Rick and I sat talking I was introduced

to Seattle police officer Tom Burns, Southwest Precinct. Officer Burns agreed to take me through the steps of a police officer responding to a report of "shots fired" and the presence of a "prowler." Officer Burns's insight, from more than twenty years on the job, was a great help to me.

Special thanks also to Bernie Dennehy, corrections program administrator, King County Department of Adult and Juvenile Detention, for explaining to me the procedures when a defendant is arrested and when a defense attorney seeks to speak to his client. As one might imagine, incarcerating human beings is a difficult challenge on a number of different levels and I'm grateful to Bernie for sharing his valuable time with me.

I also owe a special thanks to Micheal Hurley (that's the Irish spelling of Michael, he tells me), supervisory special agent, Drug Enforcement Administration (retired). Mike is a good friend who invited me to his home and explained to me much about the drug trade. In past books Mike has been behind the scenes but graciously agreed to allow me to use his name for a character in this book. I could think of no one better to lead a covert drug enforcement agency. Thanks, Mike.

Special thanks also to Adrian Coombes, who told me to ask for "the Brit" when I visited him at Wade's Eastside Gun Shop in Bellevue, Washington. Mr. Coombes was a big help with the firearms I chose to use in this novel and how those firearms would react. Finally, I'm grateful to Paula Henry, A.D.E. combat operator, who spent half a day at the Los Angeles firing range demonstrating, then teaching me how to shoot, various weapons. It was a heck of a lot of fun, but also a sobering lesson on the power and force those firearms possess.

As much as all of these individuals assisted me I am most grateful to Kirkland police detective Brad Porter. Detective Porter was the lead detective on the brutal killing mentioned above. He sat at counsel table beside Scott O'Toole throughout the months, working long days and nights, but always met with me and took my calls when I had questions about police procedure. Detective Porter even read the manuscript so that I could make it as realistic as possible. My thanks to you, Brad, for your kindness.

As careful as I tried to be, I'm sure there are mistakes. It is difficult to write a novel and account for legal procedure, which can occur over many years before a defendant ever sees a courtroom. Any mistakes are mine and mine alone. This experience, more than any other I have had writing novels, made a distinct impression on me. Those who choose to give their lives in law enforcement, be it as officers, detectives, investigators, or prosecutors, really do serve the people of the state. They are dedicated servants doing their very best at a very difficult job to keep people like me and my family safe. Too often in the news we read about one of their brethren making a mistake. Too infrequently do we hear of their heroism, each and every day, that they put themselves out in the community doing their jobs to keep the rest of us alive. We owe them a huge debt of gratitude. I hope this book depicts them as the heroes they are.

Special thanks to Jerry Willins and Virginia Dugaw for their generous support of the La Conner Rotary Scholarship program. I was pleased to use their names as characters in this novel to support that organization and the good it does. The La Conner Rotary has allowed me to share a dinner and a book signing with them since the publication of my first book, *The Cyanide Canary,* back in 2004. I very much look forward to my visits, particularly seeing Lee and Dee Carlson, my hosts. Rotaries do great work worldwide and I'm humbled to do my small part to support their greater good.

Thanks to Meg Ruley of the Jane Rotrosen Agency, my agent. Meg is simply the best. She has an infectious personality that sees the glass half-full. I am indebted to her for so much. Thanks also to the rest of the Rotrosen team who read my drafts and offer suggestions. I do appreciate all of your support. I couldn't do it without you.

Thanks to Tami Taylor, who runs my website and does a fantastic job. Thanks to the cold readers who labor through my early drafts and help make my manuscripts better. Thanks to Pam Binder and the Pacific Northwest Writers Association for their tremendous support of my work.

Thanks to Touchstone/Simon & Schuster for believing in *Murder One* and in me. To publisher Stacy Creamer, thanks for your support and promotion of *Murder One* and my career. Thanks to Trish Todd, Marcia Burch, David Falk, Meredith Kernan, Jessica Roth, Lauren Spiegel, art director Cherlynne Li, production editor Josh Karpf, production manager George Turianski, and interior designer Renata Di Biase. If I missed anyone, you know you have my thanks.

To Louise Burke, Pocket Books publisher, and Pocket Books associate publisher Anthony Ziccardi as well as editor Abby Zidle for great insight and support. And thanks to all on the Touchstone and Pocket Books sales forces. I wouldn't be writing this without you.

Thank you also to the loyal readers who e-mail me to tell me how much they enjoy my books and await the next. You are the reason I keep looking for the next David Sloane adventure, and beyond.

I've dedicated this book to my brother-in-law, Jim Fick. Jim has overcome so much in his life to become a tremendous man. He cares for all he loves, his mother, his brothers, and his own family, and he has been kind enough to include me. Jim promotes my books as hard as anyone, especially to the legal community. His law firm, Bullivant Houser Bailey, and in particular Matt Hooper and Chris Bakes, has become a big proponent of my work and source of knowledge for me. That would not have happened but for Jim. He gives so much of himself; I hope someday I can give back half as much.

And always, first in my heart, my wife and my two kids, who are no longer kids. Cristina has raised a wonderful son and daughter and they fortunately inherited many of her wonderful qualities and beauty. You work too hard. I hope to remedy that someday, too. In the interim, thanks for standing by me.

ABOUT THE AUTHOR

Robert Dugoni, author of *Wrongful Death* and *Bodily Harm,* is a two-time winner of the Pacific Northwest Writers Association Literary Contest. Fomerly a civil litigator, he now writes full-time and lives in Washington State.

www.robertdugoni.com

The employees of Thorndike Press hope you have enjoyed this Large Print book. All our Thorndike, Wheeler, and Kennebec Large Print titles are designed for easy reading, and all our books are made to last. Other Thorndike Press Large Print books are available at your library, through selected bookstores, or directly from us.

For information about titles, please call:
(800) 223-1244

or visit our Web site at:
http://gale.cengage.com/thorndike

To share your comments, please write:

Publisher
Thorndike Press
10 Water St., Suite 310
Waterville, ME 04901